PRAISE FOR *MIND'S HORIZON*

"Like *The Walking Dead* meets *Fallout* meets the Cthulhu Mythos."

— C. T. Phipps, author of *Cthulhu Armageddon*

"By all that's holy, I don't know how he does it. Another masterwork by the King of Cosmic Horror!"

— Leigh Grissom, Author of *KLS-9*

"Malikyte follows up *Echoes of Olympus Mons*, his woeful tale of Mars's untimely death, with a love letter to H.P. Lovecraft. *Mind's Horizon* features all the good apocalyptic stuff you expect from Lovecraft, notably world-ending excitement, a hint of magic, and teeth. Lots of teeth. It's a cracking good read of Lovecraftian proportion."

— Eric Lahti, author of *Road Side Attractions*

I0630481

MIND'S HORIZON

ERIC MALIKYTE

PROLOGUE

It slithered from the dark, taking long, deliberate steps across the metal floor around Val. Val's eyes tracked the thing's pace, uncertainty painting her face—her body shivering with a fear so complete that Aden could almost feel it from the grating in the corridor she'd hidden behind.

Aden shuddered at the spines on its back. They pulsed and waved through the air, smacking against themselves like the quills of a porcupine. Aden had never seen it so clearly before; it had to be at least twenty feet long.

Val's eyes found hers in the dark. Her lips trembled, tears forming in her eyes.

Aden's fingers gripped through the grating, watching helplessly as the thing coiled around Val like a snake.

Val shook her head. "Run."

It reared back like a wolf, ready to sink its blackened teeth into its prey. Aden covered her own mouth, trying not to scream.

From within its shadowy head, seven eyes pulsed with eerie gray light the moment before it snatched Val's body up in its massive jaws and dragged her to God knows where.

But she did know; she knew all too well about that other place, a place that was between physical space and that nebulous void where dreams and nightmares dwell. Val's screams filled the concrete tunnel, lingering long after her body was gone.

The lights flickered and Aden was alone.

She'd read about that place in Weber's secret book, the one she'd stolen it from his room hours before the alarm sounded. She felt the leather cover with the tips of her fingers.

There had been a time before this madness. A time spent crawling through record stores, going to the movies, and spending entire days at the beach.

She'd give anything to return to that time now.

With tears pouring down her cheeks, Aden honored Val's last request, limping down the stone tunnel corridor, following signs that read TO CORE REACTOR. The sounds of her bare feet slapping against the concrete floor and her shallow, panicked breathing bounced off the curved walls of the corridor.

Her heart skipped a beat every time the lights flickered, and she thought: *Maybe this is it, maybe I won't make it this time.*

But each time it was only a power fluctuation, or the creature was testing her resolve, waiting for her sanity to break before it made its move on her.

At the start of the trials, the creature had seemed drawn to what they were doing. No one believed what they were seeing, and Weber waved off their concerns like they were nothing.

What had drawn it to them? She guessed that the occult nature of the experiments, and the levels of energy that they were playing with, acted like a beacon to the creature, the same way it must have been drawn to its prey eons ago when its alien masters unleashed it upon their enemies.

That too, was in Weber's forbidden book.

Aden came to the end of the hall. The door was already open. She entered, and the hatch closed behind her with a hiss.

Doctors Wong, Weber, and Abrams had managed to make it. The three of them huddled around the pulsing cylindrical fusion core in the center of the chamber. They were nursing bruises and wounds and bloody scrapes. Trivial things compared to the unknown fates of the others.

In the pale red light of the pulsing core, Weber looked decrepit and old. He was a pale shadow of what he had been months ago.

"One of the volunteers survived," Wong said, rising from her seat cautiously. She was little older than Aden was.

Volunteer, Aden thought. *Is that really what we all were?*

"It appears she has indeed," Weber said, a yellow-toothed grin spreading from ear to ear. "We can't wait any longer. We have to activate the final experiment protocol."

"We don't even know if it'll work," Abrams said, holding himself close, shivering. "What if that thing gets us while we're in the tanks? You said it…you said it used shadows as a kind of gateway into—"

"It'll get us if we stand around deliberating," Weber said.

"You're not suggesting it can shut down the core?" Abrams' eyes vibrated, as if his very notion of reality had been offended. Aden understood that feeling all too well.

"I'm saying we can't possibly understand what it can do." Weber approached the activation terminal. The others looked apprehensive, but none moved to stop him from entering the passcode. "I will spare you the details, but know that the beings that created that thing are well beyond us."

That at least was true. When they'd started this project, they had been five hundred, most of them "willing" volunteers from the outside. Aden remembered it well; how she had been given the generous choice of volunteering for a top-secret research project or being sent off to some prison by two MPs in an interrogation room. A death sentence, either way. All for the great crime of looting an abandoned grocery store to try to feed herself and her sister.

Now, only the four of them remained, and the last of her family was dead.

The lights in the core chamber dimmed to a hideous crimson, creating shadow where light once stood. Abrams, Weber, and Wong moved into the light.

They knew better than to linger too long in the shadows.

Nine cylindrical tanks rose from beneath the floor, gleaming metallic red in the glow of the dim lighting. Weber peeled his lab coat and coveralls off of his hairy, withered body. The others followed his lead—except for Aden.

Wong went into the tank first. She hesitated while putting on the breathing mask. "What if it doesn't work? What if we get liquefied like Daniels?"

"Ask yourself what fate is worse," Weber said. "Flip a coin if it makes you feel better. But the protocol has been started, and once it runs its course, all systems will cut off and there'll be no way to reconnect them all without my passcode." He grinned, tapping his temple with a single yellow fingernail. "And I have them all locked safely away in here—which will be coming with me to our brave new world."

Abrams had already closed the lid to his tank, no argument, no complaint.

Say something, damn it! Aden thought. Her hand was clamped like a vise around the book in her pocket. She couldn't stop thinking about the look on Val's face the moment she'd gotten snatched up.

"Fine," Wong said, putting the mask on and descending into the tank. Her final look was one of uncertainty.

Weber closed the lid to her hatch for her, locking the latch tight before she could protest.

That only left the last subject.

Aden did not think of herself as a smart woman. How could she outsmart this man? A man who had stared into the abyss and somehow survived.

She was standing before him, hugging herself like Abrams had just been doing.

Weber's dark, sunken eyes and that look of total contempt for her was what gave her the strength to finally speak up.

"The others don't know," Aden said softly. "But I do. You unleashed that thing."

"Did I?" Weber said.

She nodded, and then did something that was a surprise even to herself. She produced Weber's tattered copy of *Messages from the Abyss* from her coat pocket and fanned the pages out. His eyes were wild now; she could see his heart pounding through his protruding ribcage. "The things I saw, the things you had us chant…they're all in here. Every…maddening detail."

4

Tears broke from her eyes.

"You must understand, Aden, I only consulted that terrible book because it was the only way to get us out of this place. Do you know what's happening out there? The world of man is ending. With each passing day, the ice sheets grow nearer to covering the entire Earth, and when that happens not even this place will survive. There may yet be life remaining on this world when that happens, but it will not be human."

She shook her head. "Then why are there only nine tanks in here?"

Weber smiled, chuckling, wheezing, falling into a coughing fit. "Even Wong and Abrams failed to question *that* little detail."

"You knew that we wouldn't survive, didn't you?"

"Something like that." He turned around and started walking up the metal ramp to his tank. She could see his spine protruding through his yellowing, wrinkled skin. "But, you drew the long straw, didn't you? How lucky for you to have been one of the few to survive. I'd only intended for the best and the brightest to survive, and you certainly were not one of those."

There wasn't much time left. She would have to act fast. But what could she possibly do? Her eyes scanned through the chamber frantically, looking for anything that might stick it to Weber and his insane plans.

Her eyes fell on a lone fire extinguisher and the console Weber had just used to activate his final experiment protocol.

She screamed and ran to the wall, ripping the fire extinguisher out of its case, threatening Weber with it while still holding the tattered book of forbidden things in her other hand. "I could smash the equipment, I could smash everything, and then you'd be stuck here with that *thing*."

"And then you'd be stuck too, wouldn't you?" Weber chuckled. "Really now, what do you have to lose by joining us? There's more than enough room."

She looked back and forth, uncertainty writhing deep within her.

It seemed that Weber was done arguing, though. He submerged himself in the tank and stretched the breathing mask over his head.

Aden was walking over to the console when it broke from the shadows, pouncing like some twenty-foot hell-cat upon a reflective floor that refused to betray its reflection. Its spines shifted, and as it padded forward, its movements were jerky, almost like a stop-motion effect in some old movie. Its very presence was an affront to her sanity. Like it was both there and not there at the same time. Its pale gray eyes focused on her. Aden could feel her heart beating in her ears, the blood draining from her face.

I can't move, she thought.

It dashed at her, carefully winding through patches of shadow to avoid the light—snatching her up in its massive jaws in one terrible sweeping motion. She screamed, tasting the iron tinge of her own blood bubbling up from her throat as its blackened teeth skewered right through her torso.

The creature slammed into the wall; she could feel its teeth grinding into her bones, sawing them and tearing at her flesh. Just before she passed through the wall, through reality, she dropped the fire extinguisher and the book.

Too late, then, she thought. *He wins after all.*

I'm sorry, Val.

The next thing her eyes saw was a gray sky that had the consistency of a cancerous lung. She felt the creature's teeth dig deeper into her flesh. She could feel the blood draining from her body. Her head dropped lower, and she could see the horizon. It was an endless expanse of land, like sand dunes the texture of leather.

There were body parts everywhere. Severed hands, feet, whole torsos, each consumed by a mouth with jagged black and yellow teeth that seemed to be part of the land itself.

Then she saw two pale blue eyes staring back at her.

It was Val.

She was being chewed by one of those mouths in the earth, the soft blonde hair Aden had often caressed streaked with blood now.

At least we die together, Aden thought.

The creature stopped moving.

She looked down at a crevice in the leathery ground. It opened to reveal a mouth filled with serrated teeth, and an acrid smell like decaying flesh forced its way up her nostrils. She could see down its throat, an endless tunnel of teeth and shifting muscles.

"Please, no," she said, grabbing at the creature as it dropped her into the pit. "No!"

Knives dug through her stomach and chest as she was impaled on a set of teeth. She stared up at the creature. Its seven eyes gave her no comfort as the mouth closed on her like an iron maiden slamming shut.

I hope he fails, she thought, as consciousness faded. *I hope the abyss swallows them all whole.*

CHAPTER ONE

A cold wind assaulted the frozen tundra and dark clouds broke above the snowy Southern California mountains, revealing a fading sun, struggling to find its noonday place in the dim Summer sky.

Frost clung to Ira's facemask, accumulating on her goggles and threatening to freeze the ventilator shut. She wiped the frost away, tossing it to the snowy ground. Even with her snow gear, the cold threatened to dig deep into her bones—like death's cold fingers. She almost wished she'd have worn more layers before embarking into the frozen wasteland she used to call home.

There was a numbness to each of her steps; the feeling in her legs had long since evaporated from her tired muscles. The frigid wind stabbed down and clawed at the layers of her clothing. She crossed her arms and tilted her head toward the ground. For a moment, she longed for a time when she could drive to the store to get what she needed, a time before the old world had been erased by miles and miles of white nothingness.

Only a little further, she thought. *I know I saw a building from the other side of the ridge.*

She forced her muscles to keep working for another thirty minutes before coming to a stop at the edge of a large icy hill. Her hands found her knees, balancing her weight as her breath steamed through her facemask. Her watch read the temperature at negative ten degrees

Fahrenheit. She couldn't linger here for long; her body was far too exposed to the biting cold. If the wind decided to flare up, it could flash-freeze her skin in an instant if she wasn't careful. She checked herself over to make sure she was fully covered, all the way up to her nose.

Life hadn't always been like this, desperately scrounging for supplies, hoping against improbability that the ice hadn't overtaken every portion of her city. The change had been rapid. The memory was fresh in her mind. One night, the stars had gone dark, the moon had clouded over, and the sunrise had become dim and tainted—nebulous.

The next morning some scientist was on the morning news talking about something called a "space cloud" and how his career was at risk just for talking about it, that the Feds didn't want the information out there. That program had left a terrible sickness writhing in her gut.

Life was over.

It hadn't taken long for the ice sheets to claim most of Canada and some parts of the upper portions of the United States. Mountains, forests, rivers, and even entire cities had been crushed beneath walls of ice four times larger than the tallest building on Earth. That had been nearly three years ago. For all she knew, the glaciers could be nearing her location any day now.

Nature's bulldozers, she thought.

She shuddered. Once that happened, nowhere would be safe—unless you were a fish.

Ira stood up, reached inside her pack for her multi-spectrum binoculars, and felt the lenses tap against her goggles. She increased the magnification by fifty percent.

There it was.

Down the hill and across a parking lot covered in about twelve feet of snow. The snow made an abnormally shaped slope over the top of the department store's roof, but it was still intact.

That snow was going to be a problem: there was almost fifty feet of it crushing down on the ceiling. The supports probably couldn't handle that much weight. Ira looked at her stomach and grimaced beneath her facemask. If the ice hadn't already caused a cave-in, she probably had enough time to find what she needed.

"Ira." Eddy's voice called over the CB. "Ira, do you read me?"

She fumbled with the CB receiver on her belt; she held it close to her mouth. *Stupid gloves.* "Yeah, I read you."

"Good, you took off so fast, I didn't get a chance to catch up with you. What's your location?"

"I'm outside an old department store, probably a few klicks away from you."

"Wow, there's a store that hasn't been covered yet?"

"Kind of. I'm gonna go in before the roof collapses."

There was a pause; she could almost imagine him face-palming. "How much?"

"How much *what?*"

"How much ice is covering the roof?"

She walked toward the building and squinted her eyes. "About fifty feet, give or take, but I think most of it's fresh."

"Ira, don't risk it. If that roof collapses while you're inside, there's not a damn thing I can do to pull you out."

"You'll just have to break the bad news to Nico, then."

"He'll kill me!"

She paused, considering the building. Crackling noises in the ice she was standing on caused a thrill of fear and adrenaline to overtake her. She persisted forward carefully. The ice had long since shattered the front windows of the store, bending and shaping the metal to its will. There was a small hole near the top of the window frame that wasn't covered in snow—that's where she could get in.

She dug around in her pants pocket for a few moments; she knew she still had a few left-over from the night before. She retrieved a few bottle caps, huddled up close to the small entrance to the store and tossed them inside. She heard them slide along the ice and fade away. That didn't tell her as much as she'd hoped, but she was still going to risk it.

She slipped her pack off the outer layer of her jacket and slid her feet into the hole. She held her breath and let inertia do its thing with her body. Next thing she knew, she'd turned sideways and impacted with an empty shelf.

Ira groaned, lifted herself off the floor, and sat for a moment; she'd move again when the agony left her side.

There wasn't much light inside the department store, save for a small amount coming through the hole she'd slid in through. The pain finally subsided, and she decided nothing important was broken. Her pack was about five feet away from where she'd hit the shelf. She retrieved it and pulled out her flashlight.

She shined a circle of light up at the ceiling. The supports looked rusted in some parts, tiny icy stalactites forming in several sections of the ceiling, pointing down at her—ready to turn her into a kebab. A large portion of the northern section of the store had suffered a cave-in, which was probably relieving weight from the rest of the structure. She moved her circle of light down to the shelf she'd crashed into. It was on its side, and it seemed that the impact had caused a domino effect on a number of other shelves, ending with a support beam—which was bent inward.

She sighed. That had been a close call.

"Ira, come in." Eddy's digitized voice made her jump.

"I'm shopping," she said. "Go away."

"No, goddamn it, there's a storm coming in from the west. You don't want to be stuck in there when it does, any added weight could cause that building to come down over your head!"

"I'm almost done, just give me a few more minutes."

"I'm coming to get you."

"Still won't stop me."

"Stubborn woman!" Eddy's final shout echoed through the dust and grime as Ira made her way down one of the aisles.

She scanned her flashlight over aisle signs; some were completely missing, probably destroyed or buried; some had ice growing on them, making them completely illegible; and others had just enough ice that they were still legible. She passed several aisles: water (which was empty, no duh), electronics (also empty, probably looted since the early days of the ice age), hardware (also useless to her this time), and finally, hygiene, the aisle she needed.

The shelves were empty, probably picked clean by panicked women, or their significant others, in the early days. She cursed, but couldn't give up just yet. She decided to check the back room, and the loading dock, to see if there might be a misplaced package somewhere.

11

She found herself climbing over collapsed shelves and carefully sliding over patches of thick ice to get there.

Two plastic doors separated the shopping area from the backroom, and they were frozen shut by a waterfall of ice. She gave them a few kicks; shards of ice flaked and scattered as the doors swung open. The corridor beyond was a darkened mess of metal and frosted concrete.

Click, click, click.

The clicking haunted the darkness above; she shined her flashlight up into the rafters and saw twisting frozen pipes that ran the length of the long corridor's ceiling, with numerous areas that opened to black nothingness. Her lunch twisted in her stomach; maybe coming here hadn't been so wise after all?

Her steps tapped and echoed through the corridor, masking the clicks. Rusted back stock-carts cascaded into the darkness, some frozen solid and others toppled on their sides. She scanned her light over them; there were a few that still had product on them. She tore through them, tossing frozen packages and boxes to the floor until, finally, she found what she was looking for.

Click, click, click.

She quickly secured the precious package inside her pack and made her way back down the corridor and through the plastic doors.

The clicking turned into a constant scraping, and Ira's heart threatened at the walls of her chest. She quickly made her way from aisle to aisle, climbing over debris and chunks of ice, and skating, sometimes gracefully, back to where she entered.

The scraping had become an ever-present rumbling; Ira pointed her flashlight at the support beam she'd inadvertently bent earlier and tried not to panic when she noticed it was beginning to give. She assessed the hill of ice leading up to the hole she'd entered from. She tried darting up the hill, but only managed to slide back down to where she started from.

"Okay, maybe Eddy was right," she said to herself. "This was a stupid idea."

"What was that?" Eddy's voice came from the light above the hill.

Her eyes found his silhouette, crouched low. "Don't be an ass, just help me get out of here. The ceiling's going to give any minute now."

"Told you so."

She tried running up the hill diagonally this time, but her efforts only resulted in her sliding back down the hill again. She heard Eddy chuckle and resisted the urge to throw a rock at his head.

"Here." His voice echoed, and she heard a light scuttling sound. "Grab onto that and climb up, quickly."

She shined her flashlight on the rope, resting halfway up the slope. The rumbling was getting louder. She took a deep breath and forced her fatigued limbs to rush up the slope. Once she had the rope in her grasp, she began climbing. Eddy pulled as she climbed; she felt small pieces of ice and frozen plaster flake from the ceiling and come to rest on her coat.

Then, the rumbling stopped. Her heart rate quickened; she had to hurry.

The ceiling finally gave with a deafening *CRACK!* and Ira leapt out to grab Eddy's hand, letting the rope fall. She felt his hands clamp down on her arm, yanking her forward, embracing her—then she was surrounded by blinding light. She felt a tremor in the ice, a gust of air frosted her back, and she turned her head to see part of the snow canopy give way and collapse.

"Eddy," she said.

"Yeah?"

"Can't breathe."

"Oh!" He released his bear like grip on her body, and let her roll free onto her back. "Sorry…"

She sat up and nodded, then checked to make sure the contents of her pack were all there, including her precious cargo.

"Let's see what you were willing to get us both killed for."

Eddy snatched the box out of her hand, and Ira felt her cheeks flush with warmth.

She could almost see his facial muscles twist into a grimace beneath his facemask when he scraped the ice off of the box. "Are you fucking serious?"

"Umm, yeah?"

"Tampons! You went through all of that, almost got turned into an icy pancake, for a box of tampons?"

She tossed a snowball at his face and watched him wipe his goggles clean with his gloves. "You wouldn't understand."

"Like, I get needing them." He tossed the box back to her, and she secured it in her pack as if she were handling radioactive material. She could imagine the shit-eating grin beneath his facemask. "But, couldn't you just borrow some from Lena? You women-folk are supposed to be on the same cycle when you live together, right?"

"That bitch wouldn't share her rations with me if I were the last person left on Earth. In fact, she'd probably eat them all slowly in front of me while she watched me starve."

"Come on, she can't be that bad."

"She is, she's the worst."

"Well, in any case—" Eddy stretched around, and Ira followed his gaze to the approaching wall of storm clouds casting long shadows on the city. "—we gotta get moving before that hits."

"You have my permission."

He stood up, and then helped her to her feet. There was a moment where their eyes met; Ira could feel her heart beating in her ears.

Eddy, of course, ruined it.

"Watch it, or I'll toss those back in the hole."

"You wouldn't!"

He chuckled. "Maybe not, but you get to explain to your brother why we were so late getting back."

"I knew you'd throw me under the bus." They began to shuffle across the frozen parking lot.

"Because it's your fault."

She stuck her tongue out at him, even though she knew he couldn't see it under her mask.

CHAPTER TWO

Before they reached downtown, the snow had already started to fall. Ira watched it descend in slow swinging arcs from the snowmobile as they made their way home. She sat behind Eddy, clutching tightly at his midsection; the constant hum from the engine was almost enough to drown out the howling of the winds cutting through the frozen and crumbling rooftops.

Riverside was a husk of its former self, frozen and withered. She was almost glad that the storm had obscured the jagged, rusted and broken city from her eyes. She always thought, maybe, the memories wouldn't come as easily that way—but they still came.

Through the falling snow, she could see bent traffic lights sticking out of hazy white hills. A swinging street sign that said COMMERCE ST dangled from beneath one such traffic light.

They weren't far from where she and Nico had grown up. By now, the snow had probably caused the roof to cave in, leaving those familiar brown walls and floors exposed to the elements. Maybe Papa was still in his favorite chair, frozen solid, staring into the eternal winter winds as they slowly destroyed the neighborhood—wiping it from the face of the Earth.

Eddy took a turn down one of the alleys, a shortcut to the warehouse. Broken chains that once held street signs clinked and clacked in the wind, snow caking atop their bent and rusting metal poles.

Ira caught the faded and flaking blue paint from the roof of a buried bus stop bench, just like the one where she'd had her first kiss. His name was Alex Ramos, and he was most likely dead now.

There was pain on every corner.

Eddy brought the snowmobile up a large slope that led to a small snow-covered warehouse. They parked in front of the garage door. Ira watched Eddy walk up and coax the door open. He waved her on in; she slid into his seat and drove the snowmobile into the building, parking it next to the other one.

Ira turned the key and shut it off, then walked over and closed the garage door. She tore her facemask off and took a deep breath, one that didn't taste like sweat and saliva.

Eddy let out a groan as he opened up the hatch that led to the place she refused to call home. They'd been living underground for so long that she could hardly recall what normal life was.

Eddy's hands and feet made plinking sounds as he made his way down the ladder; she followed after him and closed the hatch behind herself.

She remembered when it had just been Nico and her; back then they were only using a small section of the vast system of tunnels beneath downtown Riverside as shelter. Those had been lonely days. If it hadn't been for Nico's guidance, she'd be dead—they all would. The tunnels were mainly used for city maintenance before the ice came, but some of them had been used by the Revolutionists in the Second American Civil War as well. There were still booby traps all over the place, meant to take the lives of unsuspecting Feds who came searching for the Revolutionist base. Nico told her to be very careful where she stepped, and for good reason. Sometimes they'd hear a loud pop, and days later find a cougar's corpse, body twisted and wrong.

The cougars sometimes clawed their way past the lining in some of the barricades, probably drawn by the warmth from their generators— or looking for a tasty human-flavored snack.

They were resilient animals, but they were running low on food…Ira could empathize with them. Most of the smaller animals had already died off.

Her gaze turned to Eddy, who walked as if he knew every section of the tunnel. Eddy had been a Revolutionist in the war. She could practically feel the memories sparkling to life in his eyes as they traversed each corner of these tunnels. How many friends and enemies had he seen dead down here?

Eddy caught her staring at him.

"Your brother isn't gonna be happy we're late," he said.

"Let me handle him," Ira said.

Her nose picked up the faint smell that a hot light bulb produces when it makes contact with dust, and she knew they were home.

2

Nico's fingers twisted the knob on the ham radio, switching back to the frequency that they used for communications. Ira and Ramirez were way past due to be back from their supply run; they hadn't been using another frequency, as far as he could tell. He was starting to grow worried. His hand found the hilt of his combat knife, unfastened the strap, withdrew it, and spiked it into the weathered desk's surface. The sound echoed through the chamber; he let the knife stand there, sticking out of the desk. If Ramirez got his sister killed…he shook his head.

No.

They had to be okay.

His ears perked up to the sound of shuffling feet and laughter, Ira's laughter, coming from one of the tunnels leading into the chamber.

His eyebrows twisted together.

"Where the hell have you two been?" he asked as they entered the room. "I was just about to get the others to form a search party."

Ramirez came forward and removed his facemask, causing his unkempt beard to unfurl—not much of a contrast from his dark brown skin. "My fault, boss-man, we got sidetracked."

They got sidetracked. That's it? Nico's rough, weathered hands found the hilt of the dagger while his mind ran wild with scenarios that ended with them hooking up in some abandoned tunnel near home, just far

17

enough out of sight for anyone to notice. His fingers clawed into the arm of his chair, his hand squeezing the life out of the knife.

"Sidetracked," Nico said. "For five hours past your scheduled return time?"

"Yeah," Ramirez said. "No big deal, boss-man."

Before he knew it, he felt Ira's hand on his shoulder, keeping him from following through on the premeditated bloodshed he'd just been imagining.

"It was my fault," Ira said. "I left Eddy behind to enter an abandoned department store, and he had to catch up."

Nico's shoulders relaxed, somewhat...but still, Ira could be lying. They weren't exactly close. "Why didn't you radio in?"

"I forgot," Ramirez said. "There was a storm rolling in, so, after I caught up with your sister, I had to make sure we got back before it hit."

Just the sort of lack of discipline he expected of a traitor. "In other words, you didn't want to get your ass chewed out for a stupid decision that could have cost both of your lives."

"Did you not hear your sister, dude?"

"I did, and it seems like if you kept better watch over her, you wouldn't have been separated in the first place. Maybe you're in need of another lesson as to why it's so damn dangerous out there? Maybe you're just too fucking stupid to get it through your thick skull that this isn't a game!"

He watched Ramirez remove his coat and toss it over a nearby couch. Its impact kicked up dust and filled the chamber with the smell of mold and decay.

Go on, asshole, he thought. *Come at me. Let me end you, like I should have done when I first laid eyes on you.*

Ramirez's shoulders arched, his fists tightened into balls. Ira's grip tightened on Nico's shoulder, and she shook her head at him, as if she knew what he was thinking. That look was enough to soften his boiling rage.

"Just get out of my sight," Nico said, tossing the knife onto the worn wooden table. "I'll call for you when it's time to pass out rations."

18

He watched Ramirez snatch up his jacket and quickly exit the chamber in the direction of his room. "Fine by me."

"Did you really have to act like that?" Ira asked.

"How the fuck was I supposed to act, Ira?" he said. "What the hell am I supposed to think when you're missing for five goddamn hours."

"He saved my life today!"

"And if I had been there, you wouldn't have been in that situation in the first place."

Her face twisted into a grimace. She looked away, squeezing her eyes shut to hold back her tears; he knew the look too damn well. She stomped off for the tunnel that led to her room, stopped, and turned back to him.

"You know, the war's over for everyone," she said. "Everyone, except you."

Then she stormed into the tunnel, leaving him to stew in his anger.

She didn't understand. None of them understood.

3

Ira found herself sobbing into her pillow, her tears mixing with the fabric to create a smell that reminded her of glue. Her body's hormones were starting the rapid process of making her act like a psychopath. She'd allowed herself to lie there for a while, to calm herself before attempting to rejoin the rest of their less than merry group.

So far, it wasn't working.

She sat up and wiped her tears away with her jacket sleeve. She hadn't removed it since getting back, even though it felt like she was cooking inside of it. She had been too distracted by her brother's all but spoken threats toward Eddy to care.

She stripped off her layers; a loud beeping sound caused her to freeze in position. Her hands felt around for the cold sensation of acrylic, and she pulled out her thermal monitor out from her jacket pocket. The battery was low, but the charging dock was out in the hub with Nico. There was no way in hell she was going to go back out there after storming off.

There was something else, though: a small heat signature was resonating near the San Bernardino Mountains way north. She'd placed a thermal sensor near the city limits several days ago when one of their expeditions had taken them out of Riverside. She hadn't honestly thought it would do any good; after all, it was Mathias's idea.

The heat signature she'd picked up now wasn't exactly within walking distance; she'd have to borrow one of the snowmobiles.

There was no way that Nico would let her go after what just happened, so she'd have to wait till he cooled off. She'd charge the monitor later, and stand guard to make sure no one else caught wind of her little discovery.

This was *her* find. And it could be a *good* one too. A heat source like that could mean there were other survivors, generators—hell, maybe even a bigger, better shelter than this dump they were living in.

Maybe, if she found something like that, then Nicola would stop treating her like a damned child?

4

Nico called for ration distribution an hour later, and Ira found herself eating in silence. There they were, sitting around a weathered, dusty table, surrounded by the hum of the generators while everyone glared at the person they despised most. It was the closest thing they had to "dinner" anymore, a bunch of people that hated each other, sitting scattered around a single room, or retreating to their rooms, eating protein bars and MRE packs... When she thought about it, it almost sounded like home, minus all the dust and metal pipes extruding from a low-hanging ceiling. Their own unique, apocalyptic, deranged family.

Mathias came stalking down the hall; he was a small, skinny man, with short dreadlocks and dark skin. He made eye contact with her only for a moment, then took his share of the rations that were piled loosely on the table.

He didn't say much, preferred to keep to himself, and that had always unnerved her about him. Not so much his antisocial behavior, that she could definitely identify with, but the constant silence, and that annoying habit that he had where he'd just ignore Ira if she spoke to him. She'd only made that mistake a couple of times.

With a protein bar and an MRE pack cradled in his arms, Mathias sulked back to his room and shut the door, where he did God knows what with himself. Mathias was a fan of scrounging through old book collections when they went out to search for supplies. Nico hated that. In her brother's opinion, there was no use for books now unless they could teach you how to clean a rifle or otherwise survive.

Mathias had overheard him once, and grinned, baring his crooked white teeth, and said, "If books are no longer of use to humanity, then perhaps it's time for us to lay down and accept the cold embrace of extinction."

Those words made the frozen wasteland of Riverside, California seem a lot colder. Since then, Ira dreaded any time Mathias opened his mouth. Something about the way he spoke. He just seemed…unhinged.

Lena and Hugo came out moments later and they each took a seat across from Ira. Lena tossed her a bitchy look and flipped her stupid bottle-blonde hair back. Ira wondered where Lena kept her stash of hair color boxes, so she could trash it. That'd show her.

"So." Lena reached forward, clawing at one of the protein bars; her nails were covered in dirt and grime like everyone else's, and yet she still had the nerve to paint them red. "I heard that you and Eddy got lost today."

"We didn't get lost," Ira said. "I took a detour to find supplies."

"A detour." Lena chuckled. "Is that what you kids call it these days? I hope you grabbed a pregnancy test while you were at it."

Ira slammed her hands on the weathered table, causing the packages in the center to hop several inches in the air. "Look *bitch*, I—"

"Enough!" Nico raised his hand into the air, and at once they were silent. "We have enough problems trying to survive in this world without you two constantly fighting like a couple of children."

"I was only trying to help," Lena said, grinning like the devil-woman she was.

"Help less, eat more," Nico said.

21

"Yo, this reminds me," Hugo said, spitting bits of protein bar out his mouth. "I was rereading The Minotaur of Chaos again, and I noticed that the hero's group is a lot like us. You know, it's weird. Like. Everyone fulfills a role, you know? And there are these two girls that wanna kill each other, just like Ira and Lena."

"Imagine that," Ira said.

"No, really." Hugo started waving his hands around enthusiastically. "The hero's the leader, and he's real quiet, like Nico, then there's his oldest friend, an elven princess who's tough, like Ira—"

Lena rolled her eyes. "If anything, I'm the tough one."

"Only thing tough about you is how much you can fit inside you," Ira said.

Lena's mouth dropped open. If there were any forks on the table, Ira was sure Lena'd have tried to stab her in the eye.

"No, baby—" Hugo wrapped his arms around Lena, not missing a beat. "—you're the cleric, the woman who steals the minotaur's heart and tames him at the end."

Nico sighed. Hugo saw the look in his eyes and went silent.

"Uh, sorry, B," Hugo said.

That was how Nico always reacted to things that weren't grounded in the here and now. He hadn't always been like that; the war had changed him, made him distrust anything that wasn't, as he put it, *real*.

It wasn't the first time Hugo had brought the book up, and it probably wouldn't be the last. He was obsessed with it.

Ira knew that he hadn't been much of a reader before the ice came. Apparently, he'd been a big YouTube star back before the big freeze started. He'd avoided the war, of course. Wasn't his thing. Nico had discovered him at the Riverside Public Library, huddled in the corner, clutching the book tight to his chest; he'd been living off the leftover junk food from nearby vending machines.

Hugo didn't have many skills, unless you considered talking into a camera enthusiastically a skill.

Nico didn't.

It didn't seem like her brother to take someone in that he couldn't readily use. Even Lena had been a nurse before the ice came. Ira figured Nico just felt sorry for him. No man left behind, that sort of thing.

Everyone turned at once when Eddy walked into the chamber. "What'd I miss?"

"You're late, as usual," Nico said.

"Oh, you're still here? I was hoping you'd have gone back to your cave to spend the night brooding already."

Nico's eyes narrowed. The temperature seemed to shoot up several degrees.

"Take a seat," Nico said.

Eddy took a seat next to Ira and grabbed at his share of the rations. Nico watched him like a predator might watch its prey before the kill. Eddy unwrapped his protein bar and chewed it with a big sheepish grin on his face. He enjoyed getting under Nico's skin; Ira worried that one day he'd go too far, and she'd lose either of the men closest to her.

"Hugo was just telling us that the people in his fantasy book are a lot like us," Ira said. "I'm apparently an elven princess."

"You're not a princess," Eddy said. "You're the loud village girl that calls the villain a dumb jerk and gets tossed in jail or something."

"There's no one like that in the book," Hugo said.

"There should be," Eddy said. "Cause that's what she'd do."

"Can't argue there," Ira said.

"What are you trying to say?" Nico clasped his hands together. "That Ira would enter into seditious behavior, become a rebel?"

Eddy grinned. "You tell me, you're the big soldier, right? Aren't you used to spotting rebels, detaining them?"

"I could tell you were resistance scum the moment I saw you," Nico said. "Ira would never join the Revolutionists."

Eddy's grin faded. "Are you so sure?"

"Guys—" Ira stood up and wedged herself between them at the end of the table "—you're both manly men, and I love you both equally."

"I'll bet you do," Lena said.

Nico glared at Lena and stood up, brushing Ira's arm away. "I'm going to bed. Ira, you have first watch tonight, followed by Hugo."

23

And then Nico was gone. Eddy started laughing. Ira smacked his arm.

"Did you have to do that?" she asked.

"What?" Eddy said. "He's been an asshole to me all day!"

"Come on, Hugo." Lena stood up and pulled Hugo by his collar. "The lovebirds need their privacy."

"Bye, Lena," Eddy said, waving like a fool and talking in what he called his *special* voice. "It was so nice talking to you!"

Lena rolled her eyes and dragged Hugo back to her room. Ira often wondered why she'd latched onto Hugo. She guessed that it was because he was easy to control.

Ira noticed that Lena hadn't touched her rations.

"You gonna eat those?" Eddy said.

"I don't know, I'm not really hungry."

"Why? Because of what Lena said?" Eddy opened up his MRE and dug at it with his fingers. "You shouldn't listen to her, you're giving her exactly what she wants."

"Ugh." Ira leaned back in her chair. "I hate her so much."

"You should really just ignore her."

"Like you?" Ira sat back up and made a flailing gesture with her arms. "'Bye, Lena, it was so nice talking to you.' God, I could puke."

"I was being ironic, if you'd have noticed. I didn't share one word with her. You should try being overly nice to her, it'll totally throw off her game with you."

"Oh, like you were doing with Nico?" Ira said, glaring at him.

"That's different," Eddy said with his mouth full.

"How?"

"I'm right." He grinned, chocolate staining his teeth.

"Why do I hang out with you?"

"Because I'm awesome." He shoved a big piece of chocolate in his mouth and started chewing with his mouth open. "And you'd be incomplete without my wisdom."

"Chew with your mouth closed!" Ira laughed, punching his arm playfully.

They sat together, eating quietly for a while. As soon as she was done with her rations Ira retreated to her room and checked the monitor's battery life. She waited another hour for the others to sack out for the night before she attempted to charge it. It was her turn to stand watch, though she was surprised Nico hadn't made Eddy do it as punishment. Maybe he knew he was in the wrong for snapping at him? It didn't matter anymore; Nico would never apologize, and Eddy would eventually forget about the whole thing. He never held a grudge.

Ira watched the battery charge progress bar slowly increase over the course of several hours, and she mulled over how long she might have to wait before taking the snowmobile out. How long would Nico play the overprotective brother and keep her locked up tight?

After the battery was charged, she moved the monitor back to her room. It was getting close to time for Hugo to start his watch, so she went to wake him up. He was in his room, of course, and Lena was huddled up next to him. She tried not to enjoy waking her up with him, and failed. Hugo ran his hand through his short black hair, yawned, and took up point somewhere where he would likely fall asleep on watch—and get yelled at by Nico in the morning when he was discovered.

Ira retreated to her room, crawled into bed, and curled up into a ball.

Soon, she let the darkness take her.

5

Nico found himself in the ration storage chamber, taking inventory of their remaining supplies. In the early days, they'd managed to scavenge together enough freezers and refrigerators, and a few generators, to sufficiently store all of the food that they needed to survive—at least until the stuff broke down, or the supplies in the city ran out. There was a separate room for water and liquid storage. In the past three years, he'd been forced to cut daily rations by fifty percent due to their inability to replenish them fast enough. If it had just been him and Ira, their supplies would have lasted much longer, but having to feed so many mouths was costly.

He found himself opening and closing each refrigerator, each freezer, and notating how much of everything they still had. After his check on the dry food storage, the results were less than pleasing. If he had to guess, their current supplies would last them about six months.

He'd have to start pushing their search patterns further and further out of the city if there was any hope of survival, but that also meant that their supply runs would take longer, perhaps even days, and that was a risk that could prove fatal, even with every precaution taken.

In the beginning, when the ships were finally boarding regular folk to the equator, Nico and Ira'd had to deal with lots of looters, with people who were as ravenous as they were vicious in their need to survive. Those people died quickly when the real cold set in, when the world froze over for good and the city became a frozen necropolis. They hadn't run into a stranger in quite some time, but that didn't mean that there weren't others out there still. People just like them, who thought that there was a possibility that they could be the last ones left alive on the whole Earth.

The sad truth of it was, the longer they progressed into this modern ice age, the more likely it became that any food sources would become spoiled or get looted by other unknown parties, animal or otherwise.

Water was another issue. Mathias had developed a means to recycle their bodily fluids—based on a type of water purification that had been proposed for long-term space flight—but it was an ad hoc pile of shit, and they lost a small amount of water from each attempt to recycle their fluids. They had other means of getting fresh water, one of them being collecting fresh fallen snow and melting it, but as soon as it came down to boiling snow and ice that could contain harmful bacteria, or worse yet, Measure 86—the bioweapon his government had forced him to use during the war, which would see them dead in a matter of days after exposure—it was probably just wiser to let dehydration kill them instead.

Without a steady supply of medicine or antibiotics, every risk, even one as innocent as drinking boiled snow, had to be carefully considered. Eventually, without a better means of recycling, or a large source of fresh water, they'd run out completely.

The lengths of time that the human body could survive without certain things were determined by a rule of three: three minutes without air, three days without water, and three weeks without food. That rule said nothing of the resilience of a person's sanity.

Their whole group was a ticking time bomb in that regard.

His hand was shaking. He tightened his fingers into a fist and started to count down from ten.

No, he thought. *Not again.*

His heart used his rib cage as a punching bag; his head hit the cold concrete floor. He felt himself hyperventilating. He knew the symptoms well, but he hadn't actually had a panic attack in over three months. Why now?

His vision blurred, and he could have sworn that he smelled the distinct aroma of blood…

The concussive force from each bullet, shot from the barrel of his AR-15, left his ears ringing. It was the very embodiment of chaos, but, despite that chaos, they did have a strategy. The enemy was using an abandoned building as cover; he was laying down cover fire, while Hernandez flanked the Revolutionists. Before he even knew it, dirt and rubble exploded from within the abandoned building, and the firing stopped. For a second, he froze.

Those were once our people, he thought.

He couldn't help but be mesmerized.

A single enemy combatant had managed to avoid Hernandez's grenade.

The Revolutionist was trying to flee, pumping her legs and screaming bloody murder.

Three shots in the back stopped her legs and she collapsed in the dirt, silent. He never even saw her face, or the expression she might have made as her body went limp.

"Holy shit," Boyd said. "They didn't even have a chance, right, Hartman?"

Nico nodded. "Yeah…"

"What's wrong, man?"

He shook his head. "Nothing, Boyd, I'm good."

"All right, let's get back to base camp," Boyd said. "Drinks are on me tonight!"

"Fuck yeah, they are!" Martinez said. "You still owe me for that bullshit you tried to pull on poker night."

"I wasn't cheatin'," Boyd said. "I swear on my mother's grave."

"Shut up, both of you," Nico said. "Let's get the hell out of here."

The war had already been on for several months, but until now, there hadn't been any actual fighting. California, Oregon, and Washington State had each attempted to secede from the union, and had been met with warnings of civil war. Nevada, Arizona and New Mexico joined the rest of the west in response. At first, politicians from each state got together to try to negotiate a peaceful exit from the union, but the Federal Government, the corporations that had vested interests in keeping the Union whole, and the new president just weren't going to let that happen. It wasn't long after those meetings that the California Republic had declared civil war on the United States. From the couple of battles Nico had been involved in, it was obvious that the California Republic, or the Revolutionists, as the internet was starting to call them, were in way over their heads.

When they got back to base, Nico found himself taking off his Talos armor. He had the upper layers stripped, and was just about to open up the exoskeleton, when he heard a deafening explosion.

He rushed out to see what had happened, still half covered in armor. Unarmored soldiers scattered, running from a large cloud of smoke rising up from the barracks.

Fire raged from inside, and he could hear screaming...

"Nico." Hugo's hand was on his shoulder, shaking him back to consciousness. "Man, wake up."

Nico sat up and slapped Hugo's hand away. He didn't need anyone's help. It took a few moments for him to get his bearings back. He knelt there for a moment, his head in his hand.

"You okay?" Hugo asked.

"Yeah," Nico said. "Get back to work, it's your turn to make sure the generator exhaust ports are clear of snow. If those get clogged, they could blow."

Hugo shook his head and exited the food storage chamber, mumbling obscenities.

His watch read 0400. The others would be up soon, so there was no time to sit around feeling sorry for himself. With one hand on his knee, he forced himself to his feet and got back to work.

CHAPTER THREE

She dreams of an infinite plane of hills against a drifting gray sky that has the texture of a dead lung.

Mouths in the leathery ground open and close. A black shape at the top of the hill opens its jaws and drops something too mangled to be human in one of the open mouth-pits.

Screams fill the putrid air.

The silhouette turns its head to her.

That's when she realizes that she's the one who's been screaming.

The morning came with a bang—several of them. At first, Ira thought it sounded like someone had dropped a bunch of pots out in the tunnel...but, as she pushed the fog from her mind, she heard shouting.

She rubbed her eyes and sluggishly rolled out of bed. Part of her didn't want to know where those sounds were coming from.

She walked to her bedroom door.

Her hand cupped the doorknob, she twisted it open.

"You fucking idiot!" She heard Nico yelling, his voice carrying through the entire dwelling. "What did I tell you about clearing the ventilation on the surface?"

Ira found herself creeping into the tunnel, inching toward the source of her brother's one-sided shouting match. She had a pretty good guess who he was yelling at.

"You better hope they're salvageable," Nico said. "Or I'll have half a mind to send you off into the ice wearing nothing but your long johns!"

She stood at the edge of the tunnel, peering into the den where they'd had their argument earlier. Nico's face was twisted into a scowl, and Hugo was sitting on one of the couches, his eyes half-open and drowsy.

"Called it," she said. "I knew he'd fall asleep on watch."

Her brother's damaged angry blue eyes stabbed through her. "This isn't funny, Ira. This dumb son-of-a-bitch just cost us three generators."

Her heart sank.

"Hugo was supposed to check the ventilation, but instead, he decided to take a nap, even though I ordered him to get back to work."

"Man, I said I didn't mean to," Hugo said.

Nico grabbed him by the cuff of his long johns. "I don't give a damn what you meant!"

"Nicola," Ira said. "Maybe we should worry about making sure the other ventilation ports are clear, and fix the three that are broken, before you bash his skull in?"

She watched her brother stew in his rage for a few moments, his other fist shaking. He tossed Hugo back against the wall of the couch and approached the ham radio, held the receiver to his lips.

"This is Nicola." His voice echoed throughout the entire shelter, carried over a crude PA system. "I need everyone in the northern den in less than ten minutes. Anyone who's late goes without rations for the morning."

It took all of five minutes and thirty seconds for everyone to file out of their rooms and park themselves in front of Nico. Ira paced around them, finding Eddy. She poked at his back, and he acknowledged her presence with a slight nod.

"Hugo here has something to say," Nico said. "Don't you?"

Hugo looked up at Nico and shook his head. "No way, man, they'll kill me."

"Too bad," Nico said. "You're the one that fell asleep on watch!"

Hugo sat forward and cupped his hands together, exposing his pasty white palms. "We lost three generators…"

31

"Tell them why." Nico paced back and forth, like an angry General.

Hugo stirred in his seat, popping his knuckles one by one. "I fell asleep...and snow got clogged in the vents...and they exploded."

Ira saw Eddy's shoulders pulsing with his increased pace of breathing; she could practically feel the heat radiate off his body. He turned around, faced her, closed his eyes, and took a deep breath. His ritual for calming himself.

"Now, despite our collective desire to beat Hugo into an unrecognizable bloody mess," Nico said, "we have a job to do, and we have fuck all time to get it done. Three generators is not enough to power the heaters in this place, we're going to see a considerable loss of heat within hours, so we've got to take initiative and find a way to replace, or repair, the damaged ones."

Eddy turned back around. "I'll have to inspect them, but if I get the parts—and the damage isn't too extreme—I can make repairs."

"I passed one of them on my way here," Mathias said. "I can't be sure, but it looked like the block exploded. Now, I only minored in engineering, but I'd say you'd be better off replacing the whole of the unit."

"You'd be surprised," Eddy said. "If the block is the only thing that's broken, then I can probably still fix it."

Nico nodded. "We've got two snowmobiles, so fuel them up, and take them to either end of the city."

"We'll need to search for anything that can be useful, broken-down cars, lawn mowers, anything," Eddy said.

"Are we forgetting that there's a storm going on outside?" Lena raised her hands up, palms facing the ceiling pipes. So dramatic. "We'll be lucky to see our own feet out there!"

"Knees," Ira said. "You'll barely be able to see your knees. Snow, remember?"

Lena rolled her eyes. "Whatever."

"That's enough chatter," Nico said. "Fan out and get suited up! I'll inform you who you're traveling with before we set out."

Ira saluted her brother, and the irony was most likely lost on him.

2

Ira pulled her snow pants up to her waist and fastened them in place. There came three knocks at her door. She opened the door to find Eddy geared up in his blue thermal coat—and freshly shaved.

"The beard!" she said.

He rubbed his chiseled jaw; there were bits of paper covering the areas where he'd accidentally cut himself. The beard always brought out his rich amber eyes. "Shush, I had to."

"But why!"

"It's a liability out there, didn't want it turning into an ice cube."

The beard made him look at least ten years older than her, when they were only a few years apart. Ira hadn't seen him without it in months; she'd almost forgotten what his face looked like underneath that bush. She grinned.

"What?" he said.

"Nothing."

They stood there for a moment; Ira avoided eye contact.

"Hey, Eddy," she said, sitting down on her bed.

"Yeah?"

"You ever wonder what woulda happened if we left with the others?"

"Haven't we had this discussion before?" He took a seat next to her; she felt his weight sink into the mattress. "There's no way any of us here would have been able to afford a ticket."

"Yeah, but, just pretend for a moment."

"Pretend." She heard him sigh, and felt him lay on his back, shaking the bed. "Okay, well, at the time, I was still fighting. I was an enemy of the state, technically, so, it's just hard to imagine for me…"

"What if you weren't?"

"I'd still be too poor."

"Ugh, forget it." She lay back next to him, and his arm wrapped around her. Her ears felt like they were burning.

They locked eyes. Ira's heart started to pound.

She wanted him to pull her closer, wanted to feel his lips on hers.

Nico will never approve, she thought.

"Once when I was stationed near here at the end of the war, we got word about the ships," Eddy said, tearing his eyes away from her. "We knew, all of us, that we'd never be on one of those ships."

"Yeah..."

He was right, of course. Back then, when the war was starting to grind to a halt due to the impending crisis, scientists came out and announced that the equator would be the safest haven for humanity for the time being. The rich and the powerful had been first in line to take up residence in those areas. The native populations had protested, but such protests had proven moot against the will of the most powerful governments in the world.

It was a trickle-down effect, really: first the rich left, then the politicians, then the upper class, and by the time it got down to the middle and lower classes, the demand for tickets leaving the Northern Hemisphere was so great that no one could afford one. Overpopulation in the equator became an issue as well, which hiked prices even higher.

In a way, it had been a death sentence.

"You know," Eddy said, "they're probably suffering the cold now too."

"You think?"

"Yeah, eggheads on TV said this wasn't a normal ice age. Thinking about it that way, the overcrowding and all, maybe we're the lucky ones."

"That's so depressing."

"That's life now."

Unable to find the words that would clear the awkward and depressing tone that they'd set, they lay there for a while. There was a stillness in the air that drove Ira half-mad. She sat up and grabbed for her black fur coat, slipped it on.

"We should get going, Nico's probably waiting," she said.

She reached for the acrylic thermal monitor, slipped it into one of her pockets, and patted herself down. She might not get a chance to investigate, considering their situation, but she felt it might come in handy.

She walked past Eddy, and he followed closely behind.

"Yeah," he said. "Maybe with Hugo's fuckup, he'll forget about yesterday."

Ira scoffed. "Like hell, he'll hold that over your head for at least a month."

"Guess we better find something good, so he forgets."

"There's an idea."

They arrived to find the hatch to the surface open. It was roughly the size of a manhole cover, and inside of it was a ladder and a vertical tunnel that led to the warehouse on the surface where they kept the snowmobiles.

Ira looked up the tunnel, grabbed the ladder, then hoisted herself up. The sound of hands slipping over pipes reverberated through the tunnel as she climbed up. The others had already gathered in the building: Nico was rigging up the two snowmobiles with tow cables and a sled; Hugo was standing in the corner sulking like a puppy that'd just been hit with a newspaper; Lena wasn't far from Hugo, playing with her nails.

"Lena, Ira, Ramirez." Nico stood up and clapped the dust off his hands. "You'll be in group one, the rest of us will be in group two."

"Ugh, why do I have to go with them?" Lena asked.

"So you and Hugo don't get shot." Nico patted at the side-arm he kept holstered around his waist.

Lena crossed her arms and avoided Nico's stare.

"I'll be taking my group west," Nico said. "Ramirez, you'll be taking your group east."

Eddy nodded.

"You'll keep going till you've filled that sled with at least one piece of usable machinery. You know what you're looking for."

"Naturally," Mathias said.

Eddy pulled his facemask up and slipped his gloves on. "Well, we gonna do this?"

Nico walked over to the shutters that kept them safe from the harsh winter weather and pressed a button on the side panel; the shutters creaked and rattled as they were dragged up into the interior of the wall. A blast of arctic wind and snow filled the warehouse like a river spilling from a dam. Ira quickly covered her mouth and slipped her gloves on. The others did the same.

Eddy sat at the front of the snowmobile, Ira sat behind him, and Lena reluctantly took the third seat behind her. Eddy checked himself over, made sure he had a clear line of sight of his compass.

The loud buzzing sounds from the snowmobiles filled the chamber. Nico, Mathias, and Hugo headed out first. Eddy revved the engine, laughed like a madman, and let the snowmobile carry them into the blizzard.

If it was morning, Ira couldn't tell. The storm had blocked out the sun and cast a shadow across the city. The buildings and ice structures were silhouettes in the falling snow. Before the space cloud, people had called it a whiteout, but now, it seemed more like a gray shadow swallowing everything whole and plunging the world into chaos.

The winds smacked and tugged at Ira's clothes; she hugged Eddy's waist tight, then she felt Lena's arms wrap around her, like a snake wrapping its length around its prey, ready to constrict and strangle the life out of her, and a shiver crawled down her spine.

Shadows raced by them; they appeared to be traveling much faster than they actually were. The snow was so deep that Eddy had to constantly edge the nose of the snowmobile up to keep from getting stuck. It was soon very clear that trekking out into an ice age winter snowstorm was a terrible idea.

3

Nico twisted the handlebars to the left and guided the snowmobile down into a ditch, temporarily hiding them from the storm. Patches of snow had begun to stick to his jacket, which would make moving any considerable distance difficult. He opened his satchel and pulled out a set of binoculars, raised them to his face, and attempted to peer through the thick snowfall.

"Man, I can't see shit," Hugo said. "How we supposed to find anything when you can't see your feet?"

"Interesting question," Nico said. "Should have thought of that before you decided to nap and destroy the one thing keeping us alive out here."

Mathias stirred behind Nico and sank his boots into the snow.

"What are you doing?" Nico asked.

"Stretching my legs," Mathias said. "I trust that's allowed?"

"Suit yourself."

Nico returned to surveying their surroundings.

"It strikes me that we'd have better luck finding anything of use near the old RTA bus depot," Mathias said.

Nico dropped the binoculars back into his satchel, clasped it shut. "It's not far from here. Sounds like we've got an idea."

"We can use GPS to get us there," Mathias said.

"Those satellites haven't seen repairs in years—who knows if they're even working," Nico said.

"Who cares?" Hugo waved his hands above his head. "We gotta do something quick, B, before we get froze solid!"

"He's right," Mathias said. "Even if the signal from the GPS isn't precise, it's still better than going out there blind in this storm."

Nico revved the engine and waved for Mathias to get back on; Mathias nodded and hopped between the other two. Nico guided them out of the ditch and back into the storm. Stirring movement and fidgeting in the middle seat told him that Mathias was getting his GPS out. There was something odd about taking directions from a machine high above the Earth's surface. He wondered if anyone had been left stranded on the ISS when the ice came.

Which death would be worse, Nico thought. *Freezing on Earth, or dying of starvation in space?*

The GPS wasn't accurate, but it helped them get within one thousand feet of the RTA bus depot; they used the buildings and frozen landmarks to guide them the rest of the way. It got more than a little irritating, listening to Mathias's shrill voice, barking out locations and directions.

Nico found a place to park the snowmobile, but kept it running. The winds were getting worse. They swept waves of falling snow like claws raking the surface of the earth. They coiled like serpents in places, kicking up miniature ice tornadoes. The street must have been at least five feet beneath them. Nico tried not to think about his sister.

This was no place for people.

"All right, Hugo." Nico got off the snowmobile and slung his pack from the sled to his back. "You're going to stay with the snowmobile, keep the snow off of it, the sled too."

"Man." Hugo's shoulders sagged.

"Mathias," Nico said.

"Yes?"

"Let's go."

Ira was growing impatient. Eddy had taken them near the border of Riverside and Colton; the hills were hazy, white silhouettes in the distance. They found a few car parts here and there along the way, but judging by Eddy's lack of enthusiasm she didn't think they'd made much headway.

"What if Nico hasn't found anything either?" Ira asked.

"What!" Eddy said.

She repeated herself, shouting this time.

"Don't think like that. Try to stay positive." He was shouting as loud as he could, trying to overcome the howl of the wind.

"No, seriously," Ira said. "If none of us manages to find something to repair those generators, we're screwed."

"We just have to hope that—"

"What if we had another option?" Ira asked.

"What are you getting at?" Eddy said.

"Just keep driving for a second," Ira said. "I'll show you."

She tried to feel out the shape of the heat monitor near the small of her back. Lena was still holding on for dear life; she couldn't retrieve the monitor with the other woman attempting to strangle the life out of her.

"Stop," Ira said.

"What!" Eddy turned his head as far as he could without losing sight of the snowmobile's nose.

"Stop the snowmobile!"

Eddy brought them to a full stop. The snow was coming down in massive clumps. The howl of the wind came from high above in the darkened clouds, like some eons-old eldritch beast, casting its shadow on the Earth.

"Now, let go of my waist." Ira gestured to Lena, and she complied.

"What's wrong with you now?" Lena asked. "You know we're gonna freeze if we sit here for too long, right?"

"Shut your trap for a moment." Ira unzipped the compartment that held the monitor and dragged it out. The other two stood up and crowded around her to get a better look at the screen.

The homing signal was all the way north, in the mountains. It would be feasible to reach it if the storm broke part way. If not…they'd all probably die.

It would take quite a bit to convince them to follow her on this.

"What's that blip?" Eddy asked.

"It's a heat signature I picked up last night," Ira said. "It could be worth checking out."

"That's all the way in the mountains, Ira," Eddy said. "It could take all night to get there if the storm doesn't let up."

"Won't we die?" Lena asked.

"We'll freeze to death if we don't get parts for those generators, right?" Ira shook her head. "But even that's a long shot. Eventually they'll break down and need to be replaced, and supplies are becoming more and more scarce within the city limits."

"I don't see how venturing out to the mountains to check out a dot on a screen helps us," Lena said.

Ira rolled her eyes. "That dot is a massive heat signature, idiot. It could be a power source of its own, and if it is that means *heat*. Warmth. And if that's the case, we can relocate."

"What if it's a complete waste of time?" Lena asked. "What if it's another camp of survivors?"

"Then we barter with them." Eddy pumped his fist. "Get the parts we need."

"Unless they're cannibals!" Lena kicked at the snow.

"It's the best shot we have, Eddy," Ira said.

Eddy took the monitor in his hand, stared at it for a moment, probably considering his options. It seemed like an eternity, waiting for his reply; then, he nodded.

"We'll go," Eddy said.

"This is bullshit!" Lena stomped her feet in the snow, kicking icicles up into the air that got swept away into the wind. "Of course you'd listen to her!"

"Get on the snowmobile," Eddy said.

"No!" Lena said.

"Now!" Eddy pointed at the snowmobile, towering over her. "Or we can leave you behind, if you'd prefer."

Lena stood there for several moments, looking back and forth between Eddy and Ira, before she finally stomped over and took a seat on the snowmobile. Ira followed, and Eddy took the front seat again; the engine gave a sharp buzz, which cut through the constant cracking of the snowfall and wind.

Ira watched the progress on her monitor and gave directions. The snowfall started to let up after about an hour of constant travel. Lena didn't make a peep for the final leg of the journey. The outline of the San Bernardino mountains crept into view, and before Ira knew it, they were starting to drive uphill.

5

Nico gave him the signal, and Mathias smashed open the frozen grapheme cover that was protecting the bus's engine. It shattered into thousands of pieces like it'd been exposed to liquid nitrogen. Nico bent low, shined his flashlight into the engine, and felt around inside. Mathias held a knapsack to gather up the parts that Nico haphazardly tossed out of the compartment. There wasn't much time for finesse.

"I'm going to try to remove the unit," Nico said. "Get the sled."

Nico watched Mathias turn around, stumble up the hill, cut through the hole in the rusted chain-link gate, and motion for Hugo to help him untether the sled. He brought out the plasma torch on his belt and used it to sever the hoses and bolts holding parts of the engine in place. By the time he had it loose, Mathias had brought the sled back to him.

"Winded?" Nico asked.

Mathias nodded; he kept lurching over and breathing hard. "Forgive me, I'm not used to taking an EVA of this length."

Nico shook his head and resisted the urge to tell the gangly bastard to man up; he let Mathias rest for a few moments before waving him over to help him lug the engine piece onto the sled. That piece only made up the engine block, less than a quarter of the entire machine. They spent about thirty minutes loading additional parts onto the sled before dragging it back up the hill.

Nico spent several moments hooking the tethers back up to the sled, sealed up their packs, and had them take their seats.

The extra weight slowed them down, but they managed to get back home using Mathias's GPS. Somehow, he'd managed to figure out the margin for error in the GPS signal and calculate how far off the location reticle would be. Nico hated to admit how useful Mathias had become, at least when it came to using his brains.

Nico parked in front of the metal shutters and waved for Hugo to go find the lever to open them from the outside, then guided the snowmobile into the interior of the building and cut the engine.

Hugo rushed inside and closed the shutter.

"Eddy ain't back yet," Hugo said.

Nico got off the snowmobile, shaking off some of the snow that coated the outer layer of his thermal jacket and pants. "I'll raise them on the CB; you two get that thing down into the tunnels and start thinking of ways to fix our generator problem."

Nico descended through the hatch and left Hugo and Mathias to do some actual work for a change. He found himself in front of the CB again, and tuned into Ira's CB frequency.

"Ira, do you read me?"

No answer. He tried again.

"Ira, it's Nico, do you read me?"

He sank back into his chair and unzipped his jacket. If she was ignoring him again, or if Eddy was doing this on purpose, he'd... He tried to calm himself down.

Failed.

All he could do was wait now.

CHAPTER FOUR

The storm clouds started to break up, giving way to patches of dim blue sky above. The snow itself stopped about halfway through their journey. Eddy took the snowmobile through what was once the 91 Freeway, where the snow would be smoothest. He took care to avoid large expanses of raised road, where the supports were weakest from the weight of the ice.

The city of San Bernardino was practically entombed in the snow, and what buildings were still left standing were nothing more than skeletons of their former selves. Not that the city had been much better before the ice came; even before the war it had been no more than a decaying slum.

Ira imagined she was a little girl again, riding passenger with her mom, peering out the window at the sights with a slushee squeezed between her tiny legs. The Carousel Mall—not much of a mall, just a decaying mausoleum waiting to be torn down and replaced by a new housing development that would never come. Now it was just a mound of snow and ice, the once prominent—at one time, iconic—sign barely peeking above the snow to a gray sky of twisting, indifferent clouds.

The Inland Center Mall had suffered a worse fate when the war broke out. Even now, the ceiling was caved in from where explosions had detonated during an ugly fight between the Revolutionists and the

Feds. With the snow covering it, it just looked like some frozen vortex to another world.

There had been a bowling alley on H Street that Ira's grandmother used to take her to. It had smelled of used gum and shoe polish before it finally closed down in the late 2010s, and now, who knows where the hell it was in that sea of white?

The courthouse where her grandfather had gotten arraigned for his third DUI was also hard to find. Compared to Riverside, San Bernardino was practically a memory already.

"My tío's garage used to be around here," Eddy said.

"Yeah?" Ira said, resting her head against his back.

Lena snickered.

She could almost feel Eddy's eyes piercing through the layers of snow, peering down memory lane. "That's where I learned engines. He'd take me there after school and I'd help him reassemble them."

"Isn't that against child labor laws?" Lena asked.

"Shut up, Lena," Ira said.

Soon they were climbing hills and ascending what they hoped was left of the old mountain road leading up to Big Bear. The treetops that were left standing just inches above the snow line. Here, their progress slowed to a crawl.

It was damn eerie. This had all once been a forest, where bears and dear and rabbits lived. Campers and hunters alike would come here to enjoy the elements, get away from big city life. Now there weren't even ghosts, just miles and miles of ice marching up the incline, and the howl of the wind that swept razor-sharp icicles up on long sweeping arcs to nowhere. A never-ending cycle.

Slowly, a massive, icy cliff came into view over the top of the next hill. It was only dwarfed by the snowcapped mountain peaks.

Eddy brought the snowmobile to a stop. Ira got off and started walking toward the base of the cliff. She squinted her eyes, trying to see the top. It was a straight vertical climb, and there didn't look like there was any other way up.

"Your heat signature stops at the top of that cliff," Eddy said.

"Sweet!" she said.

Ira's hands scurried and scuttled through her pack, snatching hold of her multi-spectrum binoculars. What her eyes couldn't see, the binoculars easily picked up in infrared.

"What do you see?" Eddy asked.

She saw a large heat signature emerge from beneath the ice. That was a surprise...somehow she'd imagined it'd be above ground. "I think it's inside the mountain."

"Inside?" Eddy said.

"Cannibals!" Lena said.

Ira rolled her eyes from within her goggles and started digging through her pack for climbing gear. "Hope you didn't skip leg day."

"Wouldn't that be arm day?" Eddy said.

"Technically, it'd be cardio or both. I never went to the gym." She shuffled around in her pack, retrieved her climbing picks, and watched Eddy and Lena dig theirs out from their own packs.

"This is stupid," Lena said. "We're going to die."

"Always a possibility." Eddy walked over to the icy cliff face and stabbed a spike into it. The spike gave off a loud clang that sounded down the mountain. "Doesn't mean you need to remind us every five seconds."

Lena crossed her arms and pouted.

Ira laughed and followed Eddy up the cliff. Eddy was already ahead of her by several feet; she shook her head.

No you don't, she thought. *I'm getting there first.*

A smile formed beneath her facemask, stretching her chapped lips. Lena was trailing behind them, probably pissing and moaning with every foot she climbed. The cliff's top was only about a couple hundred feet above her current position, and she'd climbed higher before.

"Gotta move faster, slowpoke," Ira said, chuckling. She could feel the adrenaline pumping through her veins as she climbed past Eddy.

Ira began to climb faster; she could feel her pulse in her temples, could see her breath streaming from her facemask.

The top was so close. The bright, bluish ice chunks sticking out near the top, clawing at the air, harshly contrasted with the drifting gray clouds high above.

She was going to make it!

"Ira, don't—"

"—Shit!" Ira felt her body drop several feet in an instant. She swung a desperate arm out, stabbing her pick into a solid piece of ice. She let one hand dangle off to the side and told herself not to look down, but—stupidly—she did anyway.

The frozen landscape below her stretched on for miles. The ice sheets looked like an eldritch claw rising up from beneath the Earth to crush what was left of the city in its grip. She squeaked, tried to stifle her own fear of painting the ice below an unflattering shade of red, and stabbed her other climbing pick back into the ice, stabilizing herself.

"Jesus," Eddy said. "Don't scare me like that!"

"Right." She grunted, hoisted herself up, and kept climbing. "Because I did it on purpose!"

Eddy reached the top first and helped pull her up over the edge of the ice wall. Ira dusted herself off and took a look around their surroundings, while Eddy stayed behind to help Lena.

"Does it feel slightly warmer up here?" Ira asked.

Eddy's grunts while heaving Lena up over the edge echoed up the hill toward the mountain's peak. "No idea."

Ira walked forward, fastened her climbing picks around her belt, and waved her hands around. The temperature had risen several degrees—something you got real sensitive to when surrounded by constant biting cold. She could see a small dark area near the start of another incline. She wiped the ice away from her goggles—it was a cave! She ran over to it; her feet made scrunching noises in the fresh snow.

She stretched her hand out to the cave. It was heat all right, faint, but it was there. She tested her footing in the cave mouth and proceeded forward.

"Ira!" She heard Eddy's feet rapidly crunching across the snow. "Wait up!"

The walls of the cave looked like they had been blasted out, melted at precise angles that it looked more like a subway tunnel than anything else. She could see faint hints of pipes and rock beneath the thick coating of ice, cascading into pitch-black darkness. She was

46

starting to get the feeling that the heat signature was a generator of some sort, and if that was the case, Nico would be very happy.

Deep into the tunnel, out of daylight's reach, she thought she saw movement. She couldn't be sure; but it was as if the darkness itself moved, like some great beast stirring after a long slumber. The memory of a nightmare she'd had flooded to the surface of her thoughts; the beast turning its head to her on a leathery hill before a gray sky. Her heart seized in her chest for half a moment, but when she squinted her eyes harder, she saw nothing. Panicked, she sparked a flare, turning the interior of the tunnel a bright orange-pink.

The tunnel was empty. It had only been her imagination.

Still, for a moment, a nameless fear crept upon her, like a whisper in her ear.

"Damn it." Eddy came up behind her, then bent over hands on knees and caught his breath. "Don't run off like that!"

"Sorry," Ira said. "I got excited."

Eddy checked behind himself. "Yeah, but as annoying as her bitching is, Lena might have a point. I mean, what the hell could be buried out here that gives off a heat signature like that?"

"Careful, there…I'm getting the strong urge to run ahead and leave you both behind." A tiny voice inside her told her to listen to him, to listen to her fear. Ira silenced it. This was her moment.

"All I'm saying is that we need to be careful, okay?" Eddy looked around himself, a faraway look in his eyes. "This would have been right in the middle of the forest. If that's the case, I don't imagine many people knew about it."

"Uh-huh, exciting, right?" Ira continued walking toward the end of the tunnel.

It was a strange mix of emotions she was feeling. She was excited, yet, despite that, there was this sinking feeling in her gut. She tried to tell herself that it was just nerves.

"Ira." Nico's voice called over the CB. "Ira, goddamn it, answer!"

Both of them stopped in their tracks and looked at each other. Ira imagined both of their expressions read something like, *oh crap, we did it again.*

Eddy scrambled for his CB receiver, which was wrapped up inside his pack to keep it from freezing over; Ira's hands covered his as he raised it to his mouth to respond.

"Might be better if I answer," Ira said.

"Right…"

Ira grabbed for her own CB, squeezed it tight. "Hey, what's happening, *bruh*?"

Eddy grabbed at the CB, wrestling with her for it for a moment. "Are you clinically insane!"

"Yes, now let go."

"Thank God," Nico said. "I've been trying to raise you for an hour straight! Where the hell have you been?"

Ira pulled the CB away from Eddy's grip, giggling like an idiot. She couldn't help herself—for once she was excited.

"Something funny to you, Ira? You better have a good fucking excuse for doing this to me again. I thought you were dead!"

"We found a heat signature in the mountains."

"Mountains? Which mountains…"

"North."

"Like, Big Bear?"

"Yeah."

"You idiots went all the way out there? Do you realize how dangerous that is?"

"Yeah, we survived, so…"

Nico's voice cut out for a moment. Ira could imagine him cursing and stabbing his knife into his desk over and over again. "Do you need assistance?"

"Not yet. We're inside a tunnel, approaching the source."

"I'm getting the others, you're going to give me your exact location."

"I got Eddy with me." She rolled her eyes. "Oh, and Lena. I guess she's useful too."

"No, Ira, give me your latitude and longitude."

"Fine." She looked up at Eddy, cut her CB off.

"What are you looking at me for?" Eddy asked.

She pushed his CB into his chest and walked off. "Nico needs the latitude and longitude for this place."

"Seriously?" Eddy said. "And where the hell are you going?

"Where the hell is my sister going?"

"Down the rabbit hole."

"Give me the goddamn coordinates!"

Eddy and Nico's voices became echoes in the distance. The buzz from the CB stopped as Ira neared the end of the tunnel. She looked up, cleaned her goggles again, and was greeted by a set of black metal doors.

"Jackpot." Ira ran her gloves over the surface of the doors, felt out their grooves. That unconscious fear returned, a fear that was rooted in government conspiracies, alien abductions, and that ancient fear of the unknown that lies dormant within everyone.

After a time the sound of Eddy's footsteps came scrunching up to her. They stared at the black metal doors together for a while.

"I've never seen a door like this," Eddy said.

"Yeah, most doors open inward!" Ira covered her mouth dramatically, and Eddy flipped her off.

"You know what I mean," Eddy said.

"No, no I really don't."

He sighed. "This looks like something the Feds put up, like a base from the war."

"Which probably means it'll have food and extra supplies?"

"Maybe." He stared at the door, fists forming. "Or angry Feds."

"'The war's over, we're all just folk now.'" She tried not to grin too wide.

"Yeah, okay, maybe I'm just being paranoid."

"Ya think?"

"Why do I hang around with you?"

"Cause you love me."

"Oh, God, if you guys are gonna have a moment," Lena said as she approached from behind, "please don't."

"How nice of you to join us," Eddy said. "We were just talking about how much we missed your beaming positivity."

"Whatever," Lena said. "What is it, we found a door, now we're all happy and shit?"

Eddy pointed at the door's complex grooves and rusted markings. "This door is probably the entrance to a Fed facility of some kind."

"Cannibals?" Lena said.

"No cannibals?" Ira said.

Eddy turned back around to face the doors—which seemed more like some kind of gate, now that Ira thought about it—and tore his facemask off. There was a single seam down the middle, so they probably receded into the interior of the wall.

"How're we gonna do this?" Ira asked.

"I'm thinking," Eddy said.

She watched Eddy scratch his head through his thermal hood.

There were exhaust vents off to the left and right of the doorway, which explained where the rise in temperature had come from. Ira looked around for anything that might allow her to access the door, get inside. The access panel looked worn, rusted, and all the screens seemed to have burnt out not long after the ice hit.

Her eyes drifted to the vents, then down her own slender frame, and back to the vents.

"Maybe I can fit through," Ira said.

"You're welcome to try." Eddy swung his hand out, gesturing toward the vent.

Ira turned her pack over, and the sound of tools slapping against the ice echoed through the tunnel. She scooped up her crowbar and approached the exhaust grate. The grate was solid metal, but the ice and sub-zero temperatures had caused it to weaken significantly over time.

Ira wedged the crowbar between the wall and the metal grate and pulled on it with all her strength, but it wasn't enough. She sat down and pouted.

It had been one hell of an effort, and all she managed to do was rattle it.

"Finished?" Eddy was grinning like a jackass.

"You could help me, you know?" Ira said.

"I could, but if this is a Fed facility, you're not going to get in that way anyway without something better than your crowbar."

"Damn it."

She scooped up the CB receiver, squeezed it tightly. "I hope Nico hasn't left yet…"

"I'll raise him." Eddy grabbed for his CB, walking past Lena to gain some privacy.

"Tell him to bring his plasma cutter!" Ira said, putting her CB back.

Eddy gave her a nod.

After a few minutes of back and forth from Eddy and Nico, he dropped the receiver from his face and cut the transmission—put the receiver back in his pack.

"What'd he say?" Ira asked.

"You're in luck, they haven't left yet," Eddy said.

"He'll bring the plasma cutter?"

Eddy nodded. "So we gotta hold tight."

Ira reached down to where she had dropped her pack and dragged it closer to the door. She plopped down on top of it and picked up a protein bar.

"Good idea," Eddy said. "We should eat some rations, drink some water."

Ira glared through the gate. She hoped that whatever lay beyond those doors, that it was (firstly) food, and (secondly) was better than the protein bars she'd been forced to endure for the last couple years. She'd give anything for a nice piping hot bowl of ramen. For now, though, she would wait for her brother and the others.

That momentary fear of what might lie beyond those doors that she'd felt earlier had completely subsided, but, someplace deep inside of her, she was deeply afraid to turn around and look into the darkness.

CHAPTER FIVE

"Looks like you were telling the truth," Nico said. "Impressive."

"Yeah, okay—" Ira crossed her arms and stood up. "—less wonderment, more cracking the damn thing open."

Nico stood there for a moment, his weight shifted onto his good leg, considering the door with one hand on his chin. Ira hated when he zoned out like that. She bent down and scooped up the makings of a snowball; but before she could finish packing it together, Eddy grabbed her forearm and shook his head at her.

"Can you open it?" Eddy asked, coaxing Ira to drop the snowball.

He stood there a moment longer, then turned back to them, nodding lazily. "Yeah. I think so. Grab me the plasma cutter."

"Didn't I just suggest that?" Ira asked.

He ignored her, took the plasma cutter from Eddy, and turned to his task. She sighed and sat back down on her pack. She considered her brother while he worked; how he'd grown, evolved, since they were kids. Back then, he was always leaving her in the dust, and now…it seemed like he was carrying them all.

In the early days of the ice age, before the world had figured out what was really going on, people had just tried to go about their lives — trudging through four feet of snow, fighting their stupid civil war, adjusting to new norms, and going to work, despite the prevailing fear that things wouldn't be going back to normal. The ugly truth was, those that didn't prepare died.

Like everything in her life, Ira had found herself caught in the middle of things, unable to commit to a decision. She felt that she should have been one of those casualties.

If it weren't for Nico, she would have been.

"Got it!" Nico gave the doors a hefty push, and they crashed against a concrete ramp that trailed into an abyss. Ira shielded her face from the dust and ice particles kicked up by the falling doors.

"It's lucky that they've been sitting here surrounded by ice for so long," Eddy said. "Otherwise we'd be going home empty-handed."

Nico nodded.

Ira got to her feet, gathered up the contents of her pack, and stuffed it back up. "What are we waiting for? Let's see what's inside!"

"Eddy," Nico said. "Go get the others, they'll want to see this."

Eddy nodded and headed back out the way they'd come. When his footsteps stopped echoing through the tunnel, Nico and Ira lit their flashlights and shined them into the darkness.

From outside the tunnel, she could see a guard station and inactive red lights on either side of the ramp leading into the chamber. So far, Eddy's theory was holding water.

There was something else. For a moment, she thought she saw movement inside. She felt the hair rise on the back of her neck, like someone had just walked over her grave.

"Ira?" Nico nudged her.

"W-what?" She blinked, rubbed at her eyes.

"I've been trying to get your attention."

"I'm sorry, I must have zoned out."

"Right, well, let's focus and check the place out."

Nico gave her a lazy nod. She forced her shaky legs forward and entered first. The air was stale, not much of a surprise. The ramps and tables were all covered in a thick layer of dust.

"Looks like nobody's been home in a while," she said.

Nico looked back at the door. "No...I don't think that's it."

"What do you mean?"

"That door's been sitting there for a while, untouched, unopened." He gestured at the abandoned guard station several feet from the doors. "This was clearly a military installation. No one's called this place home in years."

"Okay, so, like the ones you were stationed in?"

"No. I was a grunt. I've never seen anything like this." Nico approached a console along the far wall and tried flipping a few switches. "Power's out."

"I detected a power source somewhere earlier, though."

"Yeah, but it's not getting to the main systems. Just atmospherics… We'll have to connect it manually."

"Should we be here…?"

He didn't bother answering.

Ira froze in place. What if this place had been some kind of top-secret research base for Measure 86? She felt like microscopic particles had gotten beneath the protective layer of her suit, crawling up the length of her arms and legs and sinking their insidious poison into her body. In and out she breathed, closing her eyes and centering herself—calming her nerves.

It's all in your head, dummy, Ira thought. *You're just being paranoid.*

She opened her eyes. She scanned her flashlight across the room. There were several doors that led out of the entrance area they were in. Without power, they'd have to pry them open.

Nico approached one of the doors and sized it up.

Good, he read my mind, Ira thought.

Nico stabbed his combat knife into the crevice inside the door, using his crowbar to pry the door open. The door gave a loud creek, a pop, and slid back into the wall. He sandwiched himself inside the doorway to keep it from slamming shut and gestured toward her. "Bring me something to prop this open."

She nodded, snatched up a metal chair, and handed it to him. With the chair holding the door open, he slipped into the next room and pointed his flashlight forward. Ira cautiously crawled through the opening after him. She chased after him down the hallway. Even in his caution, he still walked with a slight limp.

And then Nico's body just vanished into the darkness, like it'd swallowed him whole.

"Nico?"

Ira's voice echoed through the darkness. There was no answer. The dark swam in front of her, clawing at her. For a moment, she thought she saw a gray, dead sky and leathery hills.

She closed her eyes and counted to ten.

It's okay, Ira thought. *You had a nightmare, and you're just freaking out.*

She needed to get her bearings, that was all. She shined her flashlight around; the "hallway" looked more like a large concrete tunnel. Like pictures of underground government bases she'd seen of sites devoted to UFOs and conspiracies.

"Hurry up," Nico said. "Found an elevator."

"Thank God," Ira said. "Why the hell didn't you answer me before?"

"What the hell are you talking about?" Nico said. "I didn't hear anything."

She found her way to him in the dark. "Whatever."

"Put on those binoculars, will you? We need to see where that power source is located."

"Right."

She fetched the binoculars, turned them on, and raised them to her eyes.

"See it?" Nico asked.

"Yeah." She lowered the binoculars to her side and eyed her brother. "It's a ways down… How are we gonna get down there?"

"We could just reppel down the elevator shaft," Nico said, completely serious.

"Or, we could use the emergency staircase like normal people," Ira said.

"Where's your sense of adventure?" Nico said. She couldn't tell if that was one of his rare jokes, or if this was his honest attempt to motivate her.

Ira shined her light around the tunnel-hallway for any sign of an emergency staircase. "The last time we climbed down an elevator shaft, I almost died. It wasn't fun."

"You didn't, though."

"Now you sound like Papa." She stopped. There was a picture of a staircase and a stick-figure running away from a fire above a single locked door. "I think we found it."

"Move aside, then."

He grabbed his plasma torch and worked at melting the locking mechanism. After a time, the door swung inward, inviting them further into the mouth of hades.

"You know," Ira said. "I'd almost rather take my chances outside."

"You're welcome to." Nico stood up, put the torch back in his pack, and marched down the stairs. "But you'll forgo your share of the loot."

She glared at him, watching him make his way down the stairs. Just moments ago she could have sworn she'd seen him vanish into the dark. She didn't want that to happen again. She darted down the stairs, following him.

"You're an ass, you know that?"

"This was your idea, remember?"

"I'm allowed to freak out a little. Even you have to admit, it's a little spooky down here."

"I'll give you that," he said quietly.

Maybe he's scared too? she thought. That thought definitely didn't make her feel any better. *Please let this just be my nerves. Please.*

Now, she could see the shadows dancing behind her brother. The flashlight was in his teeth, and he was holding his sidearm at the ready.

They both stopped several floors down. Nico's light shined up at her, and he said something unintelligible.

Ira pointed to his mouth. "Take the light out of your mouth, dummy!"

"Use the binoculars, Ira, see how much further we need to go."

Ira nodded, retrieved the binoculars from her pack, stared down at the heat source. "Just a few more floors to go."

She heard him bite back down on his flashlight, his footsteps echoing off the concrete walls.

Nico stopped again. They'd reached their target floor, and Ira barely avoided stumbling into him. She could almost feel him glare at her.

"You should warn me when you're gonna stop," she said.

He didn't answer. Her eyes followed his flashlight while he checked out the door to this floor, grabbing his bag and retrieving the plasma torch again. Neon sparks flew, the door handle turned a bright orange and fell off, and the door swung inward.

"Binoculars," Nico said.

This time, the heat source Ira was reading was only a few hundred feet away from their location. Nico proceeded ahead, and Ira kept the binoculars handy to guide them to the source.

Nico paused and stared at one of the rooms in the corridor, where the door had failed to close all the way.

"What is it?" she asked.

"Wait here," he said.

Nico vanished into the room. Out of boredom, she pointed her flashlight at the sign above the doorway. It read EXPERIMENT 12C at the top.

"Ira." Nico's voice sounded small. "Come look at this."

She followed his voice into the room...and pointed her light at Nico, who was standing there, stoic, peering into what looked like an interrogation room from one of those old crime movies—two-way mirror and all. He removed his goggles and set them on what looked like a control panel.

"What is it...?" She moved closer. Her eyes followed his flashlight to its focal point. Her heart dropped through her chest; she felt like her protein bar was about to make a return trip.

It was a corpse, strapped to some sort of medical table, which rested inside a glass pyramid. The pyramid itself rested inside a large metallic ring, which seemed to protrude from the walls of the chamber... Her eyes found the corpse's face, peering at her with blackened pits from beneath dome shaped helmet apparatus. Its eyes were gone, but the expression on its face could only be described as abject terror. Its flesh was rotting off its limbs, which were twisted in tight leather restraints on the table. At the top of the medical table, the corpse's helmeted apparatus had wires which snaked their way into the darkness.

She fell back into a chair she hadn't known existed and stared at her brother. Maybe they had descended into the mouth of hades after all?

"This was an observation chamber," Nico said.

He shined his flashlight around the room, scanning over consoles and dead readout screens. Some life crept back into Ira when she couldn't see the corpse. She watched her brother scan through the room like he had in a hundred other buildings, looking for threats, exits, clues, assessing danger.

"Go wait in the hallway," he said. "Get Eddy on the comm and tell him to meet us down here. Keep your mask on until I say otherwise."

Ira nodded, stiff, and stood up. She couldn't shake the awful writhing in the pit of her gut. What had happened here? Were her initial fears correct? Was this the birthplace of Measure 86? No. She didn't want to know. The best thing for everyone, for her, was to leave this place and never return.

She almost felt ashamed for how she'd behaved earlier, how foolishly excited she was for having found this place.

What the hell was I thinking? she thought.

Her feet carried her out into the hallway, her free hand comforting her stomach.

2

"I don't know if they got the doors open," Eddy said.

Eddy had guided Lena, Hugo, and Mathias halfway back through the ice tunnel. It'd taken time to locate the path they'd taken. Nico had found a detour earlier, a ramp of snow that led to the top of the cliff. Hugo and Lena were waiting at the snowmobile.

Hugo claimed Lena didn't want to go back inside the tunnel. That she was scared.

They'd all stood around deliberating far longer than Eddy would have liked. Getting Lena to snap out of it had been like twisting her arm.

Even now, she was taking baby steps, deliberately slowing their pace down.

"Oh, man, I just hope they have something other than those garbage-ass protein bars we've been eating," Hugo said.

"Eddy," Ira's voice rang over his CB.

He held the CB to his mouth and angled away from the others. "Ira! What did you guys find?"

"Nico needs you down here…"

"We're on the way. Everything all right?"

"Just get down here."

Her voice cut out.

"That don't sound good, yo," Hugo said.

"What do you mean?" Eddy said.

"You don't wanna know what goes on in places like this—" Hugo eyed the entrance to the facility. "The government had, like, underground bases and stuff where they worked with aliens, man."

"Aliens," Eddy said, rolling his eyes and quickening his pace. "I'm sure we'll find Elvis down here too."

"Who the fuck is Elvis?" Hugo asked.

Eddy sighed. "Come on, man, you don't know who Elvis was?"

"Dawg, I'm talkin' real shit here, they probably had, like, alien-human hybrids down there or something, I'd bet—"

Lena smacked Hugo. "Stop it, you're scaring me."

"Don't worry, there's no such thing as aliens…" Eddy found himself staring into the looming darkness. "At least, not here."

"Naw, dawg, that's what *they* want you to think," Hugo said.

"Hugo, give it a damn rest," Eddy said.

Hugo nodded, muttering something under his breath, and they all marched into the darkness. Lena, of course, trailed behind them. Hugo'd probably scared the pants off her.

3

They traced Nico and Ira's path through the abandoned check-in station, the long, dark corridor leading to the elevator doors, and the emergency staircase.

Lena and Hugo's banter stopped at once as they made their way down the staircase, floor after floor.

For a moment, and maybe it was just his imagination, Eddy felt as though the staircase vanished from beneath his feet.

He stumbled forward and braced himself with the railing.

"What is it, B?" Hugo asked.

Eddy looked at him for a second, tempted to say what was on his mind, but shook his head. "It's nothing."

They came upon an open door, where the handle had been melted off.

"Looks like this is our stop," Eddy said.

"Oh, joy," Lena said. "Are you all just going to keep ignoring how stupid this is?"

"You could have said something before we descended however many floors," Eddy said.

"I did!" Lena shouted. "I said it over and over again."

"No, you didn't," Eddy said. "Stop lying."

"Yeah, I didn't hear shit neither," Hugo said.

"No—" There was a strange look in her eyes as she looked at both of them. "—I did, I swear, I was complaining the whole way down."

"Right." Eddy rolled his eyes and stepped into the corridor. She was probably just looking for attention.

"I didn't want to say nothing," Hugo said, "but I'm gettin' weird vibes down here."

"Hugo, what did we tell you about the conspiracy talk?" Eddy said.

"Not to..."

Eddy paused to fetch his flashlight, clicked it on, and shined the light in the dark. His eyes landed on Ira's back slumped against the concrete wall, head in hands. She was still wearing her ash-black fur coat, sitting on the floor, holding her knees close to her chest. He couldn't help but think of a Greek goddess when he looked at her. Even in her weakness, there was a strength. Instinctively, he ran his hands through her soft black hair, caressed her back.

"Ira," Eddy said. "You okay?"

She stirred, and stared at him, like the life had been sucked right out of her. Even through her goggles, he could tell that those beautiful green eyes had been leaking.

"The hell's wrong with her now?" Lena asked.

"Nico's inside..." Ira pointed to a room directly adjacent to him. "We found a body."

He could hear the quiver in her voice. That was something, because they saw corpses all the time out in that frozen wasteland they used to call home, and Ira wasn't what one might call squeamish.

"I'll go check on him," Eddy said. "You guys look after Ira."

"I'm coming too," Mathias said. Eddy almost forgot that Mathias was even there with them. As if he had vanished in the dark.

Eddy slipped into the room Ira had pointed out to him and Mathias followed closely behind.

"What's going on, Nico?" Eddy asked.

Nico turned away from the two-way mirror and waved Eddy over. "Take a look."

Nico shined his light through the two-way mirror, and Eddy gazed upon something that looked like it'd come right out of a horror film. He lurched, quickly removed his facemask, and vomited all over the aluminum floor.

"That is—" Eddy stood up, wiped his mouth and replaced his facemask. "—the most disgusting thing I've ever seen."

"What were they doing here?" Mathias approached the glass, studying the corpse with a coldness that was beyond unsettling. But it was more than that; it was the look in his eyes. They seemed almost to glint in the darkness the moment Mathias caught sight of the corpse. "Some sort of experiment…or an execution, perhaps?"

"How are you so calm about this, dude?" Eddy asked.

"We won't know what they were up to until we get the generator connected and get a look at their files," Nico said.

"You can't be serious, man, not after this," Eddy said.

"And why should this stop us?" Mathias asked. "We're in desperate need of supplies, and we're not even sure we can repair the generators at home with the parts we found. Venturing out in the city is becoming more and more dangerous with each passing day. We've seen death in the city before, and it didn't stop us from looting every nook and cranny, so why should this be any different?"

"What if this place was used to make Measure 86?" Eddy pointed his flashlight at the corpse. "I've seen what that shit can do, watched friends turn into dried-out husks, and I'll tell you, they didn't look too different from *that*."

"We'll starve sooner rather than later if we don't take this opportunity," Nico said. "So we're seizing it. There's always a risk that we'll accidentally run into Measure 86 out in the city, this is no different."

"Yeah, I can't really blame you for not being scared." Eddy crossed his arms, glared at Nico. "Since your side pulled all their forces out before they deployed it."

"Get out," Nico said.

"No!" Eddy was in his face now, screaming for the dead that Nico had helped put in the ground. "You never saw it! We had to dig mass graves, man, and wear masks twenty-four hours a day to keep from being exposed! It was a fucking holocaust, and you helped make it happen!"

Nico's right hook was so fast in the dark, he hadn't even seen it. Eddy reeled back and fell against the two-way mirror, holding his jaw. "You son-of-a—"

"Would you two testosterone-addled fools think for a moment!" Mathias jumped between them. "Whatever issues you two have, get over them. This is survival, in case you've forgotten. The Earth itself is trying to kill us, and you two are still waging war and arguing politics. Well, let me tell you a harsh truth. The ice age does not care for your point of view, your morality, your religion, or what side of the war you fought on. It is survival of the fittest plain and simple."

Eddy got to his feet, lowering his fists. As much as he wanted to find wisdom in what Mathias was saying, he couldn't just forget the dead. Even in death, they were his brothers. "I'll go along with it, but only for Ira's sake."

Nico scoffed.

"Now, can we please start using our heads?" Mathias asked.

"The plan doesn't change," Nico said. "We have to get this place turned back on."

Eddy swallowed a lump in his throat, and turned for the door. "Hope it's worth it…"

"You and Mathias will follow me to the power source Ira detected," Nico said. "Get Hugo to watch after the girls, and grab Ira's binoculars for me."

"Right..." The nerve this man had, ordering him around after slugging him in the face.

You are so lucky you're her brother, Eddy thought.

Eddy followed Mathias and Nico out into the darkened hallway. Ira looked at him; the emptiness in her eyes told him that she understood. He shook his head.

Nico didn't bother to acknowledge his sister; he and Mathias continued on down the hallway.

"We're going to find the heat source," Eddy said. "I need your multi-specs."

Ira shook her head. "No. We have to leave this place."

"Your brother doesn't see it that way—won't listen till he sees how dangerous this place is."

"That's just like him." She dug around in her pack and handed him the multi-spec binoculars. "Make sure you convince him."

"Trust me." Eddy closed his eyes, shook his head. "Freezing to death would be better than suffering Measure 86."

"Measure 86?" Lena's eyes went wide. "What the hell are you talking about?"

"I'm not sure," Eddy said. "But this place could have been a manufacturing plant for it."

"We should leave, then!"

"Tell that to Nico." Eddy turned to Hugo, who was staring off into space. "Watch over the girls till I get back."

Hugo nodded. "Got you, B."

"And try not to fall asleep again." Eddy followed after Mathias and Nico down the hallway.

"I don't know, dawg, it's real cozy here." Hugo's voice faded into the black of the tunnel. Eddy could almost imagine Lena staring daggers at him.

When Eddy caught up to them, he saw that they were both pressing their weight against a large metal door. He looked through the binoculars before Nico could ask, and saw that the heat source was very close.

"The door won't budge," Nico said.

"Have you tried shooting it?" Eddy said.

Nico caught the sarcasm in Eddy's voice, judging by the look in his eyes, but he pulled his sidearm out all the same. "Stand back."

Eddy grabbed Mathias by the arm and pulled him around the corner as Nico discharged his clip into the door. Each shot rang like a battering ram slamming into the wall of his eardrum.

Mathias shook his arm free of Eddy's grasp. "Don't know what he's thinking he's going to accomplish like that."

Eddy came out from behind the corner to find Nico loading another clip into his sidearm. "You didn't even dent the doorway, man. Give it a rest!"

Nico must have realized that what he was doing was crazy, because he holstered his gun. "The heat source is just beyond those doors. How can we get to it if the main door won't open without power?"

Eddy ran his hands across the smooth metal surface. The door was more like a hatch, a seal. "The better question is, why are all the other doors open in this corridor?" He shined his light back through the hallway, which was more like a concrete tunnel than a hallway. Some of the doors along the path were halfway open, and all the rest were completely open. "None of them look like this one either."

"What the hell does it matter?" Nico said. "It's just another obstacle in my way."

"Ah, but it does matter," Mathias said. "Eddy is asking the right questions. This door is different, so the chamber beyond must be special. Is it a reactor, a generator, or perhaps something else?"

"We can turn back now, Nico," Eddy said. "We can fix the generators back home."

Nico shook his head. "No. We're getting in that room."

"If we had a portable power source, I could probably hook it up to the door's control pad." Mathias walked up and picked at the dead screen to the right of the hatch. "That might give it enough power for me to trick it into opening."

"Where are we going to find something with enough juice for that?" Eddy asked. "No, I think we should just cut our losses and—"

"The snowmobiles," Nico said. "Remove one of the batteries and bring it back to me."

"You're really dead set on getting us killed, aren't you?" Eddy shook his head and sighed.

"Do it," Nico said, patting his sidearm.

"You're not the only one with a gun." Eddy found himself resisting the urge to draw his. What Nico was doing here was reckless. What would it say of him if he let this man lead them straight to their deaths? There was no telling what was beyond that hatch. His worst fears could very well be confirmed.

"You won't shoot me, Eddy," Nico said, drawing his gun and aiming it between Eddy's eyes. "My sister would never forgive you."

"Same goes for you," Eddy said, pushing the barrel away with his finger. "But make no mistake—if we find any evidence that Measure 86 was made here, with or without you, we're leaving."

"We'll see about that." Nico turned around and crossed his arms. "Now go get me a battery."

Eddy stormed back down the twisting tunnel, Mathias following closely behind.

"You're tempting fate," Mathias said. "Nico is not one to shy away from violence."

"Did I ask for your opinion?" Eddy said.

"No, but you seem determined to get shot."

"The man is out of control."

"You must realize that his goals are the same as ours. He only wants to ensure our survival, and this place seems like just as good a bet as any other."

"You saw that corpse, man, you can't tell me that doesn't raise alarms for you."

"No alarm could sound loud enough to deter my desire to learn all I can about this place."

Eddy examined Mathias closely. His eyes looked as if they were sucking in the detail of every corner of the tunnel with a deep and insatiable hunger. Something about the way he'd said that awakened some nameless fear in Eddy, something that was far removed from the perils of the ice age or even of Measure 86.

"I liked you better when you weren't saying anything," Eddy said.

They walked the rest of the way to the elevator shaft in silence. Eddy couldn't help but feel like there were eyes on him, coming from the dark. He shook the feeling off and cursed Mathias for being such a creep.

Once they were outside, Mathias helped him take off the front cover to the snowmobile Nico had left on the slope. The battery was easy enough to disconnect. Eddy shoved it in his pack and carried it back to Nico.

Mathias brought out a toolkit from his own pack and opened up the screen next to the hatch. He dragged the wires and connected them to the negative and positive.

Sparks flew—Nico and Eddy hit the floor—a hissing sound filled the air and a wave of stale air hit them.

The hatch was open.

Nico and Mathias were the first ones through, shining light into the darkness. Eddy was cautious, but followed anyway.

The room was spherical, with a large cylinder in the center. There were computers and dead screens everywhere, and yet there was a faint buzzing sound through the air that sent his hair standing on end. It took a moment to realize that the center cylinder was pulsing with a dim red light.

"Is that thing nuclear?" Eddy asked.

"Fascinating." Mathias was pacing around the circumference of the pulsing cylinder, shining his flashlight at every tube and wire and crevice. "It appears to be a power source, but it's clearly not nuclear. If I had to wager an educated guess, I'd say it's a small fusion reactor."

"Like the one that blew up in Norway?" Nico asked, without a hint of worry in his voice.

"That was sabotage," Mathias said. "If you're worried about it blowing up, your concerns are unfounded. Fusion reactors are really quite stable in comparison to their fission counterparts. Though it is strange for one to be here, even one of this size. There were only two reactors ever created, and as you pointed out, one of them blew up due to sabotage."

"Clean, renewable, infinite energy wasn't something our corporate overlords were going to just let happen," Eddy said.

"The benefits outweigh the damage to any corporation's bottom line," Mathias said. "No, they were very difficult to build, and the designs were only shared between a few tight-lipped scientists who had a clear distaste for the American Federalist regime."

"Then how did one come to exist here?" Nico's expression changed slightly, his eyes wide with awe.

"Your government probably stole the plans," Eddy said. "Complex spy shit."

"Yes, most likely," Mathias said. "But, why here? What could be so important in this facility that they'd require a stable fusion reaction to power it?"

"Enough," Nico said. "These questions can wait till we figure out how to get the power it's outputting back into the main systems."

Mathias continued to pace back and forth, bending and scanning every now and then. Nico's patience eroded within the first few minutes of silence.

"Can you get power to the systems or not, Mathias?" Nico said.

Mathias nodded. "I believe so. The connections to the system are all still here, but without power I'll have to reroute it manually, which will take a few hours."

Eddy paced toward the edge of the room and plopped down into a computer chair. "Great. I don't suppose anyone brought a deck of cards?"

Nico's glare told him no.

CHAPTER SIX

Ira felt the sunbeams cook her back and grew just a little bit worried about what they might be doing to her cells. She sat up and nudged her friend with her sand-covered foot.

"Aren't you worried about overexposure?" Ira asked.

Jennifer sat up and sighed. "You can't be so cautious, Ira. You have to learn to live a little."

"And why does living have to involve the sun of all things? I was perfectly happy inside. Playing games. Away from the sun."

Jennifer plopped back down on her beach towel, and Ira watched her check out all the half-naked men playing in the ocean—who in all likelihood had just learned how to read and do basic math. Ira lay back down and pouted.

"That's exactly what I'm talking about," Jennifer said. "You spend so much time in those damn games, you forget to live, gain new experiences."

"New experiences, as in, fucking a bunch of macho idiots on the beach?"

"If that's your thing." Jennifer grinned.

"You know it isn't."

Ira watched the waves roll and crash against the beach sands, giggled when a surfer wiped out. *Okay, so maybe it wasn't such a bad idea,* she thought.

She'd never admit it to Jennifer.

"I'll teach you to appreciate this Southern California weather, even if it kills me."

"Famous last words."

"No, Ira, my last words were a jumbled mess of screams as someone slipped a knife between my ribs." Ira turned to face her friend, and screamed when she saw that her torso was littered in stab wounds, her bikini bottom torn, exposing her pubic hair. "I died just one year later, when some fucking looters decided they'd rather rape me than take the big-screen TVs or any of the jewelry in the display case."

Ira's feet kicked at the sand. She was crawling back across the sand, trying to get away. She had to get away. "I didn't—"

"You didn't know?" The corpse that had been her friend only moments ago laughed. Her voice had a bubbly quality, as if there were blood oozing from her throat, cutting her words to gibberish. "Of course you didn't know! You hid away with your brother when the news hit and he came to save your sorry ass. You're worthless, Ira!"

Jennifer's face melted until it bore a striking resemblance to the face of the corpse she'd seen in the chair. Jennifer's hair was falling out in clumps, eyes sinking into a black abyss.

"But you'll see soon enough. They opened up a gateway here. If the beast doesn't get you, then Lai'thamia will!"

The sand became liquid-soft. Her arms sank first, then her legs and torso. The corpse was over her. Ira couldn't move. She could smell its rotted breath. Its skin was turning green.

"You'll see soon enough."

Its laughter was brittle now, like glass shattering.

Ira screamed into the darkness, with only a faint memory of the nightmare that had so recently consumed her.

It took her a moment to remember that she'd gone to sleep on the floor, letting Hugo keep watch of both her and Lena.

The lights came on throughout the corridor. Her arm met her face, shielding her eyes. She let her eyes slowly adjust to the new normal and scanned the hallway. Lena and Hugo were cuddled together, completely passed out. She was surprised that her scream hadn't woken them.

So much for keeping watch, she thought.

69

It wasn't enough that he'd fallen asleep on his last watch, and let the generators to explode due to his negligence; now Hugo was tempting fate—*again*—and risking Nico's wrath. She felt the urge to kick him in his pale face to wrest him from his sleep, but resisted, cursed under her breath, stood up, and started following the signs that read TO REACTOR CORE.

The lighting was a garish and uncomfortable white. The corridor was tubular in shape. Her initial impression of something similar to an underground military base was confirmed. She had never really been one to buy into conspiracy theories, if for no other reason than the fact that it would've made her the laughingstock of university, but she couldn't deny the similarity here.

She rounded a corner and began to hear a discourse of distant and muted voices through a circular doorway. There was a snowmobile battery wired to the console on the wall to the right of the door.

"And what about the entrance doors?" Mathias asked.

"It'll be a team effort to restore them," Nico said. "But I think it's doable."

"I'm not so sure," Mathias said. "It might be easier to booby-trap the entrance room and fortify the remaining doors."

"Easier, but stupid," Nico said. "If there's anyone else still out there, I'd rather them only have one door to choose from, rather than three."

"I agree," Eddy said.

"Now there's a surprise," Mathias said. "Just hours ago, you two were at each other's throats; now you're in agreement."

"Never said I liked it," Eddy said.

Ira made her way to them through the doorway, taking a quick look around the circular room.

"I see you're already deciding to set up camp here." She directed her attention at Eddy, tossing him a scornful look. "You were supposed to convince him!"

"We determined that there was no present risk to our lives." Mathias glared at Ira—his mask and goggles were off, exposing his cold, dark brown eyes.

"Your brother and Mathias swear that this place has nothing to do with Measure 86," Eddy said.

"It's not? Are you sure? If not Measure 86, then what caused that—" she swallowed a lump in her throat "—man to die?"

Nico avoided her gaze.

"Mathias thinks it was some sort of behavior experiment," Eddy said. "Nothing biological as far as he can tell."

"As far as *he* can tell?" Ira asked.

"Well." Mathias pushed his glasses up to the rim of his nose, turning one of the laptops that they had hooked into an access panel toward him. "We haven't found the mainframe for this facility yet, but the logs that we were able to access hinted at some type of non-biological science experiment. And, yes, we have found no references to Measure 86."

They opened up a gateway here. A shiver traveled up her spine. *If the beast doesn't get you, then* Lai'thamia *will.*

"Though, admittedly," Mathias continued. "Data mining and hacking is not my forte. Perhaps you'll have better luck, if you're dissatisfied with our conclusions?"

"Dissatisfied is one way to put it," she said. "Come get me when you've found the mainframe."

She turned and stormed out of the room. Only so much of Mathias she could stand in one sitting. He'd been a quantum physics major in college, from what she knew. Had a full ride, and had even started on graduate studies when the ice age started. There weren't many applications for his kind of knowledge, not with society beneath a thick layer of ever-growing ice and death. She assumed that's why he always came off like a lecturing pretentious prick.

Ira traced her path back to where she had fallen asleep and snatched up her backpack. Lena stirred, rubbing her eyes.

"The lights are on?" Lena said.

"You don't miss anything," Ira said.

"Where's Nico?"

"Go find him yourself." She stormed down the hallway, toward the elevator. "I'm going to go find a room to put my things in, since we're stuck here."

"Wait! We're staying?"

"Ask my brother."

71

She reached the elevator. With the power now on, a bright red triangle was lit up above the doors. There was a large circular button off to their right. She pressed it, and when the doors opened, she was greeted with a claustrophobic metal box to stand in.

Ira had always had a fear of elevators, ever since she was a small girl. She and Nico had rappelled down a few elevator shafts in collapsed buildings over the last couple of years, especially as supplies started to dwindle. Climbing up or down a metal cable was one thing: you were relying on your own strength. With an elevator, you had to trust that it was in good repair, that the gears hadn't rusted to pieces, that you weren't going to plummet fifty stories to your death.

Fortunately, the elevator worked. She pressed a random button and it transported her up through the facility. The doors opened to another hallway—no—another lifeless concrete tunnel that stretched on and on.

As much as the old shelter had not been home to her, this place was worse. Its walls were uninviting, and the floors were cold, metallic, and painful just to stand on. And then there was that…thing…in EXPERIMENT 12C. She shuddered.

Nico would force them to move here, and it was her fault. If she'd just never looked at the heat monitor…

She passed several rooms. This corridor looked as if it had been used as quarters for the people who'd lived here. It was eerie. Each room contained the personal effects of its former inhabitant. Pictures, posters, and personal journals. She found herself standing in the middle of one such room, holding a picture of a man and his family. They were all smiles and there were trees and grass in the image, and now they were all likely dead, covered in snow and ice—or an unwilling science experiment strapped to a medical table.

Ira set the picture down on the end table. She couldn't stay in this room, surrounded by the ghosts of someone else's memories—a peace she could never have.

Five other rooms, and they were no different. Different pictures, different faces, but ghosts all the same. Finally, she found a room that had no pictures, no journals—no memories. She set her backpack down in the corner and sat on the lone cot in the small-six-by-six-foot room.

The blank concrete walls were no comfort for her, despite the lack of pictures. She couldn't help but hope that Nico and Eddy would find a reason to leave this place.

CHAPTER SEVEN

The Second American Civil War had been a long and endless bloodbath, one many felt was necessary — the precursor to the next step in societal evolution. The onset of the modern ice age had put a stop to the fighting, but the wounds could still be felt, even in the frosted ruins of the old world.

Ira had never actually fought, having been deemed a psychological risk at the time of the draft, but Nico had. She wondered what fighting for the Feds had done to him.

Being a first-year student at MIT might as well have made her a target. Having any association with programming or technical proficiency with computers — without a security clearance, or a rank in the armed forces — came with a certain amount of paranoia. It was vivid to her, the fear of being under constant surveillance, and the threat of the Feds showing up at any point to cart her off to some unnamed prison without the benefit of a trial. She'd heard news about the conflict in school, whispers here and there, and even seen a few students detained in the middle of class — suspected cyber terrorists. She'd kept her opinions to herself, but in her mind, in her heart, she'd known that the Revolutionists were right about what the Feds had become.

She held her left arm, as if the injuries were still there…

She could still hear the rain clapping down on the skylight as the instructor droned on about the glory days of HTML; she could remember the specific lines of code she'd entered for her final.

Remembered the news: a cyber activist had shut down a Fed-operated nuclear power plant, almost triggering a meltdown. She remembered the feeling of her heart exploding, thundering through her chest, when they burst through the door.

She could still feel the hairs ripping from her scalp, and the sound of individual keys flying from her keyboard when they slammed her head into the desk. She could still feel them ignore her screams while they twisted her arm behind her back and shouted things in her ear, and she could still feel the sinking feeling in the pit of her stomach as they'd carted her off to some undisclosed location without reading her her rights.

Ira could still feel the anger she'd felt for her brother, who had joined them of his own free will.

They had suspected her because of her connection to Nico, thought that he'd let something slip, inadvertently giving her a back door to the power plant's mainframe. They'd found the real culprit days later.

They'd released her back to her family in California a week later, after the Feds had determined she wasn't hiding anything that might incriminate her.

There had been no apologies.

When Nico had come home from the war, and she saw the change in him, her anger ebbed. She'd watch as he'd elect to sit alone, staring off into space, clutching his stump, not a tear in his eyes, but the pain still clearly etched in his face.

"Ira." Eddy's voice calling over the CB shook her from her daydream. "We've found the Mainframe."

"About damn time," Ira said. "Feels like I've been going gray over here!"

"Ha. Ha. Just get down here and help us crack into it, will you?"

"Yeah, on my way."

She'd been lying in her new cot for almost two hours, staring at the concrete ceiling, imagining the shapes in the concrete were the different players in her life. She sat up, her legs and midsection protesting by shooting jolts of numbness through her body.

The elevator filled her with a sense of palpable dread. She watched the numbers decrease until arriving on the floor where Eddy and Nico had been earlier. She passed the experiment room. Visions of the corpse that she'd seen just hours earlier filled her mind. Ira stifled them as she entered the chamber where Mathias and Eddy were studying the core.

Mathias was bent over a computer terminal, mumbling to himself, and Eddy was eating a protein bar at the other end of the chamber.

"So, where is it?" Ira asked.

Eddy's eyes perked up when he saw her. "Have you eaten?"

Ira shook her head. "I'm not hungry. Take me to the mainframe."

"Gotcha." Eddy walked past her, down the corridor she'd just come from. "Follow me."

They walked back into the elevator, and Eddy entered something into the keypad. The elevator ride wasn't so bad with him with her.

"You found a room already, huh?" Eddy asked.

Ira nodded. "Hopefully we won't be staying too long though."

"I don't know…"

"Don't tell me you're starting to agree with Nico?"

He shrugged. "I mean, so far we really haven't found anything dangerous."

"We saw a corpse tied to an operating table, Eddy!"

"Yeah, but there's nothing in the logs that suggests that he died from anything that could harm us. Isn't that what's more important here? And, let's face it, the old shelter wasn't going to last forever. Hugo made sure of that."

It was an irrational fear. Sure. All fears are like that. But what she'd seen in that experiment chamber…it wasn't just frightening. No, it was as if some ancient part of the universe had reached down deep into her soul and touched her.

Something that shouldn't be, Ira thought.

"I just—" She held herself. "—I have a really bad feeling."

"Look, let's just hold off on making any snap judgments until you get a look at those encrypted files, okay?" Eddy tossed her a smile that almost melted the fear away, like the warm embrace of a blazing California sunrise. "If you find anything dangerous, I'm sure Nico will understand and we'll all go back to the old shelter."

"Promise me that."

The elevator dinged, the doors opened, and they filed out into another concrete tunnel before he could answer her.

The mainframe was tucked behind another circular door, like the one that housed the fusion core chamber. Inside it was dark, filled with black metallic towers with blue LED lights that sparkled and danced almost as if they were alive. Ira almost felt her fear evaporate, like moisture from a hot surface. The room was cold; she buttoned her coat up and strolled inside. There were no tables. This was not a place meant for human beings.

"I'm going to have to set up in here," she said.

"Are you kidding? It's freezing."

"I'll wear layers." She grinned. "But, seriously. I need to plug my gear into the main tower directly."

"If you say so."

Ira placed her backpack down on the icy floor, dragging out a small laptop and a mess of assorted types of wires. "You could help by getting me a table, a comfy chair, and some blankets, instead of standing there looking stupid."

"Ouch." He turned to face the door, chuckling. "All right, I'll be right back then."

Ira searched for a connector on the main tower, something that might give her direct access to the system, or the hard drives where any logs might be stored. Luckily, there was an array of USB ports on the side that she was able to use.

The mainframe towers all seemed to be linked on the same network, but, as she'd suspected, they were all encrypted. When she tried to access the hard drive on the main tower, a prompt for a username and password appeared. She'd have to use her rainbow tables for that later; what she could already tell was just how much data was stored on those towers. Hundreds of terabytes across every tower were being used at once.

It wasn't surprising to her that the mainframes were being used, but the sheer volume of data collected on those drives made her wonder, and simultaneously made her afraid.

What were they doing here that would require so much storage and processing power?

Something that should not be.

She shivered. She wasn't quite sure why she kept thinking of that; maybe just her nerves mixing with the memory of old H.P. Lovecraft stories she'd read as a little girl.

She almost laughed. How silly of her.

Eddy came back thirty minutes later with a large folding table and several blankets.

"Your brother gave me these." He dropped the blankets on her head and laughed maniacally about it, then set the table up in front of her. "I still have to get the chair for you, though."

Ira unfolded a warm blanket with black and green camouflage print—her heart jumped. "It's Woobie!"

Eddy raised an eyebrow at her. "I think I'll leave you two alone."

"Oh, shush." She hugged the self-warming blanket tight. "I love this thing, but he always keeps it with him, never lets me use it."

"I used to have one just like it. Never could wrap my head around how it keeps you warm during the winter and cold during the summer. We used to joke that it was stolen alien tech from the Roswell crash."

"And it's so soft!"

"I'll go get your chair."

Ira watched Eddy leave again. She wrapped her body up in Woobie while she set her laptop and things up on the desk. When Eddy came back with her chair, she was all set for a very long night.

"Here, let me help," Eddy said, smiling, and tucked the edges of the blanket underneath her, sealing the warmth in. "You missed a spot."

His breath was streaming in the air, his face lit blue by the servers, hovering mere inches from her face.

It'd be so easy, Ira thought.

"Well—" Eddy stood up, glancing around the chamber. "—your brother needs my help with something. I guess I'll leave you to it."

"Yeah..."

The hatch closed behind him, and Ira was alone again. She was tempted to run after him, to ask him to come back.

But she had a job to do too.

Surrounded by the glow of the screen and using her rainbow tables and various other hacking tools, she was finally in her own element.

2

Ira had figured it would be a long night, and she was right. She'd spent all night in there, huddled up with her brother's woobie. It wasn't the first time she'd hacked into a government server, though this was decidedly higher security than what she was used to.

It was slightly ironic to her, breaking into a Fed mainframe, an act that would have been punishable by death or life imprisonment during the war.

In the hours since calling her down to check out the mainframe, Nico and Eddy had done their own exploring, but Ira was intentionally avoiding asking them how their progress was going. She'd had enough to be paranoid about for one day, no need to fuel those fires any further.

Her stomach growled, and she frowned. They'd have to find the supply cache soon; the rations they'd brought with them would only last so long.

"There you are!" Her rainbow tables finally did the trick, she was inside. She scrolled through several files, some documents, some videos, probably logs, all of them most likely top-secret—as if that mattered now. Her cursor hovered over one of the encrypted videos. She wasn't sure if she wanted to see what any of that footage had to show her… She began the decoding process on one of the videos.

3

Eddy gave the rusted door one last pull and it finally gave way. It rocked back and slid open, revealing a dark storage room. Nico stepped inside and turned on his flashlight.

"Looks like we found the food," Eddy said.

"Yeah." Nico's light revealed a massive stock of MREs, canned food, and a bunch of fresh water barrels. "This alone will last us for years to come."

"As long as we can keep everyone to a rationing schedule…"

"If they want to survive, they'll follow the rules."

Eddy leaned against the door, crossed his arms. "What's next, boss-man?"

Nico's wounded green eyes shifted to Eddy. "We need to mount an expedition to the old shelter and start moving things over."

"I was afraid you were gonna say that."

Nicola turned around and headed back out into the corridor. Eddy stuck his hands in his jacket pockets and followed after him.

"Who should we bring?" Eddy asked.

"Leave the girls here. You, me, and Hugo will go."

"And Mathias?"

"I need him here to analyze the core, make sure it's not gonna blow up on us or anything. Besides, he bugs the hell out of me."

"Damn, never knew you felt that way about him."

"There's a lot you don't know about me."

They walked in tense silence for a time. Eddy was never sure how to relate to Nico. The war had really fucked him up, that much he was sure of, and it made every single conversation difficult. It was almost simpler when they were at each other's throats.

The only person in the group he could really talk to was Ira, and Nico didn't really seem too happy about that. Eddy wondered what Nico would do if he and Ira got any closer...

He stifled the thought as they came upon Hugo and Lena, snuggling and eating their rations for breakfast.

"Get up," Nico said. "Got a mission for you."

Hugo's muted blue eyes focused on Nico, like a lazy old dog. "Can it wait till after breakfast, B?"

"Finish it quickly and meet us in the reactor core." He glared at Lena. "You too, Lena."

Lena swiped one hand through her short blonde hair, cattily, and glared at Nico. "And does Ira get a free pass again?"

"Ira's already doing her part. So get off your ass before I shoot you in the leg for my own amusement."

Nico walked away, and Eddy quickly followed him. When they were further down the corridor, Eddy leaned in and whispered, "You wouldn't really shoot her, right?"

"You doubt me?" He patted the sidearm in his holster.

"Nope."

"Listen up, cause I'm only going to say this once." Nico paced back and forth in front of the primary readout station for the reactor. "While Ramirez, Hugo, and I are gone, you will all have specific tasks assigned to you. These tasks will need to be accomplished by the time we return with the first shipment of supplies from the old shelter."

"Oh, great, busywork," Lena said.

Nico's eyes zeroed in on her slender frame. Eddy's hand came to rest on Nico's shoulder, as if to say, "Don't do it. Don't shoot her." Nico shrugged his hand away.

"No, not busywork," Nico said. "Mathias, you will have two tasks. The first will be ensuring that the core to this facility—" he gestured behind him to the pulsing and humming central structure "—isn't going to explode, or give us radiation poisoning. We still don't know why this place was abandoned, or what they were doing here, so I don't want to take any chances."

Mathias nodded.

"The second will be rotating watch duties with Lena. We still don't have the front gate fixed, so this is crucial to our security."

"Why?" Mathias asked, adjusting his glasses. "It's not like there's anyone besides us who's survived."

"We don't actually know that," Eddy said. "And, you know, better safe than sorry."

"I'm fairly certain that this is not the case." Mathias smiled, smugly. "It's statistically improbable at best."

"Keep your educated guesses to the realm of science, where they belong, and let me worry about survival," Nico said. "You've got guard duty, end of story."

Mathias crossed his arms and scowled.

"Lena," Nico said.

"Yes, Master, do I get to clean toilets or do you want me in the kitchen preparing you men a hearty feast for your return?" Lena asked.

Lena'd had few skills before Nico and Ira came along, and Eddy hardly considered her bitchy attitude to be among them. The one skill she did have, she always pissed and moaned about having to do.

"No, Lena," Eddy said. "We've found a med bay on the third level; you're going to go through and get acquainted with the machinery, and take inventory of all the medical supplies that are left."

She sighed, obnoxiously. "Why don't you just have Ira do it for a change?"

"Ira's not a nurse, moron," Nico said.

"Ira's also working on decoding the files in the mainframe in order to understand what happened here," Eddy said. "I'm sure you'd hate to find your skin boiling cause your bed was infested with Measure 86."

"Don't even joke about that!" Lena shouted.

"Who said I'm joking?" Eddy's shit-eating grin faded when he saw how Nico was looking at him. "Right, I'll shut up."

"In any case, Ira is not to be disturbed," Nico said.

"How convenient." Lena said.

"Ahem." Ira's voice boomed through the chamber. "Is this thing on?"

"Speak of the devil," Lena said, coughing into her hand.

"We read you, sis." Nico said.

"Cool, get your asses up here. You need to see this."

5

Ira sulked back into her chair and watched the others gather round in the dim blue light of the mainframe room. Lena stood in front of Hugo, arms crossed, complete with resting bitch face; Mathias lurked at the back of the room like a ghost; Eddy came next to her and grabbed a chair; and Nico split the pack and stood in the middle.

"Let's see it," Nico said.

"Hope you didn't eat lunch today." Ira pushed play.

A small, slender man sporting a lab coat and a large messy black beard with interspersed gray stared back at them. Dark circles and bloodshot eyes accented his face, like he hadn't slept in days. He cleared his throat.

"After numerous unmanned tests of the equipment on apes and smaller animals, today marks the beginning of our human trials. This is the last hope for us avoiding this disaster... The equations are solid, all we've got to do now is test them for real.

"Soon, with any luck, we'll be able to open the gateway to another reality."

"Another reality?" Lena asked.

"Shush." Ira fast-forwarded to another part of the video.

"Experiment 5A," the scientist said.

The camera panned around to an observation room, similar to the one Ira had seen the day before. There, in the center of the room, was an operating table, and a man strapped to it. His face was painted with worry. Tubes and readout wires were taped to various parts of his naked body, just like they'd seen on the corpse.

"Daniels, are you ready?" the scientist asked.

"Yeah, doc, I guess."

"You're going to experience some pain, Daniels, but it'll pass. Remember your training in the deprivation chamber."

"Just flip the damn switch, doc."

"You heard him. Commence experiment."

An opaque green liquid filled Daniels' veins. His face tightened. His body jerked with intense violent convulsions, testing the tensile strength of his restraints. His screams filled the testing chamber; but the scientists remained calm.

The glass pyramid lit up, until all but Daniels' body was obscured by its light. Artifacts crept into the video, like a VHS tape getting chewed up.

Daniels' eyes clouded over. A high-pitched whine spread through the room, and Daniels' screams rose in octave to match it.

Ira wanted to avert her eyes.

"Remember your training, Daniels. Transference does not come from the drugs or the machinery. It must come from inside, at the mind's horizon!"

A white substance foamed around Daniels' mouth, stifling his screams into an incoherent gurgling. But the worst was yet to come. Daniels' body began to calm, and his breathing returned to normal.

"Alpha and beta waves are where they should be, Doctor Weber."

"Good," Weber said. "Turn it on."

Things seemed to calm down for a bit... Then the outer ring of the experiment chamber began to glow white-hot, and the walls vibrated with a terrible mechanical whisper. Daniels' body twitched and writhed in place; his eyes rolled back into his head, and the lights pulsed on and off, on and off.

The glowing glass pyramid around him started to shake, rattling like an old rusted Chevy in its death throes.

Daniels' convulsions managed to shake the whole table he was on; the bolts securing it to the concrete exploded. His mouth opened wide, as if something unseen had grabbed his jaw and yanked it open. Out came an impossibly loud, guttural repetition of spoken words, something like a Buddhist chant, but if Satan himself had done the chanting. His mouth remained open, but his lips did not move, as if his mouth was being used as some kind of fleshy speaker.

The chants caused terrible things to flash through Ira's mind. Her nightmare came to life, and she could almost feel the air of that dead place embrace her. The beast was still staring at her. Seven glowing gray eyes opened, regarding her with nothing but contempt.

She almost screamed, but Daniels' chants stopped, and with that, her visions of that hellish place faded like a memory.

"Sir, he's flatlining," one of the technicians said. "If we don't turn it off and administer the sedative, he'll die!"

"Don't you fucking touch it," Doctor Weber said. "We're so close."

The painted symbols around the pyramid started to shake, lifting off the ground as if they were composed of some viscous material — then wavered, tore themselves to pieces, like fracturing pages, and were sucked into the light emanating from the pyramid.

There was a loud explosion. Sparks flew from the machinery, and the glass pyramid shattered into thousands of deadly shards. Those shards fell, stabbing into Daniels' body like a pincushion. Daniels stopped twitching for a moment. His eyes were open, his chest rose and fell, but something was missing in his stare.

"Shit!" someone screamed.

"Someone get in there and take his damn pulse," Weber said. "And cut the recording, you imbecile!"

The lights continued to flicker… Then everything went dark, and the footage stopped.

"What the fuck did you just make us watch?" Hugo asked.

"I dug ahead to another video," Ira said. "Daniels died in that experiment."

"The mind's horizon," Mathias said, as if he were rolling the words around in his mouth.

"Yeah, what is that?" Eddy asked.

"I can't be sure," Mathias said. "I've never heard of anything like that. But from what the scientist said at the beginning of the video log, it seems as if they were using this base to experiment with some form of dimensional transference. Though this method doesn't make any sense to me, and frankly, smacks of the occult rather than the scientific. Truly strange."

Ira nodded: for once she agreed with Mathias.

"We need to be careful here," Eddy said.

"Yeah…" Ira turned to Nico. "Still think we should stay here?"

Nico's eyes found hers, and she saw no fear in them. She wondered if he was even paying attention. "This changes nothing. So what if these scientists were experimenting with dimensional travel? They're not here now. So, either they left, or they succeeded. Either way, we still need to survive, and this place is as good a shelter as we're going to get."

"But that wasn't just any experiment," Ira said. "Did you even watch the video? Did you hear that chant?"

Eddy nodded. "He wasn't even moving his lips."

"I have to agree with Nico here," Mathias said. "This place is a goldmine for resources, not to mention knowledge. What if these people found a way off this world and onto another?"

"I can't believe I'm hearing this!" Ira shouted.

"I'm surprised the opportunity doesn't excite you, Ira," Mathias said. "The chance to get off this icy hell and live a normal life?"

"Drop it, Mathias," Eddy said. "We're not looking to break any dimensional barriers, just trying to survive here."

"That's right," Nico said. "I don't want you screwing with anything in those experiment chambers. I don't care how smart you think you are, I won't have you unleashing a flesh-eating bacteria or blowing the damn place up on us."

Mathias crossed his arms.

"As for the rest of you," Nico said. "We've got work to do. Lena and Mathias, get to it. Eddy and Hugo, follow me."

They filed out of the doorway; Nico turned back to Ira.

"What?" she asked.

"Good work, sis," Nico said, and then he was gone.

The hatch closed behind him, and Ira felt as though she had made things worse. Why didn't they feel the all-encompassing sense of dread that she did?

Mathias was right; it wasn't science that those people had been practicing. Not with those strange symbols. It was some horrific mash-up between the occult and science.

It was madness.

And yet, Mathias's suggestion about the occult had not been made out of fear; rather, it'd sounded as if he was intrigued.

She shuddered and drew Woobie tighter around herself.

CHAPTER EIGHT

Eddy's boots sank deep into the snow. The weather was as calm as he could hope for, given the circumstances. Blue skies and only a slight stinging breeze to contend with. He almost felt like removing his facemask. How long had it been since he'd felt the sunlight on his naked skin?

Nico had managed to find an incline of snow that snaked its way around to the entrance of their newfound home. He'd parked the snowmobile at the top, but the one Eddy'd rode in on was still at the base of the cliff. Nico was busy reattaching the battery to the snowmobile and Hugo was busy standing around looking useless. There was no sense risking a climb back down the cliff, so he took the twisting path—what might have been a dirt road leading to the facility before the ice age—instead.

He stopped and took a quick glance around. He was near the bottom, and the snowmobile was just a hundred feet away, blanketed by a dusting of snow. Nico and Hugo drove past him and halted to a stop, kicking up a cloud of ice.

"You'll ride with Ramirez," Nico said.

Hugo dismounted from the snowmobile and stood next to Eddy.

"I got you, B," Hugo said.

"Try not to fall behind, Ramirez."

"Right," Eddy said.

Nico revved the engine. It stung the air with its harsh buzzing. His snowmobile took off across the snowy landscape toward Riverside.

"Why's he gotta' be such an asshole," Hugo said.

"You're asking the wrong guy, man," Eddy said.

Eddy turned back and continued to march his way through the snow toward the snowmobile. They both spent a few minutes brushing the loose snow off of it, then took their seats. The engine buzzed and Eddy took off after Nico.

He made his way over the next hill, and the decrepit and frozen skyline of downtown Riverside crept into view. Nico was just a klick ahead of them; Eddy noticed him look over his shoulder at a distance.

They continued on into the ruins of the city. Collapsed buildings, covered in sheets of ice and snow, cascaded toward the horizon on either side of their view.

While most of the destruction was the result of the incredible weight of snow and ice forming around and above the city, some of it had been left in the wake of the battle for the Mission Inn.

Eddy remembered it well. He could almost see the ghosts of those long-forgotten soldiers, their boots slapping against pavement, their guns rattling and flashing into the night, the screams of civilians and soldiers alike, echoing through the whole city like phantoms in the night.

The Revolutionists had been using the Mission Inn as a base of operations during a large-scale lockdown of the city. The hotel had been deserted for months since the outbreak of the war, as had been true for most of the downtown area of Riverside. It had been, in many ways, their last stand in Southern California. Many had speculated that, if the war had continued any further, the Feds would have won.

Eddy followed Nico up to one of the auxiliary entrances to the old shelter and brought the snowmobile to a stop. A plume of icy crystals filled the air in their wake.

They were on University Avenue, near the old performing arts center. This entrance to the tunnels was housed inside an old bar called Lake Alice, one that had seen some traffic from celebrities before the war erupted.

"Here we are," Eddy said.

Nico kept his engine running. " Hugo can help me with Cache A, B and gather up the weapons. Ramirez, head inside and grab the supplies in Cache C. Make sure you get to the west wing and grab all the batteries and miscellaneous supplies you can think of. We'll meet back here in an hour."

Eddy glared at Nico for a few moments longer than he should have; Nico's eyes focused through his goggles on him.

"Got something to say?" Nico asked.

Eddy got off the snowmobile, shook his head. He watched Hugo walk over and take a seat behind Nico, then they drove off. Eddy pushed the war to the back of his mind and considered the entrance. The large metal K was still sticking out of the snow, its protruding bits covered in rust and frost, but the rest of the Lake Alice sign had been buried. The windows on both floors had long since been shattered; the interior was worse. The bar was still there, but it was covered in ice. The alcohol that had once sat behind the counter had been looted in the early days, and the stage off to his right was covered in ice and fresh snow.

Eddy remembered going there a few times in his youth, trying to use a fake ID, and getting escorted home by the cops after getting caught.

He walked through a long hallway, which used to be covered in celebrity placards. He heard a crunch and looked down.

It was a placard.

He bent down and picked it up.

"Arnold Schwarzenegger," he said, chuckling. He leaned it back up against the wall and continued to the stairwell.

After descending the stairwell, he passed the remnants of bricks and shattered, frozen bits of stucco used by the long-dead owners of the place to seal it off from the tunnels below. Now he found himself in the basement, where a locked gate blocked his access to the tunnels. He pulled out a key from his pants pocket and unlocked it. When he opened the gate, its rusty hinges creaked so loud it made his ears hurt, ice cracking around its frame.

After walking for a while, he passed the red safety marker and removed his facemask. The smell of stale air, mold, and dust crept into his nostrils. The unique smell of home. His hand reached out and flipped a circuit breaker. Lights ignited above him, following sporadically along the path ahead, making a familiar plinking sound that filled every dusty crevice.

Their old shelter had scattered offshoots throughout most of the downtown area. Due to the sub-zero temperatures, the only place they could live, even semi-comfortably, was underground. Downtown Riverside had a series of catacombs and underground utility passages beneath the streets that had made for the perfect hiding spot to survive the apocalypse.

Eddy rounded the next corner. The food storage area was just a few hundred feet away. He passed one of the barricades to another part of the tunnel system. The chicken wire looked like it'd been torn up by something. A bad sign.

Rats and cockroaches were a common problem down here, but the mountain lions and coyotes rarely ever made it past the chicken wire.

Nico had killed the few that had made it through. Roast coyote and mountain lion ain't so bad when you've been living off of protein bars and MREs for months.

Mathias had gone on once about how coyotes and cougars were the last true survivors of the previous ice age. That they would survive this one by scavenging the carcasses of those unlucky enough to have died in the icy tundra of the valley.

As the population of prey animals dwindled, it left these animals fewer and fewer options.

Human probably tastes better than rat, Eddy thought.

He continued on to the cache. With every step, the sounds of crunching gravel echoed throughout the tunnel. Stealth was not an option.

He rounded the corner. The door to Cache C was open already.

His hair rose on end at the first sight of its silhouette, and, by instinct alone, he found his back slapped right up against the dusty stone wall. The mountain lion continued sniffing through containers, pawed at some protein bars that had been left lying around.

Shit, he thought. *Why do I always have to be right?*

Eddy's heartbeat intensified, adrenaline filled him, and his eyes frantically scanned the room for anything that might help him fend off the animal. The mountain lion sniffed through box after box, probably searching for something filled with a warm gooey center. The animal looked thin, emaciated, and its movements were slow and lethargic.

This was what made them so dangerous: most of the surviving population in the region would be starving with the dwindling population of prey animals in the area, making them desperate for that next meal. Eddy's eyes locked on a broom in the corner of the room, not exactly an ideal weapon of choice. His hand found the nine-millimeter that was holstered at his side, slowly unlatched the fastener. He had two options; either he would scare it off by threatening it, or take a shot at it and hope he didn't miss.

Eddy took in a deep breath and slowly drew his sidearm. The mountain lion's ears jabbed into the air, and its desperate, wild eyes locked onto his body. It began to pace around him, hissing quietly. His thumb cranked back the hammer, and his index finger slowly put pressure on the trigger.

It leapt forward, and Eddy fired several times before it could pin him against the wall. It reared its head back and clamped down on his shoulder. He screamed, fire engulfing his left shoulder as he shoved the barrel of the gun to the animal's cranium.

He pulled the trigger one final time.

A film of blood and brains covered Eddy's face as he grasped at his shoulder, wincing from the pain.

The animal fell limp on the ground. The blood pooled out from his fingers and around his shoulder. It soaked through his coat, quickly leaking onto the floor, and created a large puddle. It was hard to tell how much blood was his. He let the gun fall out of his hands, and, with a shaky hand, reached for his CB.

Ira was gonna be pissed.

2

There is nothing but darkness.
Endless darkness.

No horizon. No land. Nothing.

Mathias wants to scream, but finds he has no voice.

It seems like he's been drifting there for an eternity, floating like he's nothing.

Then, after staring into the dark for untold hours, he sees something begin to take shape. An oval thing. Its surface is hard, cracked, like acrylic. It pushes through the dark like it's burrowing through black clouds, until it hovers inches from his face.

It has no breath. No eyes.

His heart. He can feel it pounding, telling him to run away. Far away.

The oval shape is like a face, or the impression of one. It slowly takes shape, revealing two eyeholes and a carved mouth that's permanently fixed into a frown. The mask is covered by a hood that drapes back into the dark, fading. When Mathias looks at it, really looks at it, he gets the impression that it's older than even the most ancient of Sumerian artifacts.

Mathias wants to ask it who it is. He feels as though the figure already knows.

There are cracking sounds. The mask's mouth is moving.

Transforming into a smile.

Mathias woke up clutching at his chest, screaming.

When he saw his own fear reflected back at him in the check-in station's window, he stopped screaming, took a moment to look at his surroundings.

The florescent lights above buzzed, flickering on and off. The smell of the moldering sandwich he'd found when he first opened the door still struggled to make its presence known from the trash.

He'd started his "guard" duty session from inside the abandoned check-in station, so he'd be able to keep some of his heavy gear off.

He must have dozed off in the chair at some point.

Only a dream, he thought.

Every hair on his arms stood on end; there was a chill in the air.

The door to the check-in station was ajar, swinging open and shut, seemingly by itself, letting in the harsh air from the ice tunnel beyond the gates.

"Odd," Mathias said, standing up and closing it, making sure to lock it this time. "I could have sworn I closed it..."

He sat there for a time, reading a tattered copy of Stephen Hawking's *A Brief History of Time* that he'd found in the insignificant concrete cell he'd claimed as his own.

The chapter on black holes wasn't keeping his attention like he'd hoped.

Every time he read the word *event horizon,* all he could think about was the thing Weber had mentioned in the log entry Ira had shown them.

"The mind's horizon." Mathias rolled the words around in his mouth. Just saying it sent chills through him.

If an event horizon was the point of no return for matter entering a black hole, then what was the mind's horizon?

Perhaps it's the point beyond the mind's ability to understand its own perceived reality? Mathias thought. *No, that can't be it.*

He closed the book and set it on the switchboard in front of him.

Nothing was working.

All he could think about was that thing in his dream.

The mask. If it was a mask at all. It seemed so real. Even now, he felt like he could picture it perfectly in his mind.

"I'm a rational, scientifically minded man," Mathias said, hearing the shaken quality of his voice bouncing back to his ears off the small check-in station's walls and buttons and tables. It was an alien sound. Even as a child, he'd never feared the things that his peers did. He'd known that the bogeyman was as real as Santa Claus and Jesus Christ were.

But this was different.

He chuckled. "I just need to clear my head, that's all."

Mathias grabbed his coat and his facemask and unlatched the door.

Maybe it was time for him to tour the facility?

3

Nico watched Hugo lug the last of the supplies to the snowmobile.

There was another storm rolling in from the west, its shadow already covering what was once Corona. If Eddy didn't hurry up, they might get stuck here for the night.

"Make sure you tie those down, Hugo—"

"Shit, Nico—" Eddy's voice crackled over the CB. "—I got a problem here."

Nico grabbed the receiver and held it to his facemask. "What is it?"

"You might get a laugh out of this." Eddy fell into a coughing fit. "A cat got me. Fucker bit right into my shoulder. I need a field-dressing...maybe a shot of morphine..."

Idiot probably let his guard down, Nico thought. "We're at the warehouse over the main shelter. Can you make it to us?"

"I think so." He paused. "It fucking hurts, but I think I can make it over to you."

"Move your ass, then. Nico out."

Nico lowered his CB. Hugo looked up at him. "What's up with Eddy, B?"

"Don't worry about it," Nico said, retreating through the shutters and descending down the manhole. "Just make sure that load is secure. I need to take care of something."

"Sure thing, boss-man."

Nico made his way through the tunnel leading back to the shelter. He was certain there was a first aid kit he'd forgotten to grab.

They didn't have time for this distraction. If Ramirez didn't get the supplies packed up, then there was no way they were going to get out of here before the storm hit.

It was a miracle none of them had died in the last one.

Nico removed his facemask. Took a seat before the desk where Eddy and Ira had come trotting into the shelter just days ago—late as hell—laughing and joking.

The old shelter was cold. The generators that remained still ran, but the living space had dropped to an unlivable thirty degrees already.

Nico watched his breath steam in the air.

The first aid kit was packed underneath the desk. He grabbed it and held it close to him.

He remembered his first time giving a field dressing.

His hands had been covered in blood. Hernandez was bleeding out from multiple wounds. He didn't think she was going to make it. He desperately tried to get the bleeding to stop.

"Just let me go, Hartman," Hernandez said, blood staining her perfect teeth. "Go find someone else who needs help."

"No," he said. "I'm not giving up on you."

She tried to respond, but descended into a violent coughing fit. Her body twisted and writhed on the ground like a child possessed by a demon.

The empty look in her eyes when she died haunted his dreams to this day.

Hernandez was one of his closest friends. She had always been by his side in the trenches.

The Revolutionists that planted those explosives, that stormed the base while their guards were down, killed her.

"What the hell?" Ramirez's voice came from the other end of the room.

That was when Nico realized he was on the ground, rocking back and forth like a damned mental patient.

Ramirez rushed over to him, holding his bleeding shoulder tight.

Nico could practically smell the blood.

People like Ramirez killed Hernandez. Killed Boyd. Took his leg. They couldn't be trusted.

"Dude, are you having a fucking panic attack?" Ramirez's voice was incredulous. His dark complexion made his eyes look as if they were smoldering in their sockets.

"You killed her," Nico said.

"What the fuck are you talking about?" Ramirez said, backing away. "Dude, I'm bleeding out here, I don't feel—"

Nico barely realized he'd done it. It was like someone else was in control of his body. He got to his feet and closed the distance between them in the space of a heartbeat. His hand found the grip of his knife...and he swung.

It was a clean cut, right across Ramirez's throat.

The look in Ramirez's eyes as he fell back, gripping his bleeding throat, was enough to shake Nico out of his paranoid daze.

He'd have to act fast if he wanted to save him.

Do you really want to save him, though?

He could make something up, claim the cat killed him. Bury him before anyone noticed. Would it really be so bad to lose this traitor?

"Damn it," Nico said quietly, watching Ramirez writhe on the floor. "Ira would never forgive me."

He grabbed the first aid kit and the bandages. Saving this asshole's life was going to be painful.

4

Lena covered herself as she made her way to the med bay, or whatever the hell it was called here. The corridors were cold and unfriendly. She hated it here already, but she couldn't put off the task Nico had given her any longer. There was no telling when they'd be back.

At least their underground shelter had felt like a home. This…place…felt like they were part of some science experiment, like rats inside a maze.

Every step she took reverberated back to her seconds later, filling the tubular corridors. It was like the place was making sure she knew she was totally alone.

The med bay was its own room, separated from the corridor by glass. The doors opened for her, and she stepped inside.

There was an open MRE pack and a dead cell phone on one of the counters. A mess of hypodermic needles and other supplies were spilled on the linoleum floor—

She screamed, covering her mouth.

Two bloody handprints started where the mess was and streaked all the way to a dark corner where the harsh florescent lighting barely reached.

The lights flickered.

It must have been her imagination; she could have sworn she saw something in that dark corner. Something that was staring right at her.

"Screw this!" Lena backed out through the double glass doors and retreated to her room.

She didn't care if Nico yelled at her. There was no way she was going to clean that mess up. At least not alone.

And that face, those gray eyes…she pushed it away. It was only her imagination.

She found her way back to her room. Taking an uncomfortable ride in the elevator. She held herself tight.

Lena wished she could talk to someone about what she'd seen. But, Mathias was an emotionless brick, and Ira… Yeah, no.

Why couldn't her friends have survived? They'd always gotten her.

But that had been years ago, when the sun had burned bright in a vibrant, sometimes smog-filled sky. Where there were warm beaches filled with the hottest chicas—none as hot as she was—their smooth skin, oiled up, their asses hanging out of their bikini bottoms, breasts so full…and the shirtless guys, with their washboard abs, who worshiped the ground she walked on. She'd had a lot of fun on the beach. Taken a lot of girls home, and a lot of guys. Now, all she had was Hugo. A white boy who desperately wished he was black, in more ways than one.

He wasn't half the man Nico was, even considering his fake leg.

She bit her lip.

Lena crawled into her cot, curled up in a ball, and prayed for it all to go away, for the blazing Southern California sun to return.

It didn't, obviously.

She rolled over on her side.

Maybe she'd just take a nap? It'd be easier without the lights on…she remembered the thing she had seen in the shadows…

I'll just nap with the lights on, she thought.

Lena's eyes jerked open.

She was sitting in the check-in station that Mathias had told her about.

Must have fallen asleep, she thought.

The ice tunnel was dark…it must be night already.

Where was Mathias? He was supposed to trade watch duties with her.

There was a crunching noise echoing through the speakers… She glanced at the control board. Funny, she didn't remember turning them on.

She jumped as the door to the check-in station swung open.

"What the fuck!"

The crunching sounds…they were growing closer and closer.

Fear coated her skin like sweat as she got up from her chair, walked to the ramp leading to the ice tunnel…and peered into the abyss.

The crunching. It was footsteps.

She could make out something moving in the tunnel.

Something small.

"Hello?" Lena said, her voice shaky and pathetic. "Nico? Hugo? Is that you?"

The crunching stopped.

"This isn't fucking funny!"

As her eyes adjusted, her heartbeat quickened. The figure in the tunnel…it looked like a little girl.

"I agree, mommy." That voice…it couldn't be…

Lena backed away from the ice tunnel, down the ramp.

"This isn't possible," Lena said, shaking her head. "You're dead! I saw you die!"

"You're right, mommy, I am dead." The footsteps started up again and their pace intensified. "We can be together again. Don't you want to see me again?"

"Baby…"

"Don't you *baby* me! You were never there! Always off with one of your weekend lovers, always spreading your legs, just like Tía always said!"

"I'm sorry!" Lena broke down, curling into a ball and sobbing into the cement. "I'm so sorry!"

The footsteps stopped again.

The smell of death filled the chamber. Lena's eyes slowly rose.

The bullet wound in Sophi's head was still oozing blood. Her teeth were black. Her eyes, bloodshot. She smiled.

"Join me in the abyss, mommy!"

Lena screamed herself awake. She sat up.

It was dark.

She patted the cot to ensure that it was there. She vaguely remembered keeping the lights on before her nap.

Reluctantly, she got up and turned the lights back on.

She sat there, catching her breath and wiping the sweat from her brow.

Her head felt heavy, groggy, like she'd overslept. Was it night or day? If it was her turn to take up watch in the check-in station, she'd kindly pass. Not after that nightmare.

Sophi, she thought.

"I need a drink," she said.

5

Ira let her long johns fall to the pristine tiled floor. She rubbed at her eyes and stretched her aching back. She'd been at it for a few hours, watching video logs and reading log entries from personnel. There was only so much she could take.

There was a group shower on the same floor as her room. She'd been reluctant to go there alone, but somehow, she found the courage.

This place, facility, whatever it was called, was lonely, and she couldn't help but feel like there were eyes on her as she approached one of the showers. The fluorescent lighting didn't help much, either. It gave that familiar buzzing that the tunnel lights did, so low and ominous that it was almost like the constant irritation of a fly at the back of her skull, just out of reach.

It'd been so long since she'd felt hot, running water.

Part of her almost felt guilty as she turned the nob and let it come steaming out onto her naked body, washing the grime and the dust away.

It was almost enough to make her forget about what she'd seen.

It can't be real, she thought.

The way Daniels spoke. The strange, guttural language.

She glanced behind herself. There was a rattling sound coming from the walls.

The pipes were connected to a large water supply that was contained somewhere deep in the facility along with a central boiling unit. It was a limited supply, that much she'd seen in the mainframe files, but the supply would last a decent while, enough that they wouldn't be hurting for water enough to go without showering. At least, she hoped.

Still she felt eyes on her. She ignored the feeling, knowing that it was only her own paranoia, and soaped the pain and the dirt and the grime away. She watched it run black and red, circling down the drain.

6

Ira came back to the mainframe room with a towel wrapped around her head. She almost felt refreshed.

She sat in front of her laptop, found the next video log, pressed play.

"Update on human trials," Doctor Weber said, his words slightly slurred. "We've conducted six experiments so far using my original design, and all six have failed, resulting in some...oddities."

Weber removed his glasses and attempted to rub away the dark circles beneath his eyes. The gray in his hair had increased since the first video Ira had seen. Even presidents aged slower than this guy.

"It's no secret that what we're doing here is... unconventional, and they can't understand, can't see what I'm doing for them all. Ungrateful simpletons! The whole lot of them would be frozen corpses if it weren't for me.

"I'm their savior!

"If they only knew the burden I've taken on for them, for all of humanity..."

He paused. His eyes drifted down to a tattered book he was holding. Ira had seen that book in a couple of the experiment videos, sometimes tucked away in one of the doctor's pockets, or clutched tightly in one hand during an experiment.

"I understand now—" He chuckled. "I know now what the mind's horizon is. I've been reading. Reading so much it hurts sometimes. It is difficult to make them understand without showing them the book. If only they could see.

"Still. The book is dangerous. Reading it...changed me. It's hard to describe. At first, I tried to record the changes I felt...but I lost track...there's almost a...how can I...it's like another will inside of me."

He touched his temple. "In here. So deep inside. It wants out. It wants to be known, to be spread…"

He blinked. Rubbed his eyes. Looked around the room. It was almost like she was looking into someone else's eyes.

"The answer to getting these simpleminded subjects to reach the state the book describes may be…pharmacological. They wouldn't understand if they knew where I gained the knowledge from.

"We've since concocted a more precise cocktail of hallucinogens and morphine, all to help isolate the body's ability to perceive its surroundings. It's very similar to the effects of a sensory deprivation tank, and in fact, in the next round of tests, we'll be adding the tank to the design framework as well.

"The mental training inside the tank will be geared from this time onward toward allowing each subject to detach from this physical reality, followed by subliminal messages for the chants. Some of the other doctors have raised questions as to the nature of these chants, what they mean. Professor Kendal even accused them of being sacrilegious."

Weber started chuckling. The look in his eyes changed again. It reminded Ira of when her grandfather would shift from being lucid to having one of his Alzheimer's episodes.

"Fools," Weber said, running his hands through his hair. "They do not know how lucky they are to hear these ancient words. Even as the world freezes over, they cling to their false gods and pray for salvation. But, if there are such things as gods, they care nothing for us."

He paused again, blinking, as if he wasn't sure where he was. His eyes returned to the camera.

"Some of the volunteers are apprehensive toward the tank, following the untimely 'deaths' of a few of our subjects. I can't say that I blame them, but we must prevail."

He leaned back in his chair, reached for a bottle of brown liquid off to his right, poured himself a glass, and took a sip. He looked almost content then, like someone reminiscing on the good ol' days.

"My first experience in a sensory deprivation tank was met with some aversion too, I must admit. I remember that a few of my friends had taken a trip into Los Angeles for our spring break away from

101

Caltech, and they, after discovering the work of John Lilly, wanted to try the tank. I didn't know what to think at the time, and I was probably a bit frightened about how the experience of total submersion would affect me."

He took a long drink.

"After that first thirty-minute session, I became obsessed with his work. I spent a half an hour inside the tank every day for the rest of break, and I saw such incredible things. I must confess, though, that the mind's horizon is not an idea that I came up with on my own. No. It was the late Douglas Collier.

"Jimmy, a friend of mine, heard about my sudden, almost manic, obsession with Lilly's work. I remember it like it was yesterday, how he passed me that tattered leather book and said to give it a read, that it might change my life.

"And he was *right*. With the help of *Messages from the Abyss*, Collier's last work of note before his untimely death on Mount Denali in Alaska, and Lilly's work, my path became all too clear.

"I spent so long with my face buried in that terrible book that my grades took a sharp dive. If I'm honest, it's a wonder that I even graduated. The book was both a diary, and a manual of sorts, what the superstitious might call a '*grimoire*.' The diary aspect of the book records Collier's rapid descent into madness after bringing a statuette back to his quarters, a statuette that gave him terrible visions and enlightened him to a world where humanity was nothing more than a speck in an infinite void. Collier claimed that when he stared into the statuette, let it talk to him, that it gave him powerful incantations and scientific formulas that have only just been discovered today by normal means.

"As for the other half of the book: there was one page in particular, it spoke of a passageway through the abyss, beyond a place called the Astral Lands, through which all information and light goes to rest eternally, a passageway that was only reachable by passing through the mind's horizon."

He stared into the camera, and Ira almost felt like he was looking right at her. The lucid quality in his voice eroded almost instantly. All she could see in his stare was madness. "If an event horizon is the point of no return for matter, then the mind's horizon is the point of no return before reality itself unravels, before the curtain is finally pulled back."

Weber was shaking. He poured himself another glass.

Ira's breath was short.

She wanted desperately to turn the video off, to stop the slow descent into madness that was taking place. But a part of her wanted to know more; a part of her was morbidly curious.

"Like Lilly before me, I've met with an entity far beyond the grasp of Earth. It showed me things. Great secrets that humanity would have taken untold eons to unlock. It's all thanks to the tank.

"There are many passages in the grimoire written in what can only be described as a dead language. Impossible to decode. I know the secret is contained within the book, but…there's no telling how long it would take to make a proper translation of the hieroglyphs contained within…"

He grinned, showing his yellowing teeth. "Did you know, Tibetan monks meditate their entire lives to achieve enlightenment? I have a theory…that perhaps the state they seek is not too dissimilar to what the book describes."

His eyes became very grave, serious. "But, I do not have a lifetime to accomplish this task.

"I don't remember many details from the experience, but I remember the void of space, and the sight of an otherworldly entity with an orange glow drifting toward me…it was like it could sense me. At first, I was foolish enough to think that it was just the LSD I'd taken—I was so wrong. So naive. My mind needed to be opened up…needed to see the doorway.

"It was trying to speak to me. More impression than actual speech, as if I was being sent telepathic messages from this being, and it was receiving mine. It was incredible. Such euphoria.

"The entity seemed to be going against the orders of its directorate, which were to observe humanity, but not influence us in any meaningful way. This being, it seemed to recognize that we were in trouble, all of us, on our way to extinction. So, it did the only thing that it felt it could.

"It gave me so much. So very much. It told me that our minds are not products of the brain itself, but that organic lifeforms merely use brains as...as antennae...yes, that's it...antennae...our personality, our desires, our feelings, from another dimension, which is in the same place as our bodies—" he descended into a coughing fit "—but slightly out of phase from the rest of our perceived reality.

"And what is reality, really? Our eyes are such flawed things. There are so many holes in our universe, and our brains just paint over them.

"The key, as I understand it, is putting our minds into a trance-like state. Don't you see? Science fiction films have told us for decades that we must rely on technology alone to reach the stars, but the real frontier is within *ourselves*. With the proper training, we can use our minds to change the very frequency at which our molecules and atoms vibrate, and shift into another reality!

"This, of course, was something that I'd already read in the grimoire. But, the entity seemed to know *how* it was done. Which was something I could never decode from *Messages from the Abyss*. This entity was very likely the missing link. My last chance. The tank was the gateway.

"I had to know more."

A beeping sound erupted from Weber's watch. He checked it haphazardly. "Speak of the devil. It's time for my next tank session."

His smile spread from ear to ear as he opened up an orange pill bottle and placed something white on his tongue. "Wish me luck."

7

Ira rubbed her eyes and turned away from the glow of her screen. The video was over at last, thank God. She felt like she was going a little crazy herself while listening to the nonsense coming out of Doctor Weber's mouth.

There were still encrypted parts of the network, more secrets that she didn't want to find. Yet, there was a part of her that was compelled to dig deeper. That part of her always seemed to win out in the long run.

Her eyes opened wide when a rumbling sound came from her stomach. Maybe it was time for a break, and something to eat? She stood up, arched her back and stretched.

It was 3:00 am already.

Definitely time for a break.

She found herself alone, walking down the tubular corridor to the cold, emotionless stone-walled rectangle she refused to call home. The others could bitch all they like about the old shelter. How much they'd hated living under the city. At least that place had character, had felt like it was theirs.

This place felt like a prison.

Nico and the others had been gone less than a day, and she already wished they had stayed.

The halls in the facility were less than comforting. Cold white and black stone walls, sparsely lit by buzzing and flickering fluorescent bulbs. She tried to tell herself that her uneasiness wasn't because of the things she'd found in the archive, the video logs, or from the project summaries that told of horrific experiments that had left dozens brain-dead, or worse.

And then there were Weber's secret logs. These she wished she'd never found. Weber was insane, clearly. There was a room at the top of the facility where he'd spent most of his time. She wondered, grimly, if there was still a copy of *Messages from the Abyss* up there, and if she'd go mad just from reading it, the way he had. A stupid thought.

Books couldn't make you go insane.

She stopped walking; there was a quiet tapping behind her, like the careful footsteps of a predator. The skin on the back of her neck tightened, as if reacting to the cold; her limbs felt stiff, and some primal fear inside of her told her not to turn around. She stood there for what seemed like minutes; she closed her eyes, and, finally finding the courage, quickly turned around.

She found nothing but an empty tunnel that faded into darkness.

Ira sighed, relaxed her shoulders, shook her head and continued walking. It was probably all in her head.

She'd barely spent any time in her room at all; her cot was still unmade. It was pretty bare, considering all of her belongings were still at the old shelter. She walked over to her pack and withdrew a protein bar, sat down on the cot and took a bite.

Eddy and Nico needed to hurry the hell up and get back.

CHAPTER NINE

Mathias woke up screaming, staring into the blackened pits of that ancient mask again.

He scrambled off his cot and found the light switch, panting and raving like a mental patient. The lights came on, and the masked figure was gone.

Collapsing on the cold, concrete floor, Mathias held his head in his hands.

What in the hell is happening to me? he thought. *Why do I keep having these nightmares?*

After he caught his breath, he found the courage to stand again. The alarm clock on the room's previous owner's nightstand read 3:00 am.

It might even have been right.

Yesterday's walk had worked wonders. Why not do it again?

Mathias grabbed his coat and put it on, then opened his door and slipped down the corridor.

His stomach was growling.

In the last day or so—he couldn't be sure how many hours had passed—he hadn't run into Ira or Lena once. Not that he was complaining. Even in his aimless wandering throughout the facility, there wasn't the slightest hint that he wasn't alone.

He wondered just how large this place really was.

He found himself standing in front of a metal door with a keypad and a sign overhead that read EXPERIMENT 13A.

Nico had told him not to go messing with any of the experiment chambers here.

He'd never know, Mathias thought, as he caressed the keypad.

There was no telling what the code was, but he tried the door handle anyway. It twisted as though it weren't locked. Something clicked. And the door swung open, its hinges squeaking.

Why wasn't the door locked?

Perhaps reconnecting the core to the main systems fried the locking mechanisms?

The darkness loomed before him, beckoning him forward.

Sweat beaded above his brow.

"One peek won't hurt," Mathias said, stepping into the dark.

His hand patted the wall for a light switch, found a row of circular buttons instead. He pressed all of them in the order he'd felt them.

The lights plinked on, one by one. First, in the observation room, then, in the experiment chamber.

He almost screamed when he saw them. Two horizontal sensory deprivation tanks sat in the center of a cold stone floor, marked up by a white circle. The white circle was contained within a glass pyramid, just like the previous chamber.

One of the deprivation tanks was open. There was a skeletal arm sticking out of the solution.

Mathias scanned over the rows of keyboards, buttons, monitors, and other equipment.

Part of him wanted to get the hell out of there...but another part of him, the scientist deep inside him, wanted to know more. Wanted to know what had gone wrong.

He found himself reaching for one of the computer towers—He stopped himself.

"No," he said. "I shouldn't. Nico may be right after all..."

He gave the experiment chamber one last look before turning the lights off.

2

Ira almost turned back when she saw Lena in the food storage cache.

Lena glared at her, grabbing her rations and putting them in her pocket for her morning meal. Surprisingly, she didn't say anything.

"Morning?" Ira said, slipping past her and grabbing an MRE.

There was something else in Lena's stare, a look she was all too familiar with. Did she blame Ira for finding this place?

The look faded from Lena's face. "Have you heard from Nico yet?"

She shook her head. "I've had my CB on me just in case…still nothing. I was…" She hesitated. "…I was gonna head to the surface to look for any signs of them in the valley."

Lena stared at her for a moment, probably considering her own options. "I'll go with you."

Ugh, why? Ira thought. "Okay…"

"Don't get the wrong idea," Lena said. "I…I just don't want to be alone here. I feel like I'm going crazy."

Ira could relate.

"Right," she said, slipping out the door. "Well, I'm going to have breakfast first, then I'm headed up to the surface."

"I'll be there," Lena said.

3

Ira had to force herself to eat.

She blamed it on the log entry she'd watched last night. It had given her nightmares. Nightmares she was thankful had left only a fading impression on her as the morning droned on.

Mathias was sitting in the check-in station when she reached the facility's entrance. He nodded to her through the window, but didn't bother coming out to say hi. Not that she was bothered. It was cold as hell in here.

She'd thought it was Lena's turn to be on lookout, but she wasn't going to raise the issue.

Ira stretched her goggles over her eyes and put her facemask on. She was trudging through the ice tunnel before she knew what she was doing.

She felt the hair on the back of her neck stand on end when she heard the unmistakable sound of boots crunching on ice, coming from behind her. Footsteps that she knew weren't hers.

This time, she resisted the fearful urge not to look and spun around. It was just Lena.

"Jesus Christ," Ira said. "You scared the shit out of me."

Lena glanced at her halfheartedly and kept walking.

"What the fuck is wrong with you?" Ira whispered, following after her.

4

The valley looked empty, save for a pack of coyotes in the distance. She scanned what used to be San Bernardino and Highland with her multi-specs, but couldn't see any sign of Nico or Eddy's snowmobiles.

There was a fresh coat of snow on the ground, and dark clouds to the east.

"Looks like we might have gotten another storm last night," Ira said. "Might have forced them to stay the night at the old shelter."

"Might have?" Lena said. "But, you're not sure?"

Ira shook her head. "I'm sure they're fine. We were lucky to get here without incident the first time."

"Yeah, lucky isn't the word I'd use for it," Lena said, her eyes both accusatory and worried beneath her goggles.

"You blame me for finding this place," Ira said. "I can see it in your eyes."

"The thought crossed my mind," Lena said.

"There was no way to know what was out here…we couldn't pass the opportunity up…"

"Keep telling yourself that." Lena turned around, hugging herself, and headed back toward the ice tunnel.

Ira watched her go. *Bitch.*

5

Hugo woke up to Nico smacking him on the cheek.

"Wake up," Nico said.

It took a few moments longer than Nico probably would have liked for him to remember where he was.

"I said—" Nico gripped Hugo's arm and dragged him off the dusty, broken couch. "—get up!"

"Or what, B?" Hugo eyed Eddy's body. His chest rose and fell, but no one seemed to be home. There were bandages wrapped around his neck and shoulder. "You gonna do to me how you did him?"

"You don't say a word to them about what happened here," Nico said, his eyes full of fire. "You got that? It was a mountain lion. That's our story."

"Yeah," Hugo said, keeping his eyes low. "I got you."

"Good." Nico crossed his arms. "Now get off your ass and prep the snowmobiles. We're heading back while we have a chance."

Hugo nodded. He kept a watchful eye on Nico as he left the room. God knows he'd given him plenty of reason to put himself next on the list.

6

After slipping into his snow gear, Hugo made his way to the warehouse. He'd have to go fetch Eddy's snowmobile at the other cache too, but that could wait till later.

He found himself reminiscing about the old days. He missed the days when all he had to worry about was getting several videos out for a given week, eagerly checking his viewership, and letting the cash roll in.

He'd had it made. He could make videos on any subject he wanted, ranging from politics, conspiracies, science, religion, and even the war. His most popular videos were any dealing with the flat Earth.

How could he have let himself get sucked into that mess, only to be proved wrong by the coming of the ice? Science don't give a shit what you believe.

Now, all of that seemed trivial. If his former, flat-Earth-believing, God-fearing self could see him now…

He was just thankful Nico and the others had never seen his videos.

The snowmobile's gas tank was nearly empty. He filled it and warmed the engine up. Then, he checked to make sure the straps on the sled were in good shape.

"Help me get Eddy," Nico said, startling Hugo.

"Whoa, B," Hugo said. "Scared the shit outta me."

"We're going to tie him to the sled."

Hugo nodded.

Nico seemed different somehow.

They descended through the manhole and grabbed Eddy's unconscious body. Hugo wondered, as they hoisted him up through the hatch, whether he was in a coma or something.

He couldn't imagine that he'd survive the trip back.

When Eddy's body was secure atop the supplies they'd packed on the sled, Nico got in the driver's seat and beckoned Hugo on.

"Let's move," Nico said.

Hugo nodded and did as the boss-man asked.

The look in his eyes. He'd seen that look before for sure. Back when he'd holed himself up in the Riverside Library, rationing old bags of potato chips and pretzels to keep himself from starving.

Lena had been with him. Nico had drawn his gun on him. Hugo had been certain he was gonna pull the trigger, but Lena had stopped him. Said they should take him in. Maybe she'd been sweet on him from the very beginning?

He was pretty fuckin' baller, even now. He couldn't blame her.

They came to Lake Alice's frozen, decrepit entrance. During the war, his rep had gotten so bad he couldn't show his face here without someone threatening to beat his ass for the shit he'd said in his videos about the Revolutionists, saying they were gonna be judged by God in the end and all that. He'd just been talkin' out his ass, of course. He didn't know the first thing about politics, but it was good for business, even if all he did was blow smoke.

"Get that snowmobile running," Nico said.

It was covered in about five inches of fresh snow. Hopefully the gas tank hadn't been empty enough for it to freeze. "I'll give it a go, boss-man."

"Do more than that," Nico said. "It's your ass if we lose it."

"How's that my fault?"

"Don't argue with me. You don't have the right."

Hugo grabbed the brush and scraper he'd packed with the supplies, making sure to dig around Eddy's body, and sulked over to the snowmobile.

With his finger, he wiped off the dashboard. The tank needed filling.

He walked back and grabbed the gas can.

Nico watched him carefully as he worked. He had the snowmobile cleared shortly, and got its engine running.

Nico stared forward, revving the engine. "Follow me."

Hugo watched him take off into the frozen corpse of the city. Eddy's coat flapping in the wind, his body bouncing and shaking at every turn and snowy hill.

Maybe you should have got cut, Hugo thought. *Fucking asshole.*

He pushed the thought aside, climbed up on the snowmobile, and took off after Nico.

7

Mathias had been sitting for hours, staring at A Brief History of Time's tattered cover.

He was having a tough time keeping his eyes open. There was no real telling day from night down here. He could have sworn the clocks they'd brought with them were set to the correct time…but how could any of them be sure?

He glanced at the clock on the control panel. It read 10:00 am…and then it read 12:00 pm. Just like that.

Mathias sat forward, tapping the clock's glass casing…but the time didn't change.

It must have been a glitch. That's what it was. But, when he checked his own watch, it too read 12:00pm.

He ran his hands through his hair.

He needed sleep.

That's all.

Last night's nightmare had left him sleep-deprived.

His eyes drifted to the facility's broken doors, lying and freezing on the ramp leading out into the ice cavern.

No one was coming. Hell, Nico and the others would probably be gone for another day.

"I deserve a nap," Mathias said.

He stood up, slipped his coat on and headed toward the elevator down the next hall.

His cot felt like heaven. He didn't bother undressing.

He set his alarm for three hours. That seemed reasonable.

A black comet the size of a large sun blazed a path across a crimson sky; the waves of its ion tail had the consistency of oil, casting ripples into the infinite dark.

Mathias couldn't believe his eyes. He stood atop a canyon of some kind. All around him, towering, ancient, impossible structures, lit carmine by the sky above. Their supports were carved into the visages of massive creatures with three eyes and too many limbs.

"Where am I?" His voice echoed down into the canyon.

That's when he saw it.

The masked figure from his nightmares, towering over him like a giant.

Its tattered robes billowed in the musty winds of this strange place. Its ancient mask looked even older than the ruins. When he looked into its eyeholes, he saw nothing but darkness staring back at him.

An abyss.

"Who are you?" Mathias asked.

The mask had a grin etched into it.

The thing in the mask pointed to a series of gargantuan stone steps, which led down into the canyon. Its cloak's sharp, tattered edges glided as it moved down the steps, beckoning Mathias along with appendages which looked far too large to be hands.

His first inclination was to ignore the strange creature and strike off on his own, but, for some reason, he found himself mesmerized by its dragging cloak, following after it like some drooling, empty-headed fool.

The path became strange. When Mathias tried to look up at the canyon walls, get a glimpse at the towering monolithic buildings made—presumably—by a long-dead civilization, he saw only the roof of a square tunnel overhead.

When he lowered his head, there was a light at the end of the tunnel, a doorway, which silhouetted his newfound companion.

"Hey, what the hell is this?" Mathias asked, but the creature did not reply.

On they marched. The doorway never grew in size. The perfect tilework cascaded beneath his feet with each step they took, but still they gained no distance at all.

Then, they were at the base of a stone pyramid missing massive chunks. Those chunks floated in the sky of that strange place, reflecting red off the light of that awful sky. The black comet was so close he could feel its heat slowly boiling his skin. When he stared at the cratered horizon, he could almost make out several small worlds, crumbling into the mouth of the comet... But, that was insane. *Comets don't have mouths.*

The masked figure did not wait; it sped off toward the pyramid.

Mathias chased after it, not wanting to be left alone on the surface facing that thing.

The inside of the pyramid was oddly familiar to him. The corridors were curved, and they led to many different rooms which were blocked off. As much as he wanted to stay and examine them, the masked thing marched on, and he was compelled to follow.

They came to a large chamber, perhaps at the center of the pyramid, with immense, cylindrical tubes scattered atop a circular platform. There were dead, crumbling consoles, whose wires had long since been eaten away by time.

The strangest thing was the bottom most portion of the wall. It was a kind of tube, raised above the door in which they entered; it was not unlike a particle collider.

Mathias was so busy gawking at the room that he lost track of the masked figure. Now, when he looked around the chamber, it was nowhere to be found.

"What am I supposed to do with this?" he asked, but all he heard was the echo of his own voice in reply.

Then. The place began to shake. He saw great fissures and cracks form instantly in the stone walls, ruining the perfect craftsmanship.

Mathias scrambled for the corridor he'd come through earlier. Large stone debris rained down on the circular platform behind him. A part of him ached when he saw the place crumbling to ruins. What he'd give for just a few more minutes to study that place!

The tunnel stretched on and on and on, dust filling the air as he sprinted as fast as his scrawny legs would allow.

Finally, he made it out into the open, but his feet did not touch the dusty surface. Instead, he floated, spiraling around in the dark until he spun around to face the pyramid.

What he saw drove him slightly mad with laughter. The brilliant jaws of something his brain could not quite comprehend had cracked the moon he had just been on in two. Chunks of it were being devoured, swallowed by a black hole in the center of this thing. Staring at the pyramid's shattered face, his peripheral vision interpreted the comet's shape like he was staring at an ever-changing inkblot test.

He felt his body falling toward the thing. His screams were heard by no one.

Mathias woke in darkness. For a moment, he wondered if he had been swallowed by that thing. His head hurt, badly.

Groaning, he sat up. The air, wherever he was now, was stale. He tried standing up, found the cold touch of metal, then the slightly warmer caress of smooth stone, and finally, the hard plastic of a light switch.

Finally, something normal. But he hesitated for a moment to flip the switch, remembering the thing he'd seen. The thing that broke his mind.

He decided it was just a dream, a nightmare, probably the result of being in a strange new place, and flipped the switch.

He was in one of the experiment rooms, one they had yet to discover.

How the hell had he gotten here?

There was something oddly familiar about it.

The metal he'd touched in the dark wrapped around the base of the room. Mathias instantly knew what it was, too. A particle collider, just like the one he'd seen in his nightmare...

That had to be a coincidence, right? Surely, he'd just been sleep walking.

He decided this was the appropriate answer.

Then why was his heart racing so hard?

Mathias ran his hand over the collider's cold aluminum surface. Its touch almost erased his panic. He couldn't help but smile. His eyes traced the curve of the collider eagerly, following the wires that snaked from the metallic tank in the center of the chamber. The wiring was bunched together under coils, revealing strange symbols and shapes painted on the floor beneath them.

The symbols too were familiar to him.

He walked over to the tank, ducking beneath some copper wiring suspended in the air surrounding the tank. At a distance, the wiring created the image of two diametrically opposed triangles, forced into occupying the same space. The configuration created a certain amount of visual balance in the experiment room.

That was the major difference between this room and the one Nico and Ira had discovered. There was also no surgical table. How many other rooms like this were there?

Mathias popped the latches on the tank and peered inside.

"How odd," he said.

It was a sensory deprivation tank. The saline solution was still there, albeit discolored, with sensors and tubes running down either side of the interior—presumably for cycling fresh solution into the tank.

He closed the lid.

The chamber also featured a two-way mirror and an observation room on the other side. He made his way into the observation room, turned the lights on, and scanned over the monitors. All of the wires and components seemed to be undamaged; he pressed the power button to one of the terminals. The machine fired up; the monitor turned on and displayed several sets of numbers and bars of data. The software and interface was unfamiliar to him, probably proprietary.

The data, however, he understood very well. Each set of numbers correlated to measuring different kinds of stress on the human body, as well as graphs showing beta and alpha waves coming from the subject's brain. He clicked around on the interface and saw that there was a recording dating back just six months ago. He clicked to play the file.

Unlike the one Ira had discovered on the network, the video had no introduction. Mathias saw the chamber he'd just been examining, and a man with auburn hair and pale skin standing naked before the sensory deprivation tank. There appeared to be no sound on the recording. The man climbed inside the tank and closed the hatch, and shortly thereafter the particle collider lit up with white-hot glowing light. The wires surrounding the tank began to glow as well, creating a strange pattern within the glass pyramid. He scratched his head; where had he seen that structure before?

Mathias's eyes darted back and forth between the video and the chamber on the other side of the glass. The video seemed to distort for a second, and as his eyes returned to it, there was a bright flash inside the chamber. The camera followed another man in a hazmat suit as he inspected the tank. When he opened it, there was no one inside, but the saltwater now took on a greenish hue.

"Fascinating," he said. "Perhaps you succeeded, after all?"

"Mathias, where the fuck are you?" Nico's voice, as abrasive and full of false authority as always, echoed from his CB. "Lena says it was supposed to be your turn for guard duty!"

"Back so soon? I must have passed out..." He almost blurted it right out. It'd be best not to reveal that he had been sleepwalking. "I thought I was due for a break."

"I have no time to argue with you, we've got injured up here, and we need all the help we can get bringing supplies in. Get your ass up here!"

There was no point arguing with him, not this time. Mathias turned to leave, but before he could reach the door to the observation chamber, he caught a glimpse of a small booklet. It was resting on the edge of one of the consoles.

Mathias picked it up.

It appeared to be a diary of some sort.

He pocketed it. If nothing else, it would make for an interesting read.

Mathias retreated into the hall and found himself on the elevator to the surface entrance.

He'd return to this chamber later.

In any case, he felt that he was beginning to better understand the experiments that went on here. The idea that sensory deprivation could allow a person to break through to other universes, or to celestial beings, was not a new idea. John C. Lilly, the man who created the first sensory deprivation tank in 1954, had believed exactly that. His experiments had started with using a crude standing chamber; the subjects were fitted with a nightmarish blackout mask, which fed air into their lungs.

The mask proved distracting to the overall experience, so Lilly had refined the design to be a sitting bath with a cover to block out all light; it was filled with a salt-water solution which regulated the temperature of the body so that the brain couldn't tell where the skin ended and the water began.

Lilly had claimed that the tank allowed him to make contact with a more advanced civilization, and even dubbed the event, "The First Conference of Three Beings."

These experiments, however, were far more than that. The strange hieroglyphic symbols he'd seen in the first video were evidence enough of that.

Mathias shivered when he thought of the thing he'd seen in his nightmare. The comet's shifting, rippling edges, and the black hole that he'd seen inside of its mouth…

What if Lilly and Weber hadn't been crazy?

Then perhaps Doctor Weber had been on to something here? What if it were true? What if an altered state of mind, such as meditation, or even a state beyond that, could actually open up the gateway to another universe? The occult trappings of the experiment chambers, with their pyramidal structures and circles, were a touch silly to Mathias, but, then again, even he had to admit that there was a certain appeal to the designs, a certain *power* even.

He chuckled. Maybe it was *he* who had gone mad?

The scientists who had run this facility had all vanished. The others in his group hadn't even raised the question: where had they gone? Sure, there were bodies in a few of the experiment chambers, but it was easy to guess that those belonged to the subjects of failed experiments. Clearly there hadn't been time to clean up the mess, only time to move on to the next one. They had been desperately scrambling to find the answer, before the ice age consumed the world.

Mathias smiled.

This facility is more than just a temporary haven, a den of false hope and security, he thought. *If I don't unlock its secrets, we will all die in this frozen hell.*

The elevator came to a stop. Nico and the others were huddled around a body draped over a sled full of supplies. Mathias stepped out into the entrance and zipped up his jacket.

"Mathias," Nico said. "You took your sweet time getting up here."

The body belonged to Eddy. Blood soaked through the bandages wrapped around his throat.

"You should have left him," Mathias said. "He's going to bleed out all over the supplies, ruin them."

Nicola's eyes said it all: those dangerous, green eyes, so full of hatred for people like him. "There are two other sleds full of supplies, get them in here."

"While you and Hugo play with his corpse?"

"I am armed. Don't argue with me."

Mathias pushed his facemask up, covered his head with his hood, and watched them cart Eddy's body into the elevator.

Why was he still smiling?

❂

"Goddamn it." Ira covered her mouth. "How long has it been…can you save him?"

Lena didn't answer; she paced around Eddy's body, her eyes dancing over his wounds, like a machine analyzing a damaged engine.

"Lena, answer me."

"Get her out of here," Lena said. "We don't have much time and she'll only get in the way."

Nico grabbed Ira by the shoulders and dragged her out of the infirmary. She didn't go willingly, but even after an elbow to the groin, her brother still managed to get her out of the room. Hugo sealed the door behind them. Ira found herself pounding on the glass wall to the infirmary as Lena cleaned and dressed Eddy's wounds.

He looked so lifeless lying there.

She couldn't tell if Lena was saving him or killing him.

"He'll pull through, Ira," Nico said quietly. "We just need to be patient."

There was a quiver in his voice.

"Yeah, Eddy's tough as balls, yo," Hugo said, his voice full of conviction. The look in his eyes, however, did not seem so confident. "Shoulda seen what he did to the cat that did it. Straight alpha."

"Jesus, Hugo, will you shut the fuck up?" Nico said.

"I was just saying..."

Hugo's mouth stopped running when he saw how Ira was looking at him.

"Sorry," Hugo said. "I was just trying to—"

"Go help Mathias bring the rest of the supplies in," Nico said. "Now."

Hugo sulked away like a sad puppy. She could almost imagine his tail tucked between his legs.

Nico put his arm around her, but his embrace was hollow. He was only doing this for her; she knew he didn't give a damn about what happened to Eddy.

She felt like she was standing beside herself, watching things from the outside. Tears burned trenches down her chapped cheeks.

She remembered the first time she met Eddy.

Ira and Nico had been living in an underground bunker for several months. He'd found a way to get heat pumping into the place so they could take off their gear. Ira had been asleep at her computer, where she'd been watching the infrared readouts of the surrounding area. It was easy to become paranoid in their isolation; there were hungry predators out in the world.

It had been the ping from the sensors that woke her up. At first, she'd thought it was another mountain lion. It was large enough on the sensors, and it had wandered into their food storage area. She woke Nico up, and they grabbed their rifles.

Nico had nearly killed Eddy in that first meeting. He was pigging out on some rations and had the insignia of the Revolutionists ironed into his coat. That set Nico off instantly. The bullet burrowed into the wall, barely missing its target. They got into a short fistfight after that, which Nico won with an intense precision she'd never seen prior.

At first she didn't really understand why Nico had tossed him in a makeshift prison cell, but Nico had once been a soldier who served the Feds. He had to be sure Eddy wasn't holding onto any resentment toward his fallen government.

Eddy had been happy to comply, but she could tell there was still a bit of resentment toward Nico. She was the one who'd convinced Nico to let him out—and that had been the birth of their group. Lena and Hugo, and even Mathias, would be found later, but she'd never really accepted them like she accepted him. She'd stifled other feelings she had for him, because Nico would never approve of her fucking a Revolutionist.

Now Eddy could be dying.

She'd never get to say those things, and she wasn't sure she would, even if he pulled through. Ira found herself clutching at the tiles on the ground, crying like a hysterical fool. Nico stood, stoic, next to her, arms crossed.

Why was she such a coward?

She wiped her tears.

"He survived on his own before he met us," Nico said. "And he'll survive this."

"You're just saying that so I'll stop crying."

"Maybe."

Ira sat up. Nico didn't change his posture. Lena opened the doors to the infirmary, stepped out, sulked against the glass, and removed her surgical mask.

"I've done everything I can," she said. "I think he'll pull through, but he lost a lot of blood. You said a cat did this?"

Nico nodded, sternly. "Yes."

"Odd that there's only one cut across the throat," Lena said. "You would think there would be smaller ones accompanying the main—"

"Are you suggesting he cut his own throat?" Nico said. "I saw the animal myself."

"No, I'm not, it's just…" Lena stopped. "It's nothing."

Ira stood up, letting her eyes scan over Eddy's unconscious body through the glass. If he was breathing, it was so slight that her eyes couldn't tell the difference. There were stitches across his throat and a massive bandage on his shoulder.

"Can I see him?" Ira said.

Lena nodded. "Just be quick about it. He needs to rest."

Ira found herself standing next to him, holding his hand. He felt so cold, so weak.

"Get better fast," she said quietly.

When she emerged from the med bay, Lena and Nico were talking.

"Make sure to keep track of his vitals," Nico said. "And report back to me if there's any change, for better or worse. But for now, we need to secure the rest of the supplies and get back to our assigned tasks to fortify this place."

"Can you please stop talking about him like his life doesn't matter?" Ira said. "He's a person, he's my friend, and he might not make it."

"He isn't dead yet," Lena said. "And Nico's right, we need to make sure none of us end up like him."

Ira turned and stormed out. What the hell was the point of surviving if they all lost what made them human?

She found herself in her room, screaming into a pillow that smelled like dust.

9

Mathias and Hugo finished bringing the supplies into the new shelter. Mathias dragged the sled that had held Eddy's body off to the side. Some of Eddy's blood had managed to get onto the supplies on the sled. Mathias picked up one of the boxes. The blood was still fresh.

That's when it hit him.

"What are you doing?" Hugo asked.

Hugo wouldn't understand. He was a fool.

"Hello?" Hugo said. "You gonna answer me?"

Mathias set the box down, turned around, and began moving other boxes and supplies into the storage chamber.

"I was just thinking about how fragile we all are," Mathias said.

"Yeah, B," Hugo said. "But Lena said she might be able to save him."

"Not what I mean," Mathias said. "Eddy was quite capable as a survivalist, and still he ended up in the infirmary. Any one of us could be next."

"I'm just glad it wasn't me who got bit," Hugo said, "you know?"

Mathias nodded. "This ice age is going to kill us all."

"Don't talk like that."

"I'm serious."

Hugo wouldn't look him in the eye.

It occurred to Mathias that the others, with their limited understanding, found the experiments conducted in their new home to be grotesque. They, in their ignorance, would never agree to be test subjects, no matter how much he explained the benefits of following through.

He couldn't stop thinking about the experiment logs. He wanted to know more about what had gone on here. Maybe the reason the inhabitants of this facility were gone was because they'd succeeded in finding the mind's horizon? Maybe they'd escaped this hell?

He toyed with the small diary he'd found. During the course of the day, he'd managed to steal a few moments to read parts of it. He simply hadn't been able to contain himself. It had belonged to one of the technicians, and complained about Weber's worsening mental state. That he was rambling about communing with aliens and spending hours in his chambers at the top of the facility, doing God knows what.

Maybe his nightmares weren't nightmares at all, but something else entirely? A window into a larger world, perhaps?

He'd have to do his research, which meant reading and watching every experiment log he could get his hands on.

"Tell me something, Hugo," Mathias said. "If you had the chance to escape this frozen hell, would you take it?"

"That ain't happenin' yo," Hugo said. "The scientists said the whole Earth gonna get covered in ice, fuckin' space cloud did us in."

"Yes, I'm well aware of the space cloud. Although, to call it a space-cloud is to grossly simplify the science of what is happening to the Earth and the Solar System at large. It's true that passing through the spiral arm of the Milky Way has had a significant dimming effect on the sun, but the Earth has also been bombarded by cosmic rays left over by past stars that have long since gone supernova. This has caused cloud cover to increase exponentially, causing more and more cooling to occur."

"Yeah..."

"But what if there were a way to escape this Earth, to travel to a new one. A place where the ice age had never happened?"

Hugo blinked, probably processing the idea. "Hell yeah, B."

"That's what I thought..."

Mathias wasn't much for making friends, but Ira was the gatekeeper of crucial information. Fortunately, it was likely that she would be needing a new friend to console her on her recent loss.

"I certainly hope poor Eddy pulls through," Mathias said.

"Yeah," Hugo said.

CHAPTER TEN

It was late. The others were in their newly claimed rooms, sleeping soundly on cots provided by the dead. The fluorescent lighting in Weber's personal chamber buzzed uncomfortably overhead.

Mathias had awoken in the middle of the night again. This time his nightmare had been more intense.

Mathias had found himself in the middle of that strange red canyon again, beneath the heat of the black comet.

The masked thing was waiting for him.

"You again," Mathias said.

The masked figure raised one of its arms—but they weren't arms at all, but large, disproportionate appendages covered in dark green scales, and segmented in multiple areas, bending and twisting into two massive fingers.

Those fingers were beckoning him to follow.

He did as he was bid.

The masked creature guided Mathias through various lands, across the scorching desert of a world with a black sky, an endless forest full of carnivorous trees, where the sun appeared to be forever on a collision course with the planet, and finally, a world covered in ice, where the blue sun was almost indistinguishable from the sky's dim hue.

There was a pyramid here, too. The creature's mask twisted into a grin and it pointed its green appendage to the pyramid.

"What are you saying?" Mathias asked. "That these people faced a similar fate? That they found the mind's horizon and survived?"

The nightmare had ended shortly afterward. The masked figure hadn't answered.

Mathias looked around, his eyes burning from fatigue. The room was like the inside of a small pyramid. The walls each tilted to a point, leading to a massive image of that same intersecting triangular symbol he'd seen in the experiment chambers he'd woken up in before.

Beneath the symbol was a single horizontal sensory deprivation tank composed of cold blue metal. Resting inside, yet again, that same symbol.

There was a small writing desk near a twin-sized bed with salt-stained sheets.

Mathias took a seat at the desk and picked up one of the notebooks that were scattered about the surface. He felt the weight in his hands, opened the notebook, ran his fingertips over the words that Weber had penned by hand. He began to read from it, not scanning, but reading each word, every sentence, as if they might contain some hidden secret, a key that might answer the questions that burned within him.

The first page was far less confident than the Weber that he'd seen in that first log Ira had shown them all. *Entry 1: Life is a strange thing. I'm starting this journal in an effort to make sense of my life before I die. The future is not as certain as I like to think, and even I may prove to lack the tenacity required to solve this immense puzzle. There is always the chance of failure. We've been here only a short time, and even so we hear reports of the world falling into chaos. The war turned from a simple civil war fought over the dispute of civil liberties to absolute anarchy, a war for resources, for warmth.*

The sides and loyalties are no longer clear. Now there are thousands of sides and agendas, and each of them can change in an instant if it means victory. When victory is the right to continue providing for your children, and staying warm in an ever-colder world, then what the hell should any man care about law and order?

As it gets colder, it seems we lose more and more of that which makes us human. Or, is it that the cold returns us to our truest form?

Mathias turned the page. *Entry 2: Today we ran a test of the core systems; one of the tanks shorted out and didn't rise from its resting place the way it's supposed to. The nine tanks must all rise, even if there are not nine bodies available for the tanks. Together, they make a circuit, described throughout Messages from the Abyss. I doubt any of those that looked upon its pages ever realized it. Maybe they knew the cost was too great to obtain such knowledge. The circuit is the key, it's not the eye of the abyss, it's the bridge through it.*

"Messages from the Abyss?" Mathias felt a chill run down his spine as he said it.

The urge to put the log entry down was strong. Like standing at a crossroads.

His hands were shaking.

He kept reading the entry.

It is nearly complete.

But, with that knowledge, with things coming close to an end, I fear what would happen if others discovered it. It might seem superficial, or even overkill, but it's incredibly important that we seal off the device so it's not readily accessible to any miscreant that stumbles upon this place after we're gone. Some things should be left behind—like human barbarism. There is a reason why human beings are regarded so lowly in that terrible grimoire. What was it that the author said? "I saw the abyss, and when that pulsing green eye—with its vast tentacles that spread throughout all time, all space, and all universes—when it regarded me, it seemed unamused at what I'd done."

It's exactly that reason that I've barred anyone from talking about it in their logs, revealing passwords, or hints to passwords. One would have to have an open book to my very life to be able to tell that, and fortunately, all those libraries have been buried in the ice.

The final experiment is on a system isolated from the rest of the facility. So, I alone have authority over its operation.

It's time for my next tank session. Hopefully our friends in the Betelgeuse constellation have more to show me than before.

Mathias set the notebook down.

He couldn't take his eyes off the sensory deprivation tank.

For some reason, he felt a strong urge to rip his long johns off and climb inside.

John C. Lilly thought he was able to talk to alien beings inside a deprivation tank too, Mathias thought. *Maybe he wasn't entirely crazy?*

And if there were other entities out there, maybe they would have some clue how he could activate this final experiment that Weber had talked about? Maybe they could help him escape this frozen hell?

"You're a fool," he told himself, rubbing his eyes.

He was sleep-deprived. That was all. All he needed to do was get some sleep, then he'd be back to his old rational self.

His eyes drifted back to the desk. There were pill bottles scattered messily across the top. One was labeled LSD.

But, what if?

What if he could save everyone?

Before he knew what he was doing, he'd swallowed a tablet and was rushing over to the tank, tossing his long johns to the floor.

Mathias practically ripped the lid off the tank. He could see his own reflection in the saline solution. His eyes were red. He looked tired, crazed.

"What am I doing?"

And yet, he still climbed into the tank. Let himself sink into the lukewarm saline solution, letting it absorb him, erasing the boundaries of his flesh and the rest of the universe with a sweeping hand of warmth. He felt a strong need to reach out. To make contact.

In college he'd written off all of John C. Lilly's experiments with LSD and deprivation tanks as bunk.

But, sitting in the solution. He wondered.

His arm reached out—it felt strangely detached—and he pulled the cover over his face. He was already feeling effects from the LSD. The ground had already shattered beneath his feet, and he could see the southern hemisphere's constellations. He counted them off: Hydrus, Crux, Circinus, Mensa, and even Pictor. He'd often longed to see them, but had never had the chance to make a trip out below the equator. So much of his life had revolved around the West Coast of the United States, and he'd hardly ever questioned it. All that time spent educating himself, never enough money to take the lavish and expensive trips that his richer peers could afford.

He wondered if he'd wasted his life.

No, he thought. *I won't go back to then; that's the way I came.*

He looked to the stars, to the cross-shaped constellation Crux, and decided that he'd go there.

As quickly as he thought it, he was there, among the stars. There was no life around any of the stars that made up the constellation, at least, there hadn't been for hundreds of millions of years. There had been worlds. Yes. But they had been the victims of violent cosmic catastrophes similar to ones he'd had fever dreams about as a boy.

There was a world, not much larger than Earth, that rested within the star's habitable zone. Its surface was twisted and malformed from the violent flares that its parent star expelled, like the tantrums of an angry father, beating his child into submission. Only, the child had been long dead, and the father, the star, was allowed to keep on living, and beating, desecrating the child's corpse with fire.

He lingered for a time there, watching charred sands blow across the surface, the lava beds raging across blackened cliffs, but he quickly became bored with the sights.

Mathias moved on.

Three other worlds, each one more different than the last, all dead, and still he was restless.

He was desperate to make contact with something. Anything. Then, he saw Betelgeuse creep into view.

There, he thought.

He could feel something there, in the constellation. And he remembered that Weber had mentioned it in his journal.

It was as though something were reaching out to him, pulling him in.

And before he realized what was happening, his body...no, that wasn't right...his *essence*...his essence was moving. Stars rushed by him as though he were traveling far beyond the speed of light, until he was orbiting around a glowing orange world, orbiting a blue star.

There was a presence, floating before his essence. An orange cloud that shimmered like a nebula. It seemed to be studying him.

Mathias tried to speak, but found that his words didn't work here.

Images flashed before Mathias's mind: *a race of plantlike beings, caring for their young beneath a blue sky with golden clouds. The beings congregate in large buildings and sing. At first, he thinks it's a church that he's seeing, but soon he realizes that there's a kind of energy buildup within the room.*

Then, he's seeing what they see. Inside their collective mind's eye. What they see has made the younger aliens scream.

Mathias sees the alien world freezing over, he sees their host star dim, flicker, and then vanish, like a candle getting snuffed out.

The images stopped coming. At first, Mathias was confused.

Perhaps this creature is capable of seeing the future by some unknown mechanism? he thought. But, how could he communicate? Could he just think of what he'd like to ask, would it understand?

The nebulous orange cloud seemed to be pacing around Mathias. Studying him.

He tried thinking of his own world, what had happened to it. The civil war and the ice age that had followed it. How his species was slowly being pushed to extinction.

And, the experiment chamber, the log video, Weber's notes. The possibility of a way out.

The orange being stopped moving.

This time, only a single image flooded into Mathias's mind: *the infinite black of an abyss, and a single thing in the center—an ancient mask.*

A familiar mask.

And then, he's seeing an experiment chamber as if through his own flesh-and-blood-eyes. He's peering down at his hands. They look oddly gray.

Then he's flipping a switch.

A bright flash of light engulfs the experiment chamber.

The being pulled away from him. It floated there for a few moments before retreating to its world. And Mathias was left alone to wonder what that meant.

He clawed his way out of the tank. Colors swam before his eyes.

The effects of the LSD made getting to his feet quite difficult...but he knew what he had to do.

The clock read 3:00 am.

Everyone was asleep.

And Eddy was waiting.

2

The stream was calm today. Alone in his boat, Eddy tilted his head back, feeling the cool breeze, and arched back against the rear wall. His fishing rod hadn't moved in a while, but he was content enough with the peace and quiet. The fish would come later. They always did.

When he was a boy, his whole family would come here to get away from their slum home in Fontana. It had been hell scraping enough gas money to get up the mountain, but it was well worth it.

He remembered his mother, showing her pearly whites, resting on a beat-up pool recliner.

He and his brothers would be getting into trouble in the lake, trying to get out of sight so they could have some real fun, when they'd hear her scream something in Spanish. Then his dad, looking like an angry African god, would toss them a look, and they'd all sulk back where they could see them.

Those had been the days.

He hadn't thought of his family in so long…he wondered where they all were now…

For some reason, the thought saddened him.

He could feel the boat slowly drifting across the lake. There was more of a current than there should have been; it only added to the mood.

The tree line was silhouetted by the clear sky; the sun seemed as if it had taken up perch beneath the tops of the trees. It was almost too perfect. This view. And he couldn't help but feel a bit guilty for enjoying it while the country was tearing itself apart after the bombing in Nevada.

There were even rumors of an uprising having been stopped in the West. These were uncertain times, at least, as far as humans were concerned. The Earth might have been warming up, uncontrollably even, but nature was still nature.

At least he still had that. At least he still had his life, his family.

That's why he'd gone and done it. They'd told him he was too young to marry, but he hadn't listened, and he was better off for it. His daughter would be a full year old next month, and that alone showed how little they'd known. Even with the world falling to pieces, protests spreading from shore to shore, life had to march on, and he had to find some measure of happiness in it.

The boat continued to drift with the breeze and the current that shouldn't have been. He fought the urge to fall asleep.

3

The gurney's wheels squeaked, echoing through the curvature of the tunnel corridor; for a moment, only a fleeting moment, Mathias felt a pang of guilt. He reminded himself that he was saving this man, this longtime victim of a war long since buried in the ice.

They made their way to the elevator, and Mathias wheeled him in. The descent seemed to last forever. He found himself checking the biometric reader on Eddy's forehead, hoping that his new subject wouldn't pass on the way to the chamber. He figured that Lena had left it there to monitor his vitals from afar. At first, that had seemed like defeat, but, after discovering that the monitor had its own independent battery supply, he'd continued with his plan.

Mathias tried not to think of the aftermath of his experiment. If they discovered him in the act, it would be disastrous to his efforts. Eddy had to go, though, for him to get closer to Ira, to get the data he needed. There was only one way to make the man vanish without any evidence.

Why was he doing this?

Sweat beaded atop his brow. The most rational part of his mind, the part that still thought his nightmares were mere dreams, told him this was madness, inhumane. That he was a monster for even thinking of it.

He remembered his dream. What the masked man had shown him. The decrepit pyramid on a dead alien world. If Weber's chamber was the top of the facility, it was possible they were actually in a giant subterranean pyramid too.

It made a certain amount of sense when he thought about it.

Perhaps other civilizations had faced similar fates to that of Earth, and perhaps they had done as Weber had done?

And if Weber had succeeded, then wasn't it his duty as a scientist to find out? To unlock the secrets of this facility?

Mathias smiled.

His guilt melted away.

Sometimes, true science required making a few sacrifices for the greater good. And, besides, who knew, maybe the first time would work. Maybe Eddy would find himself in a new world.

He was almost envious.

4

There was a loud ringing sound in the sky; the birds scattered from the trees. Eddy sat up in his boat, trying to pinpoint the source of the noise. Something was wrong. He looked down at the boat and the lake; he didn't seem to be moving anymore.

The sound faded, and he felt the boat begin to move with the current on the lake again.

"What the hell?"

He remembered now. It wasn't possible for him to be sitting on that boat, fishing, in Big Bear. This whole area was covered in ice and snow. The last thing he remembered was a cougar sinking its teeth into his shoulder, and him returning the favor with his pistol.

Then…Nico. Had he really lost it? Had he really cut his throat?

Was he dreaming…or dead? A rage quaked within him that he hadn't felt since the day he'd come home to find their bodies on the kitchen floor, bleeding out from holes in their heads.

He punched the boat's wooden flooring.

"Time to wake up." A familiar voice echoed through the sky above. "It's time to save the human race."

5

"Wake up, Eddy," Mathias said.

Eddy opened his eyes to see Mathias standing over him. He tried to speak, but his neck and half of his face felt completely numb. The other half of his face could feel Mathias's hands slapping his numbed cheeks.

"I wouldn't squirm, if I were you. Lena has medicated you very heavily."

He tried to squirm anyway, but Mathias held his arms down.

"You're a lucky man, really, Eddy. You almost died out there, but you've also lost a lot of blood. You could still die. Fortunately, I have a solution, and it's going to save your life."

His eyes focused on the room around Mathias's head. Even though he couldn't turn his head to see, there were complex metallic plates on the walls, and wires suspended in the air. Lots of wires.

They were in one of the experiment rooms!

His pulse surged through the stitches in his throat, like pressure in a clogged engine.

"Now, Ira and Nico agree that this is the best possible solution, Eddy. There's a sensory deprivation tank in this chamber where your body can float without restriction. It'll be like you're weightless. This should allow you to heal faster."

Ira and Nico were okay with this? He wished he could ask to get their verification. All he could do was continue to search the room with his eyes. His head was so foggy. He couldn't tell if any of it made sense or not.

"You're wondering why they're not here? It's simple, really. They're busy securing the supplies and fortifying the entrance to this facility. There's a lot of work to do.

"You understand, right? Of course you do. You're a soldier."

Maybe he was telling the truth. Mathias had no reason to lie to him. What could he possibly gain from harming him?

"Now, to the point. I need you to help me get you into the tank. Can you try to walk?"

Mathias had probably already tried to lift him and failed. Wouldn't Nico have known that Mathias was too weak to lift him alone? It took some effort, but, with Mathias's help, he managed to sit up on the gurney. He could see the chamber better now; it was circular, with a large metal tube that ran along the wall. They seemed to be inside of some kind of glass pyramid shape. Metal wires were arranged in a strange pattern above and around them.

His eyes scanned over the tank at the center of the room. There was a staircase attached to it for easy access; Mathias helped him over to it and popped the hatch. Together, they limped up the staircase.

Mathias let out a groan as he helped Eddy slip into the water. It was warm. Comforting almost.

"Good, very good, Eddy." Mathias's chapped lips stretched into a twisted grin. "There's just one last thing to do."

Mathias placed a tube into Eddy's mouth and fixed a pair of goggles onto his face.

"This is your lifeline. The rest of the tube is going to fill up with solution. If you spit this out, you will drown."

That grin unsettled Eddy to no end. A kind of madness lurking in Mathias' bloodshot eyes. Yet, he seemed sincere.

Mathias reached up and closed the hatch. Eddy could see nothing but darkness now, a formless void. He could hear a latch snap into place, and water filled up to cover his face completely. He tried to move his hands, but the water made it impossible to tell if it was working. He felt weightless now, like he no longer had a body at all.

He wanted to scream.

He wanted to find Ira…

6

Mathias could feel his heartbeat in his temples. For a moment, he thought he wouldn't get away with it, that Eddy would see through his lies and scream for help.

What the hell was he thinking?

When Nico and the others found out what he'd done…they were sure to exile him to walk the frozen Earth alone.

He looked at himself in the two-way mirror. Sweat blanketed his skin; his eyes were crazed.

"They wouldn't understand," he said. "I'm going to save them."

His eyes returned to the gurney; he'd have to return it to the infirmary quickly for his plan to work. It had to look like Eddy had gotten up and walked away. He grabbed hold of the handles, pushed it back out of the chamber and into the elevator.

He could hardly contain himself. In some ways, it was a thrill to have a subject in such an experiment. He felt like his old self again. Useful—*important*. He stifled that feeling.

First things first.

Mathias returned the gurney to where it had been before, but made sure to push it off to the side, so that it looked like Eddy had gotten up of his own accord and pushed it back.

"What the hell are you doing here?"

Her voice shocked him from his euphoria; Mathias turned around to face Lena. "I was looking for Eddy...but, it appears as if he isn't here."

He watched her enter the room and examine it. She wasn't very bright, so as long as she hadn't heard him pushing the gurney earlier, all would be well.

"Damn it," she said. "He couldn't just fucking lay still, could he?"

She checked a device in her pocket.

"Something wrong, Lena?" Mathias asked.

"His vitals are still registering. He probably went to his quarters when he woke up. I'm going to kill him."

"That would be counterintuitive."

"Shut up." She turned to leave, but hesitated. "Why did you want to see him, anyway?"

"I couldn't sleep. Felt a little bad about what I said earlier...figured I should pay my respects, if things took a turn for the worst."

"That ain't like you."

"Depends on the day."

"I'll be sure to tell him when he wakes."

"Without killing him, I'm sure."

She left the room, finally.

Mathias sighed. His heart had felt as though it might rupture for a moment there.

He returned to the elevator and headed back to his quarters. It'd been a long night. He was certain he was going to need his wits about him for what would come next.

CHAPTER ELEVEN

The smell of burning flesh filled Nico's nostrils. Searing pain lit up his leg. When he opened his eyes, the sky was ash.

Groaning, he sat up.

"No," Nico said.

The encampment was a smoldering firepit. His comrades—Hernandez, Boyd, Martinez, even his CO—all turned to ash.

"You were right to cut his throat." The voice called to him from his right. When he turned his head, the striking image of Boyd was standing there, the musculature beneath his skin exposed.

"You were nothing but ash..." Nico said. "How?"

Boyd chuckled. "All things are possible in the Astral Lands."

"Why am I here?"

Boyd grinned. "Revolutionists can't be trusted. God gave us this great country, and they perverted it. You know this. This ice age is divine punishment. They must all be wiped out, along with their sympathizers."

Staring at the smoldering firepit that had once been home to him, he couldn't help but agree with Boyd.

"But you saved him, despite that fact." The joyful quality in Boyd's voice faded. "What happened to you, Hartman? You were once a God-fearing man."

Nico held his head. "I...if I let him die, my sister...she'd never forgive me."

"Revolutionists can't be trusted. They must be wiped out."

"It's not that clear-cut..."

"Look at me, Hartman, look at what they did to me!"

Nico turned his head back to Boyd and screamed. His flesh melted from his face, and his skull crumbled to dust, followed by his insides. The dust mixed with the air and found its way into his lungs.

"Kill them all, Nico. Kill them all."

The nightmare faded, and Nico found that he'd been sitting on his cot, staring into the darkness.

How long had he been like this?

His heart was racing, his pulse pounding in his temples. The clock read 3:00 am. Another morning in this place.

He reached for his CB. Went to the private channel they always used, and held the receiver to his face.

"Lena, status update on Ramirez," he said.

There was a ruffling sound, static.

"Lena, wake up."

He had a sinking feeling in his gut.

"He's gone," Lena said. "Found the med bay empty last night."

"Why didn't you come get me immediately?"

"I didn't want to disturb you. Besides, he may have turned up by morning. I don't know."

He let the receiver rest in his hands.

Was it his fault?

2

Lena caught Ira pacing back and forth in front of the medical ward. At first, she tried to act as if she didn't see her, walk the other way; but it was too late, Ira's eyes were locked on her, and she was heading right for her. The bitch's hair was a rat's nest, least she could do was have some respect for herself and brush it.

"I don't fucking understand!" Ira's shrill voice bounced off the concrete walls. "How the hell could he have just vanished?"

She was acting hysterical and selfish. Lena's hands bunched up into fists.

139

"Ira, calm the hell down," Lena said. "I'm sure he's around here somewhere."

Ira screamed, then lunged into her, shoving her back against the curved stone wall, making a loud smacking sound that reverberated down the corridor. "No! You were the one that was supposed to be keeping tabs on him!"

"I was only keeping track of his vitals, which, by the way, haven't fucking *changed*!"

"Why did you leave him in there unsupervised?"

"How the hell was I supposed to know that he'd just walk off like that?"

"You're the nurse, Lena, you tell me!"

"What the hell is going on here?" Nico came in from the other end of the corridor, buttoning his shirt; Lena hoped Ira didn't put it together.

"Eddy's missing," Ira said.

"I know," he said. "That doesn't give you the right to assault the only person who can stitch him back together."

Ira removed her forearm from Lena's collarbone and turned to her brother. "Why don't you organize a search party?"

"He's not outside," Nico said. "Hugo and Mathias have been helping me fortify the entrance, and that's the only way in or out of here that I know of. If you're so determined to find him, then why don't you turn on the facility's security system, use the cameras to pinpoint a location?"

"I will." Ira turned around and stormed down the corridor. "It's not like anyone else gives a damn."

Then she was gone.

"Your sister's out of control," Lena said.

"I'll handle her," Nico said. "Get back to work. I know you haven't finished cataloging the tools in the medical bay."

Lena watched Nico follow after Ira. She felt a scream threatening to burst from her lungs. Why was Ira always given a free pass to act like a total bitch, without any kind of consequence?

If I pulled that crap, Nico would find someplace to lock me up in for at least a week, she thought.

140

She'd known she hated Ira from the moment she met her. The way she flipped her hair, that fake-ass smile, and the way she extended her hand to shake. It had been obvious that Ira was jealous of Lena; before Lena had come along, she'd been the only female in the group.

Lena reached down for her CB. "Hugo, come in."

"What's up, baby?" he said. "What you need?"

"Meet me in the med bay. I got some stress I need to relieve."

"I don't think Nico would like me leaving my post right—"

"Now, Hugo!"

"I...I can't..."

"Ugh, never mind, you're useless."

Lena switched off her CB and headed for the med bay anyway.

3

Ira plopped down in her chair inside the mainframe room. There were still no lights, save for the aquatic glow from the servers, but the darkness was somewhat comforting; there was a certain amount of freedom in it, like she could imagine that she was somewhere else — someone else. She opened her laptop and started looking for the system that controlled the security cameras. She had no time to daydream if she was going to find Eddy.

She felt the pressure in the room change when the hatch opened, forcing harsh light into her eyes. She shielded her eyes and squinted to see who it was.

"You need to control your anger, sis." It was Nico, who'd come to lecture her on the million reasons she shouldn't resort to hitting people in enclosed spaces.

"She had it coming," she said. "Been nothing but a bitch to me since she joined us, and she doesn't give a damn about finding Eddy."

"You and Eddy are close." He crossed his arms like a disapproving father. "Not everyone is going to feel the same about him."

"Like you?"

"Eddy's got skills I need. Christ knows he's a lot more useful than Hugo or Mathias. But accidents happen, we all know that. It isn't as if we're living in a tropical resort. This new world is dangerous, and just one mistake out there can be fatal."

"So, what are you trying to tell me—" tears welled up in her eyes "—that he deserves to die?"

"He shouldn't have wandered off when he woke up, and it's that same carelessness that got him…" He paused, a distant look in his eyes. "Why he was mauled by a cougar in the first place."

"Get out!"

"Ira…"

"No! I said get out!"

She covered her eyes and heard him open the hatch.

"You need to remember that we're isolated here," he said. "It's easy to go crazy here, to lash out. We're all just a hair-trigger away from tearing each other apart. One mistake. That's all it takes, Ira."

The door closed, and she was left to collapse into her keyboard, sobbing like a child. She couldn't remember the last time her heart had felt like this, maybe when they'd had to leave Papa behind…

Wiping her eyes, she tried desperately to bring herself back to reality, but she couldn't stop imagining that somewhere within the facility, Eddy was lying dead or dying, bleeding out through his bandages or scrambling through bloodstained snow.

A knock came at the hatch.

"Go away, Nicola!" she said.

The knocking persisted.

"I said go away, damn it!"

The knocking persisted.

"Goddamn it." She jumped from her chair to the hatch and slammed it open. "I said go away, Nicola!"

Mathias put his hands up in surrender. "I'm sorry, I'm not Nicola."

She glared at him. "What are you doing here, Mathias?"

"I just wanted to see how you were doing."

"I never figured you to be the compassionate type. In fact, I thought you despised Eddy."

"It's true, I never took a liking to him, given my aversion to the soldier mentality, but that doesn't mean that I wanted anything to happen to him." Mathias paused. "Or you, for that matter."

Her grip tightened on the hatch. "Forgive me if I call bullshit."

"I expected that." He smiled; it looked forced. "I just wanted to see if you were okay, that's all."

"I'm not, so go away."

He nodded and started to back away from the doorway. She watched him slither back down the corridor; even his walk was arrogant.

Ira closed the hatch and sulked back to her chair. She couldn't keep feeling sorry for herself; she needed to throw herself into her work.

She brought up the interface she'd used to gain access to the facility's basic systems. The security system couldn't be turned on the same way that the basic systems were; it required some form of authorization, probably Weber's.

A shudder escaped her shivering lips at the thought of watching more of those insane experiment logs.

A dialog box came up, asking her to enter in a passcode. She placed her head in her hands.

Cracking that passcode could take all night, or all week.

Ira spent the night attempting various passcodes and watching video logs hoping that they might give her a clue to what the answer was. She found herself locked out of the system for hours at a time when she'd maxed out the number of times it would allow her to fuck up. She found herself alone with her thoughts and memories, most of them unpleasant.

The experiment logs were, as usual, more disturbing than helpful, and the security footage of day-to-day activities didn't give her any idea as to who had been in charge of security. She watched the scientists rinse and repeat their daily routine countless times. The time stamp told her that they had been conducting these experiments when the ice sheets hadn't yet reached beyond the Canadian border. A lot of experts had suggested that they'd stop there, that we'd be spared having our cities crushed by sheets of ice six times larger than the tallest building on Earth. But they *did* advance, because it wasn't an ordinary ice age that humanity was dealing with.

The United States had been lucky that all they'd had to worry about was snow and ice, in some places accumulation in the double digits; they'd be dead if the ice sheets had come to cover all of their resources.

However, the ice sheets would reach them eventually. It was only a matter of time before everything froze.

With each passing day, the sun grew dimmer, as the thickness of the interstellar cloud the Solar System was entering thickened. Eventually, the thickness of it would even out, but, by then, the course would already be set. All land-based life would be stamped out eventually. So, really, Ira felt that their struggle for survival, day in and day out, was, in a way, completely futile.

None of it means a damn thing, she thought. *At least when you were here, I had a friend. Someone to distract me from the unavoidable truth.*

The clock read 3:45 am before she finally decided to give it a rest and go hunt down some coffee. She found herself down the corridor, in a space that she'd been setting up before she heard the news about Eddy. It had been a kind of lounge intended for just the two of them. A surprise she'd wanted to spring on him. There was a coffee pot, which she had found packed away in a box one of the scientists had left behind, and enough coffee to last her till the end of the modern ice age—or the end of the human race. There were even some snacks tucked away that hadn't spoiled. She set a pot to brew and basked in the aroma as it percolated.

It was late enough that she was almost certain that the others would be asleep. Her hands cradled a hot cup of coffee. She leaned back into a soft chair, closed her eyes, tried to relax.

She couldn't keep her mind off her task, though. Where was he?

Unless Weber had been really careless and let the password slip in his personal logs, she'd have to use a code breaker program to do it. It would be risky, because it could cause the whole system to lock up. After blowing on her coffee, she took a sip. It was French Vanilla flavored. She usually preferred to have some kind of sweetener, maybe a bit of creamer, but under the circumstances, she could hardly complain. She hadn't had freshly brewed coffee since all this bullshit had started.

"I haven't smelled fresh coffee in a long time." Nico's voice came from behind her.

She watched him come in and examine the pot, grab a cup and pour himself some without asking. Typical Nico. He sat down on a chair adjacent to her. He took a sip without blowing on it and relaxed his shoulders a bit. He always took his coffee black; Ira had never understood how someone could drink it like that.

"Nice place," he said.

"I intended it to be a refuge for myself," she said.

"And Ramirez?"

She nodded.

"He'll turn up, we haven't explored the whole facility yet and—"

"Just, please, let's not talk about Eddy right now?"

Nico set his coffee on the table. "Okay, we'll talk about something else then."

They sat in silence for the better part of an hour, just sipping their coffee. Most of the conversations they had revolved around business, survival; they hadn't had a real conversation in months. And now, when they finally had a chance to connect, there was a wall between them, something that both of them knew, but couldn't bring themselves to just say.

After a while, Ira finished her coffee.

Ira returned to her task, leaving Nico behind. Ira sat down in front of her laptop and set up her code breaker program, then set it to work on cracking the passcode.

With any luck, it wouldn't fuck everything else up in the process.

Mathias woke violently, gasping air for a scream that was choked out of him. It was the masked creature again. Every night the dreams got worse. Every night, the masked creature came for him, guiding him through alien vistas, ancient structures, and impossible realms where the laws of physics held no bearing on reality.

He struggled to remember his nightmare. The last thing he remembered before passing out was retreating from the mainframe room after his failed attempt to befriend Ira. He'd retreated to his room, and...

The clouds strangling his mind's eye seemed to part, his vision focused—there was green, mucous spittle dripping from his mouth to the black and white checkered linoleum floor, and in that spittle, three gnarled, wormlike...*things*, which he must have vomited up. Glancing up, he realized that he was not in his room anymore, but Weber's personal chamber.

There was something in his hands too. A tattered, leather-bound book. The lettering on the cover spelled out *Messages from the Abyss*. He knew the title from Weber's journal.

He remembered now.

How he'd gotten here.

It was the masked creature. A creature which preyed on those possessing forbidden knowledge, *unique* knowledge...

They had met beneath the pyramids of an alien world, one long since dead. Great clouds came to cover the sky, pulsing green beneath the light of some unknown creature whose tentacles pierced the clouds in odd places.

When the green light flashed in the distance, Mathias could see the texture of the masked creature's cloak more clearly than he had been able to previously. It looked as if it had been hemmed together with rotted human flesh and covered in cobwebs.

That incessant grin persisted. It leaned in close to him. He didn't want to look into its eyeholes for fear of what he might find in their depths. Its arm unraveled into three long, segmented appendages, pointing to the pyramids.

March. It seemed to speak into his mind directly. Its voice was like spiders crawling over his skin, airy and full of the threat of death.

He did not dare disagree with this thing. His feet carried him one step at a time toward the pyramids in the distance. The masked man hung always behind him, looming like some ancient specter of death.

There were strange symbols carved in great obelisks leading to the pyramid's entrance, collapsed statues of winged creatures with too many mouths, too many eyes. The symbols on the obelisks seemed to tell some kind of story. Imagining a species of tall, thin creatures which were facing the end of their world, the coming of a great comet, a creature they'd named "the great devourer of stars."

How was it that he could understand this strange pictographic language? It was as if something had come to infest his mind, a kind of growing madness that yearned for more, more knowledge, to see more of these strange places where logic and reason were forgotten, to go deeper into the abyss.

When they reached the tallest pyramid's base, he was greeted by a wall of solid metal the likes of which was not found on Earth. Still, there were great cracks in the wall.

Enter. The masked man pointed its long, snakelike appendage to the triangular door at the pyramid's base.

"How?"

The doorway was worth three of him in height at the very least.

The masked creature's appendages pulsed with an eerie green light; the slab of metal shook violently, and vibrations traveled up Mathias's legs, shaking his very bones. Then the door receded into the dark.

"Move."

Mathias nodded and padded into the dark.

From there, he wasn't sure what he was seeing. Twisting cylindrical corridors and bending hallways, experiment chambers hidden behind triangular doors, and markings that made his mind feel as though it was going to crawl from the safety of his cranium into the ever-looming madness of the abyss. Like the one he'd dreamed of, this place seemed familiar too. What were these pyramids? What was this place? And why was the masked creature showing them to him? Perhaps among these pyramids there was one just like the facility he and his unfortunate companions now inhabited?

Yes, he did understand that beneath the ice of the San Bernardino mountains there was a pyramid, cleverly concealed as a place of military science so as not to be interrupted by the sane and the overzealous.

Were these his own thoughts? Or were these the thoughts of the masked creature? He could not be sure anymore. It seemed as though his head had filled, fit to burst.

He couldn't stand it any longer. It was hard to breathe. He felt something strangling him, twisting and slithering.

That was when he realized he was dangling in the middle of a raised platform at the center of the facility: the masked creature was holding him up, its appendages twisting, writhing around his body. There was something else, too, something above him. A gateway, or a doorway in time and space.

An eclipsed moon on the other side of the doorway, its edges blazing like the exposed corona of a star, its light bleeding onto great, twisting tendrils that threaten to strangle the sky of a once-thriving world, where strange, jagged obelisks stab up through the dusty surface like the claws of some ancient beast, trapped forever by a wall it cannot traverse.

The eclipsed moon is not a moon or a star at all. His mind expands, the doorway approaches the glowing ring in the dark, revealing it to be a black hole. The tentacles coming from the black hole are like gnarled roots of some ageless tree—one finds its way to the doorway, the sheer size of it tearing the pyramid to pieces. The gateway widens to fill the sky, clearing the clouds and scaring off the beast that once dwelled there.

Then it's staring him in the face. The tip of it is segmenting into smaller, gnarled tentacles, an infinite segmenting kaleidoscope mitosis. The smaller tentacles enter his mouth, slithering down into his core, to his essence.

After that it's only brief flashes of memory. Scrambling barefoot through the halls of the facility in the dead of night to the core chamber, where he finds the tattered book. Then he's reading it for what seems like days. The thing that controls his body won't let him blink, won't let him look away, like a mental patient forced to stare at the same clip over and over while strapped to some primitive chair.

Then, when the masked man is satisfied, it carries him through the doorway, into an impossible chamber containing that black hole and a small solar system which is being eaten alive.

You are ready.

It's going to feed him to the abyss! His body will become a lifeless husk!

He screams and yells, but he cannot help but think about how much he'll learn on the other side of that event horizon, to see all of the dead worlds and lost knowledge that await him before he finally ceases to be once the thing in the abyss devours him.

Still, what good will that knowledge do him if he's devoured by that thing? He wants to live, damn it!

Then, the thought strikes, lightning in a bottle. The thing in the abyss cares not where it gets its information from. It can be bargained with.

"*I can give you another!*"

The mask has twisted into a grinning thing with deep, bright pinpoint lights for eyes.

We know the one.

"*I'll give him to you! Just let me go!*"

The masked creature referred to in the grimoire as the harvester of the abyss nods.

That's when he'd awoken in Weber's chamber.

Mathias couldn't stop himself from laughing. How narrowly he had escaped!

He clutched the tattered book close to his chest.

There was only one thing left to do now.

Honor the bargain.

CHAPTER TWELVE

"Experiment 5D," Doctor Weber said, sporting a smile full of yellow teeth. "Today, we'll be testing out the new experiment chamber. I'm sure you're all as excited as I am."

Weber stood inside the new chamber holding a clipboard. His hair was long and messy, and the gray had erased every trace of his natural color—the same could be said of his skin. Ira couldn't think of any skin condition that could do that.

He pointed to the large, upright tank resting inside the particle collider. Ira had seen sensory deprivation tanks before in movies and on TV—hell, she'd remembered hearing about a few places in Los Angeles that actually marketed them to herbalists and yoga enthusiasts who believed in the power of meditation, crystals, and other kinds of hocus-pocus bullshit. Those had been cute pink and blue bathtubs, with rubber tops and scented candles, compared to the cold metal coffin that she saw on the screen.

It was said that if someone stayed inside one for too long, they could go mad.

"This is the newest addition to the design, a vertical sensory deprivation tank." The doctor picked up a pair of thin goggles. "The subject will be allowed to wear these while submerged inside; there's also a breathing apparatus within to supply air. The goggles and the breathing apparatus are specially made so that they adhere to the temperature of the body and the saline solution, so the wearer doesn't notice that they're there at all.

"Originally, we intended to use a horizontal tank in this room, but I thought that would break the circle. The body must be upright within the eye of the abyss."

Shivers snaked down her spine.

She'd heard Weber talking about the abyss before, about how a creature whom the mad author of *Messages from the Abyss* called The Eye in the Dark devoured lost worlds unfortunate enough to have drifted into the Astral Lands. There it lived, at the center of all realities, feeding on the memories of worlds and stars unlucky enough to be swallowed by black holes, or...

She held herself.

Or the star eater.

She'd never seen an experiment log where Weber referenced the grimoire directly till now. The other researchers, scientists, and experiment volunteers all looked at him like he was mad. Why didn't any of them try to stop him?

Maybe it had been desperation? Maybe they were a bit mad themselves?

"Sir," a voice called from behind the cameraman, shocking her attention back to the video. "The subject is ready."

Weber looked at the camera again, licking his cracked lips like some hunger-crazed homeless man. "Shall we make history?"

The cameraman followed Weber out of the experiment chamber and into the observation room hidden behind a two-way mirror. There were three men in lab coats sitting at computers and readout screens. Weber stood at the center of the room and instructed the cameraman to focus his lens on the experiment chamber.

A short-haired naked woman walked into the center of the chamber. The sound of her bare feet slapping against the metal staircase echoed over the speakers in the observation room as she walked up to the mouth of the central tank.

Ira found herself whispering to the woman not to go through with it, as if she were watching some cheesy horror film, cursing the actions of the protagonist who was most assuredly about to die at the hands of some crazed knife-wielding psychopath.

An orderly helped the woman open the hatch, and she slipped into the solution; the orderly handed her a pair of goggles and carefully attached a breathing apparatus to her mouth.

A harsh clang sounded when the hatch shut. The orderly quickly left the room.

"Okay, let's begin," Weber said. "Anthony, why don't you do the honors and flip the switch?"

A man off to the left nodded and pressed Enter on his keyboard. That familiar reverberation, like a subwoofer, poured through the observation room's speakers. The particle collider glowed red-hot, causing the video to glitch out momentarily. The group of scientists had become so used to these experiments that they needed no instruction from Weber; they were like his little drones.

"Come over here." Weber waved the cameraman over to a readout screen, which displayed the young woman's biometrics in real time. "Here we can see that Mrs. Daniels' vitals are very strong, and over here, we can see that her alpha and beta brain waves have reached the appropriate look." He pointed to a comparison graph, which showed nearly identical waves. "Now, if I'm right, the combination of hallucinogens and the tank will allow Mrs. Daniels' mind to be able to reach the mind's horizon, pushing her body into a state of flux where the mind has the ability to change the frequency at which her atoms vibrate at. Then. The collider will smash two particles together at the speed of light and the resulting quantum shock wave will push Mrs. Daniels' body and consciousness into another universe!"

"Doctor, the particles are about to collide!"

There was a power surge, the lights flickered, and then…darkness.

The lights came back on a moment later, and everyone was silent.

Weber waved the cameraman over to the readout screen, and when the lens focused in, the screen showed nothing.

"Let's have a look, shall we?"

The camera once again followed Weber into the experiment chamber. Digital artifacts crept into the video.

"There's a charge in the air," Weber said. "Do you feel it?"

Weber climbed up onto the stairwell and popped the hatch to the tank, then waved the cameraman over. The next shot focused into the now empty sensory deprivation tank.

The saltwater had turned red.

"Hmm, we'll have to run some tests on the water left in the tank," Weber said. "Let's end this log and get a team up here to take samples."

The video stopped playing.

2

Ira rubbed her eyes and stretched back in her chair. If she wasn't careful, she might develop an oversensitivity to bright lights. Maybe she'd get some form of lamp set up in the mainframe room later? There were so many rooms down in the lower levels still unexplored.

Her eyelids burned. She hadn't slept all night, and her rainbow tables still hadn't cracked the passcode to unlock the security system. Although it also hadn't locked her out.

One way or another, it was only a matter of time.

Three knocks rang out like a gong. If it was Nico or Mathias, she'd tell them to leave her alone. She got up and shuffled over to the hatch, opened it, but no one was there.

She stood there, staring into the shadows in the tubular corridor. A nameless fear told her to shut the hatch.

The hatch latched shut. She locked it and turned back toward her workstation.

Before she reached her chair, she heard three more knocks on the door.

The hair rose on the back of her neck.

What does it want with me? she found herself thinking.

Part of her wanted to ignore it, just go right back to work and pretend she'd never heard the noise at all. But the knocking persisted.

Always in threes.

She found herself back at the door, her shaky fingers on the latch, twisting it slowly.

It unlocked, and she opened the door and found herself staring at Mathias's cold and calculating brown eyes. She wasn't quite sure, but there was something different about him.

He smiled; she frowned.

"You again," she said.

"Yes, me again," he said; his smile faded. "I wanted to check on you, make sure that you were well."

"So was that you earlier too?" she asked. "Think this is funny or something?"

"I don't know what you're talking about."

"Look, just tell me what you want, okay? We both know this display is completely unlike you."

"It's true, I'm not particularly good at socializing with people, and I'm sorry if I ever made you feel like you didn't exist."

"That's putting it lightly."

He gestured in at the darkness. "May I come in?"

Ira rubbed her temple and waved him on in. If nothing else, the distraction would keep her from falling asleep at the keyboard again.

"Have you managed to make headway on unlocking the security system?" Mathias asked.

"No." She sat down at her computer station.

"Well, perhaps what you need is another set of eyes, someone who can pore through the data that the scientists here left. There might be a clue as to what the password is there."

She looked at him, cautiously. "You'd like that, wouldn't you?"

"Only trying to help, though I can't deny my curiosity."

"Those experiments were horrific and inhumane; how can you be so curious about something that led to so much suffering?"

"How can historians study ancient wars, which caused the deaths of untold innocents, with excitement and hunger? It's the same thing, really. A yearning to know and to learn from humanity's past mistakes, no matter how recent or distant."

Ira fell silent for a while, hoping Mathias would leave. He didn't, of course, he just sat there in the dim light, probably waiting for her to cave in to his offer to help.

She tried to focus on her job, make him sweat. The rainbow tables had been working on the next attempt, trying to decipher the passcode, but she'd set the program to manually accept her input when she felt like pressing Enter on the password interface was an acceptable risk to take. She tried not to think about Eddy, about where he might be. He'd been missing for far too long already.

She shook her head, rubbed her eyes.

How long had it been? She'd been holed up in this damned prison of hers, the days were running together, and she was deliberately avoiding sleep…she couldn't stand the nightmares anymore.

"You miss him, greatly," Mathias said.

She nodded. "He's my only friend here."

"That's no secret, and it's doubtless something that your brother knows as well."

"What do you mean?"

He seemed to hesitate. "I probably shouldn't say it…I'm sorry."

"No, if you're gonna say something, spit it out!"

"I only mean that your brother and Eddy have never gotten along, and have been close to coming to blows on more than one occasion. Everyone was talking about how close Nico was to hurting him after your recent sojourn out into the tundra. I may not like partaking in gossip, but I do listen very carefully. Lena was especially keen on suggesting that the two of you were engaging in some form of secret romance."

"Of course she was." She punched the arm of her computer chair.

"Yes, ironic that she's the one in charge of maintaining our medical facilities, isn't it?" He smiled. "I mean, she's useful in that regard, no doubt, but it makes you wonder if she's some sort of idiot savant."

Ira almost chuckled. It *was* ironic.

"Anyway," he said. "Nico is no stranger to war, and if he were to suspect that you and Eddy were—" he cleared his throat, coughing into his hand "—copulating, then who knows what he might do?"

"Nico would never *kill* Eddy, if that's what you're suggesting."

"I'd hate to think it a possibility, but, in these uncertain times, you might be surprised what horrific actions we might be capable of."

155

Ira's eyes narrowed. Maybe it was just the glow from the server towers…but did Mathias's skin look a little gray? "Speaking for yourself? You spend an awful lot of time alone."

"Indeed." His face seemed to sulk, his shoulders hunched, and those large lips of his curled in on themselves. "Perhaps that's why I've reached out to you?"

"Afraid you might hurt someone?" Her fingers clawed into the rubber armrests.

"No, no." He smiled and put his hands up defensively. "But, madness, that's something I fear. As a scientist, it would be worse than death to lose one's grip on rationality, you know?"

She nodded, glancing back to her screen, where the most recent log entry had been playing. "I guess I understand."

"When I first came here, I was fearful of your group, as I'm no stranger to the unknown quantity that human behavior is when the rule of law has been tossed out the window. My quiet aversion to interaction was a subconscious defense mechanism, in a way, a way of trying to remain out of Nico's sight."

"You failed there."

"Yes, that much is clear to me now. I suppose I was lucky that my limited knowledge of engineering proved useful to him."

"Or what? He's not as big of an asshole as you and Hugo seem to think. He *cares*. He wouldn't just kick you out. Hugo's living proof of that."

"Yes, but after Hugo's latest flub, Nico did threaten just that."

"That's different!"

"Is it?"

She slouched back in her chair and tried not to look him in the eyes.

Her computer beeped at her. The code breaker program halted in its constant shifting and changing of characters on the screen. Her finger hovered over Enter.

"Here goes."

She pressed it.

She gasped and thrust her hands up into the air. "I'm in!"

"You are?" Mathias shot up and quickly moved behind her; a shiver wormed its way up her spine when he did. "Try one of the cameras."

She didn't answer him, but activated the camera feeds in several of the facility's corridors. The first one to come up was an empty corridor near the reactor core, the second was just outside of Hugo's new quarters, the third was outside of a room just a few floors short of the top level of the facility. Her eyes locked onto that third camera feed. She tried not to cover her mouth when Nico emerged from the room wearing only his long johns.

"That's not where his quarters are," Mathias said.

Nico paused, wiped sweat off of his brow, and sat for a while in the corridor; his chest was falling and heaving, as if he'd been doing something strenuous.

"Why does he look so tired?" Mathias asked.

Ira shrugged. They sat there for a time, watching him do nothing. Then, after ten minutes, Nico got back up and reentered the room.

When the door opened, the room appeared to be completely dark inside.

"Can you find a camera inside that room?" Mathias asked.

"I'm not going to spy on my brother!"

"And why shouldn't you?"

"Because he didn't do anything to Eddy!"

"Then why was he so sweaty there?" Mathias edged around to the other side of the computer, the glow from her monitor making him look like a wraith. "Aren't you the least bit curious?"

"He was probably just moving around things from home, some of that stuff is pretty heavy."

"Not likely. We finished cataloging and bringing that stuff in before nightfall."

Ira placed her head in her hands. Why was he pressing her with these questions?

"Murder is, after all, a tiring act," Mathias said. "I find it odd that the slash across Eddy's throat consists of only one wound. Last I checked, cougars had more than one claw."

She shot out of her chair and threatened her finger at him. "Get out!"

"I'm sorry," he said. "I didn't mean to offend—"

"The hell you didn't! Get out, before I force you to!"

He shuffled off to the door, opened it, but turned to her one last time.

"If you won't ask the important questions, who will?" he said.

She held her head and sobbed like a stupid little girl.

3

At first, he'd seen only an infinite darkness. He was still aware of the pain in his throat, but little else.

Now, after untold hours floating in tank, the darkness was no longer purely black, and Eddy had lost the ability to tell whether he was awake or asleep. He saw the convincing likeness of Alli, wearing her favorite purple cardigan, floating, smiling, before him in that formless void. She was clutching something wrapped up in a blanket. Her eyes rose and met his. The thing bundled in the blanket wasn't a thing at all, but his one-year-old daughter, Elena.

He tried to reach out, to touch her, like he'd done the night before the looters broke in and murdered them both, but his hand wasn't there.

He had no body; his essence was everywhere.

Her smile faded into a twisting frown. Tears ran down her cheeks. She offered the child up to Eddy, but no matter how much he wanted to, he couldn't embrace her. He tried to call out to her, but he couldn't speak, and before he knew it, she'd fallen deep into the darkness, never to return.

He pushed himself forward, chasing after them. The darkness was like a doorway, like the canvas of a quarantine tent, thick and membranous. He pushed and reached and screamed and shouted.

When the barrier finally gave way, he was greeted by a phantasmagoria of color and sensation. A vortex which ended in a single point of light.

He seemed to fall for an eternity before being spit out into a blanket of stars. Now he was alone, and Alli and Elena were nowhere to be seen.

Their phantoms had opened up an old wound, one he'd thought that he closed long ago. If he had eyes, he would have been sobbing.

More faces from his past appeared around him; some had died in the war, fighting alongside him, and others were childhood friends whose fates he could only guess at.

They seemed to be shouting, warning him of something.

Was that it? Was he dead? Was this his own personal hell?

He tried to close his eyes, but he had no eyelids. He tried to sleep, but the phantoms continued to pass him by.

Then, the starscape faded into something else. It was still dark, but something blue pulsed in the darkness, and then, that dim blue light spread until it became slightly more recognizable. He'd recognize Ira's disheveled black hair anywhere. She was slumped over her keyboard in the mainframe room, probably passed out after working all night. He tried to call out to her, but his voice wasn't there.

He wanted nothing more than to go to her, put his arm around her, embrace her…and now he'd never get that chance. He was trapped, or dead, or who the hell knows what.

Something welled up inside of him; he tried screaming at the top of his lungs.

Ira stirred and sat up in her chair. Her sleepy eyes turned around to face him…but he saw only confusion written on her face. She didn't see him. She left the room in a tired shuffle.

His heart sank, and he couldn't help but wish that he would cease to exist.

There was a tapping sound now that he was alone. Like the gentle clicking of a cat's claws rapping on the floor as it padded closer to its prey. It seemed to be coming from the shadows of the chamber. When he stared at it, he felt as though it stared back.

Curious, with nothing left to lose, he approached the darkness.

It was like a window into another world, and what he saw broke his mind into pieces. He saw hills, land with the consistency of a leathery hide beneath a pulsing, gray sky that had the texture of decaying flesh. Open mouths in the ground with sharp, black and yellow teeth, opening and closing, chewing on rotting body parts...human body parts.

Then, at the top of one of the hills, a great black shape. It seemed to be asleep. It was twenty feet long, or a hundred, or a thousand—he wasn't sure which—and had great spines, spiking off its back into that terrible pulsing sky. It seemed to be breathing in from its head, growling, rumbling, which made its shape rise and fall as though it was in many places at once. If it had eyes, he couldn't see them—

A single gray eye at the center of its head jerked open, revealing multi-segmented pupils.

He backed away from the window, tearing his eyes away from that beast and fleeing.

He tried to find Ira. He had to warn her about that thing!

But he found himself in the center of the void again, unable to move...

Maybe he was just imagining all this stuff?

Maybe he was still in the tank, alive and well, healing as Mathias had said he would.

Ira let the bittersweet aroma of the coffee wrest her from her own sleepiness. She sat down at the table in the lounge and rubbed her eyes.

The warmth radiating through the ceramic cup into her hands was almost enough to comfort her.

Now, even her dreams weren't safe.

She could have sworn she saw Eddy naked, strapped to some apparatus, screaming for her to help him...

There was more to it. A descent through an elevator shaft, the deeper it went, the stranger it became. There were moans near the bottom. Shapes she couldn't make out—didn't *want* to.

One of the shapes came for her, scrambling up the steel traction rope with fingers which were bent and wrong.

She fled into a corridor, deep below where they had taken up residence, found an experiment chamber.

160

That's where she found Eddy. Only, he wasn't Eddy anymore. Something was coming out of his mouth.

She shuddered.

A fucking nightmare.

Maybe she should stop watching the experiment logs. But they were her only clue as to how many rooms there were in the facility, and those rooms gave her a better idea of which cameras to focus on. The facility itself was too damn large to cover everything in any reasonable amount of time. Hell, it had once housed an impressive crew of over five hundred people, and about five percent of them had been devoted to managing security.

She hated to admit it, but Mathias might have been right; she needed some help.

"Can't sleep?" Nico's voice came from the doorway.

She shook her head.

He nodded, walked across the lounge and grabbed himself a cup of coffee, sat opposite of her. He wasn't sweating anymore, but he was still only wearing his long johns.

"Make any headway?" he asked.

"Got the cameras running," she said, taking another sip of her coffee.

His eyes opened wide. "That soon?"

"Yeah…" She couldn't lie, the look on his face was almost alarming. "Got a problem with that?"

"No, not really."

She took another sip—but paused, almost spitting out her coffee when she noticed it. There was a splotch of fresh blood soaking into the collar of his long johns.

"Something wrong?" he asked.

She swallowed deep. "Did you hurt yourself?"

She gestured to the front of his collar; he arched his back and examined himself, wiping at it with his thumb. When he removed the material, she could see the faint outline of scratch marks on his collarbone. Her face flushed with heat; her pulse quickened.

"I must have cut myself shaving again," he said.

"Right." What if Mathias had been right about Nico? "You should be more careful."

He nodded and let his collar flap back down into its natural position.

"I just remembered—" She set her coffee mug down and stood up. "—I have something I have to do."

"Yeah, good talk."

She rushed out of the room and sprinted down the corridor into the elevator. She entered the numbers for floor B-2 and waited for the doors to close before she allowed herself to collapse, sobbing, on the cold aluminum floor.

She caught her breath and fought off panic. She had to keep her cool. If Nico had done what Mathias suggested, she'd need more proof than a little bit of blood—but—how else could it have happened? And the scratches—

The elevator dinged. She stepped off into another corridor, rounded the bend into a darkened tunnel. Her feet felt numb, like they belonged to someone else.

She'd have to check the room she'd seen Nico exit first! Where was it again? Second—or third-to-last floor? To hell with it, she'd just search all the rooms.

She stopped.

Something wasn't right. She heard footsteps further down the hall.

They opened up a gateway here. The words from her nightmare echoed in her mind.

"Is someone there?" she asked.

The footsteps got louder.

Tap.

Tap.

Tap tap tap.

The peach fuzz on the back of her neck stood on end. She thought she could make out a shadow in the dark.

Her legs had a mind of their own. She backed up.

If the beast doesn't get you, then Lai'thamia *will.*

"What are you?"

The shadow seemed to snake around in the dark, as if it wasn't totally aware of what it was doing or where it was. It avoided direct contact with the light. She thought she could hear faint laughter, or a deep snarling breath, as it snaked away out of sight. Out of mind.

She backed off and sprinted down the corridor in the opposite direction.

It was strange, because she didn't realize that she'd been screaming.

Then she found herself pounding on Mathias' door, wondering how she'd even gotten there.

He opened the door. "What are you doing here at this hour?"

"I panicked." She stormed into his room; it wasn't much, like her own, just a cot and his backpack. "I saw something, and I ran."

"What did you see?"

"Blood." She covered her mouth. She'd been about to tell him about the shadow, but how could she be sure she wasn't just going crazy? All those experiment logs. She hadn't been sleeping much. What if this was a nightmare too? "Blood on Nico's long johns…and scratch marks on his collar bone, signs of a struggle."

Mathias nodded, his eyebrows furrowed together. "I see."

She took a seat on his cot and let her head fall into her hands. "What the hell? What if you were right, Mathias?"

"What I said was out of line, and a result of pure paranoia," he said. "I'm sure there's a perfectly logical explanation for this."

"Yeah? Like what?"

"Well…" He fell silent for a while. "Well, I don't know, but it's decidedly uncivilized to jump to conclusions."

"He's my brother, you think I didn't fucking think of that?"

"I know, I know."

"I don't think you do know. He's my brother, but sometimes I don't even know who he really is. Not since he returned from that god forsaken war. The way he looks at Eddy, it's like he thinks he's trash. When I lashed out at you earlier, I did so out of love for him, but…if he murdered my Eddy, I—"

"Don't do that to yourself." She felt a blanket cover her and Mathias's scrawny arm find its way around her shoulders.

She convulsed and lunged into Mathias's chest; her tears drenched his shirt. The sorrow twisted inside of her, heaving and writhing. All she could see when she closed her eyes was the image from her nightmare: Eddy's mouth open, gnarled roots growing from deep within, his eyes aglow, bulging, and her brother, she remembered her brother had been in the nightmare too, laughing incessantly.

It was all out of her control, wasn't it? As it always had been. Ever since she was a child, she'd always been too reliant on others, keeping to herself, nose in a book, staying quiet. Even when the ice fell, all she did was stick close to Nico, afraid to stray too far from him.

She owed him everything.

Scratch marks on his neck, redness on his pale skin, blood on his long johns. And he just expected her not to question him?

She remembered watching Lena stitch up Eddy's neck wound. Now that she thought on Mathias's observation, it was clear that it couldn't have been made by a cougar. But her brother's tactical knife...

She sobbed until her tears were spent and she felt only a deep and unrelenting rage. Mathias's arms were not a comfort, as much as he tried; his weak grip only reminded her of the embrace she'd had with Eddy, and the fact that she'd probably never feel it again.

"Look, maybe we can summon the others and discuss our fears?" Mathias said.

"No." She stood up, wiping the last of her tears away. "I'm not taking that risk."

"What do you intend to do?"

"I'm going to kick his goddamn ass!"

She stormed out of the room, heading for the elevator. She was tired of being pushed around—and aside—by everyone and *everything*. This was the last straw.

Her fists clenched up tight; she entered the elevator and returned to the floor where Nico would still be sipping on his coffee.

His back was turned from the door.

He didn't see her coming, not when she pulled the chair out from behind him, and not when she picked it up and threatened to beat him with it.

"What the hell, Ira?" he said, his eyes wild with shock.

164

"You son-of-a-bitch!"

He stood up, his hand extended out at her. "What's wrong with you? Put that thing down!"

"No, not this time. We're going to get to the bottom of this."

"Bottom of what?"

She lunged out and attempted to hit him with the chair, but he twisted, grabbed it, and struggled to wrest it from her grip. They spun around, struggling to gain the upper hand. He'd trained her to fight, but he was far stronger than she was, and far more experienced.

Still, he had one serious weakness.

She pulled him forward and kicked at his prosthetic leg, then, when he was off-balance, grabbed at it and ripped it off his stump. He tumbled to the floor, and she towered over him, threatening it at his face. Now his back was to the open door again. His eyes opened wide, his teeth clenched, and for a moment, there was a vague doubt in her mind…

Then, a loud smash sounded through the room, and before she knew it, Nico was on the floor, lying lifeless.

Mathias stood above him with a small frying pan in hand.

"I didn't know what he'd do," Mathias said.

Ira found herself at Nico's side, feeling out his pulse.

"Is he breathing?"

She nodded, relieved. "But he's going to be really pissed in the morning."

"Let's move him somewhere secure where we can question him."

She nodded, and they moved to grab his leg and arms.

CHAPTER THIRTEEN

The rattling and shaking caused Ira's head to shoot up. She struggled to remember why she wasn't in her cot; once she saw the iron bars, she remembered. She was in a detention room, one of two scattered throughout the facility that Mathias had helped her find.

The clanking was coming from Nico, banging on the bars from within his cage.

"Let me out of here," he said.

She really wished she could. "I can't do that."

His knuckles turned white with his grip around the bars. "You better unlock this cage right now, Ira. I'm not fucking playing!"

"Or what?"

He bared his teeth and slammed his arm against the bars. "Let me out!"

"Did you kill Eddy?"

"Are you fucking kidding me?"

Her grip tightened on the metal seat. "Answer the question."

"You know that I didn't kill him! Lena's still getting vitals from him!"

"Actually, no, she *isn't*, they flatlined last night, probably about the time you showed up in the lounge in your long johns."

"What the hell makes you think I killed him?"

166

"Think about it, Nico. You fought for the Feds, he fought for the Revolutionists. You may have tolerated him for his abilities, but deep down we both know that you hated him."

He was quiet for a moment. His cold, calculating green eyes searched the room, searched *her*.

"That doesn't mean that I'd just kill him, and besides, you have no proof."

"What about the blood on your long johns, or the scratches on your collarbone?" She shook her head; it took everything she had to hold her composure together in front of him. There was a time when he would only have to bark an order, and she would have followed it without question. For so many years she had been ordered around by him and stomped on by so many others. She was done being led around by the whims of others, done being made to follow someone else's plan. "I told you that I got the security cameras running, remember? One of the first feeds I saw was *you*, coming out of some dark room in your long johns, sweating profusely."

Nico backed away from the bars and fell back on the barren, stiff bed inside the cell. He gripped at his prosthetic leg and smiled wryly. He must have put it back on when she was asleep.

"You went straight for my prosthetic," he said. "That was pretty smart."

Was he actually proud of her? "Answer my question."

"I can't."

"Why the hell not!" She jumped from her chair and approached the bars. "You owe me an explanation!"

"I owe you nothing!"

She stopped just short of arm's reach from the bars. "You knew how I felt about him!"

"If it weren't for *me*, you'd all be *corpses* six feet under the snow. So. Yes. You owe me your trust, your loyalty, if not for the fact that we are family, then for the fact that I've saved your life more times than I can fucking count!"

"The wound in his throat." The air in that dead chamber seemed to freeze when she said it. "I know what a knife wound looks like, thanks to you."

167

His eyes opened wide; his face almost looked red.

"You cut his throat, didn't you?" she said.

He was silent for a while. He wasn't making eye contact.

"Just admit it, Nico!"

His eyes stabbed up at her. "It was a fucking *accident*! I was having a panic attack and he snuck up on me!"

She fell to her knees, tears hitting the concrete. "I didn't want to believe it. I didn't want to believe that you could."

"He was a traitor," Nico said. "Maybe it was God's judgment?"

She wiped her tears and stood.

"Listen to me very carefully."

His eyes stabbed at her, quavered with a miserable loneliness, but as much as she wished things could just go back to normal, her anger raged through her like a wildfire. There was no backing down.

"If you killed him," she said. "Then you and I are strangers, and I can't be blamed for what I do to you."

"Sweet little Ira," he said. "Gonna get her hands dirty?"

"Yes. After all, I had a damn good teacher."

"I didn't teach you everything. I guess I know why now."

"One way or another, I'm going to find out."

"And what happens when you find out that I'm innocent? Huh?" He chuckled. "I brought him back alive, didn't I? I told you it was an accident, and that's the truth."

"Fact is, I still can't trust you."

They sat for a while, not saying anything. Nico crossed his arms and eyed his stump.

2

The time was near.

Mathias ran his hand over the page. There were strange ink drawings of symbols, triangles and circles and ornate markings which he would likely have scoffed at in his college days.

The fool he was.

He looked up from where he'd set the book down, through the two-way mirror, into the room where Eddy now rested, soaking in a vertical tank. Somehow, he knew he needed this page to complete the circle in the experiment chamber. To complete the bargain and stop the nightmares. To stop the harvester of the abyss.

Then, he would be free to unlock the secrets of the grimoire and escape this frozen hell.

Still, it would take some supplies and planning to make the necessary preparations for the circle around Eddy's tank. The symbols Weber had used in this room were all wrong. Somehow he knew that. That fact alone simultaneously frightened him and caused him to chuckle.

There was still one piece of the puzzle missing. He could feel it coming, though. Yes. It was almost time.

3

The great waking dream.

That's what Eddy started to call his time in hell. It wasn't that he had ever been very religious, but what else could he really call it? He couldn't tell how long he'd been forced to endure it; but in the time that he'd been floating there in the void, he'd witnessed the deaths of his comrades as well as his wife and child; the birth of stars; the death of galaxies; and the soul-crushing cries of an alien species whose lives were extinguished by the awe-inspiring collision of a massive comet.

The world which the aliens had inhabited, though, kept turning, kept orbiting its parent sun, and that sun continued to glow a bright red-orange. It was a thing he'd never really taken time to think about when he was alive, but, now that he wasn't, it was all he could think about. He understood now. Humans, when you thought about the size of the universe, were painfully insignificant. A speck of dust to be swept away by the ever-growing push broom that was the cosmos.

The void was quiet now. He saw nothing but an endless blanket of stars and galaxies. Maybe, unconsciously, he was gaining some control over where his soul wandered? If it was wandering at all.

He hadn't thought about his former life in a while, about Ira... His heart still ached, of course it did. But, if there was nothing he could do, if this was his existence now, perhaps it wasn't so bad?

He caught a faint glimpse of a massive shadow across the vast blanket of stars. It was so big, his mind could barely rationalize it. It reached out a clawed, tentacled hand, scooped up a cluster of stars, and pulled them into its own bulbous blackness. When he looked again, they were gone—just gone. A void, light-years in diameter.

He tried to look away, fearing that it would notice his gaze and swallow him too.

Could souls be eaten by such beasts? Was he a soul at all?

It seemed to shift, as if noticing him, and its mass began to grow, enveloping the blanket of stars until it was all that encompassed what he could see. Two crimson eyes opened, peered down at him.

He tried to ask it what it wanted, but no words came out.

It squinted its eyes at him.

If there had ever been a time to contemplate the existence of God, now was the time. Was this terrible thing *it*? Or, was *it* something else, something *worse*? He couldn't be sure, but the shadowy thing seemed to have a great amount of contempt for him, or perhaps, maybe, it was indifference?

Even in death, his mind was not built for science, or for existential questions. He just wanted his life back, even if it had been miserable, even if it was insignificant in the grand scheme of things.

He cared nothing for stars, or planets, or aliens, or gods.

Do you hear me? He thought. *I don't care about you.*

The great shadow closed its eyes, sank away into the distance, and vanished into the stars. It hadn't noticed him after all.

No.

He wasn't worth noticing. The stars seemed washed-out in the wake of that cosmic beast.

No.

He was falling somehow. Eddy could see ripples echoing from where those stars had been consumed. He could feel his essence getting dragged in by something, a portal or perhaps a gateway.

Before he could say anything, he found himself lying on the surface of a broken platform of some kind. Looking up, it was almost as though he were at the edge of a dead star system. The star did not brighten the sky; somehow it made the air feel colder to him. He could see the remains of broken moons and asteroids drifting high above the horizon, dimly outlined by the scarce light.

He peered down and found that he had hands once again; in fact, the rest of his body was intact as well.

Where was this place?

Was this just a dream? Another aspect of the afterlife?

There were pyramids on the blackened horizon, their triangular bodies reflecting the sparse blue light of the star.

He tested his feet, found he had weight in this place, and—as if by instinct alone—started towards the pyramid in the distance.

Nico had been lying with his back against the steel wall for hours. Ira hadn't moved from her seat either. It was no use trying to convince her to let him out; she was dead set on getting a confession out of him. In a way, this was exactly what he'd feared would happen if Ira and Ramirez got too close.

The fact of the matter was, when the fog of his panic attack had left his mind, when he'd stared at Ramirez's bleeding throat and realized what he'd done, he'd felt glad.

He smiled.

In a way, he knew Ramirez had finally gotten what he deserved.

His thoughts were disturbed by several knocks on the door to the brig, and Nico sat up attentively. There was another person in this equation. Someone had hit him from behind. Who would it be?

He watched Ira get up and cross the room, open the door.

"What is it?" Ira said.

"I need to talk to him."

It was Lena's voice…he clenched his teeth. Now was not the time. If he could help it, he'd get out of this cell without having *that* information come to light.

"He's busy," Ira said.

"Look," Lena said. "It's really important. I won't let him out or anything…"

"Is there a problem?"

He recognized that voice, thin and nasally; Mathias.

"Lena says she needs to talk to Nico," Ira said.

"Alone," Lena said.

"I'm afraid that we can't do that," Mathias said.

"Well, I don't want *her* to hear," Lena said.

"Why's that?" Ira said. "Got something to hide?"

"Yeah, and it's *private*," Lena said.

"What if I take Ira's place?" Mathias said.

"Are you serious?"

"I'm not one for spreading gossip, trust me—as long as you had nothing to do with Eddy's death."

They seemed to go quiet for a while, but every now and then Nico heard Ira raise her voice at Lena. Eventually, he saw Ira leave the room—shoulders hunched, a scowl painted on her pale face.

Lena and Mathias came in.

Mathias carefully descended into Ira's chair and opened up a tattered book, started reading.

Lena came forward. Her face was a bit pale, her short blonde hair was more messy than usual, and she was clutching her stomach.

Oh no, he thought.

"Nico," she said.

"Don't you dare say it!" Nico found himself clutching at the bars.

"Why the hell not? What? Is it too *inconvenient* for you?"

"You know damn well why you shouldn't!"

She crossed her arms, her eyebrows creased. "I'm pregnant."

Mathias's head perked up at that, then he quickly went back to reading. Maybe he'd have the sense to keep quiet?

"It could be Hugo's." Nico walked back to his bed, stared at the wall.

"No, I haven't slept with him in three months."

"Tell him it's his anyway, he's dumb enough not to notice."

"See, that's the kind of shit that got you tossed in a cell!"

"You and I both know I didn't kill him. What I did was an accident."

"Yeah? So, why don't you tell them all what you were *really* doing in that room?" She placed her hands on her hips, arched her back. He

172

turned to face her. "Go right ahead and tell them you were busy *fucking* my brains out on a gurney!"

"*Shut up!*"

"Why don't you want it to get out, Nicola? Why? Are you ashamed of me?"

"You want the honest answer?"

"Oh, *this* should be *good.*"

"Because it'll upset morale."

"Oh, it'll upset morale! Is that all?" Her eyes shot open wide; he could almost feel the anger radiating off of her like flares from the summer sun. "You sure you're not worried about what a certain traitorous little sister of yours is gonna think about it?"

He avoided her eyes.

"I knew it."

She stormed for the door and Ira let her out.

"Your brother's an asshole," she said.

Nico rested his head on the bars, listened to Ira enter the room and switch places with Mathias.

"What was that about?" Ira asked.

"Nothing," Nico said. "Just drama."

CHAPTER FOURTEEN

Mathias rapped gently on the door and Hugo took his sweet time answering.

Hugo cracked the door open. "Yo, what do you want?"

Mathias barged past Hugo, clasping his hands behind his back. "I have some rather distressing news to share with you, my friend."

"Man, we *ain't* friends." Hugo turned around and crossed his arms. "Me and you have shared maybe one word in all the time I known you."

"Yes, my fault entirely."

"Say what you got to say and get the fuck out here."

"Well, that makes this much easier. The others didn't want you to know, they thought you might do something foolish with the information I'm about to give you."

"Get to it."

"It's about Lena and Nico."

Hugo's eyebrows came together, his tiny lips creased. "What about them?"

"There's no easy way to say this." Mathias let out a dramatic sigh and sat down to add to the effect. "Lena's pregnant."

Hugo stood there for a while, clenching his fists, his eyes darting about the room.

"I'm sure you've guessed already that it isn't yours."

Hugo screamed and punched the wall. A sound not unlike a wooden fence snapping into pieces bounced off of the stone walls. Hugo dropped to the floor, clutching his bloody hand. He let himself fall into the fetal position and started sobbing like a child.

Mathias observed his behavior. His expression: completely neutral. He knelt down before Hugo and held his injured hand.

"I'm no doctor, but you definitely shouldn't have done that," Mathias said.

Hugo retrieved his hand and buried his face in the sleeve of his long johns. "Just leave me, B."

"I don't expect you to do much with the information I just gave you," Mathias said. "But, I'll tell you one thing, if it were me that Nico had done this to—well, I don't know what I would do. I mean, come on, we aren't savages or cavemen! And here he goes acting like your typical alpha male, stealing another man's woman!"

Hugo stopped sobbing for a moment, let one reddened eye focus on Mathias.

"I can see you understand my point." Something caught Mathias's eye; it was a fantasy novel featuring a massive dragon and a single warrior wielding a sword, and it looked as though it'd been read over and over and over again since Hugo had found it. "Were you always into bargain-bin fantasy?"

Hugo shook his head. "Used to beat the shit out of people that read stuff like that."

"And now you enjoy it?"

He nodded.

"I suppose escaping into a fantasy world would be quite comforting for any of us, given our reality. But, ironically, you find yourself being abused by one who feels he's superior to you. Maybe it's a poetic justice?"

Hugo's eyes widened. Mathias could almost feel the anger wash through him as understanding washed over his face like a damp rag.

"Unfortunately for you." Mathias slouched back against the edge of Hugo's bed. "You're a coward. You'll cry yourself to sleep in here, maybe end things with Lena, and seclude yourself from everyone else.

Maybe you'll just try to ignore it, stick your face in this book for the thousandth time to escape."

Hugo buried his face in his sleeve again.

"I was once a lot like you, Hugo. Much smarter, less crass, but I too was a coward at one point. You'll grow out of it, perhaps, but only when you snap, and do something you might regret." He paused. "This place can be maddening, can't it? The cold concrete walls, the tunnels, the hum from the environmental systems, and the careful footsteps of your so-called friends, lovers, monsters, who steal from you, and lie to your face. Quite maddening."

"Mathias, come in." It was Ira's abrasive and sassy voice, calling over the CB; Mathias leaned over, plucked the receiver from his belt.

"Yes?" Mathias said.

"I thought it over last night," she said. "And I think it's a good idea."

"I'm afraid I don't follow. What's a good idea?"

"I need help analyzing the logs." There was a quiver in her voice. "So, I thought you could handle that job, while I check the security cams for any sign of Eddy. What do you say?"

Mathias smiled. "Of course, just call my CB when you'd like to get started."

"I figured we could get started right away, actually. There's no time to lose."

"Right, I'll be right up to join you."

"Thanks, Ira out."

The buzz from the CB went quiet, and Mathias rose from his crouched position.

"Well, it appears as if I have a job to do," he said.

Mathias made for the door, leaving Hugo to sob himself to sleep.

2

Ira didn't have to wait long for Mathias to arrive. Within ten minutes of cutting the chatter with him on the CB, he'd arrived and asked how he could help. She only had the one laptop, but there were lots of spare computer parts around the facility, and she'd managed to scrounge enough parts together that could be assembled into a new machine for Mathias to do his searching on—which she'd found an hour earlier in one of the storage rooms down on one of the basement levels.

Mathias's gangly legs carried him into the dim glow of the mainframe room; his sharp brown eyes cut a line straight to the computer parts lying on the tarp she'd laid out on the floor.

"I hope you know how to put a PC together," she said.

"Of course," he said.

"Then get to work, I've collected all the parts you'll need, but I don't have time to assemble it for you."

"You've done enough already."

She watched him sit down cross-legged in front of the collection of parts and begin rummaging through them to find the ones he liked best. There was an empty case waiting for whatever parts he chose. She took her seat at her laptop, took a sip from her coffee mug, and began calling up security feeds.

"Have you slept?" he asked.

She shook her head. "I passed out for an hour while keeping watch over Nico. Not sure that counts."

"Hardly." She glanced over to him and saw that he'd put together a motherboard with an onboard CPU and video card, and was fitting it into the case. "Speaking of which, what do you plan to do with him?"

"Assuming he's actually guilty?"

"You have doubts?"

She sulked, took another sip of her coffee, and nodded. "He said he was having a panic attack when Eddy snuck up on him. We live in a dangerous world now…some part of me has to realize that it's possible that Eddy just got up and wandered somewhere he shouldn't have and got lost."

"Very unlikely, considering how Lena had him doped up."

"What do you mean?"

"Think about it." He inserted several sticks of RAM into the motherboard. "He was so doped up with morphine and pain killers, it would have taken a miracle for him to get up and walk away without some form of help. And I don't believe in miracles. Nicola claims it was an accident, but I think he was caught cutting Eddy's throat, and had to make arrangements to ensure his survival, albeit temporarily. And once Eddy was alone in the med bay, he was able to make his move and finish the job."

Ira stared at her screen and held herself. The thought that her brother could even be capable of something like that was very hard for her to process.

Whatever the case was, she couldn't help but feel that something was off about the whole thing.

"I still have hope," she said.

"Hence why you continue to search," he said. "But I wonder if what you're searching for is confirmation, rather than a sign of life."

"Just say it, just say I'm searching for a body."

"Sorry." He shook his head, rubbed his eyes. "I didn't mean—"

"You did mean to." *You cold-hearted bastard.*

She paused for a while, allowing herself time to process what he'd said. Her eyes scanned over the security videos, one at a time.

One of them showed Lena in the medical bay, still cataloging their equipment. Her hand resting over her stomach.

The next feed showed Hugo, curled up in his quarters, clutching his hand.

Wonder what's eating him, she thought.

The next feed showed nothing but a blank hallway, and the one after that, an empty corridor, like the one where she'd seen that…no, she couldn't think of that.

It had only been a hallucination anyway. Something from her nightmares. That was all.

She switched to the next feed; it featured an empty experiment chamber with a vertical deprivation tank at the center. And no sign of Eddy still, just emptiness.

No bodies, living or otherwise.

"But, you're right…" she said. "I need to know one way or another."

But can I live without him?

Mathias nodded, connecting the last of the cables inside the case, then closed it up.

"Where shall I set this up?" Mathias asked.

She pointed to another corner of the room, where she wouldn't have to look directly at his face while he worked. "Over there."

"Ah, excellent."

He stood up and meandered where she'd pointed, carrying his newly built tower.

She heard the sounds of him scuttling back and forth, grabbing a monitor, keyboard, and mouse, to complete his setup. Then came the inevitable booting noises that the machine made. He returned to her side, a question no doubt on the edge of his lips.

"Yes?" she said.

"The disk is blank, do you have a copy of your OS?"

"I'm insulted you had to ask." She dug around in her laptop bag next to the chair, retrieved a few thumb drives, and thought long and hard about which one to give him; she picked a black and yellow drive out, and handed it to him with only a faint grin. "Take this one, it's Linux, but you should be familiar with the interface."

He took it and lumbered back to his station, completely unaware of the malware on the drive. The drive had a special background virus that would infect his machine along with the installation of the OS, and would allow her to see everything he was doing. She may have needed his help, but she still didn't trust him for shit.

Ira had no doubt in her mind that Mathias thought that he was greatly superior to her, but he had no idea how stupid it was to boot anything straight from a thumb drive.

She'd learned that basic bit of info when she was a kid, before the war, when cyber warfare was in its infancy. But even when she was in college, it had been a common problem for unknowing students to spread malware through interacting with other machines with their thumb drives. She shook her head. It was like a mechanical STD chain, for which there was no cure, except abstaining from using school-owned machines altogether. Later, she'd use that little trick to infect the systems of large companies to get a look at their files and their bank information. She'd done some stupid shit after college, and a lot of it could have landed her a one-way ticket to a detention camp or a prison cell, but goddamn was it fun.

She opened up a tab on her system, a virtual machine that would serve as her window into what Mathias was doing. She could see that he was already fully set up, and was looking through the experiment logs.

She couldn't help but smile. It made her feel like her old self.

"Hmm." Mathias's voice echoed through the chamber. "Ira, this is curious."

"What is it?" She asked.

"Come here, I want to show you something."

She got up and made her way over to him, making sure to keep her blanket tight around her body. When she was next to Mathias, she peered over his shoulder and pretended to be surprised at what he was looking at.

"It appears as though we don't have admin access for the system," he said.

"Yeah, the account I'm in is one of the lower tier ones. Why?"

"Wouldn't we be more secure if you took advantage of the admin status?"

Her pierced eyebrow raised. "I was thinking about it before Eddy went missing, but I haven't honestly had time to take over. And I'm not sure how Lena or the others would feel about everything being coded to my biometrics and voice authorization."

"You should do it." Mathias smiled wide, and in the dim blue light of the mainframe room, she thought his teeth looked a bit yellow. "After Nico and Eddy, you're the one with the most survival experience, and should be the leader here."

"We are so fucked."

His smile faded. "I wasn't kidding."

She went quiet for a moment and allowed the gravity of their situation to fully sink in.

"I'll prep the system," she said, and returned to her seat.

She called up the interface that would allow her to gain access to the admin profile for the facility. First, she'd have to actually crack into it. She already had associate access in the security system, but this would allow her total access to every system in the facility, and she would be able to assign a status to everyone based on their skills.

That part was a comfort, given the growing amount of distrust she felt for the others.

The rainbow tables had tried several combinations to gain access to the admin profile, and all of them had failed.

At first, she thought it could be hopeless...but then, she remembered that Doctor Weber had been the admin, and she'd had all sorts of windows into what sort of man he'd been.

Maybe the password wasn't random, but something personalized? It sounded stupid. Everyone knows not to use a personalized password.

Would Weber be arrogant enough for that?

His logs weren't filled with anyone in particular; he never mentioned friends, family, or even coworkers who worked with him on the Mind's Horizon project. But there was one person whom he admired and couldn't shut the hell up about.

She stopped her passcode cracker, and typed into the password field: JOHNCLILLY

That was rejected.

She tried again: JOHN C LILLY

Failed.

Again: Mind's Horizon Lilly

Failed.

She sat back in her chair, supporting her head with her palm.

She'd make one more attempt, and if that failed, she'd turn it back over to her programs.

She entered: The First Conference of Three Beings

ACCESS GRANTED

She pumped her fist. "I am a badass!"

"Made some progress, eh?" Mathias said.

"Yep," she said. "I'm gonna set up voice authorization now."

The prompt came up, telling her to speak into the microphone. She spoke a single sentence she'd learned in theater. There was no way to key her biometrics into the system from her tiny laptop; she'd have to go down to the main security station for that. It could wait anyway voice authorization was good enough.

"It's done," she said.

"You're now the proud owner of a top-secret military research base," Mathias said. "Have any thoughts?"

"We're still fucked."

"Hardly. The others aren't even close to qualified. Besides, there's the fact that Lena... No I shouldn't say anything."

Her eyes stabbed in his direction. "What about Lena?"

"I really shouldn't say anything, it's a private matter between Lena and your brother."

Something snapped inside her, and she found herself at his side, grabbing hold of Mathias's collar, nearly lifting him out of the chair. "What the hell did that bitch do?"

"It's not what she did, it's more of what *they* did."

Ira thought back to when she had been watching over Nico's cell, how Lena had been so adamant about seeing him.

She kept touching her stomach on the security feed, she thought. *And Hugo...*

Then, she thought about the last thing Lena had said to her...the way her brother had been buttoning his shirt that time she'd slammed Lena against the wall...and the scratches on his neck, the blood on the collar of his long johns...

"She was screwing him," she said quietly.

"Indeed, and your brother didn't want that little secret getting out, because he thought it would sour the morale between us."

She let him fall back into his chair. "He was right."

"There's something else." He straightened his collar.

"And what's that?"

"She's carrying his child."

3

The explosions caused dust, rubble, and dirt to fall from the sky, and a ringing assaulted Nico's ears. He stayed low and clutched his rifle tight. The ringing persisted, but he peered over the edge anyway.

The battlefield was littered with corpses, both enemy and comrade alike. The constant gunfire filled the street; through his helmet they sounded like miniature firecrackers popping in the distance. The silhouette of one of his boys caught his attention as they ran out into the crossfire—the bullet caused blood and glass to explode like grotesque glitter as his body hung there, like it was frozen in time, before it came crashing down lifeless in the dirt.

So much for full-body armor coverage.

Nico shook his head. This was no time to close off, no time to be a coward. He summoned all his strength, picked himself up, and charged toward the building.

His courage was short-lived; his heart sank through his chest, when he heard the hair-splitting whistle of a missile careening through the air toward him.

He watched it, as if time had slowed to a crawl; it collided a meter ahead of him, but its blast radius was still in range to knock him clean off his feet. He felt his exo-suit slam into something, and heard the sound of metal bending and grinding against metal.

His HUD went dark, and he couldn't feel one of his legs. Which leg was it again?

"Wake up, Nico." He could have sworn the voice was his sister's. He tried to move, but his exoskeleton was dead, and soon he would be too.

"Wake up, you son-of-a-bitch!"

"Wake up, you son-of-a-bitch!" Hugo said.

Nico sat up and resisted the urge to scream and clutch at his stump, but only found Hugo standing before his cage, his arms holding his own AR-15.

"You're holding it wrong, jackass," Nico said. "If you're gonna shoot me, at least stop chicken-winging it."

Hugo was shaking, heavy bags beneath his eyes, bandages around his steadying hand. "Shut up!"

"I'm guessing Mathias told you about me and Lena." Nico stood up and started inching toward Hugo; if he could get close enough, he might be able to reach through the bars, offset his aim and get the weapon from him. "That fucking coward."

"You're the bitch who had to take my woman!" Hugo backed up, aimed the weapon with his shaky arms; his left arm was out supporting the barrel, and his right hand was holding the receiver, finger shaking over the trigger, his right elbow still out to the side—with that grip, even the light kick from the AR-15 might be enough to miss on a first shot.

"Listen to yourself, Hugo." Nico put his hands up. "I've been locked up down here, where I received the news. I would have told you, man to man, if I wasn't—"

"That's a fucking lie!"

"I give you my word!"

"Your word ain't shit! Mathias told me that you wasn't gonna say shit, that you didn't want to upset morale! Sound familiar, B? Same shit you told me after you cut Eddy's throat."

"And look at that." He rolled his eyes. "The morale is all upset, just like I predicted."

"Motherfuck—"

Nico lunged in just as Hugo started pulling the trigger, grabbing for the barrel through the bars.

4

She and Mathias were making their way to Nico's cell when Ira heard five muffled bangs. She instantly recognized the sound, even through solid concrete and metal.

"That's coming from Nico's cell!" She started sprinting, leaving Mathias behind her.

She rounded the corner and slid to a stop at the door to Nico's cell. She threw the door open and saw Hugo standing before the cell's bars; Nico's hand was clutching the barrel, and Hugo's eyes were wide with primal anger.

Ira's mouth dropped wide. She felt her insides hollow out. The barrel of the AR-15 was in Nico's chest, smoking from the recent discharge.

Hugo's eyes focused on hers, blood spattered all over his face. Ira rushed at him as he attempted to focus the barrel on her—she grabbed it, still hot from murdering her brother, and shoved it sideways just as Hugo squeezed the trigger two more times. She knocked him off his feet with a right hook, keeping hold of the barrel, even as his body hit the floor.

"Let go of the weapon, you fucking bastard!"

"Fuck you!" His fingers were struggling to get to the trigger again. "You and your brother can go to hell!"

Ira reared her boot up and stomped on his face. His hand went limp, and he fell back against the wall, probably unconscious. Her body fell to the floor, clutching and hugging at her brother's rifle.

"Ira." Nico was coughing, wheezing, his words bubbling, oozing; Ira's mind ran wild with possible causes as she stood up and made her way to the bars, dragging the gun with her like a child clutching their favorite teddy bear.

She fumbled for the keys, unlocked the cell, and dropped to Nico's side. Crimson rivulets flowed out from his mouth. Blood gushed from three wounds in his chest and soaked his long johns.

"Oh my god." Her hands hovered frantically over his body, unsure what to do.

She looked around for anything that might help stop the bleeding, then tore part of her shirt off and desperately applied pressure to the three wounds. Her hands were barely big enough to cover them all.

"Do they go all the way through?" Ira said.

"I tried." Nico coughed, creating a fresh stream of bloody rivulets running down his cheeks. "I dodged the first two. Asshole can't shoot. Still nailed me with the last three."

"Don't talk, damn it, save your breath."

"What should I do?" Mathias asked.

"What the hell do you think you should do, Mathias?" Ira said. "Call Lena now!"

"Hang on, Nico," she said. "We're gonna get you some help."

His hand clutched at her arm, shook his head. "I'm done, sis."

Her lips began to quiver, tears warming her cheeks. "No! No you're not!"

"Now—" He started to laugh and it transformed into a coughing fit. "—I bet Hugo told you all about what I did."

"Yeah, but shut up about that, save your strength." She covered her mouth. "I'll scold you later, when you're better!"

"All things considered, much as I deserve it, what a shitty way to go…"

"No, you're not going anywhere!"

"I'm a pretty…pretty terrible person, Ira…what I deserve…"

"No, no, no, you can't go! We need you! I need you!"

His chest started heaving, up and down. His coughs got worse. Blood was coming out his mouth. Ira tried to keep the pressure on his wounds, stop the bleeding, but she knew they probably ran all the way through. Her tears were nearly blinding her.

"Where the hell is she?" Her voice seemed to echo, and Nico's eyes rolled back into his head.

Her bloody hands reached up, slapping at Nico's face as she tried to keep him from going into shock, tried to keep him focused on the sound of her voice. When Lena finally did arrive, she shoved Ira to the side and attempted to stop the bleeding.

When that wasn't enough, she tried CPR in an attempt to revive him.

They were too late.

Nico lay there on the floor of his cell, eyes open wide, a grin on his bloody face, lifeless. She crawled backward, her brother's blood still fresh on her hands, creating a trail leading all the way back to the wall. Her hands dug into her hair and she rocked back and forth, back and forth.

She couldn't stop thinking about how she'd been the one to put him there.

CHAPTER FIFTEEN

"We're so close," Doctor Weber said. "I can feel it."

Weber sat at his desk in the pyramidal room Mathias had awoken in before, scratching at his beard, rubbing at the purple and green bags which hung beneath his eyes like swelling egg sacs, fit to burst at any moment.

Mathias spent the night watching log after log. He had plenty of time for research with Ira and Lena so distracted. The logs gave him great new insight into the man's theories and ambitions—and prepared him further to complete the bargain.

"And as I feel us drawing closer to the end, I can feel his presence...and something *else*," Weber said. "At first, only a couple researchers went missing, volunteers, and that seemed to satiate its appetite, but it always comes back. It's only a matter of time before it gets to me. Carries me off into the shadows to that place which still haunts my dreams.

"I wish I could say that it was luck that protected me so, but it is not. I knew that it would find its way to me eventually, as it did the author of *Messages*. I've surrounded myself with lights and warding symbols as much as is feasible; I've even placed them around my personal deprivation tank.

"Still, I did not anticipate the arrival of the Harvester. He waits for me every time I travel in the tank, snatches me up and drags me to places my mind cannot quite handle. My warding symbols have an effect on him.

"I have not met with the beings Lilly described for a very long time. And I fear that the Harvester will feed my essence to the Eye in the Abyss before long if I do not offer a substitute sacrifice, someone with equal knowledge. Few options exist in that regard.

"Though I do not relish the idea of sacrificing one of the people I'm attempting to save, there is an option. She's seen much of my work, and though I've protected her from the details contained within the grimoire, she would be a ripe substitute if her knowledge were to be...completed."

Mathias thumbed the pages of the grimoire in his hands carefully, caressed its aged leather surface.

"Even if I managed to conduct the experiment successfully, the grimoire is clear. The harvester of the abyss can travel anywhere it so chooses. There is no escape."

A being with the capability to travel anywhere in the universe— no—the multiverse? Mathias couldn't help but glance around the mainframe room, carefully pausing on the shadows.

Then there really is no choice?

He opened the grimoire to the page he'd been studying. There were occult symbols, triangles, all-seeing eyes, strange hieroglyphs, all meant to do one thing.

Summon the Harvester to his world and complete the bargain.

The text that was written in English was very specific. The symbols had to be arranged around the intended sacrifice exactly as it was laid out on the page. If one single, minute detail was off, the text warned of absolute disaster.

The energy requirements were also insane, requiring point-zero five percent of the Sun's total power.

Fortunate we have a fusion reactor, then, Mathias thought.

But the question remained...would the Harvester even honor the bargain? It seemed strange that a being like that would even allow itself to be summoned. It seemed archaic.

It was his only hope, though.

"If I'm unable to contact those beings again, it may become difficult to finish the preparations for the final experiment."

Mathias had seen strange things too. Perhaps even Lilly had, and simply had not reported on them? It made Mathias wonder—*a flicker of doubt*—whether perhaps Weber had been insane himself. And if Weber was insane…what did that say about *him*?

The stress of the experiments had taken its toll on Weber's body in such a short period of time. His gray hair was falling out, and though he was young, his already wrinkled skin was beginning to yellow. Weber's eyes had seen the most change.

"I'll take another session in the tank." Weber rubbed his tired red eyes. They had once been a vibrant green; now they were a dull, lifeless gray. "It's the only kind of rest I can seem to get these days."

It was a curious thing, to hedge your bets and hopes on a potential madman's design, and yet, what choice did he have? After all, madness was no stranger to him. A healthy combination of schizophrenia and Alzheimer's had plagued his family's genetics since the early 1800s.

"I've made tank time mandatory for all research facility personnel. It's my hope that this will give new insights to how the mind's horizon works, how we can finally activate it and pierce through the veil." He shook his head. "But, research personnel, specifically those chosen to be subjects in the Mind's Horizon experiment, are beginning to experience strange things inside their quarters…

"Some have complained about hearing footsteps, disembodied voices, and even claim to have seen personal objects being moved of their own accord. At first I believed that this was nothing more than paranoia; perhaps the combination of being secluded inside the mountain and the nature of our experiments was causing them to imagine things. Wishful thinking. It would seem that the grimoire has a profound effect on everyone around it, even if they themselves know nothing of its existence.

"Now, however, three people have vanished, and the volunteers are starting to ask questions. Since I'm the only one with admin permissions, I'm the only one who has access to the security footage from their rooms. If only they could see what it was that snatched their friends and lovers up.

"It's awake!"

Weber slammed the top of the desk with his fist, then took a lengthy drink from his bottle.

"I remember the first time I saw it. Its eyes, seven of them, pulsing with eerie gray light as it regarded me in the tank, in the darkness of the abyss.

"Did I call it here?"

Another drink. Weber started to slur his words.

"No. If it is the being that killed the grimoire's author, then it is likely tied somehow to the book. I can't let guilt hinder my progress. It is better to be down here than to be up there. The new ice age is beginning to bury the northern states, and I have reports that the northern ice sheet is forming much earlier than climatologists had predicted it would. We thought we had more time, and we were so wrong. The government has decided to give us as much of an operating budget as we'd like, when in the past we were an afterthought.

"I suppose I should be grateful to them, but this definitely is not a good sign. It means they've lost hope that any of their other projects will bear significant fruit."

He paused, and took a drink from the bottle.

"It won't be long before food and gas prices shoot through the roof, and by God, there will be looters, and militias, and if they think the Revolutionists were bad, well, they're about to see the entire country— *no*—the world, fall into a similar conflict. But now, wars won't be fought over land, religion, or ideals. They'll be fought over food, energy, heat, and the right to simply not freeze to death.

"We're fortunate to be down here with our monsters, hidden away from the world and its woes."

Weber checked his phone. "Ah, 6:00 pm, time for my tank session."

He reached for the camera's controls. "End log."

Mathias leaned back in his chair and stretched. He'd watched twelve videos since Lena and Ira had taken Nico's body to the surface to give him a snow burial. Mathias had told Ira that he should get back to work, but he wasn't quite sure she'd heard him. They'd locked Hugo up in Nico's old cell; the blood was still fresh.

That little bit of encouragement he'd given Hugo had done its job well. Though he'd never expected him to go so far as murder. That part was regretful, but the ends would justify the means.

He was going to save them all.

Z

The wind spiraled down, dragging ice crystals into the air in wide sprawling arcs. The dim sunrise was snuffed out by storm clouds, desperately clawing to shut out the light. With the wind and ice stabbing into Ira's facemask, it was almost enough to mask the drying tears pooling in her goggles.

There was a fresh mound of snow covering her brother's corpse. Lena stood bundled up next to her. The tears had stopped, either because she had no more to shed, or because she was so dehydrated that she couldn't physically form them.

They stabbed their shovels into the snow, and Ira fell to her knees, heaving.

"He was a good man," Lena said; an uncomfortable jolt shot up Ira's spine when she felt Lena's hand pat her back.

"No, he wasn't," Ira said.

"What?" More surprise than anger in Lena's voice. She hadn't actually loved Ira's brother; to her he was probably just a fucktoy.

"He was, once, before the war, before all of this. He had demons, and he could be cruel."

"Doesn't mean he wasn't good."

Her eyes stabbed up at Lena; for once, her body language wasn't hostile. Maybe she was feeling guilty for her part in his death. If it weren't for her not being able to keep her legs closed…

"I never liked funerals," Ira said.

"Who does?"

"Not for the obvious reasons." Ira stood up and took a deep breath. "I never liked how we seem to rewrite their lives, to shape the dead into someone we can live with. People's lives are so much more complicated than that. In some ways, we're all monsters."

"For what it's worth, I'm really sorry."

Part of Ira wanted to strangle Lena, wanted to knock her teeth out and make her face look as ugly as she was inside. "Whatever. Maybe you two were made for each other."

Lena nodded. "Maybe."

"I always knew this was a possibility. And, goddamn it, it hurts so fucking much. How do I manage without him? Without Eddy?"

Lena hugged her, held her close, and she tried not to go completely stiff. For what it was worth, Lena was trying to comfort her, even if she was only doing it to make herself feel better about what she'd done.

"I wish I'd never found that damn heat signature," Ira said. "Then Eddy and Nico would still be with us."

"You can't know that," Lena said.

Ira shook her head. "I should be blaming you and Hugo...but if I hadn't locked him in that cell...if I'd listened to his pleas, and believed that he was innocent..."

"I don't even know if he was. He didn't talk much, and he spent a lot of time alone."

Ira broke free of Lena's grip and kicked at the snow, causing a wave of icicles to wash over Nico's grave. "Damn you, Nico! Goddamn you!"

"Come on." Lena tugged at Ira's coat. "Let's go inside."

"You go. I want to be alone with him."

Lena nodded, and Ira watched her trudge back to the mouth of the cave.

Ira let the harsh wind beat into her, tugging at her clothes and threatening to expose portions of her skin to the violent cold. Part of her wanted to rip her clothes off right there, to dive into the snow and join her brother. But that probably wasn't what he'd want.

He'd want her to push on, no matter how much it hurt.

"I remember when we were just kids," Ira said. "I was always so jealous of you. You with your achievements in sports, track, all those trophies. Mom and Dad always praised you for that, and never once me for maintaining my grades, even when I got straight A's and got on the honor roll. I hated you for that sometimes.

"And then high school ended, and you went off to fight for the army, before the war, before the divide. I wasn't much for politics, but I knew things were changing, and not necessarily for the better." She shook her head. "I hated that you left us, but goddamn it, I missed you so much. Because, even when we fought, I always knew we loved each other. I remember the good times, and the bad, and I won't try to change who you were in my mind. You were a monster, created for the new imperial regime, and you never once questioned their orders, even though part of you knew they were wrong. You killed innocent people and violated the Constitution for nothing more than your twisted sense of loyalty.

"But, you were also my brother, and you saved my life, and I loved you."

She crossed her arms, held herself.

"No one's coming to our rescue now, and you're gone. I go back and forth. I have to find the strength to protect Mathias and Lena, even though, in some ways, I couldn't care less about them. But it's what you did. I can't give up looking for Eddy, either. If there's one good thing that came out of your death, it's that I have a reasonable doubt that you did it. What kind of irony would it be if I gave up, when there might still be a chance to save him?"

She could see a few buildings off in the distance, what was once known as San Bernardino; the skyline looked colder now.

She was a long way from home.

"Rest in peace, brother."

3

The stars were quiet today. Eddy's mind felt numb from the nonstop visions he'd seen. The monsters were silent now. It was the closest thing to peace that he'd been allowed to experience in what felt like years...maybe eons.

He was orbiting a red giant, standing on the boiling surface of a planet whose landmasses were breaking apart. Solar flares arced from the star, stabbing into the planet's crust, pulling it into a deadly embrace.

No, not *he*.

He wasn't anything. *He* was consciousness. A phantom wandering the eternal void. That's what the entities had told him—or—at least, that's what he thought they'd told him. If they were a thing at all. These were different than the dark things he'd encountered, the one he'd seen cons ago, the one that swallowed stars to spread its own darkness. These were bright, luminous beings, who wanted to help him, help him transcend beyond his current state. They tried to tell him he was alive, that what he perceived as real was only an illusion of the mind.

That he was in danger.

There are things beyond gods, beyond time.

He didn't believe them. He had to be dead. If he wasn't, why hadn't he woken up yet?

They claimed to have been in contact with others of his species, that the human race was headed for disaster. Claimed that they were violating their government's directorate in reaching out to him. That there was only one way for humanity to survive at their current technological level.

They told him he wasn't ready to travel, wasn't ready to move beyond this universe. He didn't understand…wasn't he already traveling?

A bright light came from above, and suddenly the stars were silenced, replaced by something he felt couldn't possibly be there. It was the face of a man he'd once known when he was alive, eons in the past on a world that had to be long since dead. His image was murky, like he was being viewed through a tank filled with water.

Mathias.

That was his name. He was talking, but Eddy didn't have ears to hear anymore.

Eddy vaguely remembered being lowered down into the tank. He could see the bridge of his nose, and the hose Mathias had fed him to keep him breathing air.

Could he still have been in the tank all this time? Was he still healing?

It had to be a lie. He wasn't really there. This had to be a trick, another vision given by the entities.

The image faded, and darkness returned; the stars came back.

Mathias grinned and locked the tank's hatch tight. Eddy was still alive and well, vitals still strong. He'd returned a couple times before to give him food and water. Each time, Eddy had looked more and more confused. He'd refused to speak the last time, even.

He was going mad inside the tank.

Fascinating.

The readouts in the observation room showed that his heart rate had spiked a few times in the last twelve hours, probably due to hallucinations brought on by his experience. Mathias chuckled to himself. Or, maybe he'd made contact with those same entities that Weber and Lilly spoke of? Had he seen the Harvester as well?

Mathias placed the grimoire down on the table inside the observation room, opening it to the appropriate page. He opened his pack, spreading its contents across the table; a paint brush, black and white cans of paint from one of the storage rooms, and a spool of wire to add to the pyramidal formation surrounding the tank.

It took quite a while to mark up the circle around the tank. He had to account for the tubes and wires snaking from the center of the chamber.

He hoped that Ira and Lena would still be busy. Too busy to go poking around the facility.

The circle consisted of hieroglyphs from before even the dinosaurs had existed on this world, before the time of the Earth even. To look at them was to invite things into this world that would drive weaker minds insane. Their names whispered through his mind as he etched them.

The Harvester's true name caused Mathias to shudder as he painted its markings on the surface of the tank.

Lai'thamia.

The word echoed through his mind like a disembodied whisper.

Lai'thamia.

Lai'thamia.

Lai'thamia!

The concrete floor rumbled with each symbol he painted, as if, at any moment, the walls would crumble away to reveal a hellish landscape where pyramids rule a burning sky circling a black hole. Where tentacles reach out from the event horizon to grab at knowledge not fit for weak minds. Where crumbling buildings older than the Earth itself float toward the dark.

Lai'thamia.

Lai'thamia.

Lai'thamia!

With the last symbol painted in the circle, he stood up. His hands were covered in black and white paint, but even he had to admit that his skin looked…lighter.

Lai'thamia.

No. Grayer. His skin looked *gray*.

He smiled so wide it hurt.

It was time.

He retreated to the observation room, safely tucked away behind the two-way mirror.

With a shaky hand, he turned the machines on and said the words.

Then, it seemed as if time itself was altered.

The Earth itself shakes, Mathias falls to his knees. The rumbling reverberates in his very bones. He claws his way back to his feet.

The walls inside the chamber are cracking, rumbling, then they're falling away into the dark. It is not the burning sky from his vision, however.

Something is wrong.

The walls continue to crumble and fall away into the Astral Lands, into a starscape where frozen planets drift aimlessly through the dark, where cloudy tendrils block out dim, faraway stars and galaxies.

There's something else in the dark.

It's not Lai'thamia, or even the creature Weber described. It's something else entirely.

Crimson eyes ignite in the dark like cosmic forest fires. Its eyes find Eddy's body. Mathias sees a dark mass silhouette and eclipse the surface of a gas giant.

Then, with tentacles like clouds of ash, it reaches out, into the chamber where Eddy drifts inside the tank.

It wraps itself around the tank. Then it's opening the lid, feeling its way inside.

Mathias is worried for his life now.

He scrambles for the door, but it won't open.

Eddy's screams make him turn back and watch. The cloudy tentacles rip the metallic lid off the tank, and then they force their way inside...until Eddy's screams are silenced.

CHAPTER SIXTEEN

Somehow, Mathias made it back to Weber's chamber at the top of the facility. He found himself on all fours, lethargically tearing his clothes from his body, crawling toward the deprivation tank at the center of the chamber. It stood inside a powerful warding symbol, which Weber referred to as the eye of the abyss—the same pyramidal shape Mathias had seen in some of the experiment chambers.

He could scarcely recall what had happened after he got the door to the experiment chamber open. It was like a nightmare. He hadn't dared look behind him as the door slammed shut, hadn't dared look back at what might have happened to Eddy as he ran screaming down the length of the corridor.

Scrambling down the hall, he'd felt tremors in the floor, echoing out from the experiment chamber. He desperately hoped that Ira and Lena had not felt them.

He'd failed, and Eddy had paid the price.

With shaky gray-skinned hands, he removed the lid to the deprivation tank and slipped the breathing mask over his head. The saline solution was discolored. Drunkenly, he brought up the controls on the side and had fresh solution cycled into the tank via tubes on the sides of the tank that receded into the floor. Once it was filled, he allowed himself to sink backward into it.

He hadn't even closed the lid and could already see why being inside the tank was so disorienting. Maybe he'd never get used to it.

He allowed himself to float there, adjusting to the feeling—the unique sensation of not being able to feel where his skin ended and where the universe began.

He chuckled and closed the lid on top of himself, bathing himself in infinite darkness.

It was freeing, in a way.

2

"What the hell was that?" Lena said.

Ira could have sworn that she felt the Earth shaking. "I'm not sure…"

She'd been outside, visiting Nico's grave, when it happened. Lena came running to her shortly after. They both retreated back into the cave mouth.

It wasn't like any earthquake she'd ever felt. As if the universe were opening up to swallow them whole.

The sky had seemed to darken for a moment.

Lena caressed a large crack in the curvature of the wall. "Was this here before?"

Would these tremors become more prevalent? Would cracks in the walls be the least of their worries?

She had a terrible feeling in the pit of her stomach.

"I need to check on our prisoner," Ira said.

Lena nodded.

Ira found herself in the elevator, holding herself.

Was the air conditioning running? It seemed colder for some reason. She'd have to look into it later.

She stepped off and headed toward the holding cell.

After opening the door to the brig, she couldn't help but breathe a sigh of relief when she saw that Hugo was still locked safely behind the bars.

Her footsteps echoing off the walls didn't bring his attention to her.

"You're a coward." Ira's voice was cold; she could feel the anger rising within her just from seeing him, like pressure beneath a volcano, ready to erupt.

Hugo's hands tightened on the bare mattress. Her brother's blood was still wet on the smooth stone floor. She found herself fantasizing about bashing Hugo's skull into the wall. Repeating it again and again in her head.

His hands clasped together; those muted blue eyes met hers, his teeth bared.

"Open that cage," he said. "Find out."

Ira squeezed her fists so tight they started to go numb. She could almost taste it. Imagining herself pummeling him to death, his teeth broken and scattered across the pale gray floor, his blood, washing away Nico's, becoming one with the stone of this hellish place.

Or, she could drag him kicking and screaming from his cell, and put him in one of those experiment chambers. Liquefy his organs with shock therapy, fry his brains with meds.

There were no courts here. The world was mad. Why shouldn't she judge him? Why shouldn't she get justice for her brother's murder?

She thought of Nico.

How much he had changed after coming home from the war. How his PTSD had made him violent or irrational. How he'd eyed his stump in his room.

No, she thought. *I won't become like you, brother.*

"You're going to rot in there forever if I have anything to say about it," she said. "And I do. This entire base is now keyed to my voice and biometrics. If I wanted to, I could leave and command the facility to suck out all the air from this room. I could watch you suffocate to death on camera while I drink a hot cup of coffee and enjoy the show."

His angry expression eroded; his mouth hung open, eyes wild, desperate. "You wouldn't!"

She rushed the bars and pounded on them with her arms. "You murdered my brother! Don't tell me what I will or won't do to you, you fucking monster!"

"He took my woman and killed your man!"

"You lost Lena by being a useless slob, by being a coward! And, instead of owning up to your failure, you took his life, shooting him through these bars while he could do nothing to defend himself!

Leaving you in there, rotting until you starve, or suffocating you, would be a goddamned mercy compared to what you deserve!"

"I found him after he did it." Hugo let his eyes rest on the floor. Was it remorse or satisfaction she saw in his eyes? "After he cut Eddy. He made me swear I wouldn't say anything, or else."

"He was having panic attacks, he couldn't control himself—"

"You really believe that, B?"

"If you're trying to justify what you did, it won't help you. Besides, Eddy is still alive."

"Open the gate." Hugo's eyes met hers, pleading, remorseful.

"No."

"Open the gate!" He stood up, pumping his fists to his chest.

"If I do that, you *will* die."

His skinny frame was shaking; he reached a hand up to the fresh bruise that her boot had left on his face. For all his taunting, she knew he was afraid of her.

"Think about that," she said, "while you rot down here in the darkness."

She was standing in the doorway, Hugo begging at the bars.

"Facility AI: engage," she said. "Turn off all lights in solitary confinement cell 2."

The lights faded until Hugo was plunged into darkness. She opened the door and stepped out into the light. The last thing she saw were his pleading eyes—and something else...seven gray eyes in the dark...but she was too angry to feel remorse or fear for her own paranoid hallucinations.

She closed the door behind her and locked it.

3

Mathias lost count of the hours inside the tank.

For some reason, he saw his classmates from Caltech; he was sitting in a familiar seat, in a familiar lecture hall, for a class which he hated. The only one that he'd ever come close to failing: ethics.

One of his classmates, a religious woman who had no love for science (and hadn't she hated him most of all?) would always ask inane questions that Professor Adams couldn't help but answer, distracting the class and derailing the Professor's lectures for an hour or more at a time.

She wore modest clothes that befit a woman twice her age and born several centuries before.

He remembered one derailment above all others: "When do you think science has gone too far? Do we dare to play God with our cloning, or the strange things we're doing with our particle colliders? Will we only be satisfied when we open a portal to hell itself?"

Some of the students had actually applauded her.

Fools.

He recalled how he'd stood up in the middle of her soap box: "We are God."

He'd watched as her mouth dropped open, ready to tear into him with some religiously fueled diatribe.

"We are gods. Not because we are all-powerful," he had said, "but because the existence of a God is brought about by the very reason why we experiment, why science was born: the need to explain the unknown, the need to understand that which hasn't been explained yet.

"But, we mean to progress beyond mere superstition, to use evidence instead of faith. It wasn't long ago that your ancestors believed I should be made to pick cotton, and serve a master, where my intellect would've been wasted because of someone's inability to form a reasonable thought. Their *belief*, as it were. So, yes, I choose science over God, or gods, and there isn't a damned thing you can do about it.

"Your beliefs will erode as our progress spreads, and you will be left behind to clutch at your Bible as you shame our progress, and predict the coming of the end of the world by fire and brimstone, which will never happen. The end of the world will be by chance, by an ice age, or by an asteroid, or a comet, but humanity will survive, because that's what we do, and it has nothing to do with faith."

Her eyes were wide, her mouth agape. She had sat down and crossed herself, and a few of his silent colleagues had clapped for his speech. Professor Adams had not been as impressed, but he'd attempted to get the class back on track at last.

Was that how it had happened? He couldn't be sure. Perhaps his speech hadn't been nearly as eloquent, perhaps it was only what he'd wished he'd have said? After that semester, he heard that the religious woman had dropped out of school to become a missionary. He hadn't even bothered to learn what her major was, but he'd been glad she was gone.

Now, when he saw her, her complexion was pale, frost clinging to her dead skin. Her eyes drifted slowly, her cataract-filled pupils focusing on him.

"You were right," she said. "In a way. But the human race will not survive this."

"We will," he said, grinning. "I will."

She laughed, revealing her rotted and stained teeth. "No. You will not. I've seen the truth, Mathias. There is no God. But, there are other things. I've seen them. I've seen them.

"One of them has its sights on you.

"It won't rest until you're gobbled up by the abyss!

"The Harvester is coming for you, Mathias, coming for you!"

A foul wind carried by her sickening cackle filled the classroom. The walls cracked, shattering and peeling away into the starless night sky.

When he turned back to her, she was gone. He was standing on the cliff, facing the ice cave that led into the facility. There was a mound of snow roughly the size of a human male.

The soft cries of a little girl filled the freezing air. She wept, bundled up and on all fours, her tears floating away into the freezing wind like snowflakes.

There was someone else, too. Mathias saw the back of someone's exposed head, standing over the grave as if he'd just materialized there. The mohawk was familiar. Nico turned to him, but his eyes were black, his mouth oozing something dark and insipid; his bullet wounds were festering, becoming frostbit.

"It's your fault." Nico's voice echoed through the tank, through the black. "You killed me."

"And how do you know this?" Mathias said.

"You were the only one in the cell who could have heard Lena say what she said. You told Hugo about me and Lena."

"I did," Mathias said. "Though it's regrettable that you had to die, sometimes that's what progress is. I'm going to save everyone. I'm going to do what you never could."

"I will be with you for the rest of your life."

"Too bad I don't believe in ghosts." Mathias chuckled. "Now go away, be forgotten like the rest of humanity."

Nico turned around and sat down atop his grave.

A creature sprung up from his shadow. Its seven eyes pulsed from the darkness. The eyes seemed to be arranged in a diamond on its rather large head. Thin, dark spikes shot off from its back, silhouetted by the purple ice and the dim glow of the moon above. It was like a panther, or a salamander, or both, but it seemed to be out of phase somehow, like it was both physically there and made from pure shadow.

It crouched low, like a cat ready to pounce.

All reason fled from Mathias's mind as he turned, running straight into the mouth of the ice cave. The creature's growls reached him, bouncing off the ceiling and walls of the cave.

The cave transformed before his eyes. Gone were the familiar doors to the facility, the tunnel ending in a ledge, a cliff overlooking a familiar stone room—built around a hole in the floor that housed a black hole. There was a staircase to the left of the icy cliff. He felt compelled to walk down, to face the black hole at the center of the room.

It was finished devouring a star, its tentacles reaching out to find other sources of sustenance.

The Harvester was standing at the edge, a frown carved in its ancient mask.

"I know I botched the ritual," Mathias said.

The Harvester nodded.

"If Eddy isn't gone, I can try again!"

The Harvester shook its head. *No.*

The Harvester's hollow whisper of a voice crept through his mind like maggots eating away at his brain stem. His knees buckled and he fell on all fours. "You don't have to take me yet, there are others!"

The Harvester turned to him. Its appendages reaching out, grasping at his frail body, lifting him up into the stale air of that ancient place, dangling him over the edge of the black hole.

"Give me more time! Please!"

Mathias closed his eyes, but even then he could not unsee the truth of the abyss.

At its center, he could see a dim green light. An eye encircled by like impossibly juxtaposed pyramids. The Harvester's master.

The Harvester pulled Mathias's body back over the edge and flung him across the floor, back toward the cave mouth high above the room.

Then, the creature was gone.

Was it toying with him?

If so, why?

He had to get out of there, he had to run, before it changed its mind.

You will never be able to hide, the Harvester said, filling his mind fit to burst. *You are all but playthings.*

Mathias screamed, tossing the lid to the tank onto the floor. He clawed his way out of the tank, his heart pounding through his chest, the harsh light from Weber's personal chamber causing him to shield his eyes in reflex. He sat on the cool linoleum floor, allowing himself a moment to come back to reality.

He was running out of time. Just like Weber.

Ira scratched her chin and leaned back in her chair.

She was watching Mathias on the security cam. He was at the top of the facility, in Weber's own personal chambers. He'd just climbed out of a sensory deprivation tank screaming. She watched him dry himself off and find his clothes. He looked like he had been spooked by something, and his steps were hurried.

Why was he using the tank?

She felt like she didn't want to know the answer.

CHAPTER SEVENTEEN

*S*omething is calling him from the shadows of the facility, radiating out *from a central point high above him, carried through lines, triangles, pyramidal shapes, waves, and curling, twisting things.*

There's something else too. A voice. It tells him to leave his chrysalis. It's so loud and violent he feels it may crack his skull in two if he does not obey.

With fingers that aren't his own, fingers that stretch and flow and wrap around things like snakes constricting on prey, he feels. The lid to his chrysalis is loose.

Yes. Open it.

With a push, it flops open, allowing the sounds of the room to fill his one good ear.

His body is much larger now. Much *larger. His considerable mass spills out from his chrysalis, down onto the cold metal stairs and floor. He finds his way to the mirror.*

He caresses the mirror even though his eyes are blackened, leaking pits of ash. It spills out from his rotting sockets and down his ruined cheeks. Yet, even so, he is not blind. He can feel the chamber even better than he could before, feel the energy pulsing through the entire facility, feels it deep in his bones.

He lumbers out into the corridor with legs like tree trunks, leaving ashen filth in his wake.

Only one thing matters now.

He must feed.

2

At first, it seemed like a normal session inside the mainframe room. Ira was at her console, observing Mathias's actions at his station. He seemed to be avoiding Weber's personal logs now, instead digging into the scientific papers, blueprints, and the final experiment logs. What was he up to? A sickness began to rest in the pit of her gut.

Mathias clicked on the last log file that wasn't corrupted.

"They called me a madman," Weber said. "They said that this work was the work of a desperate fool, that I was grasping at straws! But after today those straws will have borne fruit, and the human race will be saved.

"Sure, there's been sacrifices. That *thing* has been hard at work to make sure that none of us survive this, but I intend to win out, as I won out against the Harvester."

The video was playing in the left-hand corner of her screen, where she could minimize it should Mathias wander within line of sight of her monitor. She turned, looked at Mathias, but he didn't notice; she readjusted her headphones, and kept watching.

Weber's hair had begun to fall out; his skin was splotchy, dark blue circles hung beneath his eyes, and his yellowed teeth had black splotches growing beneath infected gums. Was this the effect that his obsession was having on his body, or did it have something to do with that grimoire?

Could something like that actually have a physical effect on someone?

A voice deep inside of her said: *Only if it's real, only if the things whispering to you are eons old.*

Eldritch things.

She shuddered.

"I do not pretend to know what the outcome of this grand experiment will be," Weber said. "But, once the core is primed, and I have the necessary calculations made, the remaining staff and I will conduct the final experiment. This time, on our selves. If it's—when it's successful, the limited automation within the facility will cut off all of the facility's systems, except for atmospherics, and everything besides the fusion core will be shut down.

"I haven't bothered alerting the government to our progress. I've decided that they can come search for it, if they wish. But I suspect all they'll end up doing is feeding themselves to that *thing*."

The thing she'd seen. The thing with the diamond pattern of eyes, seven eyes that had pulsed gray in the dark as she closed the door on Hugo.

Maybe he was dead?

Things like that don't exist. Like ghosts and demons and all that stupid crap. Only children believed that stuff. But why, then, was she so damned scared?

"If humanity is to survive, then it is our right, as scientists, to save it, and leave the filth behind to perish on frozen Earth."

Weber's chest was heaving. He was laughing.

"I have to agree with him." Mathias's voice made her jump up as he forced his hand over her mouth.

Soft fabric brushed over her lips. She struggled, kicking and grabbing for Mathias's face, but it was already too late. Her vision blurred. She tried to stand, balancing her weight on her table, and collapsed on the floor.

"I have to say," Mathias said. "It was rather smart to plant that malware on my machine. I almost would have fallen for it, if it weren't for how you acted whenever I came into view of you. You're a terrible snoop, Ira."

She couldn't speak, the chloroform did its thing, and soon she let darkness swallow her...

Seven eyes, pulsing gray in the dark.

3

Her nostrils flared. She reeled back at the sharp, stabbing aroma of smelling salts. Her head hit the back of something metallic, causing a loud bang to echo off concrete walls.

She tried to scream, but something was jammed in her mouth. Moving her head too far in any direction threatened to tear her hair from her scalp. Her hands and feet were restrained as well.

Her mind was in a fog, but she knew there was only one person who could have done this to her. She took a quick glace around the room to get her bearings. She was seated next to a metal table, and there were workstations and monitors directly in front of her, as well as a blacked-out two-way mirror.

Oh no, she thought.

"Ah, you're awake." Mathias's voice came from behind her; he sounded far too excited for her comfort. "I'm so glad. Truly. Now we can get down to business."

She tried to mouth a few choice curses at him, but only managed garbled nonsense. Mathias walked out from behind her; he was sporting a white lab coat over his long johns and a smug shit-eating grin that stretched from ear to ear.

"I do apologize, Ira, but you left me no other choice. You were getting too close." He pulled up a metal chair and sat down next to her. His right arm rested on the table, his hand clutching something tightly. Maybe a remote, or a small knife? "You forced my hand, but you'll see that it's all for the best."

She tried to ask him why he was doing this, what he wanted with her, but again all she managed to produce was incoherence.

He shushed her and shook his head. "I'm getting to that. Everything I've done here has been carefully planned and orchestrated."

She stared into his fading brown eyes, watched the sweat bead across his forehead. He almost looked remorseful. That was it. It made so much sense now. He must have been the one who told Hugo about Lena's pregnancy.

She shook her chair, testing the tight hold the tape had on her limbs. She wanted to reach out with clawed hands, to wring that scrawny little neck until his eyes popped from their sockets!

He seemed to be taken aback by her expression and leaned back in his chair, toying with the thing in his right hand.

"I feared you might be like this." He frowned and pressed a button at the end of the remote he held tight in his hand; the lights on the other side of the two-way mirror revealed one of the experiment chambers she'd seen in so many log entries. This one featured a vertical sensory deprivation tank in the center of a glass pyramidal structure, which was housed inside a particle collider. "Do you want to know who's inside that tank?" He smiled. "I'm sure you could use a happy reunion after all the hardship you've seen."

He clicked another button on his remote, which woke the screens at each of the workstations. One of the screens showed an infrared view of the interior of the tank; she couldn't believe whose face she saw.

"That's right. Eddy's in that tank, waiting for you to rescue him."

She struggled with her restraints again. She'd stretched the adhesive enough to be able to wriggle her left wrist a bit.

"I've been taking very good care of him, I assure you, and making sure he gets the minimum necessary nutrients this whole time. Well, until I encouraged you to gain admin access to all systems in the base." He stood up, walking back toward the consoles at the other side of the room. "Which is where my game comes to a head. You might be wondering why I risked letting you gain so much power, but I needed to witness how you did it. How you were able to hack into the other databases and systems, yes, but most of all, the password to the admin network. It was the look on your face that gave it away really. John Lilly was the key. Though I'm sure you've since changed the password to something that reflects your own obsessions…no, you wouldn't be that stupid, would you?" He chuckled and moved back toward her, placed his hands next to the tape that wrapped around her head. "Now, I'm going to remove this, and you're going to do exactly as I say, or else I'm going to activate this experiment chamber, and you'll never see Eddy again.

"Nod once if you understand."

Her heart thrummed, her face flushed with heat, and she felt control of her emotions snap like a rope carrying too much weight. He meant business; she didn't think she could handle seeing Eddy vanish in one of those experiments so soon after losing Nico.

She nodded once. It took every ounce of willpower for her to do it, but she did.

"Good." He ripped the tape off; fire raged across the lower half of her face.

She spat a wadded-up sock onto the floor. "You're a sick bastard, you know that?"

"And here I thought you were going to be compliant," Mathias said. "I'm disappointed—"

"I'm going to fucking kill you!"

"No, no you're not." He held up the remote. "Because one press of this button, and you say goodbye to Eddy, disappeared into another world, another Earth. Or, maybe, a pile of gelatinous goo? Who knows for sure. Although, either way, one might say that I would be saving him from this hellish icy Earth."

"Save him? Do you fucking hear yourself?" She shook her head. "He's trapped inside a tank, you idiot!"

"I don't expect you to understand the science behind this. It's far more complicated than you know. Rest assured that I'm quite certain this will work."

"Oh, great, you're convinced, that makes me feel *so* much better about liquefying my best *fucking* friend!"

He held up the device, his thumb hovering over the button. "Shut up and listen."

She bit her lip until she tasted the copper of blood spilling onto her tongue.

"Now for my demands. You're going to turn over all voice and biometric access to me, and you're going to give me the password to the admin system."

She held her words and stared at the remote he held in his right hand. She wondered if she could get her hand free, if she would be fast enough to knock it out of his grip and strangle him. Then she wondered if it was worth the risk. Her eyes drifted to the tank at the center of the experiment chamber. Where the man she loved had been kept this whole time, probably slowly losing his mind inside a formless abyss where seven-eyed abominations dwelled. She could only imagine what he'd been through, what was going through his mind now.

Would he even be the same Eddy she'd known?

Her eyes drifted to the readout screen that was monitoring his vitals. They seemed weak.

"You're trying to think of some way to stop me," Mathias said. "It's against your best interests, I assure you. I'm going to save us all."

"Even you have to have figured out that Weber's experiments were insane!"

"Were they? If that were so true, then where are their bodies? We see some corpses left over from the first few experiments, sure, but none from the final experiment. Why is that? This facility once housed five hundred personnel. The door logs show that a lockdown went into effect some time into the spreading of the ice sheets. No one was permitted in or out for some reason."

"What he was trying to do made no sense! You can't put someone in a fishbowl and expect them to pop into another dimension!"

"But you can!" Mathias slammed his fist into the table, the clanging sound echoing through the chamber. "You smug little woman. You know nothing about what is and isn't possible. Nothing!" He spat at the floor. "I've seen things that would drive you mad!"

"I'm sure you think you have."

"You'll see soon enough. When we're all safe on another Earth. Then you'll thank me." Her eyes drifted over to the readout screens. The impression of Eddy's face looked odd to her. Mathias's voice shocked her back to attention. "It's probably over your head, but there's a theory in quantum physics called quantum non-locality. In quantum non-locality, local realism breaks down and contradicts what we perceive at the subatomic level. Matter behaves differently when it's observed, and vice versa. But, most of all, human consciousness, an effect we so incorrectly ascribed to merely being a product of our complex brains, is non-local as well. This consciousness is what affects reality: it bends it, influences it like a probability generator, and makes the evolution of complex life possible. Your perception of reality affects everything."

"What the fuck does that have to do with transporting us to another Earth in a metal tank?"

Mathias sighed, rubbed his eyes. "The tank is only a catalyst to finding the mind's horizon."

She rolled her eyes. "Oh, great, this again."

"No—" He grabbed her chin and forced her to look him in the eyes. "—you *will* listen to me. You people are so smug in your ignorance, the way you ignored me this whole time, talking behind my back as if I were crazy long before we even found this place. I'm sick of it!"

Her heart knocked against her ribcage again and again. "Fine, fine, I'll listen."

He relaxed, his expression softening. "I'll make it simple for you to understand. There are three different types of horizons that are important to us. There's the local horizon that we perceive on Earth, and it's represented by a circle on the sphere. The higher a person is in the air, the larger that circle is."

"Right, a circle..." She glanced back at the readout screen. There seemed to be a glitch in the video output. Eddy's expression looked unchanged.

"Yes, a circle. Pay attention here, Ira, it gets better. I'm sure you know what a black hole is, yes?"

She nodded.

"At the center of a black hole, there's something called an event horizon. The event horizon is something we don't really understand, but it's the point of no return for light and matter, essentially. There are some who believe that black holes are gateways to other universes, and this may be true to a point."

"And the third?"

His eyes lit up. "Ah, you *are* listening. The third is the cosmic horizon. The furthest light that has reached us from the known edge of the universe. We've observed galaxies older than the universe, moving faster than light from our relative perspective. Suggesting that the universe may have no end. Are you ready for the fourth?"

She shook her head. "I don't want to know."

"Oh, I think you'll find this fascinating." He leaned closer; his breath stank like day-old coffee. "The mind's horizon is the point of no return, the point at which the mind loses the ability to perceive its surroundings. If consciousness manipulates reality around us, then what happens to reality if we lose the ability to perceive it?

"This universe is a strange place, Ira, filled with even stranger beings. Some of which have no love for our species.

"Now, imagine if there was such a device that could free your consciousness from the trappings of our perceived reality? If you could change the frequency at which your molecules vibrated at and access another universe?"

"I've heard all of this in Weber's logs, you're not going to convince me that he was right by giving me a science lecture. All you're missing is his talk of eldritch demons and grimoires from dead Alaskan researchers. You sound just like him."

"You're probably right." Mathias frowned. "I've never been particularly good at explaining these things to the lay person. But, in the end, it doesn't matter if you believe me. You'll hand over the password for Eddy's life.

For a moment, she thought about telling him to go to hell...but her eyes drifted to the tank that Eddy was confined in. If she gave Mathias what he wanted, he wouldn't stop there. He'd lock them all up and force them to participate in his sick experiments.

On the other hand, if she didn't give into his demands, Eddy would be the one to suffer.

"What's it going to be, Ira?" Mathias asked.

She sighed, closing her eyes; she could feel the blood from her lip flowing onto her chin, caressing her neck. "As long as you let Eddy go, I'll do it."

Mathias's thick lips spread into a twisted yellow grin. She couldn't help but think of Weber's physical condition at the end of his log entries, how he'd let himself fall to pieces chasing his mad obsession.

Maybe Mathias had found the grimoire. Maybe that was the source of his madness?

"You made the right choice," Mathias said, smiling.

She wriggled her wrists. "Can you untie me now? I'll have to get my laptop from the mainframe room..."

"Oh, I'm afraid not." His smile quickly faded. "I'm not sure I trust you. Even though I've got Eddy, now that you know, you could use your control over the facility to shut down the systems in this chamber, removing my bargaining chip from the board. That's why I chose this location. The experiment chambers have no voice authentication software, and they don't require biometric access from the admin."

"Then we have a problem; I can't give you access without my stuff."

He reached behind the desk and retrieved her laptop. "How fortunate for you that I brought it with us for this very purpose. How forward-thinking of me."

Her eyes smoldered inside their sockets. Every possible way she could think of to maneuver around Mathias had been countered; in their time working together, he hadn't just gotten to know her, hadn't just helped her, he had been studying her, how she thought, how she reacted, so he could plan around that and counter any move she might make. It was like a god damned game to him.

I have to do something, she thought.

Mathias opened the laptop and the screen woke instantly, bringing up her password interface. "Care to tell me the password? I'm not going to untie your hands."

She could feel the skin on her brow wrinkle from her eyebrows creasing. She wanted to stall him somehow, wanted to scream for help...but no one would hear her down here.

She had no choice.

"The password is..." It was like she was being violated. Her computer had always been an extension of her own body. Where it went, she went—even after the world had ended. She took in a deep sigh. "48373FGH space 7820A20J."

"You really do value your security." He entered the two sets of numbers and letters she'd told him. "I'm not surprised you would choose something this random. Even Weber personalized his passwords. It makes me wonder. Do you have any favorite books?"

"Just shut up and release Eddy."

"Oh, come now, you can answer the question, can't you?"

She paused, staring at the floor. This fucker just wouldn't quit. "I liked Gibson."

"I imagined you played more video games than read *actual* books. I should have guessed that Gibson would be at the top of your list though, even if his work is a bit dated."

"Please stop talking, you'll ruin my nostalgia."

"Fine, have it your way." He turned the laptop to face himself. "Tell me how to gain access."

"You'll need the password I made for the admin account first. I have a shortcut on my desktop."

"Ah, now what?"

"Now I give you the password."

He waited there, straight-faced, while she mustered up the courage to betray Lena and Eddy.

"SEVEN-SIX-D-TWO space S-D-SIX-ZERO space A-TWO-J-NINE space THREE-D-D-Y," she said.

"Ah!" He smiled again. "Now. I'll reset the admin password and change over the voice authorization and biometrics. You've been so helpful, Ira."

"You'll release Eddy, right?"

He frowned, avoided eye contact with her. "Of course I will. I'm going to release both of you soon enough."

"What the hell does that mean?"

His face softened somewhat.

Her eyes drifted to the screens which showed Eddy's face...

That's when she figured out what looked so strange about it. The footage seemed to be looping. Then there were the painted hieroglyphs on the tank, the broken padlock hanging from the lid. Her heart sank. "He's not really in there..."

"No." Was it shame or fear that she saw on his face? "I'm afraid he escaped hours ago."

"Escaped?" She struggled in her restraints. "Let me the fuck out of these, I have to find him!"

"You won't recognize him, I'm afraid."

"This is your fault!" She stared down at her immobile hands and feet. How much effort would it take to tear herself free? Every inch of her wanted to see Mathias die, to crack his skull open on the cold cement and watch his blood pool dark and red beneath her.

"You're probably thinking of ways to try and kill me," Mathias said. "But that would be foolish, I assure you." He picked up a washcloth and dabbed it against a bottle filled with chemicals, most likely chloroform, and walked behind her. "I may be generous. I may desire for you to live, to travel to a new Earth with me, but if you upset me too much, well, I can't be held responsible for what happens to you."

He forced the washcloth over her mouth; she tried to hold her breath, tried not to breathe even if it meant she'd die from suffocation. But even in that first breath, she'd already inhaled too much, and her vision was beginning to blur.

"For what it's worth, I didn't despise you," Mathias said.

She focused her eyes on the deprivation tank through the glass, her heart reaching out to Eddy...wherever he might be.

Somehow that's worse, she thought.

CHAPTER EIGHTEEN

For a moment, she thought it was all over; but the air blowing from the ventilation system told her otherwise.

Her eyes failed to adjust to the total dark, failed to see the thing that was staring back at her.

She felt out her surroundings: smooth concrete across her fingertips, a thin bed beside her, and a cold metallic wall at her back. She crawled forward on her hands and knees; her hands passed over a spot that felt textured and flaky. Her head banged against something metallic; her hands grabbed at bars, and then she knew exactly where she was.

"Don't bother." Hugo's accent was ice in her veins. "Been at it for days, no luck."

"Mathias locked me in with you?"

"And your homie."

"Eddy!" Her voice rang out, but there was no reply. The thought flashed through her for a moment like a surge of white-hot fever, *Maybe Mathias lied after all?*

"No, the other one, the pregnant ho. Your boyfriend's dead, B."

"Shut up!" *Keep talking*, she thought. *Let me find you in the dark.*

"I ain't the problem. Maybe you heard, but that Mathias has a few fuckin' screws loose upstairs."

"You're the one who listened to him, you're the one who took his words and decided to murder my brother." She wobbled to her feet,

218

using the bars as support, keeping her ear turned in the direction his voice was coming from. "You ask me, you're both guilty."

"And what about what he did to me? Huh? Did you ever think of that? No. You didn't. You just sit there judging, even though you know he wasn't no saint!"

"That didn't give you the right to take his life!"

"Ain't no law out here, it's survival of the fittest."

With every sound he made, it gave her a better idea of where he was. Her hands itched, twitching, hungry. "I guess you're right about that."

"Where you goin'?" She heard him shuffle to his feet. "I hear your feet moving."

Ira was right in front of him. Her stomach turned at the vile mixture of body odor and rank breath, but she kept calm, balling her fists up tight. His breath was shallow; maybe he knew she was standing there?

She tossed a right hook out and caught something bony. Hugo wailed and recoiled into the wall. She kicked, and kicked, and clawed, and pounded at his disgusting face until she was on top of him, grabbing at his throat, feeling the life evaporate from his body.

"It's natural selection, Hugo," she said. "Isn't that what you were getting at? You fucking bastard."

His cries stopped, and she could feel his strength leaving his body. Her heart battered against her ribcage. The feeling was almost euphoric.

You deserve this, she thought. *This is what Nico would have wanted!*

Ira reeled back when the lights came on, covering her eyes. She staggered back onto the floor, struggling to adjust to the harsh sudden light.

"Ironic how you've resorted to violence so quickly after being confined." Mathias's voice was coming from every direction; Ira felt like she might go mad if she had to hear it for too long. "Much like a caged animal, no?"

"What, it isn't enough that you've got us locked up together, now you're watching us too?" Ira said.

"I need you all alive for what comes next," Mathias said. "So, if you would please, don't kill Hugo."

"And what will you do to stop me?" she said. Hugo dragged himself to the other end of the cell, leaving behind a crimson trail in his wake, clutching for the bars.

"I can suck all the air out of the cell, for one. Kill you, Hugo, Lena, and her little bundle of joy."

Her face tightened, teeth clenched. "Damn it."

"I got that one from *you*."

"Don't remind me."

"I believe I just did."

Her eyes darted across the room: she saw Lena in the corner, holding herself, staring at her with wide disbelieving eyes. Justice for her brother's murder evaporated from her mind almost instantly... *What about Eddy?*

"Where is Eddy?" Ira asked.

"Who knows? The ritual took a wrong turn...I'm not sure what happened to him."

Tears fell from her eyes, scattering the rivulets of blood on her hands like mini Rorschach tests. "The ritual? You turned those fucking machines on him?"

"I had to, Ira, the Harvester was going to get me."

Something was wrong. There was genuine panic in his voice, not unlike herself as a child, running to tell Mommy and Daddy that slenderman had been under her bed, that he was going to get her. "What the hell are you talking about?"

Silence. Crackling sounds echoed over the speakers in the walls.

"And just like that, you forget justice for your brother's killer, and rush to find the man he might have killed were he still alive."

"Shut the hell up!"

"I'm growing bored of this conversation anyway."

She paused for a moment, staring at Lena. "Wait."

"What is it?"

"Let us search for Eddy. If he escaped the tank, he's gotta be around here somewhere."

"No chance in hell."

"You'll do it, or I'll kill Hugo and myself, then you'll only have one subject left to get your experiment right. That is what you're thinking, isn't it? You want to activate Weber's final experiment?"

"I'll have to think about it. I'm very busy right now with the preparations."

"No, Mathias."

"Or, I can just turn off the air right now until you all fall asleep. I'm not sure I like your attitude."

"Then do it. But if Eddy dies, then you lose me, period. I will make it my final mission in life to make your life a living hell. Believe me, you may have control of the facility now, but all I need is one console, an old phone, hell, I could probably hack you out of the system with a fucking Gameboy!"

There was a clicking noise, and then static.

"A Gameboy?" Lena said.

"Did it sound convincing?" Ira said, quietly.

Lena shrugged.

The static persisted for what seemed to be hours. Lena retreated to her corner, and Ira sat on the bare mattress at the other end of the cell. Hugo seemed to have fallen asleep on the bars, his face black, blue, red and swollen—drool hanging down his cracked lips. She tried to occupy her thoughts with revenge plots, how she might thwart Mathias's plans, but all she could think about was Eddy. Where was he? What was the ritual that Mathias had spoken of?

She remembered the thing she'd seen in this very cell, the seven glowing gray eyes.

What if that was the Harvester Mathias seemed to be so afraid of?

Before long, Mathias shut the lights off in their cell, cloaking them in darkness again. She wouldn't allow herself to sleep, though.

Her thoughts ran dark as she sat there, staring into the abyss.

She's clutching Eddy's hand, feeling his clammy, fevered skin.

He won't look at her.

There's something wrong with his skin, it's splotchy in some places. His breathing is harsh. Erratic.

She stands up, moves around to get a better look at him. She screams when she sees what's left of his face. His eyes are gone, replaced with blackened pits,

221

leaking a dark substance that smolders and smokes and smells like burning matches. His face seems to be melting into something larger. His mouth is forever open, teeth crooked and wrong, always frowning, always sad.

He'll never smile again.

"Eddy..."

He stands, towering over her, with massive legs like tree trunks whose roots wind and coil.

When he stands, he gestures with fingers that wave like snakes at the ceiling.

The ceiling to her cell crumbles away to a clear night sky, where a black comet darkens the stars.

She woke up.

It was still dark in the cell. No telling if it was day or night above ground.

The dream left her feeling empty inside, as if part of her knew it was true in a way, that a part of Eddy would be gone, even if they found him.

She wished she could go back in time, to a time before the ice age...

Her life had been a struggle before discovering this monstrous facility, tucked away in the mountains, but now it was even harder to recall a time when the sun shone bright in the sky, and grass grew green in front of suburban houses.

She tried to remember the way a sidewalk felt in the middle of summer when she'd run out barefoot to catch the ice cream man before he left their cul-de-sac, the way her childhood home smelled like breakfast sausage and pancakes on a Saturday morning, or even the irritation of high school and the drama of college romances. Hell, she'd have lived through her parents' last days all over again if it meant she could see them one last time.

Any time but now.

It was getting harder and harder to remember any of their faces, her parents, former lovers, childhood friends...

Ghosts buried in the snow.

Maybe this is what it's like to go mad? she thought.

She rested her head on the concrete, stared up into the dark.

2

Mathias looked up from the notebook and stared at the tank at the center of Weber's chamber. He'd seen terrible things inside the tank, and still he'd found no answers.

So far he'd been unable to establish contact with the aliens again.

Would another tank session prove fruitful? Or, would the Harvester find him, would it drag him off to the Astral Lands?

He was out of time already. The Harvester could come for him at any moment, and then it would all be over. Maybe escaping to another world, another reality, was his only hope?

Even the tattered grimoire that Weber regarded so highly would be unable to give him the information he needed. Only the tank held the answer. He had no choice. His eyes drifted to the medicine cabinet that contained all of Weber's recreational drugs. Before he knew what he was doing, he was reaching for a bottle of ketamine and stripping his clothes off, like he'd done so many times before.

The act seemed strangely empty this time, however. It was no longer a thrill for him to dip his legs into that lukewarm solution, to feel the physical connection to his body wither away as he pulled the cover to the tank overhead.

He focused on the stars. But, unlike that first time, there was nothing.

Every time he tried to focus on Betelgeuse there was no reply, no transportation like last time… He almost felt like he was being shut out.

How dare they ignore me! he thought.

Mathias screamed into the void. He wished war and blight and destruction on the aliens.

There had to be another way. There had to be other entities, other forms of consciousness in the universe that would be willing to give him the information he needed. He tried searching, scanning the cosmos for anything, he didn't care how powerful, how smart, or how malevolent they might be, without them he was lost!

All hope of contact seemed to be lost, and his essence had wandered near a black hole, when he felt it. The black hole wasn't a black hole at all, but a massive black void, swallowing stars, maybe even galaxies. It had an essence, cold and dark and malign. It seemed to regard him with faint disinterest. He tried to call out to it, but it did not hear his call. He tried to impress upon it what he needed, what he wanted, by flashing images of the core chamber, and recreations of the images he'd seen of Weber's team climbing into the tanks. But the entity did not pay him any mind.

The star it was consuming began to fade, a spiral vortex of plasma stretching for an entire astronomical unit into the mouth of the void. Soon, the star's light faded, until the rest of its mass broke down and became one with the entity as well.

He attempted to call to the entity once more, and still it ignored him, moving on to another star in another system. Mathias was not going to give in that easily, though, and his essence followed the entity to another star, a red giant that had consumed its inner planets and had begun to eat away at the outer layers of a Jovian-class world that orbited dangerously close to its parent.

The black mass moved close and began to feed.

Mathias called again.

Hear me! he thought. *Hear my cry, please, I need help!*

The entity whirled about. He could see various gradients of gray and black spinning at a fraction of the speed of light—hints at the thing's true form—and at once his essence was consumed by that very darkness, by a void that had no end and no beginning. He saw his life pass before his eyes in reverse, until he was nothing, an embryo, and then just essence—

The light was like needles in Mathias's eyes. He groaned and sat up; the crinkling of plastic wrappers and containers filled his ears as he moved. His hands found his eyes, rubbed them. His head felt heavy, and there was a throbbing pain that pulsed through his entire cranium. He imagined that was what a hangover felt like. He'd felt that pain before, the last couple of times he'd taken a trip inside the tank. How many had that been now?

The trips had faded into a blur. Was that the memory of his first trip, or the fifth? If he was honest with himself, he'd lost count.

His head turned, almost not of his own will, and he scanned over the open wrappers of protein bars and MRE packs, and his hands came up to feel the crumbs and dried chocolate on his beard.

Again? he thought.

How had he gotten here? He tried to remember the events of the trip he'd just had, and came up with nothing. Had he gained anything? Perhaps he had been successful in attaining Weber's password for the final experiment?

No, he thought. There was no answer, no password in his mind's eye.

There was something else. A vague memory of a presence within his mind after the trip.

A black comet. Hungry and immense.

How many rations had he consumed in that altered state? The last time he'd awakened in the rations room, he'd counted twelve empty MRE containers and ten protein bar wrappers. He looked around and tried to count, but held his head instead. It hurt too much to count yet.

He got off the pile and moved through the door. The air conditioning was cold on his naked body. He was dry, though; the salt was the only thing left of the saline solution that had covered his body earlier, and it cracked and sprinkled on the floor as he shuffled to his chamber at the top of the facility.

Mathias stepped through the doors and saw the tank at the center of the room, the lid shoved off onto the floor, and he instantly felt the memory of his own shaky steps, stumbling out from the tank after the conclusion of his failed meeting with an entity. He shook his head and found himself in front of Weber's cabinet of drugs.

Instead of ketamine or LSD, though, he went for the painkillers and took two. The bed called to him, but he had much work to do. Ira and the others would need rations soon, as well. He wondered how long he'd been asleep.

The digital alarm clock next to Weber's bed told him it was three in the morning. He couldn't remember what time it'd been when he climbed in.

Something struck him odd about the whole experience. Something familiar about that black mass, that devourer of stars…

Then he remembered the ceremony he'd botched only so long ago, how the walls of the experiment chamber had crumbled away into another reality, revealing a dark shape, like a comet that swallowed all light.

He was shaking there, standing naked inside the symbol that surrounded the tank.

I need to find Eddy, he thought. *I need to know how much damage has been done, how much time we have.*

3

The lights woke Ira before she even knew it. She removed her head from the concrete floor and rubbed it. She hadn't even felt herself go back to sleep. She glanced around the cell: Hugo was still in the corner; unfortunately, he was still breathing. Her eyes drifted over to where Lena had been. She wasn't there.

Ira bolted upright, panicking, thinking for half a heartbeat, *maybe he called my bluff? Maybe he's taken her too?*

Then she noticed that Lena was outside the cell, curled up in a ball against the far wall, unconscious.

It felt like it'd been days since their conversation with Mathias. Had it really taken so long for him to arrive at a decision?

Maybe it was just the confinement?

Ira felt like she was going crazy.

She approached the bars.

"Not so fast, Ira," Mathias said.

Ira felt his gaze from every angle of the room. "What?"

"You're not going."

"The hell I'm not. I need to find him!"

"You said it yourself. You could hack into any terminal in the facility if I only give you a chance. I'm not going to give you a chance. No, I'm afraid that Lena will be searching by her lonesome."

She could feel blood rushing to her head, her face boiling. "You have to let me go."

"No. Lena goes, you stay. That's the deal. Unless you'd like me to keep the door locked, and let Eddy die out there? Who knows what condition he's in?"

Lena stirred, her head lifting, confusion in her eyes. "Where am I?"

Did Mathias really come in here and drag her through the cell doors? she thought.

"I moved Lena while you two slept…"

There was an odd quality about his voice. Was he lying?

"Okay, what the hell for?" Lena held herself, glancing around the room nervously.

"He wants you to search for Eddy," Ira said.

Lena stumbled to her feet, rubbing her hand through her rat's nest of hair. "What?"

"He's not letting me go with you."

"That's right, now if you'd be so kind to move toward the door. I'm a very busy man."

Ira kept her mouth shut, watched Lena walk over to the door. Her hand shot out and snatched at Lena's arm. "Find him."

Lena nodded, her matted blonde hair swaying in the steady, mechanical breeze from the ventilation. She padded the rest of the way to the door. It opened by itself, and she walked through.

Coward doesn't even have the guts to face us in person, Ira thought.

The door shut on its own, and she heard a clicking sound, signaling that the lock was in place.

"I trust you'll be good?"

"Yeah, whatever."

She shuffled back to the bed; she sat down, holding her head.

"Now, was that so hard?"

"Go fuck yourself."

The static returned, and her eyes felt heavier than they had in years.

CHAPTER NINETEEN

L ena's legs felt weak. The unsettling sound of flesh slapping on stone echoed back to her ears as she paced down the corridor, trying not to betray the fact that she was shaking. Mathias's eyes were everywhere, down every hall, his voice coated her like an endless fog, smooth and tempting like a snake's hiss. But that wasn't all.

There was also that *other* thing she'd seen.

She remembered it vividly. There, in the darkness of her bedroom. Seven eyes had pulsed in the shape of a diamond, pupils too numerous to be anything from this world. She thought she could see an open maw, filled with thousands of shadowy teeth, ready to devour her.

Maybe it had been her imagination? But, if it was, why had she seen it again in the cell?

No. It *had* to be her imagination.

Mathias and Hugo were the only monsters here.

"The door to your right is unlocked," Mathias said.

She stopped and tested the door; it opened.

"Go on through," he said.

Sweat beaded across her forehead. Could she really pull this off? "I thought I was supposed to be searching for Eddy? How am I supposed to search for him if you keep leading me around like a damn lab rat?"

"Your search is being supervised."

"I need to get to the med bay."

"And why would you need to do that?"

"If Eddy's hurt, I may need to treat him."

"His condition is no concern of mine."

"I think it is—Ira already warned you what she'd do if he's hurt. No offense, but I wouldn't doubt her if I were you."

"And why would I give a damn about such idle threats from trapped mice?"

"Because she's got too much of her brother in her."

He paused for a second. *"Fine. Point taken."*

It wasn't the usual way to the med bay; it was like he was testing his control of the facility, forcing her to walk through a maze.

"You look nervous," he said. "You've been awfully quiet."

"You give a shit?" she said.

"Of course I care. I wouldn't have kept you alive if I didn't." Shuffling sounds echoed over the speaker. "After all, the future of the human race swells within your womb."

Icy fingers snaked down her spine and prickled over her swelling belly. "Stop the small talk, just guide me to the med bay."

"I figured you could use some verbal company, considering how much you're shaking."

She stopped, holding herself in a futile attempt to stop herself from shaking. Why hadn't she noticed that she'd been doing that? She glanced down the corridor, into the dark, and quickly turned back. "Not from you."

"How rude. And here I've been kind enough to let you search for Eddy."

"Yeah, the *let* part is the problem."

"Round the next corner and take the door on the left."

She found herself in one of the hallways that led to the med bay. She approached the glass automatic doors, but the sensor didn't react to her presence.

"The doors aren't opening."

"You might not approve of my methods now," Mathias said. "But one day you'll thank me for doing this."

"I'm sure I'll be ecstatic. Can you open the doors?"

"Say thank you."

"Excuse me?"

"Say it, or I'll let you sit out there for a few days to mull over how disrespectful you've been to me."

She stood there, listening to the static over the speakers, the way it filled every corner of the corridor, every shadow.

I have to stay strong, she thought. *What will Ira do if I don't find him?*

It was funny, in a way, how people could come together when faced with a common enemy, a threat. They used to hate each other, and maybe they still did. The fighting was over between them, though. They were going to be family soon. As much as Lena didn't like the idea, she couldn't help but think about her abuela. Whenever her family would get together, her uncles would end up getting too damn drunk and causing trouble. She'd hated her uncles sometimes. But her abuela had always told her to try to see at least one good quality in family that she was angry with. She was always the peacekeeper; without her abuela, the family might have fallen apart.

There *was* one quality in Ira she could admire, and that was her strength. Lena had to find her own strength now and use it to get Mathias to do what she needed him to.

"Open the doors or lose another body for your stupid experiment." She caressed her stomach. "Scratch that, two bodies."

"You'd seriously threaten to kill yourself? Isn't suicide a sin?"

"Do I look fucking religious to you?"

"Fine. What's one body? I'm sure I can get it right with only two subjects."

"One might mean the difference between the human race surviving or becoming extinct. You know that. You've already lost Nico, that reduced your odds of success by ten percent."

"Ten percent is a little much, you're pulling numbers out of your ass."

"Bet I'm right, though. If you thought you were guaranteed success just from the remaining three of us, you would have let Eddy die, and you would have already done your little experiment. You haven't, which means that you're not sure you've got it right."

"You assume too much, Lena. I activated that experiment chamber on Eddy already."

"What?"

"Unfortunately, things didn't work out like I'd hoped. The Harvester is still after me."

"What the hell are you talking about?"

Silence; crackling noises came over the speakers. She held herself. It felt like thousands of spiders had hatched from her pores. He was going crazy, like that doctor in the recording she'd seen on Ira's laptop.

"Tell me," Mathias said after a time. "When you stare into the dark, do you by chance see seven gray glowing eyes pulsing in the dark? Do you see it stalking your cage, salivating for the taste of your flesh?"

She gasped. Had he overheard her talking about it in her sleep, or somewhere else? "T-that was just a dream!"

"Afraid not. There are things in this vast multiverse beyond the limits of our understanding, beyond time, space, and our pitiful notions of God and divinity."

"So what? Even if I believe you, what's that got to do with me?"

"Well, it's simple, really. That thing uses shadows to travel into our world, to *hunt*. I've seen where it lives, Lena. Rolling hills covered in a leathery hide beneath a sky like a cancerous lung, with open mouths scattered across the landscape, each one filled with serrated black and yellow teeth, waiting for some poor soul to be dropped into them to feed whatever beast lives at the center.

"I wonder. What if I were to turn the lights off where you are? How long do you think it would take for it to find you and drag your useless carcass off to the Astral Lands?"

Lena heard a loud plinking sound. She turned to see that Mathias had turned off the lights at the other end of the corridor. "What do you want from me?"

"Say you're sorry."

"Are you fucking serious?"

"SAY IT!"

She hesitated.

Another light plinked off.

She wasn't as strong as Ira.

Another one. She thought she could see something looking back at her.

She couldn't beat him. Her lip curled, tears threatened to break from her eyes. "Sorry!"

He went quiet for a while. Her hands found her arms and she hugged herself, tried her best not to look back at the darkened end of the corridor. She hadn't noticed how cold it had gotten since Mathias locked them all up.

The automatic doors opened, and the lights turned on inside the med bay. "See, now was that so hard?"

She limped forward.

Lena knew she wasn't as bright as Ira, but she wasn't an idiot. Something about what she'd said had gotten under his skin. Maybe they could use that, whatever it was?

She might not have had a mind for science, but there had been plenty of learning involved in becoming a nurse, and she hadn't shied away from it, even if it bored her half to death. There had to be *something* in this room that could help Ira get control back.

"I need silence so I can think."

"I promise nothing."

"You owe us that much after all you've done…"

Static over the speakers. Maybe she'd gotten through to him? Her hands were trembling. She balled them up in fists, closed her eyes, and tried to calm herself.

You can do this, she thought.

She grabbed an open medical bag. Inside, there was some gauze, bandages, and a half-empty bottle of generic pain medication.

Her shaky hands found a scalpel, dropped it in the bag.

She made her way to the shelf, picked out a bottle of penicillin and several others. She listened to them clacking together in the bag, not bothering to read the labels.

There was a first aid kit fixed to the wall; she walked over and yanked it off, then strapped it to her shoulder. She rolled a chair around and sat down, took a deep breath, considering anything else she might need.

"Are you finished?" Mathias asked.

"What, like you weren't watching me?" she said.

"I have other things to do, so let's get you moving."

Scanning the room, her eyes caught the gleaming screen of a small phone—probably left by one of the researchers. It was resting on one of those wireless charging stations. She couldn't help but think of the streaks of blood she'd found on the floor the first time she'd come in here. Nico had begrudgingly cleaned it up for her one night, so she wouldn't have to think about it; but it was always in the back of her mind. Maybe it had belonged to whoever died in here?

If she could just get to it, slip it in the bag… "Can I just take a breather?"

"No."

"And why not? You have complete control of the facility, it's not like I'm going to run off. You can leave me here for a little while, let me rest, and go do whatever it is you were going to do."

"I don't trust you. Now, get up and continue your search. Unless you'd like to return to your cell."

Maybe if she could just knock it into her bag on her way out of the med bay? She stood up, trying not to let her line of sight betray her intention. "Fine."

The chair creaked when she stood up. She licked her lips. Then, after taking a deep breath, she walked toward the automatic doors, taking a moment to swipe the phone into her bag—

The air seized out of her lungs before she even reached the doors. The lights shut off, and she fell to her knees.

Mathias was still talking, but the blood was rushing to her ears, turning his words to whispered nonsense. Still, she got the hint. It took everything she had to dig the phone out and toss it to the linoleum.

Air filled her lungs. Her head felt like it was filled with white noise as she lay there coughing—

That's when she saw it. Not the creature with the seven eyes, but something else.

Was she safe on the other side of the med bay's glass walls?

The lights seemed to flicker and die around each of its lumbering steps. It was massive, its head nearly scraping at the ceiling of the corridor. She was too terrified to look away…what if it found her? Was this the Harvester thing that Mathias spoke of? Was he going to replace himself with her?

Tears broke from her eyes…then she caught a glimpse of gleaming reflected light off two eyeballs. There was a face, drifting off to the side of a massive silhouetted bulge of flesh and shadow, a face that seemed to be melting, twisting, cracking into madness.

A face she recognized.

It lumbered down the corridor, down the way she'd come. It seemed to be heading for the elevator.

Before long, it was gone.

The lights plinked back on one by one.

2

It took Ira a few breaths to notice what had happened. Each breath was shorter than the last, a struggle to find the air to fill her lungs, then there wasn't any at all. She fell to the floor, clutching at the bed with a death grip. There were sounds, her heartbeat, her brain cells committing suicide from the lack of oxygen. She rolled over, clutching at the bedding, and noticed that Hugo was doubled over as well.

A smile traveled across her face.

If she were to die now, fine, as long as her brother's murderer went with her.

Then it was all over, the air returned to her lungs, and Hugo sat back up, holding his stupid head.

Static echoed over the speakers. She thought she heard Mathias's voice. He'd been quiet since Lena left. She'd rolled over, content to let sleep take her, when the door slammed.

She sat up too fast, giving herself a head rush as the gate opened and Lena fell into a ball, rocking back and forth on the floor next to Nico's dried blood stain.

"What happened?" Ira asked, coming to her aid. Lena was shaking violently, staring at her hands.

"W-we…we found him…"

Her heart jumped. "Eddy!"

Lena nodded. Something was wrong. Ira sat up, holding her breath.

"I saw his face, Ira, I saw it melting into that thing…it was so big…it looked right at me! I can't get it out of my head!"

234

She couldn't help but think of her nightmare.

His eyes are gone, replaced with blackened pits, leaking a dark substance that smolders and smokes and smells like burning matches. His face seems to be melting into something larger. His mouth is forever open, teeth crooked and wrong, always frowning, always sad.

"I'm afraid she's losing her grip," Mathias said.

"What the hell is she talking about?" Ira stood up, pleading with the cameras. "Why is she telling me you found Eddy?"

"I don't know what she's talking about. The security cameras blacked out shortly after I turned the air back on. If she's telling the truth, then…it's possible…but he'd be changed…"

"What the fuck does that mean?"

Static. No response.

Ira fell to her knees, staring at the dried, crimson filth on her hands and the flaking bloodstain she was sitting in.

CHAPTER TWENTY

*I*ts *warmth calls to him, reaching around bending, twisting, never-ending pathways and corners. Like the faint remnants of a solar flare at the border of interstellar space. He searches on and on for the source of it all.*

His hunger grows more and more insatiable with each passing moment, growing to fit his new body.

It strikes him that these halls are familiar, that perhaps in another life he knew them.

2

Mathias thrust the lid off of the sensory deprivation tank, screaming for air. Clawing his way out of the tank, the linoleum tiling like ice on his skin.

He could still feel its grip around his throat, twisting, applying just enough pressure to keep him alive, conscious. Proving its point. Somehow, Mathias knew that if the Harvester wanted, it could end his life in the Astral Lands.

The LSD he'd taken before the tank session was still playing tricks on his eyes. A phantasmagoria of light and sound, shapes and patterns, endlessly attempting to distract him from the horror of his situation.

I'm going to die, he thought.

There was no telling when it would happen. The next time he fell asleep, or the time after? Maybe even after that?

Unless he could find a replacement.

Now.

He attempted to stand; the pain bunched up in his throat like he'd swallowed a bag full of needles.

The warding symbol, the eye of the abyss, spun around him. He thought of the beast it had been designed to keep Weber safe from. He'd seen its pulsing gray eyes just hours ago, both in the corner of this very chamber and the cell where he kept the others. It seemed to be watching them all, studying them. But, why?

If Weber was right about it, if it had indeed dragged most of his five hundred staffers off to some otherworldly place, why hadn't it attacked *them* yet?

Does a predator hunt when it isn't hungry? he asked himself.

It was the Harvester's fault.

If he'd had more time…he'd been so close to getting through to the entity. So close to having his answers. The key to the final experiment.

He remembered how he had felt his nose migrate down to his stomach in the tank, how he'd questioned why human beings needed bodies at all as his essence rose up into the atmosphere. The mountains and the ice were no longer visible, but he could tell he was leaving, could feel his essence pass through the Van Allen radiation belts, past the moon, beyond Jupiter, the rings of Saturn, and even beyond Pluto and Charon. Stars rushed past his eyes, out to that familiar system near Betelgeuse. There, at last, the glowing, nebulous, orange entity was waiting for him. Was this the same entity that Weber and Lilly had conversed with?

No. And maybe. They were all connected somehow.

The last time he'd met with this thing, it had reached out to him willingly. Now, however, it was resistant, maybe even hostile.

Mathias felt the luminous cloud studying him, studying his very core.

As before, his words didn't work in this place, in this form.

Images flashed before his mind's eye. Thousands of them. One element remained constant. The central core of the facility.

In one image, he sees researchers climbing into vertical sensory deprivation tanks—coming up from circular slots in the floor. In the next, he sees their bodies liquefy from inside the tank. Then, there are more researchers, alterations made to the tanks, occult symbols painted on them. Another test, resulting in a fate worse than death for the subjects inside.

He sees them transform into hideous creatures, their faces melting into an expanding biomass that was part human, and part something else...

More images flash into his mind.

He sees more alterations being made to the tanks in the core chamber. Substitute symbols, complex equations written and rewritten on whiteboards, Weber slaving for days on the tiniest details before the final experiment is set to take place.

The final experiment.

Weber himself standing naked before the tanks with surviving colleagues.

A single woman stands before them. She's holding the grimoire in her hand, threatening Weber with its secrets.

Weber disrobes and descends into the tank, not at all concerned with the girl.

The creature charges across the chamber toward the girl. It's almost twenty feet long, its teeth snatch the girl up, and with its meal in its maw, it plunges into a portal to another world. The girl's hand slams into the wall at the last moment. She drops the grimoire and a fire extinguisher. Mathias's eyes trace their trajectory as they fall beneath one of the consoles.

That must be where I found them before, *he thinks.*

Mathias's vision doesn't end there. He sees the girl get dragged into the Astral Lands.

The ground is the color of sand and has the texture of leathery skin. He sees mouths opening and closing across a vast and infinite horizon, and at the horizon, he sees that familiar, cancerous gray sky trail above him.

The ground is littered with the decaying bodies of hundreds of men and women, some wearing torn jumpsuits and tattered lab coats.

The creature sits atop its new meal, who is still somehow alive in that terrible place, clawing at the sky and ground alike. The creature watches the girl's movements with what Mathias thinks of as a form of amusement before it opens its mouth, releasing the body from its maw.

The body falls to the leathery ground, where a mouth opens up and swallows the remains of the girl's body. The creature stalks away, sitting atop a leathery hill before that terrible, pulsing gray sky, paying little notice to how the land has eaten the rest of its meal.

Then it regards him, and it seems to be charging at the instant before he's yanked back through the portal, the event horizon.

Within the core, he can see what the remaining three saw, what they visualized inside their tanks: another world, another version of Earth, a new home—then he sees them vanish, and there are no other images.

But not before he hears them chanting. Something that is at once familiar to him and completely alien. Something which echoes through their very souls across the fabric of time and space.

"Aml'cath na ule'th ada hote' tekke."

His view of the planetary system, of the luminous entity, returned.

He tried to ask the entity if the researchers had succeeded, if it could show him the other world. A vision of a Rubik's Cube suggested that they didn't know, or, the answer was unknowable.

Maybe this presence wasn't like the previous one he'd dealt with? What if the entity was just a man? A man belonging to a race of aliens who were far more advanced than humanity?

A man and his daughter playing in a park, a woman jogging by them while listening to music, animals running free, rivers and forests, mountains, humans living in harmony with nature, with science. The image fades quickly with a pang of regret and longing left in its absence.

Yes, Mathias thought. *It is. The risk is worthwhile. It is!*

The entity started to circle his essence. *He sees an image of Nico's body on the floor of his cell, then Hugo lying beaten and broken on the floor of the cell hours later.*

The feelings he got from the entity were anything but good ones. Perhaps it was trying to shame his actions? Trying to make him feel remorse for the steps he'd taken to ensure the survival of his species?

No, he thought. *You are a fool. Humans are not so easily persuaded to hedge their bets on a thing like this, especially when success isn't promised.*

He sees the images of the Hiroshima and Nagasakie explosions, the thousands dead and dying in Nazi death camps, soldiers storming a local hospital in San Bernardino, opening fire on recovering Revolutionist soldiers, and the deployment of Measure 86 on Revolutionist forces as they sleep unawares.

This is different, he thought. *You wouldn't…you wouldn't understand. My species is almost gone…extinct…*

He sees a static image of the Harvester's hooded form, the mask's expression twisting into a hideous grin, showing ancient, carved teeth.

A moment later, and it seems as if the Harvester's appendages are reaching, clawing for him.

The images ceased and the entity retreated back to its glowing orange world.

Mathias's essence lingered for a time, pleading with the entity to tell him the answer.

It seemed to pause for a moment. He could feel it deliberating with an answer.

Yes! Tell me!

That was when he felt a twisting around his neck, pulling him through time and space to that other place. His body felt as though it would shatter into thousands of pieces as it slammed into the dusty surface of a familiar moon.

The Harvester's mask was frowning at him. Its grip was tightening. Lifting him into the air.

He was screaming. He felt like he was drowning. The warning was clear.

That's when he woke.

When he was *permitted* to.

The colors were still dancing across his vision. He could see patterns in the linoleum, something he hadn't noticed before. The pyramid formation now danced before his eyes, stunning, and in three dimensions he could make out every detail, and at which point the opposite-facing pyramids became one. Their union was proportional, perfect, and seemed to have some otherworldly quality to it.

The eye of the abyss.

He stood there for an eternity, staring, considering the pattern, the symbol, and the meaning of the formation. The symbol was all over the grimoire. Weber believed that it was a warding symbol meant to keep lesser creatures like the Amarath at bay.

If his younger self could see him now, he'd balk at the things he was doing, researching, *believing*.

He peeled his eyes off of the dancing eye of the abyss and followed the shifting patterns on the floor that led to Mathias's bed.

Standing before the bed, he found himself fighting with himself, fighting with his body's intense desire to collapse into its soft embrace. The death of stars and galaxies took place in the span of time it took him to give in, to feel the sheets on his skin, to crawl beneath the blankets and shut the doorways to his brain and allow the darkness to finally take him.

His eyes were half-closed when he thought of the Harvester. Its enlarged appendage wrapped around his neck, constricting.

It was too real; he couldn't breathe.

No!

He sat up in the bed, tossing the blankets off of himself.

I can't sleep! I have to find a substitute!

His clothes were neatly draped over the back of a chair. He put them on haphazardly and made his way down to the experiment chamber where he'd kept Eddy.

He'd been trying to isolate what had caused the last attempt to fail, and so far he'd had no luck. He'd been over the symbols again and again, repainted them, rearranged them, and still he was no closer to understanding.

Maybe there was nothing to understand. Maybe the madness in these things was that there was no coming to understand them. That they were all at the mercy of forces they could never hope to control.

I am twice the scientist that Weber was, he thought, shaking his head. *I will succeed, I will unlock this mystery!*

Still. Even if *this* attempt failed, he could just try it on Ira or Lena. As long as one of them survived, things would work out.

There was no time for further deliberation.

3

He feels he's getting close. The waves crashing into his body are stronger than they were in the chamber of his birth, feeding his hunger.

But, there's something else now too. It's like…music.

Yes. Music!

241

They're like voices, chanting, pained and yet somehow beautiful to his malformed ears. They prove to be enough of a distraction from his hunger that he turns and starts moving in their direction.

Lumbering through corridors and hallways, searching rooms where the singing seems to be strongest, clawing open vents and doorways.

He finds himself in front of the elevator. His fingers reach out, the bones sinking into the crack in the doorway, shadows gripping, tearing the metal to shreds, ripping it away.

The shredded, metallic pieces of the doorway clack and clank in the hallway until they lie still.

He stands before the darkness. The singing seems to be coming from below, in the dark at the bottom of the elevator shaft. Then he's falling through the dark. The way he fell before.

There is little pain when his body hits the bottom. His body is a puddle of shadow, ash, and crumbling flesh.

There is a cable stabbing through what's left of his skull.

He tears it free.

Blood and tar drip from the wound. Clawing for support, he notices that he's missing fingers. Something is growing in their place, shadows reaching, extending past where bone and flesh once were. Soon there won't be much flesh left in him. The thought is at once welcome and terrifying.

He's not sure why.

Ira had taken to pacing back and forth in the cell. Hugo still wasn't making eye contact, which she was thankful for. She'd lost count of the hours since Mathias had cut off contact with her. Focusing on the sounds of her echoing footsteps was all she could do to keep herself sane. The sound from the static had her disoriented, especially when Mathias decided to turn the lights off and leave them in a pitch-black void.

Sometimes, when staring into that void, she felt she could almost get up and walk into the darkness for untold miles. And maybe she could.

At times she'd wake in the middle of the night—or the morning, afternoon, there was no telling—and she'd see those pale gray eyes pulsing in the dark. The diamond pattern moving toward the bars, a steady rumbling sound drowning out the static from the speakers.

Then it would be gone, and she'd drift back to sleep, her heart pounding through her chest, sweat beading moist on feverish skin.

There was madness in the void.

Then, other times, she'd wake screaming from her nightmares. Nightmares where she saw terrible things; terrible landscapes, horizons dwarfed by tentacles, black holes in impossible places—at the center of a small room, thousands of them scattered across a sea of sand.

"Now you've taken to pacing," Mathias' voice over the speakers was like nails on a chalkboard. "Interesting."

"You're watching us in the dark now?" Ira asked.

"Infrared," Mathias said.

"Turn the damn lights on," Ira said.

The lights plinked on. Her perceived space shrunk. She was almost tempted to beg him to turn the lights back off. Sometimes, there was freedom in the void, in madness.

"What do you want, Mathias?" Ira asked.

"I require Hugo for an experiment."

Her eyes drifted to Hugo. For once, he made eye-contact with her. He shook his head frantically.

Lena was still asleep on the bed.

"Oh, it's almost as if he thinks I'm giving him a choice." Mathias's laughter was distorted over the speakers, sending shivers up her spine. "I'm going to knock you all out now and collect my subject."

"Are you crazy?" Ira pointed to Lena. "In case you forgot, Lena's still pregnant. You can't just gas us or turn off the damn air every time you get angry or want something from us. She could have a miscarriage."

Static over the speakers.

"Very well, I will open your cage and Hugo will move into the other part of your chamber."

"I'm not going!" Hugo said. "I don't wanna end up like Eddy, B!"

243

"You won't. I've fixed that little error."

"You're lying," Hugo said, holding his hands over his battered ears. "You're gonna kill me."

Ira was disgusted with herself for empathizing with the bastard. She found herself standing over him, her fists balled up. "We don't have a choice. Get up and do what he says. I won't lose another family member because of you."

"Yes, Hugo, think of this as penance for your crimes."

"You put that shit in my head, yo!"

Ira grabbed him by the arm and forced him to his feet. "And yet, you have a mind of your own, don't you?"

He struggled all the way to the gate. She heard it unlatch and pop open. "No, please, don't do this. I'm sorry I killed him, yo, I'm sorry! I don't know what got into me! Please!"

Ira pushed him into the next part of the chamber. Considered running in with him. This could be her chance...

"Now, Ira, close the door."

Her hands found the bars on the gate...she hesitated. "What if it doesn't work, and he *does* end up like Eddy?"

Hugo's eyes went wild.

"It's best not to think of failure."

"You'll need another subject, won't you?"

"If this fails. Yes."

"Take me, then."

At least then, we could be monsters together, a part of her thought.

Lena shot up from where she was resting. "You can't!"

Ira put her hand up to silence her. "I know what I'm doing."

"That's a tough one there, Ira, truly. I don't think I can risk such a useful source of information just yet."

"Useful source of information?"

"You know far too much about Weber's experiments, about the systems here, for me to risk you being swallowed by the abyss just yet. Close the gate."

Reluctantly, she let it latch closed.

"Good. Now, Hugo, move to the door."

He shook his head. "No, man, I don't want this. I don't want this!"

"Move now, or suffer."

He stood up. His bruised, fearful eyes found Ira's before he went to the door. She said nothing to him.

The door popped open.

Hugo stepped into the light.

The door shut by itself.

That familiar static started to permeate the cell, and Ira knew Mathias was gone. Or was he? Maybe he was still watching her somehow, waiting for them to start plotting against him?

"Were you really gonna do it?" Lena asked.

Ira nodded. "It would have been our best chance to get out of here. He probably knows that."

"That fucker controls everything, even the air we breathe!"

"Yeah, but we need to outsmart him somehow."

"I tried to get you a phone…he caught me, though, sucked the air right out of the room before I saw…you know."

"Is there any reason why you think he'd let you back out? If you can sneak me a screen, a tablet, anything, then I can get us out of here."

Lena sat there looking at her feet; her eyes were red with tears. "Maybe. I was really trying to get supplies for us. We still need them."

"He's not stupid, that's something we need to remember. But, he *is* arrogant. And you're pregnant. We can use that."

"I don't know about you, but I barely finished two years at a community college to get my ADN, I'm not that smart." Lena stood up and walked to the bars, gripping them.

"Maybe you haven't noticed. But you're feeding for two right now, and that is *my* blood, my *brother's* blood, that grows inside you! So you are going to suck it up! And you're going to help me, help *us*, get control of this facility so we can go back to surviving this hell!"

"And what then?" Lena whipped around, eyes wild. "What happens when our rations run out, Ira?"

"I'll go out and find more, we'll figure something out."

"And what if you get hurt like Eddy did? What if you die? What will we do then? Hugo's probably going to die, the fucking murderer, and Nico was the glue that held us all together…I'd be alone, raising his baby in this hellhole. Alone."

"Now I'm the glue."

"You're not half the man he was."

"Last I checked, I wasn't a man at all."

That won her a smile from Lena, even if it was fleeting.

They were silent for a while. Ira leaned her head against the bars and slid to her knees; Lena sat back down on the bed and rested her head against the wall. Maybe Lena was right? Maybe she didn't have what it took to lead them. Especially if it was just the two of them.

Maybe Mathias was what they deserved.

"What if he's right?" Lena asked.

"What?"

"What if he's right about saving us…"

"Are you insane!"

"Have you thought about it?"

"No!" Ira banged her head against the bars a couple of times. "It's madness!"

"You saw that thing in the dark. You've spent as much time as he has watching those videos, right?"

"And it's madness! That's all it is!"

"What if you're wrong?"

She was.

"I'm not, Mathias has lost his damn mind to this obsession, the experiment was made by a very desperate and depraved man."

"But you don't know what happened to the people who made this place."

"Doesn't matter…"

She knew what Weber had claimed happened. That a creature with seven eyes had dragged them off somewhere to be devoured. Maybe that was why she kept seeing it? Why all of them kept seeing it…? That had to be it…it just couldn't be real.

But hadn't she seen it before she'd heard him mention it too? The nightmare she'd had beneath the streets of Riverside?

Ira shook her head.

"And Eddy…what he's become…" Fear dripped from Lena's voice.

Ira could almost picture what she'd seen. "We don't know if what you saw was real, Lena, Mathias didn't see anything on the cameras."

"The lights darkened around his…body…maybe the cameras shut off too?"

"That's convenient."

"It does matter," Lena said.

"And even if it isn't crazy, if you think I'm going to throw in with that bastard, the one who killed Nico and did *that* to Eddy without a single shred of remorse, then you've got another thing coming."

"I've forgotten what it's like to feel the sun on my skin."

"Trust me, it's overrated."

"I used to go to Huntington Beach every weekend with my homies in school." A faint smile traced across Lena's cracked lips. "Hell, sometimes we'd ditch days at a time and just camp out there, dodging pigs, making campfires, drinking and fucking. Living, you know? Of all the things I miss, my daughter, my girlfriends and boyfriends, that's the thing I miss the most. To feel the sand between my toes, you know? Feel the tide washing over me again and again."

Ira chuckled. For all their differences, they could agree on one thing. They missed living. "Now I know why you almost failed college."

Lena chuckled. "And I'd do it all again."

"At least we agree on one thing."

"I'm not saying we should trust Mathias."

"Then what are you suggesting?"

"We should take the place back, but we shouldn't throw it all out, everything he's said, without considering it just because he's a monster, or just because we don't understand it."

"Careful, Lena, that's starting to sound a lot like wisdom. You're not supposed to do wisdom."

"Shut up, I mean it. If there's a chance we can feel the sun again, run the sand through our toes again, live our lives, isn't that worth it?"

"And what if it's a pipe dream?" There was something else in her voice now. "What if the door can't be closed once it's open?"

"Then it's been fun, I guess." Lena's cracked smile faded into a solemn frown.

Lena stared at her for a time. There was something between them, like an invisible mass. The look on Lena's face said it all. That blank look that betrayed the moment of a hidden truth being learned, a knowing.

"So much for the human race being able to adapt to anything," Ira said finally.

"Can't adapt to this," Lena said.

"Damn well tried."

"Just prolonged the inevitable."

"Maybe."

Ira rested her head against the cold metal wall, felt her eyes dragging shut.

"He was scared, though," Lena said.

"Of what?" She could almost hear music at the edges of her consciousness.

"That Harvester thing he was talking about. It's got him spooked. Maybe we can use that?"

"Maybe..."

5

The singing is getting louder. He can feel them, how near they are.

The corridors are dark here. The waves of energy that guided him before are quieter, almost silent.

The singing guides him to a door.

The door is dark, metallic. There are black, lifeless screens and buttons.

He touches the door. Lets his fingers grow and stretch into the crack in the doors, just like he did to the elevator. He feels his fingers wrap around metal, bending it, shaping it to his will. There's a crumpling sound as the doors are crushed in his grip.

The room beyond is dark. There are glowing eyes inside.

The singing stops.

CHAPTER TWENTY-ONE

Mathias smiled, staring at the screens in the security room. The hum from the electronics buzzed deep into his eyes, into his brain. The security room was one of three in the entire facility. It was nothing more than a small, four-by-six-foot concrete rectangle. He'd found it shortly before confining Ira and the others to their cell.

There were no overhead lights in this room; he'd had to get a desk lamp from one of the abandoned rooms in the upper levels. At first, he hadn't felt safe sitting in here. The desk lamp and the screens cast shadows everywhere.

Gateways, he thought.

Drawing a copy of Weber's *eye of the abyss* in the center of the room had helped alleviate his uneasiness. Most of it. His chair sat at the edge of the symbol, just inside its influence.

Hugo looked confused on the screen, standing in the corridor outside his cell. He was holding himself tight, checking the shadows.

One of the screens showed a complex grid outline of the entire floor, as well as operations commands Mathias could use to control Hugo's path to the experiment chamber.

"You look nervous, Hugo." Mathias spoke into the microphone at the edge of the metal desk.

"Let's just get this over with, man."

"Very well."

Mathias opened up a door at the northern end of the corridor, drawing Hugo's attention like a mouse catching a whiff of cheese. "Move through that door."

"What are you gonna do to me?"

"Don't worry about that. Move into the next corridor. I don't have all day."

Hugo rubbed his arms like a junkie craving his next fix and reluctantly followed Mathias's command.

Once he was in the next corridor, Mathias closed the doors behind Hugo and opened another set up to his right. "Go into the next room."

Hugo complied. He hoped the man wouldn't require a command for every door he opened. Hopefully Pavlov would win out.

"You must really get off on this shit, yo." Hugo glanced around himself, staring at the cameras with paranoia burning deep in his dimwitted eyes.

"No more than you did when you killed Nico."

"That was you, man!"

"Really, Hugo, you mustn't blame others for your crimes."

"Man, just wait till I see you, see how tough you are when you ain't sitting behind a desk."

"By the time you see me again, it'll be too late."

"You just wait, B, your number's comin' up." Hugo's eyes kept dancing around the sealed corridor. "And where the fuck is that noise coming from?"

"I haven't drugged you, if that's what you're implying. If you're experiencing auditory hallucinations, then I would look to your cellmate if you want someone to blame."

"Man, I ain't hallucinating this, why are you playing music?"

"I assure you, I'm not."

"Whatever, man, I'm not falling for it."

"Clearly."

Mathias opened another door. Hugo moved forward without needing coaxing.

"Thank you, Pavlov."

Something else caught his eye as he entered the command for the next door. Another camera feed from the basement levels, below where

Eddy and Nico had found the rations and storage caches, a place that was never officially on any maps.

The screens showed a series of power outages. Lena had mentioned that the thing she claimed was Eddy had caused the lights to darken around his body...but, this was on a scale much larger than what had happened outside the med bay...

He remembered how the walls had seemed to crumble away to reveal an alien starscape, where the star eater was busy fulfilling its namesake.

"What's the holdup?"

"Wait. Something's happening..."

Mathias turned up the audio feed from the chamber Hugo was standing in.

"Tell me, Hugo, are you still hearing music?"

Hugo stared suspiciously at the camera dead in front of him. "You know what I'm hearing."

"Just answer the question."

Hugo sighed, staring at the floor. "Yeah, I still hear it."

And indeed, *he* could hear it *too*. It was quiet. So quiet that he had to turn the volume up all the way for it to register on his speakers.

Z

They move as one. Through ever-darkening corridors, up stairwells.

Their purpose is one.

Their goal is clear.

The waves are getting stronger, the edges of their flames licking at the incorporeal bits—their true bodies, which gestate, feeding off of the flesh that once governed their being—beckoning them ever forward. He can feel the others as if they are physically connected to his ever-changing body.

He can feel their hunger growing to match his own. It's almost loud enough to drown out his own thoughts.

Soon.

Soon they will feed.

3

"Where the hell are you heading?" Mathias asked the monitor, watching the power outages progress from corridor to corridor. He'd tried shutting the doors, but still they progressed. The cameras were useless, even after reconnecting to the network.

"Yo, man, this shit's getting louder! What the fuck is going on?"

"I'm not sure myself."

"Yo, don't mess with me, man, I'm sorry for what I did, man, but don't mess with me!" Mathias glanced back at the monitor: Hugo was actually sobbing. Something about what he was hearing was clearly driving him mad. Fascinating. "They're in the next room, man, they're fucking coming for me! Do something!"

There was indeed a power outage in the next room. Mathias scanned Hugo's surroundings. He was completely exposed. If there was something otherworldly beyond those doors, then Hugo was doomed, and so too would he be, if the Harvester had anything to say about it.

He said the only thing he could think of. "Hide, you moron!"

##

Hugo wasn't sure he could handle much more.

Something had darkened the lights around the doors at the end of the corridor. The singing was muffled, but he could tell that it was coming from behind the doors.

There was a creaking, bending, breaking noise. Long shadowy tendrils seeped through the middle crack in the doors, snaking through them. There were hundreds of them, like a pit full of vipers in some old movie.

He found himself backing away, his heart drumming into his temples.

"Hide, you moron!"

The doors crumpled like aluminum foil and sank into darkness like two derelict ships plummeting to the bottom of the ocean.

He could see light reflecting off of bubbling, tumorous masses, eyes glowing yellow and green in the dark.

His screams caught in his throat. Urine warmed the inside of his long johns.

They lumbered out of the dark, and as they did, the dark followed them. The singing got so loud that Hugo felt his eardrums rupture, the blood flowing down both sides of his neck like sacramental rivers. Still, his eyes were open, and he recognized the one-eyed face that stared at him from the front of that monstrous pack.

It was *Eddy's* face.

Broken and bleeding and fading away into the side of a hulking monstrosity that was more shadow, more fuming ash, than it was human, but it was him all the same.

Was that what *he* was to become?

Their legs were massive, like nothing he'd ever seen.

They were inches from him when he cowered on the floor and covered his head. He couldn't hear the singing anymore, but he could feel the vibrations from their massive feet.

He was waiting for the moment when they would notice him on the floor and scoop him up, tear him limb from limb, and then fight over the scraps…but the moment never came.

The darkness turned red.

He opened his eyes. The lights had turned back on. The creatures were gone, having torn their way through the door behind him.

Sitting there in a puddle of his own piss and blood, he was thankful to be alive.

5

Mathias slammed the table. "No, no, no, no!"

He hadn't been sure where the blackouts were proceeding, where the so-called creatures that poor Hugo had witnessed were heading before.

Now he knew.

There was no mistaking it. They were heading for the fusion core. It made so much sense, he wanted to kick himself. Eddy had been sacrificed to the star eater. His body must be taking on some of its characteristics.

There must have been more of them; perhaps Weber had made the same mistake many times before he had? But why had they chosen to awaken now? Had Eddy's transformation somehow triggered something?

Mathias glanced at the stack of journals sitting on his table. Maybe one of them held the answer?

Would he even have time to look through them?

How long until they reached the core...what would happen then? He'd lose control, that much was certain.

He had to do something.

But what?

He eyed the microphone at the end of his desk, toggled with the controls to communicate with Ira and Lena's cell...

6

"You're pacing again," Lena said.

Lena had watched Ira pace back and forth for nearly an hour from the bed. It was beginning to drive her nuts.

"It's been way too long," Ira said. "What happens if he fails with whatever he's trying to do with Hugo?"

"I don't want to think about that," Lena said.

"I hate this, being at the mercy of that fucker." Ira stopped, held herself. "If something happens to him out there, if he dies, overdoses on LSD during one of his tank trips, whatever, we'll be stuck in here."

"I could use a good trip."

"He's not using it to get high."

"Where's the fun in that?"

Ira shook her head, her eyes were dead serious. "He's trying to commune with aliens, like Weber was doing."

"You think he succeeded?"

"What?"

"Nothing..." Lena shook her head. Ira was obviously in no mood to ponder the value of madness.

"I have bad news," Mathias's voice was different than it had been before. Lena couldn't put her finger on it.

"Let me guess," Ira said, her head resting on her arms. "Hugo's dead."

"I can't confirm that yet."

"Then you're useless to us," Ira said. "Why don't you go take another LSD trip and leave us alone?"

"I can't do that. It's a bit hard to explain, but Lena was right. I didn't want to believe what she saw was real…but it was…and those things, whatever they are, are heading for the fusion core. I have no idea what will happen when they get there."

"What the fuck are you talking about?" Ira shook her head. "Are you on drugs right now or something?"

"No, he's not," Lena said. "When I saw Eddy…when I saw his face on that thing…it was causing the lights to darken as it moved down the hall."

"Indeed, near as I can figure, whatever went wrong with the ceremony I performed on him caused him to take on the characteristics of the star eater in Weber's journal entries. If they consume the core to this facility, not only will I lose control—"

"But we'll be stuck in here," Lena said.

"I'm going to open the doors."

Lena watched Ira shift off the bed, staring the camera dead-on. "Then I'm coming for you."

"That would be ill advised. Once the power is out, this place will be one giant gateway for the Amarath that killed Weber's researchers. It may not be interested in hunting us yet, but that may change at any time."

"You think that's going to stop me? If we're going to die, I'm taking you with me."

"Ira, stop," Lena said.

"Stop? That bastard imprisoned us! Chloroformed me! He's the reason why Eddy and Nico are gone!"

"I realize that I've done terrible things to you…but, I implore you…don't do anything rash…I've lost control of the situation…"

255

"Shit's hitting the fan and you want to let 'bygones be bygones'?" Ira said. "I don't fucking think so."

"Ira…let's agree to a truce."

The cell gate clanked open. The door to the surrounding chamber followed shortly after that.

Lena could see murder burning in Ira's eyes. *Maybe there's more Nico in you than you thought?*

"Ira…"

She watched Ira stand up and consider their now-open cage. Her fists were balled up so tight her skin was turning red. Or maybe that was Hugo's blood? Lena couldn't be sure.

Ira's eyes closed tight. She drew in a deep breath. "No."

She bolted through the open gate and the door to the chamber before either of them could reply.

Lena stood there in disbelief…utterly alone.

"They've reached the core. There's nothing I can do. Power's already fluctuating. I've failed."

"Mathias, if the core dies…what happens to us?" Lena asked.

"The entrance to this place was never secured. We'll be dead in days. If nothing else kills us first."

"Part of me hopes she finds you. Gives you what you deserve."

"It's too late for me, I'm already doomed."

"We all are."

"And yet, I'm your best shot at survival."

"Ain't that a bitch."

"Quite."

The lights flickered.

"Lena, I—"

The lights flickered again. Then they died. Now, she was alone and surrounded by complete darkness.

Seven gray eyes pulsed to life on the other side of the chamber. She heard growls rumble through the air, loud, lumbering steps, scraping.

Her breath was short. She wanted to scream, couldn't. Something was different this time.

She wasn't sure why she ran and there was no telling where she was headed in the dark. She just knew. Knew that if she didn't run, then she would wind up in that thing's jaws.

Her hands found the bars to the cell, then the gate. Her bare feet scrambled forward. She heard something scurry behind her as she shot through the doorway, slamming her shoulder on the doorframe and tumbling into the corridor.

She caught a glimpse of gray eyes when she picked her head up from the floor and scrambled to her feet, sprinting down the hall— holding her pulsing shoulder as tears spilled down her cheeks.

I don't want to die! she thought, as something unseen raked its claws across her ankle, leaving pulsing fires in its wake.

Limping and sprinting down the darkened corridor, somehow, she'd managed to get away. Her ankle felt wet, like there were pins and needles festering inside her flesh. It was probably bleeding out.

Just keep moving, she thought. *Just keep moving, don't look back!*

CHAPTER TWENTY-TWO

The waves cascade out from the star in flares, bouncing —
caressing the way lovers do
— off concrete and metal, feeding into tubes, wires, machines made by simple, desperate creatures — where their endless fuel is wasted on things that don't satiate his *hunger.*

The others are chanting. They stretch out around the source. They call to him to join them —

a part of him, the part that's still human, does not want to merge with them, does not want to do this thing which he feels so compelled
— to feast.

Another flare erupts from the tiny star inside its protective cage, its warmth, its power, caressing his flesh, what's left of it. The new parts of him, the parts made of shadow, of things unknown to man and man's science, drink that warmth.

It's not enough to satiate his appetite.

The others reach hands out to each other. Shadows stretch, bone and flesh long since consumed by the eldritch thing inside which claims more and more of him —

his human mind shudders, thinks desperately of a woman he once knew, a woman whose name he can't recall
— he cannot resist.

The hunger is too great.

Fingers of shadow embrace, becoming six points around the glowing metal cage.

Together, they stretch their fingers into the sun's cage. Through tiny fissures and cracks in the steel, their shadows snake and slither their way to the warmth. It's so close, he can feel it. They all can.

Then, they touch its surface. At first, it burns. But soon, as all of them take on its power at once, that pain transforms into a euphoric sensation eclipsing any he has ever experienced.

Ghostly faces of beings he has long since forgotten fade from his memory as the energy surges through his new body, satisfying his hunger at last.

Then, all is dark.

In the dark, the others start singing a different song. Though he has never heard it before, somehow, he finds himself singing it all the same. At once, he knows what needs to be done.

They must call to it.

They must call to their father.

2

Ira pumped her malnourished legs as fast as the anger burning through her veins would allow, and then lights plinked out—leaving her in a black void.

She shrieked, tripping over her own feet. Her hands broke her fall, skidding against concrete like worn, rusty brakes grinding to a stop. Her palms pulsed with the impossibly loud rhythm of her own heartbeat, fresh blood mixing with dirt, grime, and Hugo's dried DNA as she sat there surrounded by absolute darkness.

What now? she thought.

For the moment, the thought of wringing Mathias's scrawny neck faded from her mind. Her eyes drifted this way and that, searching for anything that might help her get her bearings while a nameless fear burned from deep within her. A fear that spoke whispers in her mind, whispers which told her not to look too closely, that the only light she might find would be gray.

Where was she? How many doorways and corridors had she sprinted through? How many had Mathias opened? If he'd opened all of them, it was possible that she'd be able to find a flashlight. Even so, it would be difficult in the dark.

But she couldn't give up.

She wasn't sure why. Fuck, enough shit had happened that no one would be able to blame her if she finally lay down and said to hell with it—let that *thing* drag her off to who-the-fuck-knows-where.

No.

She got on her hands and knees and crawled to the wall, using it as a brace and a point of reference in the dark as she stood up and continued down the corridor.

Part of her blamed Lena. If it weren't for that stupid baby growing inside of her, Ira imagined it'd be so much easier to lie down and quit. But that was a lie and she knew it. She was too damned stubborn to die without a fight.

She had too much of her mother in her.

The curvature of the stone wall was her only guide. She followed it, walking her hands one by one.

Left

Right

Left

Right

Her thoughts drifted to her mother. Standing in the living room, her gray hair glistening in the dim morning sunlight as the first summer snowflakes touched the withering lawn. Her lips were parted in a warming smile. *This is a gift from God, Ira,* her mother had said, half-mad. And she could almost see her here as if she were still flesh and blood.

When Ira had argued with her, told her how this snow was a terrible sign, a harbinger of things to come, her mother's smile had faded. *Change is inevitable, Ira. God gives us only what we can handle.*

She'd died in that house. Content to be surrounded by the memories she held dear. Ira remembered the day she and Nico decided to leave, how content she seemed to be with her decision to stay, even as the snow threatened to trap them.

Ira barely recognized her mother in the end. This world, the death of Papa, the mounting toll from so many friends, neighbors, and family lost to the ice had changed her. In her youth, Papa had said she was tough as nails, that catcallers in New York always thought twice about whistling at her with one look at the fire in her eyes.

Change is inevitable.

She remembered the house when looking back over her shoulder, covered with piles of snow. It had looked more like a coffin than a home at that point.

Her brother had touched her shoulder. She could almost feel it now. Stern, authoritative, *warm.* If he hadn't touched her shoulder then, if he hadn't said what he'd said, she would have run all the way back to die with them.

The house, the hills of snow, the collapsing buildings of downtown Riverside, it all melted before her eyes, transforming into something else. *Somewhere else.*

It was a city. One unlike any she'd ever seen before. There were two suns in the sky, both dim and distant. The buildings seemed to be made from some kind of crimson stone, with strange symbols etched into their crumbling relief. Something stretched high above her, darkening the sky.

It was a black comet. Like the one she'd seen in her nightmares. It seemed to be moving quite quickly, like it had somewhere to be.

An appointment, a disembodied voice not too dissimilar to her own said. *A date with destiny.*

Standing there staring up like a fool, she lost track of time, lost track of the wall at her side, and reality got lost right along with everything else. She felt almost as if the black comet knew she was there, as if—from all those millions of miles above—it was peering down on her, and it was not impressed. Not impressed at all.

I must be going crazy.

"Shit, yo!" Hugo's voice broke her trance in the dark. He had a flashlight in one hand and was backing away from her.

"You're alive." She was both grateful and repulsed by that fact.

He didn't seem to hear her.

Here we are, she thought. *Nothing but shadows to witness me if I were to feel the life drain from your body, and no omnipresent voice to stop me.*

She stood there, staring at him in the dark, remembering Nico. Hugo seemed to understand what she was contemplating. His lips were trembling, fumbling to create words.

Her hands balled into fists.

Stepping forward, Ira raised her arm up to cave in his skull—and then he spoke. "I saw Eddy!"

Her fist stopped just short of smashing into his cranium. "What?"

Hugo shrank away, dropping the flashlight at her feet—tears pouring down his dirty face. He slumped against the curvature of the tunnel, curling into the fetal position. "It was…it was unreal, yo…like, I don't know, the gates of hell or somethin' got opened up. I saw them all, they looked wrong, like they weren't human no more. The music was so loud, too loud! His face, *God*, his fucking *face!*"

Ira bent over and picked up the flashlight. Her anger eroded, and she hated herself for it. What good would it do to kill someone who was already so broken? What justice was that?

All she could think about was how much she loved Eddy, and about how she'd never see him again.

It took all the strength she had to offer her hand to him. "Get up. We need to find Lena."

3

The constant crunch of massive footsteps in snow reaches his one remaining ear. The sky is a dim blue, the sun rising over eastern slopes—above places he once knew. Dead places.

The others march right up to the edge of the icycliff and stare at the burning circle of yellow fire as it makes its way higher and higher—perhaps for the last time.

Their arms reach high into the sky, hands and fingers stretching and waving like snakes chasing after prey…

And they sing.

How they sing.

They sing to their father.

The one who took them and molded them in his image.

The sound is so powerful that it spills down the cliffs and slopes and fills the valley like an ocean of otherworldly whitenoise. Down frozen and crumbling roads, through broken buildings and collapsed bridges, across snow-covered plains where fields of flowing yellow grass and proud weeds once grew. It fills every space, it wakes every soul unlucky enough to still be alive —

and it reaches her ears too, deep in the dark recesses of that place where he was reborn.

What was her name again?

He's suddenly very afraid for her.

Very afraid —

and their song grows louder still, calling to Yog'Elios. Calling to the black comet that devours suns.

It was as if Lena was in a trance. She'd been limping down darkened corridors, searching for nothing in particular but for refuge from the thing that seemed to be stalking her. If Mathias had treated them like mice in some giant maze, now she felt like she'd graduated to prey — a meal unlucky enough to be tortured and toyed with by her predator.

Where could she go in the dark?

Where was she?

And what was that music?

It was different than the music she'd heard days ago, but somehow it was familiar as well. Those choruses had seemed sad, longing. They scared her, made her think she was going nuts. These chants, songs, whatever they were, were almost triumphant — *safe* even. Before she knew what she was doing, she found herself following them — limping on her bad ankle — searching for their source.

She chose corridors and hallways where the singing seemed strongest, *loudest*. She didn't know what she'd find at the source, but she hoped it might be light, safety from the thing whose eyes she could feel stabbing into her back. The thing she feared would be there, staring at her in the dark with those seven glowing eyes — if she wasn't too scared to look.

5

"Where the hell is that coming from?" Ira asked.

Hugo shrugged. He was even more useless to her now that he was deaf. If she wasn't hallucinating, she thought she heard some kind of music—*singing* even. It was quiet, just at the edge of recognition, but she swore it was there.

"Damn it, Lena, where are you?"

So far, they'd combed through several corridors and still hadn't heard or seen any sign of her. She wasn't in the chamber where they'd been held captive.

Hugo avoided eye contact with her. She was thankful for that. When she looked back at him, he seemed to be mumbling things under his breath, scratching at the bloodstains that coated his neck and soaked into his long johns.

The darkness rang out from all sides, as if it were attempting to strangle the small circle of light made by her flashlight. That had to be her imagination, her paranoia. She had to force herself to keep looking onward, no matter what her eyes might find in the dark corners of her vision.

Three more corners turned and still no sign of Lena.

Wait. No.

There was a light shining at the end of the corridor.

Carefully, quietly, she picked up the pace. Hugo was left behind in the dark. As she advanced on the light, she wondered what she might find. Lena cowering with a flashlight? Some autonomous instrumentation which had yet to die in the wake of the fusion core's death? Or, more likely, would it be Mathias, stalking the corridors with a bottle of chloroform and a cloth in hand?

She rounded the corner and was unsurprised to see Mathias toying with the lock of an experiment chamber door, cursing lightly under his breath. He was a shadow of his former self. His hair was almost white. She could see protrusions of his spine through his sweat-stained long johns.

His yellowing eyes looked to her flashlight fearfully, "No! Please, don't take me! There's still time yet!"

Ira rushed him, grabbing him by the collar. "Give me one good reason why I shouldn't bash your head into the concrete!"

"I-Ira?" His breath stank to high heaven—his teeth had started to rot, just like Weber's had. "Y-you don't want to kill *me*. I *know* how *it* works. H-how to get it started again. I wandered for so long searching for the answer, but I know now! I *know* now!"

There was something odd about his voice. Like he'd aged two decades between the time she'd last heard his voice over the speakers of their cell and now. She remembered her vision before Hugo's flashlight and voice brought her back to her senses.

It's not possible, she thought. *He's just losing it, that's all. Just like Weber did.*

"I thought I'd never see you again, Ira," Mathias said. "How terrible it was, wandering the dark, running from *him*. It was my penance, yes, that must be true. I see that now. To wander without sleep through the Astral Lands.

"I'm..." His eyes and furrowed brow looked crazed and yet, strangely remorseful. "I am truly sorry for what I did, all of it. Truly sorry. Can you forgive me?"

God, just shut up!

"Why were you trying to get in there?" Ira gestured to the door Mathias had just been fiddling with.

He cackled; she resisted her gag reflex at the smell. "The fusion reactor. It runs off of saltwater to produce the reaction. I saw it. I saw it in the blueprints before I got lost. The byproduct is helium. I think that room is where they kept concentrated sodium chloride used for the creation of new saline solution for sensory deprivation tanks. If we can get the core restarted, we can start the final experiment protocol."

"You're still going on about that?" Ira asked.

"Don't you see what's happening? The world is dying at last, I've seen it...heard the song calling to it. The Harvester and the creatures that seem to stalk this place are the least of our concerns.

"You've seen it too, haven't you?"

"Seen what?" Ira asked.

"The black comet," Mathias said, grinning wide and yellow.

Ira's grip released. She held her head. "What the hell is going on? Is this what hell is?"

"Maybe," Mathias said. "I think it...yes...I think it's that thing, the Amarath. The creature creates portals in the dark to its own little corner in the Astral Lands. But, now—" he chuckled, "—now the shadows are joined, they are *one*. How fortunate that we have not stumbled into its domain."

6

Lena found herself half-limping, half-running, across a desert of decrepit, rotting leather. Sometime after she'd turned that last corner, the sky had turned gray. Somehow, she knew it always had been there, hiding behind whatever protected sane people from *demons*, *la chupacabra*, and *UFOs*. The ground seemed to go on and on and on. Yet, it was also as if the horizon was *moving*, like a convalescent home resident taking deep breaths off their respirator. There were things in the distance she couldn't quite make out. They looked like pits, or craters, but they seemed to be moving too.

And the singing...the singing was quieter here.

She could feel it coming from behind her...and to the right of her, just over a hill, and in several other directions too. She wanted so desperately to get away from this place, to get back to the singing, find its source. Then, maybe she'd be safe?

She certainly couldn't turn back. There was a constant pressure bearing down on her, like the feeling you get when you're being watched. The temptation to glance behind her was strong, but she couldn't bring herself to do it. She was too much of a coward.

Somehow, she knew that if she did— It'd be the end of her.

She'd have to find another way.

There was a sound like heavy breathing behind her. She felt the ground shake with each step it took after her. Her heart fluttered, threatening to seize in her chest from pure terror. It was biding its time with her. It didn't have to rush, did it? No. It could find her any time, around any darkened corner, or it could wait for her to wear herself out, or to sprain her ankle in one of those holes —

They *weren't* holes.

She could see *teeth* in them, black and yellow and rotting, jagged things that opened and closed.

They were *mouths!*

If she tripped and fell into one of those, she'd have a lot more than a sprain to worry about.

That's when she noticed the smell.

It was a persistent stench, the faint aroma of death and rotting human flesh. She knew that smell all too well. She found herself captivated by the decomposing body parts that were littered carelessly across the land. Some of them still had their bloodstained lab jackets and long johns on. She watched one of the mouths open up wide, causing a nearby bloody female torso to fall in. It chewed and chewed and chewed. Even from this distance, she could hear the brittle sounds of bones snapping. She wondered how long it would be before there were no more body parts left to feed the land.

Not long, a voice said in her mind. *Not long at all.*

She could scarcely hear the music over the crunching of bone —

"Shit!" She teetered on the edge of one of those mouths. It opened so wide it had crossed her path in the time it took for her to blink. She could see deep inside the pit. It was like looking inside the biggest throat she'd ever seen. The walls of flesh had rows of razor-sharp teeth embedded in them; they pulsated as she shuddered.

She backed away from the edge of that mouth, careful not to upset it. When she was a safe distance away, she ran.

At first she just wanted to get away from that thing! Then, she heard the singing again, coming from a place over to her right. There were more mouths, all of them opening and closing in some sick kind of anticipation at her approach.

There was no way of knowing if moving toward that choir of voices would be her salvation, but she had no other choice. Tears spattered down her cheeks as she limped as hard and as fast as she could. There was a mouth expanding directly in front of her path.

I'm sorry, she thought at no one in particular. *I'm sorry I was such a fuckup! Sorry I let so many people down! Poor little Sophi...I'm sorry I couldn't take care of you!* She placed her hands over her belly. *But your sister, or your brother, will be different. All I need is to survive this. Get past that thing, and I promise I'll devote my life to them! Just, please, God—if you exist—don't let me die here!*

The mouth in front of her seemed to respond by opening wider. As if to say, *there is no God, and I will devour you here.*

At first, Lena's despair hit its peak. She was almost ready to walk over to that hole in this unholy land and throw herself in if it was inevitable...but, something inside her snapped.

No, I'm not gonna die here!

She clenched her fists and pumped her legs harder, wincing through the pain and the fatigue until she got herself up to a proper sprint.

The hole, mouth, whatever it was, drew closer.

And closer.

She'd have to jump at the last second and hope she reached the other side, if she tried to run around it she knew it would just open wider.

She was almost on it.

Then, she took a deep breath, jumped...and screamed as loud as her lungs would allow.

Was it all a dream?

Lena could feel the cold concrete floor beneath her hands and feet. She could feel a slight pressure at the back of her skull, the same kind of feeling you get when someone's watching you.

Can't look back, she thought. *Gotta keep moving forward. It's the only way.*

There was a dim light coming from down the corridor; she could just barely make out a sign in front of her.

It said TOP FLOOR, and below that it said LEVEL 1 STAGING and SECURITY with arrows pointing this way and that.

How did she get here? Had she really just been running through that hellish place?

The elevators were out, and she hadn't gone up any flights of stairs that she knew of. Yet, she was near the entrance to the facility. It was colder up here, too. Much colder.

The singing! She could hear the singing again!

It was louder here too, almost *painfully* loud.

Lena had the strangest compulsion to get up off her hands and knees and follow the voices to the source of the singing. Any thoughts other than those pertaining to following that compulsion seemed to ebb as quickly as they came. It was as if the space inside her brain could only contain the choruses coming from down the hall, and little else.

She obeyed, standing up and following the arrow to the main gate. She thought briefly of the freezing temperatures outside, that she'd need protective gear, but those thoughts too were silenced.

Before she knew it, she was staring at the long icy tunnel that led to the mountain's surface. The singing was so loud that her eardrums felt like they might burst.

The pain was almost unbearable, even here.

Still, she stepped out into the icy tunnel. Each step forward on the ice was like stepping on hot coals. She started laughing at this thought. The laughter seemed to persist long past the point when her mouth had chattered shut from the severe cold.

If she could think, she would probably be thinking about how foolish this was. How, once she emerged from that cave, she would likely die.

The light grew and grew. She felt cold rivers of blood dribbling down both sides of her neck.

Soon, she lost the feeling in her hands and feet. The cave entrance loomed. The singing was so loud it felt like she was being bombarded by constant microbursts.

With the feeling in her limbs gone, she emerged from the tunnel.

There they were, gathered at the edge of the cliff. Raising their limbs to the sky. They were massive. Their bodies had grown great tumorous masses, exposing shadows which seemed to betray an infinite space beyond. It looked as though each of their hands were composed of snakes.

Her eyes followed their gesture toward the sky, to the dim circle of the sun, and just below its noonday position in the sky.

It was like someone had torn the sky open, revealing its truth. It stretched halfway across the sky. She thought briefly that it looked strangely like a dark comet.

It was headed straight for the sun.

The comet seemed to collide with the sun, wrapping itself around it like a serpent coiling around a mouse.

And then the sun went dark, vanishing as though it had never been there at all.

The singing stopped.

The sky got darker and darker.

One of the creatures turned toward her with its featureless, bulbous head. Eddy's remaining, decaying eye, focused on her, his face nearly swallowed by the thing he was becoming. The creature's massive body split away from the pack, stomping through the snow toward her, its snakelike hands reaching out to do God knows what to her body.

She screamed.

The pain in her limbs couldn't stop her from running back into the cave.

She knew she wouldn't get far.

CHAPTER TWENTY-THREE

"You commanded all the doors to open," Ira said. "Why didn't this one?"

"One can only guess," Mathias said.

"How are we going to open it?" Ira asked.

"I was working on that before you grabbed me," Mathias said.

Ira turned back to look for Hugo. He wasn't there. Maybe he was lost in the dark? Maybe that *thing* had gotten him?

"Why can't we take some solution from one of the tanks?" Ira asked.

"We need an exact mixture that matches what was used to produce the fusion reaction."

"We can just walk through here." As if coming out from the depths of the abyss, Hugo walked right past them and placed his hands on a wall shrouded in shadow. Then he was pushing them *through* the wall and was gone.

Ira blinked, thinking it was just the pitch-dark playing tricks on her eyes. She backed up, shining her flashlight around for any sign of Hugo's body. "What in the fuck?"

Mathias straightened up. "The fool...but, yes...yes, maybe he's right?"

"What are you saying?"

Mathias walked forward and placed his gnarled hands in the wall, then, with a low, rumbling chuckle coming from deep inside his throat, he pushed himself forward and vanished too. Ira watched his gnarled feet get swallowed up by the wall.

She stood there, rubbing her eyes, hyperventilating, disbelieving. Maybe she was going mad? Maybe they hadn't been by her side at all?

"Hello?" Ira said quietly, hoping she was right. That the apparitions had gone away.

"I'm not following you," She said, shaking her head. "You're not real. This isn't real."

It *was* madness!

That was it. Some kind of fever dream that she couldn't wake from. All of this couldn't possibly be happening...could it?

Ira meant what she said, she really did. She was adamant about not following after them...

But now she was alone. Or was it that she was now aware of her loneliness? The darkness around her seemed almost to be alive, as if it were closing in on her. Part of her wanted to curl into a ball, find some place to hide with her flashlight clutched close to her, but she knew that wouldn't save her.

The maddening thing was, part of her thought they were right, that Mathias and Hugo had really phased through some kind of portal, that it wasn't all in her head—part of her could even rationalize it as if it were completely natural.

It almost made her laugh.

She inched closer to the wall, shining her light briefly across the surface. The wall didn't catch the light the way other surfaces did. Maybe it was just her imagination? Maybe Hugo and Mathias hadn't been here at all and she was just going mad talking to herself?

She placed her hand on the wall, just as Hugo had. Then, she screamed as she felt something grab her hand and pull her through.

Then she was falling. The sensation was like those nightmares she'd had as a child where she'd fall from the top of the Empire State Building, only to wake up when she hit the ground.

Only there was no ground here. Just endless dark.

Then, all at once, there *was* ground and she was lying on it. The sky was black, with two dim stars shining in the distance. One red, and one white.

"Good of you to come," Mathias said.

Hugo waved a shaky hand at her. She was disgusted by the fact that it was almost comforting. These men—no *not* men, *boys* playing at being men—who were her enemies. She'd rather embrace them than all of this madness, or her own loneliness.

"I almost fell through before Hugo found me," she said. And at that thought, she was very worried for Lena. "Oh my God."

Mathias nodded. "You're worried for Lena."

Ira nodded, getting to her feet. "How do we get back?"

Mathias shrugged. "This isn't an exact science."

Hugo smiled, turned around, and started walking. "This way."

There was an uncomfortable moment when she and Mathias made eye contact. Did he suspect something was wrong with Hugo too?

Hugo was already trudging through the crimson sand, thousands of feet away, when she finally said it. "He's not acting normal."

Mathias nodded.

But they followed Hugo all the same. That voice deep inside Ira screamed for her to turn back, to run from these madmen. But, she'd tumbled through the wall too, hadn't she?

Hugo led them down a staircase of crumbling, ancient steps composed of red stone. The steps twisted and snaked down into a massive canyon. It was the same place she'd seen earlier, she was almost certain of that.

The towers with their crumbling relief were there in the distance. And, something she hadn't noticed before, too. A massive pyramid at the end of the canyon, situated just below the dim pair of stars.

It seemed like they'd marched for days. The towers on either side of the canyon appeared almost to be peering down at them, and maybe they were.

"Who do you think lived here?" Ira asked.

"The Astral Lands are not home to ordinary creatures," Mathias said. "They are often under the sway of a particular entity, or the mirror of a place in our world."

"How do you know that?"

Mathias grinned. "Because—"

"Because he has seen it," Hugo said. There was something she didn't like about his voice, something otherworldly.

"Seen what?" Ira asked.

"The fruit of hidden knowledge," Hugo said.

They didn't say another word for the rest of the journey. Hugo led them up a stone staircase leading up to the pyramid.

Mathias seemed eager to get inside. She could see the madness that festered beneath his crazed eyes and grinning mouth, like so many maggots crawling beneath the surface, consuming what little grip on sanity the husk of the man—*the monster*—had. She would have to remain on guard around him. There was no telling what he might try to do.

It was after me! she remembered him say. *The Harvester was after me!*

They reached the top of the winding stone staircase and gazed upon the awe-inspiring face of the pyramid they'd seen from untold miles away. There were two rows of pillars leading all the way to its front face. The pyramid was black. The material seemed to drink in the dim light from this world's host stars in totality.

"Our answers await inside," Hugo said, marching forward.

Ira waited until he was out of earshot before she said, "Hugo is seriously freaking me out."

"He's been changed by his experience with…" Mathias paused.

"With what?"

"Eddy."

Mathias followed after Hugo. Ira stayed behind briefly, squeezing the life out of her flashlight.

The path leading up to the pyramid was almost as long as the canyon had been. How long had they been in this place? She was almost certain that she'd seen the suns change position more than once.

If they really had been here for whatever passed for days, how was Lena fairing back in… It struck her that this wasn't her world. That, indeed, all of this was happening. It was not just some elaborate fever dream of madness brought on by the dark as she had thought when arriving here. That thought alone caused a part of her mind to break, something she would never recover from.

No matter how long they marched, the pyramid only seemed to climb higher into the sky, swallowing it with its immense darkness.

"Behold the entrance." Hugo's possessed voice shocked her to attention.

The pyramid was so massive that it touched both horizons. An oppressive triangular doorway loomed before Hugo, its frame carved with ornate serpent-like things with too many eyes. A hieroglyphic symbol stood above the doorway.

Hugo walked forward and placed his hand on the doorway. Three shadows danced up the wall and retracted into Hugo's hand.

Then, as if the entire planet were shaking, the door faded into darkness.

Hugo gestured forward. "The way is open."

Mathias and Hugo disappeared into the doorway. Ira hesitated a moment, looking behind her, before she followed them.

It struck her that the hallways, rooms, and corridors were all laid out in a very familiar fashion. The corridors were curved, just like the facility they had been living in. The rooms had observation areas and strange experiments where what looked like the dried-up carapaces of massive insects stood decomposing in the stale, dead air. It was like a maze, but familiar. If Hugo hadn't been guiding them, she might have been able to find her own way. The only difference between this place and the facility—besides scale—was the ornate imagery etched on the curvature of the walls.

The imagery seemed to come alive as Hugo led them deeper and deeper into the pyramid, taking on an almost organic texture. Perhaps the facility they'd been living in was also a pyramid? But what would be the point of hiding something like that?

She felt she knew the answer to that question.

"The walls," Mathias said. "I've seen several of these pyramids in other lands...yet, none of them had anything like these hieroglyphs."

"They are a telling of the origin of the first oros," Hugo said. "One version of it, anyway."

"What's an oros?" Ira asked.

"The closest word in...our language might be somewhere between horizon and universe," Hugo said.

"Why between them?" Ira asked.

"What is a universe if not a horizon, a limiting circle of mortal sight?" Hugo said.

"What does it say?" Mathias asked, his voice eager. Too eager. She wished he hadn't asked.

"If you had the necessary means to activate the message it would tell you that the original universe, the one that all others are mirrored from, was created by the formation of a consciousness so powerful that its birth cry brought physical existence into being in a baptism of fire, and its anger at what it had inadvertently created fractured it into untold and unquantifiable others, like a mirror smashed in its center."

The carvings in the wall reflected only part of Hugo's telling of the story, she guessed because it was meant to be activated by some unknown mechanism. Its face was full of tentacles, mouths, angular hieroglyphs, and other unspeakable creatures which she didn't dare look at for very long. It was also segmented like a mirror, just as Hugo had said. It seemed like it would never end.

"Its true name has been long lost, and even if you could pronounce it, all mortals but those with the strongest of will would be driven insane by its mere mention. But, I suppose it could be likened to your big bang."

They rounded another corner. The mural continued.

"It is said that each universe has a mirror of that original being, one that is decidedly the lesser of it."

"How do you know all of this?" Ira asked.

Hugo smiled. "It is as Mathias said. I have awakened."

Somehow, she doubted it. When she stared into Hugo's bloodshot eyes, she saw only darkness. An abyss staring back at her.

2

Lena felt the Earth moving beneath her. It shook and waved and passed her by. It seemed somehow appropriate. They say that there's a white light, or a rush of stars, at the end. That was all bullshit, though. At the end, it was nothing but blackness.

There were sounds, though. Though, those sounds seemed to be reaching deep inside her mind, past the ringing in her ears and into her very soul.

Snarling, and thunderous beats, as if the devil himself were calling to her soul—just as her mother always warned her would happen if she didn't "learn to close her damn legs." If she was headed to hell, she could already feel the flames roasting her skin.

Then, she opened her eyes to the blackness and saw there were no flames. She was, however, sure that she wasn't on the ground. It took her a few moments to figure out that she wasn't dead, and that she was being carried.

She looked up. The snarling was coming directly from something above her. There was a faint light, silhouetting a massive bulbous form. She couldn't feel her arms, or if her back was lying against anything. Then, she realized that the flames she thought were baking her skin were actually an intense fever.

What happened? She couldn't remember being sick before. She couldn't see very far, but the faint aroma of recycled air told her that she was inside the facility…again.

She remembered a nightmare, where she had been separated from her body. She had watched herself wander through the dark until she found the entrance to the facility. She'd appeared to be following something, but what that was, she couldn't be certain.

Why would her body wander off on its own?

Her body had stepped out into the tunnel. She'd screamed at herself to not go out into the cold unprotected. But her body wouldn't listen. It walked through the icy tunnel barefoot, paying no attention to the pain she felt. The circle of light that marked the end of the tunnel was her death. When she emerged from the tunnel, there were hulking monstrosities with shadows for skin, calling to the sky with hands that wriggled like worms.

Their arms were reaching to the sun.

No.

They were reaching for the black comet that was heading toward the sun.

Then, she'd dreamed something even more impossible. The sun actually went out, turned off, like a lightbulb burning out, or a candle getting snuffed out.

What if it wasn't a dream?

She chuckled.

What a funny thought. Her chuckling turned into a laughter so painful, it felt as if her throat might be torn to shreds.

The growling presence from above silenced her. She felt something beneath her; it had the consistency of mucus. Her body slid in the dark, landing hard on concrete.

She looked up, staring into glowing crimson eyes. The light that cascaded from those eyes revealed a familiar face.

Lena tried to scream, but her voice was barely a whisper.

No one would hear her cries for help.

No one was coming for her.

3

The corridors inside the pyramid looked cracked, worn. As if there'd been a massive earthquake in this place eons ago. The ceiling was so tall, Ira couldn't imagine that anything human had walked these halls.

"Where are you leading us?" Ira asked Hugo.

"You shall see soon enough," Hugo said.

"I-I have a confession to make," Mathias said, stopping in his tracks and falling behind.

Ira hesitated to turn around and face him. The shadows lurked behind them, dancing around their flashlights, and she feared what she might see if she dared to look past him. "What is it?"

"I'm afraid I've done something," Mathias said, his voice shaking. "Something unforgivable..."

"And that's news?" Ira asked.

"He has summoned something to your world," Hugo said.

"What do you mean, *your world*?" Ira said, but knew that she didn't want to know the answer to that question.

"He's right," Mathias said. "There is something coming...if it's not already here."

"What?"

"My panicked cries for help were the beacon, my memories the map." Mathias ran his shaking hands through his white hair. "I was such a fool. Yes. That's what I was. The others shut me out…I had to find the password to the final experiment." He repeated *final experiment* for a while as he leaned against the stone wall, pulling out white, wiry hairs from his scalp and staring at each strand as if it were the last. "So I sought out something that would be similar to my own essence — yes — and I *found* one. But it was a being that was capable of consuming entire stars, and it had no love for sentient life. It must have followed me."

"Eats stars?" Ira shook her head. "That's crazy!"

"All of this is crazy, Ira," Mathias said, opening his hands, letting the hairs he'd pulled from his scalp fall to the alien floor. "How much further is it a stretch for *that* to be real?"

"He has been carrying a dangerous grimoire," Hugo said, pointing to a lump in Mathias's lab coat.

"Weber's book?—" Ira shot forward, fighting with Mathias for the thing that rested inside his coat—"You've been carrying it this whole time!"

She didn't know why she was so apprehensive toward the idea, she just knew somewhere, perhaps unconsciously, that they needed to get rid of it. Despite how scrawny Mathias was, his grip was fierce, his strength nearly unbreakable.

"No! We *need* it, it's the only way we'll survive!" Rotten spittle sprayed from his mouth.

"Don't listen to him," Hugo said, chuckling. "He means to sacrifice me to the Harvester."

Then, two books fell from Mathias's coat pocket, smacking against the floor. The echoes reverberated down the dead corridor. Mathias let go almost instantly, dropping to cradle the books.

Ira almost felt sorry for him. "Is that true?"

"What the hell do you care?" Mathias shot up, holding the grimoire and a notebook as a mother might hold their child close to their chest. "He murdered your brother, or have you forgotten *that?* So what if I want to exchange places with him?"

"I—"

"You all hide from the chaos, covering your eyes from it, as if that will save you," Mathias said. "I'm the only one who dared to stare into the abyss, despite the toll."

"None of this would be happening if it wasn't for you!" Ira shouted, getting in Mathias's face.

Mathias tapped the tattered journal. "Come now, you can't possibly believe that. Those creatures that accompanied Eddy in destroying the core? Weber created them, just as I did. I found a journal entry. He failed, time after time, to sacrifice a substitute subject to the Harvester. Their bodies morphed into hideous, monstrous things, and they became catatonic. He locked them up down there, just in case they woke up.

"Eventually, it would have come down to this. I at least gave you a fighting chance at survival!"

Ira grabbed him by his collar. "Survival? Is that what you call this? All your machinations!"

"We must go," Hugo said. "Now that his plans are exposed, he is powerless to execute them."

"What?" Ira turned back to Hugo...something was off. She felt as though she couldn't really focus on his body. As if his movements were somehow imperceptible to her eyes. "But what about the grimoire?"

"The beast is already after us," Hugo said, turning and heading—*gliding*—down the corridor. "It matters not whether we have the book or not. Once its master hungers for prey, there is no stopping it."

Mathias clutched both books closely as he followed after Hugo.

Ira wanted desperately to shout at them to turn back. But being left there—like an island of light in a sea of darkness—would be too much, and she hurried to catch up with them.

The corridor funneled out into a large chamber. Ancient dust particles, perhaps older than the Earth itself, fell from the ceiling high above in the dark. Hugo seemed to vanish into that all-consuming dark.

"*Now, we can really begin.*" Hugo's voice seemed to be coming from everywhere at once.

"No," Mathias shook his head, backing away. "No-no-no! Why didn't I see it earlier?"

"What the hell are you talking about?" Ira shook her head, looking for Hugo in the dark. Her flashlight seemed not to reflect off of anything, as if the shadows themselves were feeding on the light.

What's the matter, Masku? The voice that she heard no longer belonged to Hugo, but something else, something whose voice seemed to shake the very fiber of her being, the outline of her existence. Had it been inside her head this entire time? Had she only imagined it speaking audibly? *You failed to find a suitable substitute and complete the bargain, now you must pay the price.*

When Ira turned her head, it was as if a veil was lifted from her eyes. She saw at the center of the room a hooded figure, cloaked in rotting flesh and cobwebs, its face—a mask eons old, eyes of blackened pits and a carved mouth, grinning deep with malicious intent. Its arms were raised to the ceiling, high above in the unknowable depths of that darkness. But they were not arms at all, but great, segmented appendages which had the consistency of a serpent's skin, ending in three massive grabbing fingers.

The darkness washed away. A hellish green glow seemed to emanate from the creature.

Ira found that she was screaming, backing into Mathias.

"No!" Mathias screamed in her ear, his hands clutching at her shoulder with a deathgrip, forcing her forward. "Take *her* instead! Take *her!*"

"What the hell are you doing?" Ira shouted.

"I don't want to be swallowed by the abyss!" Mathias said, his eyes crazed, bloodshot.

The thing in the center of the room was reaching for them. Its appendages seemed to have no limit to their reach. *You will find peace in nonexistence, Masku.*

"We have to run!" Ira didn't know why she grabbed his hand, why she decided to save him. She yanked his hands off of her and bolted for the entrance, dragging him along with her into the corridor. The green glow gave chase through the corridor, spreading like a virus.

"Why?" Mathias asked. "I was ready to give you to him, why would you save me?"

"*Shut* the *fuck* up and *run!*"

You cannot run from me, Masku. I will always find you, no matter where you turn, no matter where you hide. You are but playthings, and the abyss will have you tonight.

She should have just left him behind. But, no, she felt that she might need him—and all the mad knowledge he possessed.

Sharp pains erupted through her chest, cascading through her lungs and lining her throat like needles. She couldn't stop. Not if she wanted to outrun that thing.

There seemed to be no end to the corridors. Where once they had been familiar, now they seemed to be arranged like a maze. Ira didn't think that it had been like this the first time through.

A sickening, inhuman laughter filled the stale air around them.

"He won't let me go," Mathias said, chuckling lightly.

"How is this possible?" Ira shook her head, stopping to catch her breath.

"Are you still so foolishly attached to your notions of what is and isn't possible with all of this as evidence?"

"I keep thinking it's just some kind of nightmare…that I'll wake up in the cell you put us in."

"No such luck." Mathias's back hit the wall, and he slid into a crouch. "Just leave me…I'm doomed anyway."

Ira glanced behind her. The green glow was snaking its way toward them, forming into jagged, serpentine shapes. "As much as I'd like to, I think I may need you before all of this is over."

He shook his head. "I've failed…I've failed at everything…made a mess…made a mess of the whole affair."

Ira walked over and slapped him. "Snap the hell out of it! You deserve worse than death for the shit you've pulled, God knows, but you can still try to make up for what you've done by helping Lena and I get out of this mess!"

Mathias sat there, staring at her with his yellowing, bloodshot eyes, and nodded. "Yes…yes, you're right."

Ira grabbed him by the wrists and yanked him to his feet. "How do we get out of here?"

"The book…" His eyes sparkled with madness. "It names this place as the Astral Lands. We must leave it through a door in our minds."

"What the hell does that mean?"

The green light was almost upon them. Ira started moving down the hall, pulling Mathias along with her.

"How did we get here?" Mathias said. "That thing was pretending to be Hugo, it opened a doorway. The book says that we must think on the place we wish to reach."

"That's it?" Somehow she doubted it.

"The darkness…even now the Amarath is using the dark as a means of getting to our world…perhaps, if it followed us here, we can use the dark to return to our world?"

"If you say so."

They rounded another corner and Mathias stopped.

"Here," Mathias said, approaching a wall with a crack running down its surface to a place which appeared to be shrouded in darkness.

Ira couldn't tell if he was reaching for a doorway, or simply part of the wall that was covered in shadow.

"Are you sure?" Ira asked.

The green light snaked its tendrils through the darkness, gripping like ancient fingers.

Is it toying with us? she thought.

Mathias's gnarled hands found the dark; he exhaled in complete ecstasy.

The sickly green light seemed to transform from mere light into actual tendrils, of the same consistency as the Harvester's skin. They glowed with the dim light of dying stars, and they reached, clutching for Mathias.

"Grab onto me!" Mathias yelled.

Ira hesitated only half a second before the tendrils stabbed out for Mathias; she grabbed onto his back as he pulled them through the darkness.

It was like waking up from a nightmare.

There they were. Their breath steaming in the air. Sitting in the darkness. Their flashlights flickering against what looked like salt deposits. It seemed like such a long time ago, days, even, since they had been outside that door, trying to find a way in.

How had they ended up here?

"That will not stop him for long," Mathias said, shining his flashlight around the room. "Just as I imagined, salt deposits. We should be able to start the reactor with this."

"Did...did that really all just happen?" Ira shook her head, hugging her knees tight against her body. "Why does it feel like it's so far away? Like it's fading?"

"None of that matters right now." Mathias was standing up, offering his hand to her. "We don't have much time."

She nodded, taking his hand.

They gathered as much of the salt as they could, stuffing it in their pockets.

"This should do," Mathias said. "Now we need to find our way out of here."

"How do we do that without power?" Ira asked.

"Each of these rooms has an emergency failsafe, just in case someone gets trapped inside." Mathias shined his light up and down the walls, scanning them with crazed eyes. "Yes. Here."

Ira watched him pry open a small compartment in the wall; there was a lever and a series of instructions. He pulled the lever and the door seal popped, sliding open just enough so Mathias could pry it the rest of the way.

Ira followed him into the corridor, where they found Hugo waiting.

"Yo, what happened?" he asked.

Both of them recoiled at Hugo. Ira had almost screamed.

"You don't remember?" Ira asked, forgetting that he was deaf. "You..."

But, had it really been him? Was this even him now?

"I got lost back there," Hugo said, talking like someone who isn't aware of their own volume while listening to headphones, "you two were talking to someone, and when I got here, you were gone."

"How long did you wait?" Mathias asked.

"What?" Hugo shrugged.

"He's deaf," Ira said.

"Oh, well, that doesn't help us," Mathias said.

"I was stuck out here for a few minutes, B, thought I was gonna lose it..."

"It felt like a lot longer than a few fucking minutes," Ira said, shivering. She was thankful that the memory of that awful place was fading. Maybe she wouldn't go completely mad after all?

Wishful thinking.

Mathias was starting to back away down the corridor. "We must find the core chamber."

Ira was set to agree with him when she remembered Lena. "No...we've got to find Lena."

"There may not be time," Mathias said.

"Then you two go ahead," Ira said. "But I have to find her."

"As you wish," Mathias said.

"I'll meet you in the core chamber," Ira said, turning around.

"I'm sure you will," Mathias said.

Ira stopped, clenching her fists tight. "Don't think this makes us friends, Mathias. I still haven't forgiven either of you. If you cross me, you will regret it."

"I'm sure I will," Mathias said. "More than even the abyss."

Ira ignored his last comment and left them behind. She heard Hugo shouting, asking where she was going, but soon their voices faded into the abyss.

CHAPTER TWENTY-FOUR

Mathias watched Ira disappear in the dark.

"Come boy," Mathias said. "We have no time to waste."

Hugo stuck his finger in his right earhole, made a face, and shook his head. "Man, I think I heard that…maybe my hearing is coming back?"

"How fortunate for me," Mathias said, turning away from Hugo and heading down the pitch-black corridor.

They walked in silence. Mathias couldn't tell how much of Hugo's hearing had returned, and he didn't much care. Hopefully the words would find a way into his feeble little mind.

"Now, let's see, how do we get to the core from here?" Mathias shined his flashlight along the wall.

Hugo stopped. "Man, I ain't forgetting what you did to me."

"As I recall, I was simply a messenger. What you did with that information is your cross to bear, as it were."

"You knew damn well what you was doing."

"Maybe. But we've got larger problems here in the dark than all the terrible things you all think I've done."

Hugo went quiet; Mathias could hear him quietly shuddering.

"The creature you thought was Eddy," Mathias said, "the music you heard it singing. I think it was a chant meant to lure something to our solar system."

"What?"

"And I'm afraid that that's my fault as well."

"What the fuck are you talking about, B? I can barely hear you. Talk louder."

"I read something in one of Weber's journals after the fact. It said that Weber had made an awful discovery inside the tank. He blamed himself for not having taken precautions, thought that he should not have sought to question the other entities to commune with, to reach beyond. They warned him as they warned me, that there are other, far more ancient and malevolent forces out in the depths of the cosmos—and he found such an entity. The black comet.

"I remember how he described it, terrible and beautiful simultaneously, he said he'd *'found it resting beyond the veil of a large nebula, its body like a spiral galaxy, but completely devoid of light.'* He went on to describe how it moved *'like a poisonous cloud,'* spreading its insidious tentacles to every star that it could and consuming them whole. He watched it for a great deal of time, too horrified to move his essence away. I wonder if watching entire civilizations get destroyed in the wake of this being was what finally broke his mind."

"You're freakin' me out, B," Hugo said.

"Do you know what Messages from the Abyss calls it?"

"I don't wanna know…stop."

"Yog'Elios."

Hugo stopped walking in the dark. Mathias turned to him. The sounds of their footsteps echoed into the dark and faded. "I said stop it."

"Yog'Elios, Hugo. That's its name."

Hugo placed his hand over what Mathias believed was his remaining functioning ear. But, if he was correct, Hugo would not be able to unlearn that name.

"Just take us to the core, like Ira told you…"

Mathias shrugged and kept walking. "Suit yourself."

They walked in silence for a time. The only sounds to accompany them were the echoes of their footsteps and Hugo's pathetic whimpering.

Mathias tried to focus on the core. To guide them through the shadows toward the image he held in his mind's eye, just as he'd done when escaping the Astral Lands.

This place is like a maze now, he thought. *Normal traversal of these corridors will be impossible. If Ira doesn't figure that out for herself, then perhaps there's still a chance to perform the ritual?*

He glanced back at Hugo. His eyes looked crazed.

Mathias did not believe in fate, or miracles, but it was quite fortunate that Hugo had survived his encounter with Eddy.

It was hard to tell if he was ready in the dark. How gray was his skin? His eyes? Would the Harvester even care about his physical state, as long as his mind was broken?

This is my chance, Mathias said, his heart rate increasing with every step they took.

"What is it?" Hugo asked, his words cut to bits and pieces by his fear.

"Just an observation," Mathias said, pausing in the middle of the darkness that permeated around them.

"What's that?" Hugo's eyes vibrated, his lips quivering. He looked absolutely terrified.

"Weber didn't consider the black comet to be an entity at first," Mathias said, smiling, inching closer to Hugo. "Had he not felt such undeniable malice and indifference coming from it, he would have categorized it as a cosmic force of nature, like an asteroid, comet, or a black hole.

"He didn't think it took notice of his presence at the time. But, considering the creatures Eddy unleashed after his...transformation...I wonder. But, one thing is clear—Weber knew that if it were to find its way back to our solar system, it would be the end for what was left of humanity, for the Earth itself. He claimed he wasn't mad enough to consort with such an entity."

"What's your damn point?"

"Simple, really. Science is all about deductive reasoning. About observation of our natural world. Isn't it?"

Hugo looked nervous. "You're doing it again, man, stop!"

"The universe is far more complicated than we could have ever imagined. Think about all we've seen in our brief existence, the horrors of war, the Amarath, even the Harvester, and all the infinite scope of the Astral Lands…it all leads one to one simple truth…"

"What the hell, man," Hugo said, playing with his right ear. "I said stop it!"

"Do you know what that truth is?"

"No! I don't wanna know!"

"It's that this is the truth of reality. The universe is a cold and unfeeling thing, dreamed up by a sleeping blind idiot God, and filled with horrors that would just as soon step on us as take notice of our pathetic existence. Why should we be any different from those who are not our intellectual equals?"

"What? Like me?"

"Weber didn't want to consort with the black comet, but I *did*. What does that say about me, then?"

"That you're fucking crazy, B!"

"Call it whatever you like, Hugo." Mathias took a step forward, feeling his tattered lab coat for the book.

"Yeah? And what happened to finding the damn core? Ira gonna kill your ass if you pull shit!"

"We're already here," Mathias said, gesturing to Hugo.

"What the hell?" Hugo looked around, glancing wherever Mathias's flashlight happened to be shining. He looked worried. He was right to be.

The chamber had manifested itself around them as they'd been walking. At first, Mathias hadn't realized it. Not until his flashlight shined across the cylinder of the dead fusion core at the center of the chamber.

"It's you, you know. I thought it was Eddy before, but I was wrong. *He* was meant for so much more. *You're* the one that must take my place. You alone know this is no mere fever dream. You know, because you faced down madness firsthand, and you still bear the scars it left on your soul. He'll like that."

"Man, do you even hear yourself?"

289

Mathias smiled. "We've some preparations to make. Will you help me, Hugo?"

Hugo looked at him suspiciously, backing away. "You think I don't know what your game is? You say you sorry for what you done to Eddy, but I know that's a load a shit. You smell desperate."

"Oh, you're right, I *am* desperate." Mathias withdrew his copy of *Messages from the Abyss*. "I don't have the tools, or a deprivation tank, but hopefully the words will suffice."

Hugo put his hands up. His eyes were wide, knowing. "Get the fuck away from me!"

"I hope you know, this isn't personal," Mathias said, opening the book to the appropriate page.

Hugo did something he should have seen coming, tackling him to the floor. Mathias's head smacked against the smooth paneling, the book and flashlight flying from his hands.

Mathias felt Hugo wrap his hands around his throat. "You think I'm just gonna let you do it? Just like that? After everything you did to us? How you got in my fucking head?"

Mathias felt pinpricks dance on his cheeks. "Without me...they *all* die..."

Hugo's strangling grip seemed to intensify in response.

"I told you what would happen when I found you, bitch!"

There was a deafening roar, one that instantly drew Hugo's attention, causing him to loosen his grip.

Mathias scrambled to get out from under him, clawing in the dark to find his flashlight, to find the book and complete the ritual.

If I can just say the words, he thought. *I have to try. I have to try!*

Then, his hands brushed against plastic. He cradled the flashlight.

The roar erupted through the chamber again.

He switched it on and started sweeping the floor for the book.

"Just let it go, man! There's something here!"

There were loud thudding sounds coming from deeper within the chamber, but he didn't have the mental fortitude to process them.

This was his last chance to complete the bargain!

Finally, he found it, lying open on the floor; he scooped it up in his free hand, quietly rejoicing.

There was a dripping sound coming from directly in front of him. That's when he saw the crimson eyes light up in the dark atop a tumorous mass of flesh. Something which, at one point, may have been a man.

There was something in its arms—*someone*.

Mathias screamed.

2

Ira had been wandering in the dark for what seemed like forever. She found the elevator shaft, but it was sealed. The emergency stairway was nearby. The door had been opened somehow, the seal breached. There was a slimy, black substance dripping down the surface of the door.

She stood staring at it, remembering what Mathias had said about the creature that was stalking them. Was that substance from the Amarath?

With her heartbeat thundering in her temples, her breath steaming in the ever-cooling air, Ira climbed the stairwell. There were great, oozing footprints of that strange black substance on each of the steps; she was careful to step around them.

Don't look back, she thought. *Don't look back!*

She searched several other floors, and still no sign of Lena.

Then…

The smell of salt and sweat and urine filled the air next to an open doorway. It was the food storage room…but hadn't she just been going up? This room was supposed to be near the basement level. Nothing made sense anymore. It was like this place had become some kind of sick maze.

Just like that place in the Astral Lands, Ira thought.

She entered the room.

Her boots crunched beneath empty protein bar wrappers and MRE containers. She scanned her flashlight through the room; it looked like a hoarder's mess. Tears welled in her eyes and carved a path through the dirt and grime on her face.

That bastard, she thought. *How is it someone so small could have eaten so much?*

Mathias had managed to make a significant dent in their ration and food supply. There had been plenty of food to sustain them...if they got through this madness. Now? She couldn't be sure.

Jesus. She could hardly rationalize what she was trying to do. Find the core and start the final experiment? Would it even work?

Maybe once the reactor was restarted, they'd be able to survive down here still?

How long would the rations last?

Maybe a year? There was no way to be certain with Lena's baby on the way.

It wasn't that he'd eaten so much that hurt her, but the fact that he'd let them starve for days at a time while he tripped on LSD or ketamine inside that damned tank. She had half a mind to go back and put him out of his misery. And maybe she would.

No, she thought. *I have to find Lena.*

She slammed the gate to the storage room shut and found herself seething out in the darkness of the corridor.

Her anger faded quickly; her hair stood on end. She had a feeling that there had been eyes lurking, staring at her in the dark.

Maybe it was that seven-eyed thing they'd all been seeing? *The Amarath*. Maybe it was the thing Mathias called the Harvester? At this point, she was so tired, she hardly cared which monster reared its ugly head.

Then, she thought she saw movement in the dark ahead. It seemed to slither around the beam cast by her flashlight.

Ira stopped, her heart pounding through her chest.

Seven pulsing eyes.

And sure enough, there they were, glowing in the dark. Its multi-segmented pupils seemed to dilate at the sight of her. Its mouth was open, revealing blackened teeth against the small amount of light her flashlight gave.

Was it avoiding the light?

"I'm not afraid of you," she lied, shaking her head and backing away.

There was a kind of half-growl, half-laughter emitting from its terrible head as it took several slow steps toward her. It seemed to swell and fill the cylindrical corridor, dwarfing her in size. Its claws raked at the cement floor. Its great spines spiked back and rattled as it closed the distance. It had to be nearly twenty feet long.

"What the hell do you want?" she asked, her shouts cut to stutters by her own terror. But she knew what it wanted. Mathias had told her that much.

I'm dead! she thought. *It's going to snap me up in its jaw and carry me off to hell!*

It pawed closer, the growls rumbling deep in its throat. Its seven pulsing eyes were almost hypnotic, pacifying.

Then she remembered what Mathias had said, in that strange place that still seemed like a faraway dream. If the creature was using the shadows as doorways, then maybe she could escape through one?

Ira turned and bolted down the corridor. She heard the thing give chase, heard it panting, chuckling, as if it were toying with her. And maybe it was?

She didn't dare check behind her. Pointing her flashlight ahead of her, she tried desperately to find a path leading to the core.

I'm sorry, Lena, she thought.

Sign after blurry sign came and went. She had no idea if she was making any headway. There was no telling in the dark. She tried desperately to focus on the core chamber: its pristine metallic floors, the consoles, the way the central reactor pulsed crimson—like a heartbeat.

Then, she heard it panting, laughing, its imperceptible jaws right next to her head—teeth clicking shut over and over again.

There was a rush of wind.

She screamed.

She felt something slice at her back, and she dove forward, hoping for a means of escape, of safety.

Her arms clanked against a metal wall, and she dropped her flashlight. It spun around, revealing that she'd just tumbled into the elevator.

"No," she said, panting, feeling the still-stinging pain from her bleeding back. "No, no, no, no!"

She crawled around, pounding on the walls in the dark. Hoping that there was still some way out, even without power in the facility.

Then, as if something had walked over her grave, she felt it moving above her, staring at her from the ceiling.

The flashlight was still in the center of the elevator. Just in reach.

Would she have time to grab it? Would that stop it?

It seemed like it predicted her movement; they lunged at the same time. Its massive black claws, hit the elevator's flooring, rattling it as she snatched the flashlight up.

Its head reared back as she lifted the flashlight, shining it directly at its face.

She screamed.

And then there was silence.

When she opened her eyes, it was as if it hadn't been there at all.

Ira practically collapsed on the elevator floor, sobbing like a stupid child.

There was no telling how long it would stay away. She had to move.

She tried standing up. Her back felt like it was on fire, but she managed to get up.

Mathias had gotten them out of the Astral Lands by thinking about the place they were trying to get to. It hadn't worked for her the first time, why would it work now... Maybe it took focus? Maybe she had to hold a clear image of the place she intended to reach in her mind?

She shut her flashlight off and placed her trembling hands on the wall, thinking of the core as she did so...

And then...as if waking from a terrible nightmare. She saw it. Not as it was, but as it had been. She could see her brother, Hugo, Mathias, all huddled around Eddy, who was carrying Lena in his arms.

Ira stepped through the doorway and stopped. Tears welled up in her eyes. "Eddy?"

He smiled at her, setting Lena down.

"I thought you were..." She couldn't even finish the sentence. She was just so glad to have him back.

Eddy approached her. She couldn't help but notice the strange smell in the air. The others, they seemed so strange. She couldn't focus on them.

He got closer.

The smell got worse.

It was coming from *him*.

"No," she said, backing away from him. "This isn't real!"

THIS ISN'T REAL!

The mirage shattered before her eyes, and she was confronted by the truth. It towered over her. Its skin had the consistency of some kind of blackened jellyfish. Its legs were hulking, blobular things that seemed to have no sense of structure to them. Its arms were disproportionate, but nearly as massive as its legs.

It extended its hands to grab her. Its fingers were like swimming eels, dripping with that same blackened slime she'd seen on the stairwell.

She screamed, but it was too late.

It grabbed her.

Ira could feel her body sinking into the creature's filth. Could feel the empty spaces of shadow open up, ready to consume her flesh the way it had probably done to Lena.

Lena, Ira thought. *The baby!*

Ira opened her eyes to find herself staring into the drooping eye of something which had once been human. It was sinking into the creature's flesh, black lines of filth threatening to absorb its face. Its one good eye regarded her with what she almost thought was adoration…

That's when she recognized who that face belonged to.

It was Eddy.

His mouth had been forced open by the blackened filth that threatened to consume his face. It made him look like he was forever screaming as he sank further and further away from his own humanity.

She felt the creature's arms slithering around her, drawing her closer.

"Ira!" It was Mathias's voice. She struggled to get a good look at him. "Get away from him, he's lost all sense. Poor Lena has been mangled!"

"No-n-no!" Lena's voice was wounded, like she'd inhaled liquid nitrogen. "H-he didn't…saved me…"

"Don't listen to her," Mathias said. "She's clearly delirious, *mad*."

Then she saw it, as if seeing through Eddy's eyes:

Tentacles of twisting dark clouds reach out, wrapping themselves around and eclipsing the sun. Filaments of plasma dance with shadows around the sun's outer layers. Jagged black teeth scrape across the surface, sending coronal material off into the vacuum of space.

They rejoice, ending their song.

Even the sun's light isn't able to escape. The light collapses back inward toward the star eater, until there is nothing left but darkness.

He turns and notices her dirty blonde hair blowing in the wind. Her face is red; she's been screaming.

Ira opened her eyes, shouting and screaming at the creature who had once been Eddy.

What Mathias had said was true. He'd discovered something deep in the dark, and now it was here.

"Let me guess," Mathias said, rolling the words in his mouth carefully. She turned around in the creature's arms to see him grinning yellow and mad in the dark. "The sun went dark, and you just saw it?"

"How did you know?"

"I saw it too." He laughed, pointing at his head. "I'm too far gone, I'm afraid. I can't control the visions I see, or where my essence wanders."

"You're insane."

"Am I?" He chuckled. "You're the one being held by a monster, seeing the end of the world!"

"Eddy…" She turned to him…he hadn't crushed her like she'd thought he would. Perhaps the vision she'd had wasn't so wrong after all? She reached up to caress his malformed face. She couldn't be sure, but she almost thought there was a hint of recognition in his remaining eye. "Tell me, big guy, that you're still in there somewhere?"

The creature grunted, removing her from its grasp and backing away as if it was ashamed of its own existence. Blackened goo dripped off her arms.

"Listen," Mathias said, drawing Ira's attention. "Without the light and warmth of our parent star, the atmosphere itself will freeze, compacting in layers on the frozen Earth; the oceans too will freeze, until the Earth resembles Europa's fractured and frozen shell. Even this

place won't save us, unless the Feds designed it to survive a vacuum—
something I highly doubt. So, we can't dawdle."

"How long will all that take?" Ira glanced at Hugo, who was staring
at Eddy's body dumbfounded, then to Lena, who was barely conscious,
her skin turning a bright red in places.

She saw it firsthand, she thought. *Went out onto the surface without any
protection. Without proper treatment, she could die.*

"It hardly matters, considering." Mathias sighed. "There's no
telling how long we've got. Nothing like this has ever happened, it's
the stuff of science fiction."

"Give me your best guess then," Ira said.

"Less than a month, at the earliest, and maybe three at the latest.
We've got to activate the final experiment."

"We still don't know if it will work…"

"We have to take the chance. If we die…then at least we tried."

"Great…"

"Now you see the importance of my and Weber's work here.
Without the Mind's Horizon experiment we will all die."

"Can you get the reactor started again?" Ira asked.

"We've got the salt deposits," Mathias said. "So, I'm more than
certain that we can."

"Do it, then." Ira knelt at Lena's side. "Hey, can you hear me?"

Lena nodded, moaning.

"Damn, yo," Hugo said. "She don't look so good."

"No thanks to you two," Ira said, glaring at Hugo and Mathias.

3

Mathias approached the core, watching Ira and the creature in the dark.
He didn't trust that *thing*, not one bit.

There was a hiss in the air when he removed the reactor's fuel tank
and carried it over to a nearby table. Next he removed a hose from a
nearby sink (no doubt put there just in case someone was doused with
dangerous chemicals) and turned the knob. The water flowed into the
fuel tank slowly. He used his flashlight to read from Weber's diary and

the grimoire he kept so close to his chest as he scraped salt deposits into the tank.

It was regrettable. He'd thought he'd have more time to perform the ceremony on Hugo...when that *thing* showed up with Lena in its arms. And then, Ira had showed up too...there was zero chance that Ira would let him perform the ceremony.

And Hugo seemed to be watching him carefully in the dark. Mathias was surprised that he hadn't raised more alarm at what he'd almost done...

"How can you be sure you've got the right mixture?" Ira asked.

"I've studied Weber's work and the schematics to this pyramidal structure extensively," Mathias said.

No, not just that, a voice echoed through his mind. *You wandered aimlessly through lands untold, saw floating, broken worlds, the tentacles of great beasts the size of galaxies, impossible dimensions the mind was never meant to see.*

"I'm sure you have," Ira said, crossing her arms.

He was about to mouth a reply when he saw it.

That same eerie green light they'd fled from in the Astral Lands, now at the chamber's circular hatch. Mathias's eyes drifted to it slowly, hoping against hope that he was only hallucinating. His mouth twisted into a scowl. His eyebrows clenched in pure terror. His pulse thundered, threatening to choke him to death. *"No!"*

"What is it?" Ira asked.

The otherworldly green glow swelled in the doorway, became two-dimensional apparitions of light that snaked across the wall like a reverse silhouette in the dark.

Mathias cradled the solution he'd developed in his arms and rushed over to the dead core. "No, you won't take me! You won't take me!"

Desperately fumbling with the fuel chamber, he glanced back.

Like gargantuan fingers gripping at the top of a cliff, glowing green appendages materialized, became flesh, gripping at the circular edge of the doorway where previously there had only been the silhouettes of light. Mathias shook the fuel tank vigorously, opening the compartment on the side of the reactor and sliding the cylinder inside.

Then, emerging from the mouth of the doorway like a wraith, the harvester of the abyss's hooded figure came into the core chamber. Its enormous appendages seemed to retract to its sides. The expression etched into its elegant, terrible mask was not a happy one. It seemed to glide atop the metallic floor, as if it wasn't really there at all.

The Harvester stopped to regard Ira with those blackened pits for eyes. She felt her heart seize in her chest for a moment.

In that moment, she had a vision of a monster at the center of an infinite black abyss. It pulsed green in the dark, its tendrils innumerable, stretching through black holes, tearing through both three-dimensional reality and that place Mathias called the Astral Lands. Surrounding it were the broken shells of dead planets, floating islands and pyramids from lost civilizations, and dead stars.

Then, as she came back to reality, she realized that it was creeping toward Mathias.

He's the only one who can start the reactor, she thought, her heart clawing its way up her throat.

"No, you can't take him!" she screamed, running after the Harvester.

The Harvester's laughter was like spiders swarming over her skin as it shifted its attention from Mathias to her. She felt a shame greater than any she'd ever felt fill her up like contaminated water poured into a broken glass. How could she save this man? This man who had murdered her brother, had turned Eddy into that *thing?*

She glanced at Lena…her swelling belly…her shallow breath.

That's why, she thought.

"No!" Mathias fell backwards, scrambling to escape.

There will be no escape, the Harvester said, reaching a twisting, segmented appendage across the entire length of the chamber.

Mathias screamed and struggled, but he couldn't fight the Harvester's grip. Its appendages wrapped around his body, dragging him across the floor. His feet kicked at the air as the creature lifted him off the floor and drew him close.

"No!" Ira stood up, fighting with her own terror, and got in front of the Harvester. Its torso twisted around to look at her, its twisting, snakelike appendages still wrapped about Mathias's midsection, its mask's grin showing teeth now, white lights glowing in the infinite blackened pits of its eyeholes.

No? it said, its voice shaking all that she was or ever would be.

"We need him!" Ira said. "Without the reactor started, we'll die here!"

The Harvester rose, towering almost twenty feet in the air. *This one is mine. The bargain cannot be undone.*

"Then take me instead." She shook her head, tears pooling in her eyes as she thought of her essence being snuffed out by the eye in the abyss. "He knows how to get it started, none of us can. At least with him here, my brother's child will have a fighting chance…"

The Harvester stared at her for a moment. Then, its terrible laughter filled the chamber like maggots in a rotting wound. It turned its back from Ira, dragging Mathias into the shadows.

Ira gave chase. "No! Take me instead! Take me! Take me!"

It spun around and lashed out with its free appendage, twisting, gargantuan fingers wrapping around her body, threatening to crush her bones to dust.

Yes, do it, she thought. *Take me instead, end it.*

"Yes, take her!" Mathias seemed overjoyed, even in his terror, trying to pry the Harvester's fingers away. "Put me down and take her! I'll save everyone, I promise! I promise!"

The Harvester stared at her for a moment. Its mask's expression twisted into a frown at first, and then a grin. *No.*

"Why not?" Mathias asked, squirming, tears dripping down his chin, lit green by the Harvester's glow. "She's seen things, terrible things, too!"

We will give you the required knowledge necessary to save yourself, the Harvester said, its mask too close to her face. She could smell something beneath it, a stench that was neither rot nor death — something older, far more ancient. *The price will be heavy. Your mortal mind may not survive for long. And, in exchange, we shall one day visit upon you a fate worse than death.* Its grin widened, the mask cracking and

300

readjusting to its newfound proportions. *Do you accept this bargain, Masku?*

"That's not fair! You're still taking him!"

Ours is a new contract, it said. *You have nothing to do with his, nothing to bargain with in exchange for his essence.*

Do you accept?

She thought long and hard...her eyes drifted to Eddy's monstrous silhouette, Lena's body on the floor...she had no choice.

Do you accept?

With a lump in her throat, she said, "Fine...I accept..."

Its appendages retracted, save for a single finger, which hovered above her forehead. *Very well then.*

It touched her forehead; Ira collapsed to the floor, cradling her head and screaming. It was like someone had opened up her scalp and bathed her brain in dry ice, the pain both hot and cold at the same time. She tried desperately to crush her own head with her hands to stop it from getting worse.

And it *did* get worse.

The visions flooded into her mind as the Harvester turned back toward the shadows, dragging Mathias kicking and screaming into the Astral Lands. She saw the gateway open and watched the Harvester step into a room no bigger than her mother and father's family room. There was a hole in the crumbling stone floor. The hole in the floor gave way to darkness, and in that darkness, there was a star and several planets, their atmospheres and heat twisting in beautiful concentric circles around a black hole. There were great, impossible tendrils reaching out of the event horizon, like some gnarled roots from an ancient tree.

Mathias reached for her. And she heard his bones snap as the Harvester crushed his pathetic mortal body and dropped him into the abyss. His body stretched and twisted and seemed to freeze in place above the event horizon, his face twisted in unimaginable pain and terror.

The Harvester turned to her, its mask's expression twisted into a foul grin, its eyes sparkling with the light of dead stars. *Remember, a fate worse than death.*

The gateway closed.

Its laughter echoed in the chamber.

That's when it happened.

Fires ripped through her mind, and she saw the darkness twist and form into visions as the knowledge gifted to her by the Harvester took hold.

She stands on the Earth, peering through it as though it isn't there at all, her eyes fixed on the southern constellations. Even those melt away as she reaches out beyond. Where she's going, she doesn't know.

All of her doubts fade away once she leaves her body behind.

She arrives before she can see their world. She can see a blue star shining bright, casting daylight onto a lush, green world.

Like ours once was, *she thinks.*

The entities appear as glowing orange masses and they swarm her, flooding her mind with visions; she sees them in their cities, about their daily lives. They appear to be some kind of plantlike creatures, like mobile Venus flytraps. They dwell in massive cities that appear to cause no harm to their world.

They're people, *she thinks.*

She sees a family of them entering what looks like some kind of cathedral.

Inside, the aliens are chanting, their vines and flora twisting and vibrating in the air.

They speak of things that she knows, somehow, have yet to come to pass.

They were beings who had the ability to reach beyond time and space and see things that gave them great insights into the mysteries of the universe. Things which allowed them to avert disaster time and time again.

Disasters like the one her world now faces.

Maybe they reached out to her to ease her troubled mind, as if to say: "See? We're real, just like you. Calm down, come and sit with us and talk of the end of the world."

She returns to the present, surrounded by the glowing orange forms.

I need help, *she thinks.*

They seem eager to communicate, but they are apprehensive to her presence.

She sees a vision of Mathias floating before them, and knows instantly that Mathias's cruelty and negative energy made them wary of dealing with humans.

The largest presence of the three entities comes to her.

She felt images flash before her: *Tentacles wrap about the sun, jagged black teeth scraping across its surface. Then, another star, one that was blue and bright and enormous. The black comet sets upon it, blocking out their constellations.*

Plantlike creatures stretch their bulbous heads up to the sky as it goes dark. There is no panic. Only a knowing fear of what is to come, because it was foretold.

"No," *she says, trying to communicate with them using her language.* "I know the risk is great to you, that you fear drawing its attention, but we're dead without your help!"

She feels the images flash before her again: Mathias in the event horizon, twisting and turning and screaming. The Harvester grinning, pleased with its work for its master. And all at once, it's not Mathias who's stretched to his limit, frozen in time as he enters the event horizon, it's her.

"Please! Please help us! I'm not like him! I have to save what's left of my family!"

The entity seems unconvinced at first, but, after a time, reaches out. Touching her essence…and then she sees it.

The core of the facility. Weber and his remaining team each take a different position by a vertical sensory deprivation tank. His body looks like a husk; his wiry gray hair reaches down his back. Weber approaches the terminal and enters a password into the screen—he stands before one of the tanks and disrobes, while a girl in coveralls yells at him. Weber ignores the girl, climbing into the tank and shutting the lid while she threatens to destroy the consoles with a fire extinguisher.

The girl's holding the grimoire in her free hand as she approaches the console, ready to swing.

Then the Amarath emerges from the darkness. It snatches the girl up in its jaws and jumps through a portal in the dark to that other place.

She doesn't want to see where it goes.

She knows where it goes.

The lid to Weber's tank latches itself shut with a loud CLICK.

303

The whole core begins to glow and pulse. White light obscures her vision. The light fades, and the tanks pop open one after another—empty. They retreat to their hiding places, sealed by circular metallic disks. The systems shut down. The core pulses in the dark.

What was the password he entered? She tries to think back to the motions his fingers made, the letters on the screen, their orientation. She replays the sequence in her head a thousand times.

D3ath IS a Myth.

That's a stupid password, *Ira thinks, chastising herself for not figuring it out.*

She tries to mouth the words, memorizing them.

Then, she sees other things. Perhaps a gift from the Harvester's touch? She sees sweeping, alien vistas, floating mountains, twisting tentacles, rotting pyramids composed of flesh, glass prisons filled with terrible things, evil eyes, black and yellow teeth.

Madness.

She knows, no matter where she goes, that madness will follow her. It will haunt her dreams for the rest of her life. She will never be the same again.

Then, she sees Eddy's twisted, monstrous form, along with others like him, around the pulsing core, as they drain it of its power.

The core darkens.

Then, she sees herself, directing Eddy toward the darkened core.

What was done, can be undone.

The knowledge hurts her brain; she knows what to do.

Then, the visions seem to fade back to the familiar darkness of the core chamber.

Something slimy caresses her cheek.

She glances up into Eddy's remaining eye.

Her sense of self came back slowly, almost eroding the madness of the visions.

"I need you, my love," Ira said. "I need you to do something for me."

The thing that had once been Eddy groaned, and somewhere deep inside her she thought he understood. His massive, hulking body twisted around, facing the dead reactor.

"Wait," Ira said.

The monster stopped, turning back to her.

She felt for his oozing hand in the dark. Grasped it and drew him close to her. As his towering form bent toward her, she reached her free hand out and found his mangled face, caressing his cheek. Before she could stop herself, she kissed his cracked and decaying lips.

"I should have done that long ago," Ira said.

The creature made no sound as it turned for the reactor once more, as if it had already seen what she'd seen. Her hand fell to her side, dripping with blackened slime.

Its hulking mass stood next to the core, and it reached its snaking fingers deep inside it. The edges of the thing's lopsided, tumorous silhouette started to glow with the light of an eclipsed sun. And then it faded, and the creature that had once been Eddy collapsed on its knees as the reactor roared to life.

The lights in the chamber plinked on, and she saw him as he was now.

Eddy's blackened skin seemed to drink the light, his body slowly being engulfed by stretches of shadow, like the gateways the seven-eyed beast had used to traverse their world.

His remaining eye was closing, tired.

"Thank you," Ira said.

Then, out of the corner of her eye, she spotted the console she'd seen in her vision, the one Weber had used to start the final experiment.

With the password held tight in her mind, she approached it.

"Yog'Elios has killed the sun," she said, breaking the silence. "We don't have much time."

When she looked up from the console, the metal walls were not metal any longer, but a leathery skin that still pulsed with her increasing heartbeat.

She saw mouths open in the skin, mouths filled with thousands of teeth, whose throats retreated into the abyss.

But when she blinked, she thought she saw the skin rot away, worms crawling out of those mouths until they were no more.

She entered the password and almost recoiled in abject terror when the room dimmed with crimson light, casting shadows, portals to that other place, in every direction.

"Hugo, get Lena," Ira said.

He leaned his head to the right, playing with his ear. "Got it."

"We need to strip down and climb into the tanks before the beast comes for us," Ira said. "Hurry!"

The tanks rose from their resting place, gleaming like beautiful glass prisms, catching the crimson light. Wiry metal staircases shot out from each tank as Ira and the others tossed their clothes to the floor.

She watched Hugo make his way toward Lena, who was still lying on the floor, her breathing shallow.

Her eyes found the spot on the far wall where the Harvester had dragged Mathias into that other place. Though he wasn't here anymore, Mathias had won. His machinations and madness might even be the reason they had a fighting chance at survival now. Thinking about that too much would drive her crazy.

Her eyes drifted back to Hugo, who had Lena slung over his shoulder. He was going to be allowed to survive too, while her brother's corpse was freezing beneath the snowy grave she and Lena had dug for him. She felt a great, murderous urge to grab him by his hair and yank him down to the smooth white floor and bash his temples in.

To leave him for that thing to drag him to hell with it.

But, the thing that had been Eddy stopped her. Its mass pulsed in the crimson light; his face had nearly been absorbed by its flesh. The creature loomed before her, its fingers twitching, writhing.

"Eddy?" Ira said.

It made slow gurgling sounds, coming from the human mouth in what might be its neck. Whatever it was trying to say, she wasn't sure.

Tears filled her eyes, catching in her throat. "I never got to tell you. I was such a goddamn coward, afraid of what would happen to you or Nico if I did, and now look at us all." She shook her head, wiping the tears away. "I love you, Eddy."

The monster raised its massive hand, caressing her face with snakes.

Ira left him behind. It was probably the hardest thing she had ever done, next to burying her brother or leaving her mother and father to rot in their tomb of a house all those years ago.

But the Eddy she had known was gone. Mathias had made sure of that.

Ira started toward the staircase. There was a part of her that wanted to stay with Eddy, monster or not. She reached the bottom of the staircase, touching her hand to the cold metal railing.

That's when she saw Hugo staring at the darkness. She turned around and saw it too.

Seven eyes pulsed, and she could see it pacing around the core chamber, stalking its prey.

She was its prey.

The still-bleeding wounds in her back pulsed as it circled her. It was going to get her, drag her off to that hellish place in the Astral Lands.

Why couldn't she move?

It stopped, opening its mouth, hissing with otherworldly hunger. It reared back, all twenty feet of it seeming to pulse at once, its spines shaking with murderous intent. Like a cat ready to pounce.

The shadow beast snapped at her, its thousands of razor-sharp, blackened teeth open, ready to clamp down and drag her to hell.

Ira closed her eyes, and for the first time in her adult life, she prayed for a miracle.

Then, a moment later, there was no pain. There was only a deep, rhythmic growling. She opened her eyes. She stared directly into one of that beast's seven gray eyes. It snapped its jaws at her, but couldn't quite reach.

That's when she noticed the hulking black mass over the beast. Eddy had grabbed it by its tail, pinning it down with all his strength.

Eddy's good eye found her in the crimson light. His human lips mouthed something. Even with no sound to escape his lips, she knew what it meant.

The beast and the thing that was now Eddy struggled, wrestling in the pulsing crimson light.

With her heart pounding in her throat, she rushed up the wiry staircase to her deprivation tank.

She fumbled with the cold metal latch to the hatch, opening it. She snatched up the breathing mask, put it on, and glanced over to Hugo and Lena.

Hugo had helped her into her own tank. Lena glanced at her weakly.

Ira nodded to her.

Hugo stumbled down the staircase, rolling on the linoleum floor. He screamed when the Amarath's head hit the paneling, just inches from his feet. Eddy had body-slammed it.

"Get up, damn it!" Ira shouted, pulling the mask just far enough from her face to get the words out.

Hugo rolled to his feet and sprinted, screaming, hyperventilating, up his own staircase.

Ira clawed at the lid to her tank, looked over and saw that Eddy was losing his grip on the beast. Those terrible gray pulsing eyes were zeroing in on Hugo now.

Hugo's expression softened, like he was in a trance, just as she had been before.

"Hugo, get in the fucking tank!" Ira screamed. There was no telling if Eddy's grip would hold long enough for him to climb inside his tank. Maybe the beast was just too strong?

Ira closed the hatch to her tank.

A strange taste filled her mouth, and moments later, perhaps an eternity later, she saw the abyss that surrounded her shatter into a swirling crimson vortex.

It was strange, as if she were peering through some other window. Perhaps another effect of the knowledge gifted to her from the Harvester?

She could see Lena's naked body and her own, glowing together there in their tanks. The symbol of the bridge through the abyss pulsed with its nine points of light, and they were two of the points of light in that circle.

She saw Eddy wrestling with that terrible thing. Smashing it with his free hand. The beast thrashed out, biting down into Eddy's arm and tossing him like a gigantic ragdoll into the floor, shattering the paneling and causing sparks to dance from the circuitry beneath the floor.

It stared at Hugo for a moment.

Hugo was mesmerized. All her shouting hadn't done a damn thing for him.

Eddy was struggling to stand up. His body seemed to be falling apart, dripping into clumps, like mounds of mud and tar.

Then, to Ira's horror, she watched the beast maul him with its teeth and its claws, splashing black filth everywhere.

The creature reared its long black head, showing its teeth—and in that moment she thought its hide was all scales, with patches of blackened spiny fur that spiked and stabbed at the sky. Its seven gray eyes pulsed in the dark and it clamped its powerful jaws down on what remained of Eddy's face.

She screamed into her breathing mask, thrashing at the walls of the tank.

Eddy's monstrous body stopped moving.

The creature rose, locking its eyes on Hugo.

Hugo drifted down the metal staircase, a dead look in his eyes.

You idiot! Turn back! Don't do it!

The beast charged at him.

He screamed, as if he'd regained his sense at the last moment.

But it was too late.

It clamped down on his skinny body and dragged him into the darkness, through a window in time and space.

Ira saw through that window now, saw the terrible skin that passed for land, the way it crawled and seemed to sweat as if it were salivating for the meal that the Amarath had brought into its realm. The sky in that terrible place was the color of a graying, dead lung.

She looked away. Looked to the creature who had been Eddy. His face was gone now, even the one good eye that had so recently regarded her. The creature twitched, writhing, rising from its spot on the cracked floor.

Are you still in there? she thought.

The creature struggled to its massive feet, pulling itself back together.

Eddy's face was nearly gone. An oozing, thick tar-like substance, was threatening to consume what was left of it.

The creature's roars made the tanks shake and reverberate. With its crimson, inhuman eyes, its attention drifted to the pulsing reactor.

Ira glanced at Lena.

We have to go, she thought.

The creature's hulking mass lumbered toward the reactor. If it absorbed the radiation from the reactor, they'd be stuck here.

She tried to think of a bridge to another world. The way that Weber and his team had. She rolled the words given to her by the Harvester around in her mind.

Aml'cath na ule'th ada hote' tekke.

Ira felt those words echo in the crimson vortex and felt her mind open up. She saw her core. The little girl inside that still yearned for her parents' recognition. She sat a while with that little girl as she built things with her Legos.

The girl looked up at her and smiled. "Time to let go, Ira."

Ira nodded. The girl shattered, and she was at the center of her own being. Chanting the words.

She saw a bridge open up in the vortex. A blackened abyss stretched out before them, and her heart shuddered when she saw the thing at the center of dying stars and broken worlds, the pulsing protoplasmic eye with its stretching tentacles in the dark. Tentacles that snaked their way into every universe, creating black holes in the dark of space and swallowing everything around them, even the light.

The eye of the abyss pulsed green in that infinite dark, and its gaze seemed to focus on them. Its pupils weren't pupils at all, but geometric shapes with uncountable angles, uncountable vertices.

She broke her attention away from the eye and reached out to the creature that had been Eddy. The fear of losing him to this world, or to that terrible abyss, suddenly stabbed out into her mind.

Her hand opened up. But the creature had lost itself in its own instincts and was stretching its shadowy fingers through the reactor's walls.

The little girl had been right. She had to let go. She had to let go of him.

She closed her hand and lowered it to her side.

Ira said goodbye to the thing that had once been her love for the last time.

There was a great force in that infinite dark. Several worlds around the eye of the abyss shattered as it moved forward. She couldn't be sure, but it looked as if that thing had a mouth of its own, and it looked like it was coming after them.

She got the feeling that it wanted to trap them there. To close the door in their faces so they would be forced to live there in the abyss for all eternity while it fed off of their memories and their madness.

She stretched and struggled, reaching for Lena's hand. But she was alone in the dark, drifting toward a single point of light. The end of the bridge, a vortex of crimson energy that had no true form in that darkness, like an eldritch bullet train, running straight to hell.

"No," she whispered. "Not without her, not without the baby!"

The eye of the abyss came to fill all that she could see beyond the bridge, ready to consume her essence, as it had likely done to Mathias eons ago.

Time is meaningless here, she thought, as it descended upon her, opening its imperceptible jaws.

Then, even as she was distracted by its immensity, white light came to fill her, and she felt such pain…as if she were being born…

She cried out for Eddy…

For Nico…

EPILOGUE

The white light hurt her eyes. She felt the stillness of the air, and it all came flooding back into her. The terrible, maddening dream that had possessed her.

She sat up in the bed and felt her face with her aching hands.

Had it all been a nightmare? She wondered if she'd just woken up in the facility again, that if she walked outside she'd find only stone tunnels and lonely metal-walled rooms where impossible things stalked in the dark.

There were machines beeping and an IV steadily dripping fluid into her veins.

Maybe she was in the med bay? Maybe she'd had an accident?

But, when her eyesight cleared, she saw that she wasn't in the facility's med bay at all. The walls of this place were...ordinary. There was a sterile smell, something she couldn't quite put her finger on, but recognized as the telltale smell that accompanies a visit to a hospital.

She was in some kind of recovery room.

She closed her eyes and tried to sleep, but when she did she only saw seven gray pulsing eyes in the dark, and that was enough to cause her to scream and open her eyes for fear that the thing might find its way to her again.

With her screams, the door—an ordinary wooden door—opened, and a lanky, elderly black man came in holding a clipboard. He smiled at her, and for some reason, she felt that he was somehow familiar to her.

"I see you're awake," the doctor said. "We even made bets as to what you'd say when you woke up. Now, don't disappoint me, I've got twenty bucks riding on this."

She was silent for a while, trying to figure out why he looked so familiar.

"Where am I?" she finally asked.

Where's my Eddy?

"Damn, I guess I'm out twenty bucks," he said, chuckling. "You're at Saint Bernardine's Hospital."

"Saint…"

"You don't remember how you got here?"

She shook her head.

"Damnedest thing, some truck driver brought you in, claiming he saw a white light and then you were standing in the street, naked as the day you were born."

She looked down at herself, saw that she was wearing a hospital gown. Of course she'd come in naked.

"Now, at first I didn't quite believe the man, was tempted to call the police, but then you looked up, wrapped in a blanket, and said something that caused me to second-guess myself."

"What did I say?"

"You asked if it was gone, if the thing with the seven eyes was gone." His face became grim. "Normally, I'd just admit you to the psych ward, but…between you and me…what you said reminded me of a nightmare I'd had the other night, and I decided to admit you."

"Thank you…" she said.

"Now, for the other matter." His voice became serious again. "I ran your fingerprints through our systems and came up with something peculiar. Something you'll thank me later for not alerting the other staff members to."

He gave her the chart he was holding. She saw her name there, and something else, an age that didn't make sense to her. The chart said she was seventy-seven years old. The last name was also peculiar, and yet somehow familiar.

IRA RAMIREZ

"You're an old soul." He chuckled. That chuckle made her scan the sheet frantically for the doctor's name. When she found it, her heart seized in her throat.

DOCTOR MATHIAS BANNING

She looked up to the man who was not the madman she had known, but bore a striking resemblance to him.

The final experiment worked, she thought, shuddering. *I passed through the mind's horizon into another world. And now I'm alone, faced with the reality that these ghosts are like the people I once knew, only they're not ghosts, they're old, and I'm the one who's a phantom.*

Maybe Lena and her baby were still out there, maybe they were floating through the abyss between universes, crying out for her to help them? Maybe they had spilled through to other worlds, where they too were alone.

Part of her wanted to crawl back through that white light that she'd seen and find them. Even if it meant facing that thing with the pulsing green eye.

But that was probably impossible.

"Can I go now?" she found herself asking.

Doctor Mathias Banning nodded. "Of course. I've taken the liberty of paying your bill, you're in good shape, physically, but..."

"You worry about my mind?"

He nodded.

"I'll be fine," she lied. Not without Eddy, not without her family.

Their final, strange embrace, and that kiss that had promised of things that might have been, filled her mind, and she felt a rusty metal wire tighten around her heart and constrict.

"Give me a few minutes," he said, heading for the door. "I'll bring you some clothes."

She was glad when he left. Different Mathias or not, his presence still sent shivers crawling through her and reminded her of the things that lurked in the darkness, beyond the veil.

He came back and set some baggy clothes on the table. "A Jane Doe left these behind. I realize that's a little disturbing, but under the circumstances, I'm sure you won't mind.

She nodded. "It's fine."

She just wanted him to leave.

His dark brown eyes regarded her for a moment. His lips pursed, a question dangling at the edge. "Where did you come from?"

She didn't want to answer. She didn't want to give him any reason to go searching for those terrible things, that grimoire or the truth of the mind's horizon. She saw in the glint of his eye that he *needed* to know. Needed to hear something.

"I came from another world," she finally said.

He nodded, as if that's what he'd guessed too. "I see." Then the inevitable question came, and a hunger crept into his face, his posture. "How?"

"I don't remember."

"Curious." He scratched his head. "You must tell me if you ever remember, though."

She nodded. He retreated to the door and looked back at her suspiciously. As if he knew deep down that she had lied to him.

Ira did remember. She felt like she was living through that hellish reality, forced to replay the events in her head over and over again. Forced to watch Lena and her baby drift off into the blackness of the abyss, just out of reach of her grasp. Forced to leave the creature that had been Eddy behind to languish on the frozen corpse of the Earth.

She preferred the lie. At least in the lie she could be happy.

2

She'd taken longer to leave the hospital than she'd planned. And when she finally did dress herself in the baggy clothes left by Jane Doe, she found herself standing in the warm Southern California sunlight, basking in it and watching the clouds drift across the brilliant blue sky that was now completely alien to her.

"*I'll teach you to appreciate this Southern California weather, even if it kills me.*" She heard Jennifer's words, the real Jennifer, in her mind, and, for the first time in years, she found herself missing her.

There was a light breeze in the warm air, and she marveled and relished every moment of it.

That painful rusty wire that had tightened around her heart squeezed once again, and she hoped that Lena had found a world where the sky was as brilliant as it was here.

A terrible feeling told her that she was writhing in agony, but it passed.

She hitched a ride to downtown Riverside and found herself digging through a phone book. She found her own name next to an address and tore it from the book.

In her time, phone books had been a thing of the past. This seemed to be a world that hadn't crawled past the 1990s in terms of digital technology. People weren't constantly absorbed in their cell phones or tablets, or anything else. The one time she saw someone talking on a cell phone it was the size of their forearm.

"Jesus," she said. "I've found my way to the digital dark ages."

She walked around for a while, clutching the torn page of the phone book, daring herself to seek the address out.

She wandered her way into the suburbs eventually, and sometime during sunset, when the sun was casting bands of red and orange light across the horizon and silhouetting the trees black in the distance, she stood before the house where her other self had lived the life she could only dream of.

Her feet were heavy. Each step was difficult. But she knocked on the door all the same, and found herself staring face-to-face with a seventy-year-old man, a man who looked strikingly familiar.

"Can I help you?" Then a wave of shock passed through his face, a knowing.

Maybe, maybe if she heard their story...

Maybe if she heard that she'd be able to find a reason to live.

A MESSAGE FROM ERIC

Thank you so much for reading *Mind's Horizon*. Before you get on with your day, please do me a massive favor and leave a review on Amazon and Goodreads! This book took nearly eighteen years to bring into the marvelous thing it is now, and I couldn't be prouder to have brought it to you.

Also, if you haven't done so yet, head over to bookfunnel and sign up to my mailing list to receive a free copy of my debut cosmic horror novel, *Echoes of Olympus Mons*!

ACKNOWLEDGMENTS

The idea for this book came to me during a blizzard in 2015. My brother and I had run out of beer and decided that it would be a good idea to walk to the grocery store (which was a mile away) to get more. For over an hour, we trudged through snow that came up to our knees. It was tiring to say the least. We got our beer, and many jokes were had about our lack of preparedness, as well as how stupid it was to march out into a blizzard like that (just for a 24-pack)—but I would do it again. I think that's where the idea for a modern ice age came from. I thought about what it might be like to live in my old hometown of Riverside if an ice age were to hit. How would people survive a modern snowball Earth scenario?

The insane cosmic horror elements came shortly after.

I'd like to thank Michelle, James, Jenny, Kat, Max, Erin, Jacob, Philip, Frederick, Ashe, Aleah, Schinell, Leigh, and Clara for contributing to the GoFundMe. Without you, this book's original cover would not have been made. And extra special thanks go out to Eric Lahti, for designing said cover (which has now been updated to reflect market trends).

I'd also like to thank Elise, Serena, Eric, and all of my patrons, (especially Lisa), for reading the pre-copy-edited version of the book.

And to Phoenix. Thanks for putting up with my madness. Your insight always proves to be invaluable.

A Sneak Peak of

CTHULHU GRIMOIRE

The look in his eyes. They're still open. There's a smile on his face. Lips, chapped and cracking. His neck is bent at a forty-five-degree angle... Must have broken the instant his body hit the grass.

Detective Hunter tosses his coffee on the campus lawn and curses under his breath.

What a waste.

"You all right?" his partner asks.

Hunter takes a moment to compose himself, wiping the beading sweat off his forehead with his shirt sleeve. Even at night, it's unbearably hot here.

"I'm fine," Hunter says.

"The evidence technicians photographed the room already. We should get a look before they bag and tag everything." Shirley is excited. It's almost sickening to him, how exhilarated she gets in the presence of death. How she bounces at the opportunity to examine a new crime scene. A new corpse. Even if the techs have already documented it. She loves her job. Treats it like some kind of escape room thrill ride.

He nods anyway.

The red and blue lights strobing in the sweltering night draw unwanted attention from across the campus. Three squad cars and an ambulance will do that.

He looks up. There's an open window five stories up.

"You gonna say something tonight, Hunt?" She's got that look in her eyes. The look that betrays what's lurking beneath.

"Is the victim's roommate here?" he asks.

"He is. Says he wants to talk to a lawyer before he talks to any cops. I told him that makes him look like a suspect. He didn't budge."

"He's got good reason to be worried."

321

She stands there and stares at him like there's a smart-ass comment on the tip of her tongue. Her pasty white skin catches the red and blue strobe like a blank canvas drinks paint.

"You want a crack at him?" she asks.

"What do you think?"

Most of the students who live in this apartment complex turned student housing are asleep at this hour. Some of them are up late, cramming for exams. Distracting themselves with video games. Avoiding responsibility with terrible booze and worse music. Hunter can hear some of that music still blaring at the other end of the building, totally oblivious that one of their own is slowly rotting away on the front lawn of the complex.

Not everyone is oblivious. Hunter's eyes scan over gawking faces, watching the fiasco unfolding from behind caution tape.

He doesn't care about them right now, makes a beeline for the ambulance.

The kid's huddled in some blankets, sitting on the ambulance's bumper. The physicians are asking him the standard psyche questions, making sure he's mentally stable after seeing...that.

The kid's eyes meet Hunter's. Thin fingers strangle a well-worn and cracked phone.

Several angles Hunter can approach this from. Police officers are allowed to offer a potential suspect false promises in order to get them to confess. Hunter wants to feel it out first. Maintain his distance, be friendly.

Something doesn't feel right about this.

Then again. It never does.

The kid's already glaring at him.

"What do you want?" the kid asks. "Already told you people, I want a lawyer."

The kid can practically smell the bacon. His eyes and body language don't relax. It doesn't matter that Hunter is black. A cop's a cop.

"I'm Detective Hunter, I need to ask you a few questions."

"And you thought I'd answer without a lawyer just because you're black?"

There's never an easy way to start this conversation.

"You're not in trouble, Dean."

Not unless you did it, he thinks.

"I've seen how this goes," Dean says.

"Look, we need answers. We've got a dead kid on the lawn, and countless people gawking from behind that police line--and you sitting here with a pissy look on your face. It won't take long for stories to start circulating, and most of them probably end with you shoving that poor bastard out your dorm room window."

A pregnant pause stretches between them. The kid avoids Hunter's gaze, like he's hoping he'll get the hint and just leave.

"Fine," Hunter says, nodding to his partner, who's busy taking statements from residents. "If you don't want to talk to me, I'll go fetch my partner. I'm sure she'll be a lot more understanding."

"That what you think happened, Uncle Tom?"

Dean's still defensive, but he's shaking. He unfolds his arms. Places his palms on the ambulance's bumper. Less hostile body language. Progress.

"In your nine-one-one call, you claimed that you came home from class to find that your roommate had jumped out the window. How did that happen?"

"Don't know where to start," Dean says.

"Start at the beginning," Hunter says.

He fidgets for a minute. Like every fiber of his being is telling him not to run his mouth, but that other voice wants to clear himself of any responsibility for Kevin Wallace's death.

"Kevin's been acting sus..." He pauses, as if catching himself. "Suspicious. Like, he's always been kind of weird. But we got along. He hasn't..." His eyes open wide, as if he's just now realizing that he has to refer to this person who he shared a home with in the past tense from now on. "Hadn't. He hadn't slept in a week. Or, if he did, he was cutting classes and sleeping during the day. Man, it was really starting to tick me off. He was on his laptop every night. I have a hard time sleeping with lights on, even a screen will wake me up. I tried to tell him to stop, but then he'd just stare at me with this blank fucking look on his face. It was like...he wasn't there anymore."

They always tell you not to trust your first instinct on a case, that it's almost always wrong. Hunter starts to wonder if maybe Kevin Wallace *was* pushed from his window. If, maybe, this is going to turn into a confession.

Could he have snapped at his roommate? An altercation that simply went too far? Is that motive enough?

He prays it isn't.

"Then I come home from my Friday night class. I was planning to go over to a friend's place and celebrate the end of a long week. And the window's open. I told Kevin not to leave it open. Told him he'd catch these hands if I caught him smoking joints by the window again. I've worked too damn hard to get expelled for someone else's habit." Dean pauses. Eyes drift across the lawn. He's looking at Kevin's body. "Never seen a dead body. Not like that."

So, not a confession. He's more than a little relieved. If the kid's telling the truth.

"What do you think happened?"

"I think he jumped."

"Did Kevin have any enemies?"

"Shit, I don't know. He didn't talk much. Started hanging around with a bunch of emo kids or some shit."

"Do you know his major, what his family was like, anything?"

Dean nods. He's getting more comfortable. "He...was Media Arts and Animation. Like me. We didn't have no classes together. But, I seen some of his recent work, and it was getting weird."

"Weird how?"

"Ever heard of H.R. Giger?"

Detective Hunter shakes his head.

"Well, he's famous for designing some movie monster from the Seventies. We learned about him in my concept art class. Demonic, hyper-sexual bullshit. Can't stand it. Apparently the guy worshipped some satanic dude named Crowley. Kevin was obsessed with him too for a while."

For some reason, that Crowley name sounded really familiar to Hunter. He jots the name down in his notepad for later.

"How was Kevin's relationship with his parents?"

Dean shakes his head. "Kevin didn't say much about his family before coming here. But I know he never went home. Not even for holidays or summer."

"Why do you think he jumped?"

Dean shrugs. "Maybe he couldn't take the pressure no more? Who knows?"

The room is small, barely large enough for one person, let alone two. There's two beds on either side of the dorm, books scattered all over the place.

Shirley's scratching her chin as the evidence techs are bagging and tagging items for examination. Hunter wonders if they'd even care if it wasn't a white kid growing stiff on the lawn.

"Well, looks like this is an open-and-shut case," Shirley says, clapping her hands together like she's cracked the case. Everyone's treating this like the kid's guilty.

"I don't think this is a homicide," Hunter says, scanning the room.

"Well, we're being as thorough as possible," Shirley says. "You should have been here when the kid's parents showed up. The father slugged the rookie. Won't believe what we found on him. Never thought someone would be dumb enough to bring coke to a crime scene. Had to book him."

Hunter's fingers twitch at the mention of a search. No way in hell a black man would risk slugging a cop, not if they had a sense of self-preservation. He wonders if they planted it on Dean's father. Part of him doesn't want to know. "Which rookie? Jameson?"

"Yeah. Or maybe it was Wilkins? I can't keep them straight. If they don't get fired for screwing their paperwork up, I'll bother to remember their names."

Hunter nods. The one thing she's said tonight he agrees with.

"Still… can't believe you got him to talk," she says. "So, you think he's telling the truth?"

"He didn't push him, if that's what you're getting at," he says.

"How do you know?"

325

"Just a feeling."

"You don't think it's possible that he could have gotten sick of his roommate's bullshit and pushed him out the window?"

"Possible? Sure. But I don't think this kid is capable of that. He's got no priors and decent grades. Why would he risk murdering his roommate?"

"Crime of passion. If Kevin Wallace was going nuts, like he said he was, then who knows what the kid's not telling you?"

Hunter ignores her as she drones on. Something catches his eye. Kevin's laptop is open, the screen's turned off. The techs haven't dusted it or bagged it yet. There's a sketchbook next to it, and it's open.

He puts on some gloves and flips through it.

The sketches are all in ink. His wife would call them "washes." They're monstrous things with too many teeth, tentacles, and odd, sexually charged forms.

The drawings send shivers down Hunter's spine.

"We should get into his laptop," Hunter says. "Take a look at his social media activity and contact the building's ISP."

"Want my bet?"

"No."

"Probably lots of gay porn or something like that."

"Just because he's a loner, doesn't mean he's in the closet."

"Just saying, maybe that's why he never went home? Maybe his family's religious, thought they'd disown him or something? You know how these artist types are."

"That's pure conjecture."

"Still, we should take a deeper look at the family. Both of them."

And they'd have the perfect opportunity while they've got Dean's father locked up tight in an interrogation room. They'll use the trumped up coke and assault charges to get him to spill on all the family's dirty laundry.

If the man's smart, he's already lawyered up.

Hunter doesn't say any of that. Doesn't think about the strange look the other officers are giving him, that Shirley is giving him.

"…Agreed," Hunter says.

Shirley yawns, stretching. "Welp, I'm done here. Let's let the techs finish bagging and tagging this shit and call it a night."

"How can you be so calm about this?"

She shrugged. Something odd about the look in her eyes. Like her connection to humanity's long since been disconnected. "After a while, you just get numb to it all. It becomes a job. I don't know how you can still be so moved by things like this after all these years."

Hunter moves for the door. "Some of us are still human."

She's staring at Kevin Wallace's laptop. There's a faraway look in her eyes. "Maybe. Or maybe you're the outlier?"

"What?"

She shakes her head. "Oh, nothing. Just being morbid. You know me."

Sometimes he wonders if he does.

"Goodnight, Shirley."

"'Night, Hunt."

Hunter gets home to find his third-story apartment dead quiet. It's almost 3:00 AM in Downtown Los Angeles. The wife and kids are most likely asleep.

The faint smell of rice and pan-fried chicken with a hint of kale lingers in the air.

He missed dinner again.

Moonlight bounces off the living room furniture. His recliner's calling his name. A covered easel stands out when he enters. It beckons him to look. A white pallet speckled with paint dries on the coffee table.

Fingers stretch out, grip the sheet.

He wants to tear it away. See what his wife was working on, maybe bring some much-needed color into his dreary world.

Something deep inside tells him not to look. Can't stop thinking about the inkings in Kevin Wallace's sketchbook. The writhing and twisting amorphous silhouettes.

When he shuts his eyes, he can see them moving.

Fingers tense, then release the cloth.

Hunter rubs his eyes. Tells himself he needs a stiff drink and a hot meal. That Janet will show him the painting when she's done.

The kitchen is spotless. A note on the fridge reads "It's your turn next time. No takeout."

He hangs his blazer up and looks in the fridge. There's a plate with his name on it. A little heart's Sharpied next to it. He grabs the plate and a beer. Pops the plate in the microwave. Opens the beer and takes a long sip from the can. Tries not to think about the look on Kevin's face. His graying skin. The way his lips stretched and cracked. Almost like he was smiling.

There's an odd, melancholy thing about the way a microwave sounds in the middle of the night.

The microwave dings and he pulls his food out, sits at the kitchen counter, and brings his hands together to say grace. He's halfway through scarfing the plate down when he notices her on the stairs. Her eyes look almost black, her pale skin is a near-perfect silhouette against the moonlight-kissed windows.

"I had a nightmare," she says.

The hair on the back of Hunter's neck stands to attention. He doesn't know why. Doesn't know what to say.

Janet crosses the room and hugs him tight enough to restrict his lung capacity. "I just…need to feel you. Know that you're here."

"What is this about, Janet?"

She's silent for a time. Her touch is cold. Clammy.

"Janet?"

"I don't want to talk about it."

He touches her arm. She jerks back for a moment before relaxing. "Go on back to bed, then. I'll be up soon."

A lie. He's going to spend the next hour running over case documents. Maybe the next two hours.

"You promise?"

"Swear to God."

God will forgive him.

She slinks back to the stairs. Moonlight halo's her nighty. Makes her look like a ghost.

Janet looks back at him. Sighs. And makes her way back up the stairs.

It's 5:00 AM before he finishes poring over the case files. Nothing new springs to mind. But he still can't get Kevin Wallace's paintings out of his head…

Hunter climbs into bed, careful to not disturb Janet.

He's nearly settled, closing his weary eyes when her disembodied voice fills the room.

"It was so strange," she says. "You looked like you hadn't eaten in weeks, your skin looked…well, it looked awful…and you were in some basement, drawing these weird symbols."

"Just a nightmare, honey," he says. "Go back to sleep."

"You weren't you."

"Well, I'm me now. I'm here. It was just a nightmare."

"Are you? Is it? You said you'd be right up to bed. You spent the last two hours working again, didn't you?"

"Are we really having this conversation right now?"

She shrinks away from him, holding herself tight. "No, I guess not."

"We'll talk about this in the morning."

"Heard that before."

Before long, she's asleep, and all he's left with is the quiet of a dark room and the horrible things from Kevin Wallace's sketchbook.

The silence is nearly unbearable.

———————

The alarm blares through Hunter's temples. He wakes from a nightmare. He's naked. And his wife is already up.

Hunter doesn't remember taking his clothes off.

The sun is coming up and his phone has about thirty text messages and twice as many missed calls.

They're all from Shirley.

He skips the texts and jumps right to calling her back.

The phone rings. He walks to the blinds and opens them. Light bands of red, orange, and purple cascade against the Los Angeles skyscrapers. A morning sunset made possible by the smog trapped in the valley. The sun will be up in little more than ten minutes.

He used to love sunrises. Used to be undeniable proof of God's creation.

Now?

Shirley answers the phone.

"Fucking hell, Hunt," Shirley says. "Were you asleep or something? I've been trying to reach you for hours."

"I've been asleep for exactly two hours. I'm not due in until 9:00 AM. What do you want?"

"There's been another suicide."

There's a buzzing at the back of his brain, like static filling the room. Every hair on his body stands on end. "What? Where?"

"The L.A. Institute of Commercial Art again. Kid hung himself from his balcony."

"Jesus...another artist?"

"And get this. You know those weird drawings that Kevin Wallace was into? Well, guess what this kid's art looks like?"

His wife comes in, wearing her nightgown, holding two cups of steaming black coffee. Just the way they like it. "What's wrong?"

He looks at her. And gets the feeling she knows.

ABOUT THE AUTHOR

Eric Malikyte is a neurodivergent author, illustrator, science communicator, and video editor. He has published works in various genres, including Lovecraftian horror, dark fantasy, and cyberpunk. He has written for YouTube channels such as TopTenz, Geographics, and Biographics. He lives in Richmond, Virginia, with his wife and two cats, where he spends his spare time exploring used bookstores, Irish Pubs, and terrorizing the neighborhood children on Halloween.

BIBLIOGRAPHY

Echoes of Olympus Mons
Neo Rackham 001: Ego Trip
Into the Astral Lands

Suleniar's Enigma Series:
The Man Without Hands
Rise of Oreseth

Coming Soon:
A Colour from Interstellar Space
Gr1mo1r
The Observatory

Neo Rackham 002
Neo Rackham 003
Suleniar's Enigma III: The Transit of the Kultari

Anthology Contributions:
Neo Cyberpunk Volume 1
Neo Cyberpunk Volume 3

Curious about other Crossroad Press books? Stop by our website:
http://crossroadpress.com
We offer quality writing
in digital, audio, and print formats.

Subscribe to our newsletter on the website homepage and receive a
free eBook.